THE WATCHERS

A Story of Undying Love

C. DE MELO

"Is God willing to prevent evil, but not able? Then he is not omnipotent. Is he able, but not willing? Then he is malevolent. Is he both able and willing? Then whence cometh evil? Is he neither able nor willing? Then why call him God?"

—Epicurus (341 B.C. – 270 B.C.)

"Religion is regarded by the common people as true, by the wise as false, and by the rulers as useful."

—Seneca the Younger (4 B.C. - 65 A.D.)

DEDICATION

Thank you, D.

PART I

THE ICON

After Dark Times the Icon shall come.
She will walk the Earth as a Sage, but will only provoke rage.
Our Mark she will bear on the Tenth and Twentieth year.

—First Prophecy of the Sacred Oracle

PROLOGUE
PRESENT DAY
LISBON, PORTUGAL

Sooty clouds conceal the moon in a starless sky as a white vein of lightning illuminates an anchored caravela. The fast and mighty sea vessel bobs like a child's toy upon the angry waves of the Tagus River. The sight fills me with dread.

My beloved stands tall and proud, the fierce wind tugging at the strands of his dark hair. Deafening thunder fills our ears only moments before icy water spills from the heavens. We are surrounded by imminent danger. My tears mingle with rain as I desperately plead with him. The thought of losing this man forever pierces my heart with excruciating pain...

I cannot bear it.

I awoke with my own sharp intake of breath and, as the cobwebs of sleep dissipated, the fragile echo of a memory slipped—yet again—from my grasp.

The gloomy light of dawn filled the bedroom. The packed suitcases by the door drew my gaze. Thousands of miles away, a new life awaited...

Could it save me from this madness?

Chapter 1
Lisbon, Portugal
November 1, 1510

"The church bells are ringing in honor of my birthday!"

"As they do every year," my mother reminded me with an indulgent smile. "Now go out and fetch some chestnuts."

I snatched a basket and ran outside with eager steps. All Saint's Day was a holy day of celebration in our kingdom. My mother had already promised to bake apple tarts, so the roasted chestnuts would be an extra treat. Unable to resist their sweet flesh, I usually ate them the moment they were extracted from the fire, inevitably burning my tongue. My mother often scolded me for my lack of patience, but today I would surprise her by waiting for them to cool. After all, as a ten-year-old, I should start displaying a certain measure of maturity.

I followed the footpath through our vegetable garden and slipped through a cluster of trees. The sun-kissed leaves were as translucent as the stained glass windows of the great cathedral. Sunbeams seeped through the branches to create a mosaic of light and shadow on the soft grass beneath my feet.

We lived on a hill just outside of Lisbon, and I could clearly see the fortress of the Castelo de São Jorge. Soldiers moved to and fro along the battlements like industrious ants. Hugging the narrow trunk of a sapling, I admired the sparkling water of the Tagus River and glimpsed the faint silhouette of a merchant spice ship heading out to sea.

A butterfly landed on a nearby branch and I became instantly lost in the intricate maze of its wings. When it flew away, I continued toward the clearing where the chestnut trees grew. I sank to the ground and began collecting the prettiest chestnuts.

The sun warmed my back, making me drowsy, so I stretched out on the grass. The sunlight's pressure against my closed eyelids evoked a riot of colors in the blackness—tiny explosions of bluish red and greenish gold in fantastic patterns. As the lazy drone of bees filled my ears, I imagined my body liquefying and seeping into the earth. I remained in this trance-like state for a long time.

I wasn't sure when the birds stopped singing, but I could no longer hear the insects or the wind. Opening my eyes, I sat up and shivered in the unnatural, disquieting silence. Clouds had gathered in the sky above, blocking the sun.

"Veronica."

Startled, I looked around.

"Veronica..."

This time, I heard my name uttered softly in my ear, causing the tiny hairs on the back of my neck to stand on end. I peeked over my shoulder and saw him standing on the opposite side of the clearing. His serene face reminded me of the Christ figure adorning the altar of our parish church. A long cloak partially hid his powerful body and his shoulder-length hair and goatee were black as pitch.

How did I hear his whisper from so far away?

I was too stunned to move or speak as he held my gaze within the leafy shadows, his yellow eyes glowing in the dimness. Suddenly, the inside of my right wrist burned as a cluster of tiny dots in the shape of a spiral broke through the delicate skin.

"Mama!" I cried.

A moment later, my mother called out, "Veronica, where are you?"

"In the clearing!"

My mother ran toward me. At the sight of my pale face, she demanded, "What is it, child? What do you see?"

"A man is hiding in the trees over there."

Yanking me to my feet, she stood in front of me. "Hello? Is there anyone there?"

Silence.

Gripping my shoulders, she shook me slightly. "Did he speak to you? Did you speak to him? What did he look like?"

8

I showed her the inside of my wrist. "He had eyes like a wolf, and he did *this* to me."

She recoiled at the sight of my strange mark and shoved me toward home. I bent to retrieve the basket of chestnuts, but she hastily pushed me forward, causing me to stumble through the grass. She locked the door as soon we entered the cottage and led me to our icon of the Virgin Mary.

"Kneel, child," she said, sinking to her knees and forcing me down, too. "Hail Mary, full of grace. The Lord is with thee…"

I lost count of how many times we repeated the prayer. My mouth became dry but I didn't dare risk my mother's anger by asking for water.

She stood abruptly. "Did the man speak to you?"

I nodded. "He said my name twice."

My mother paced the room and eventually paused before the Virgin Mary. As she stared at the statue, her expression went from fear to worry to anger. "Three decades of faith and devotion—I've been nothing but loyal, yet you turn your back on me!" She fixed me with a strange look, making me squirm in my seat. "Veronica comes from the Latin *Vera Iconica*, meaning True Icon. I endowed you with this holy name hoping that it would protect you from harm."

My name held special powers?

My mother's eyes slid to the Virgin Mary's sweet face and she frowned. "Why didn't you spare my precious child?"

As the ensuing silence grew, so did the tension within our cottage. The bland gaze of the Virgin Mary combined with her mocking silence caused my mother to unravel. My father had carved the wooden icon shortly before he died—it was the most treasured material possession in our home. I cried out in shock when my mother violently struck the statue and sent it flying across the room. The figure splintered against a storage chest containing our winter supply of salted cod, and we gasped in unison as its head snapped off. It rolled along the floor and came to a stop at my feet, face up. Mary's eyes glared accusingly, as though blaming me for her current predicament. Impulsively, I kicked the head into the flames. My mother screamed in protest but it was too late. Mary's serene face became blackened and distorted as the fire greedily consumed the wood and melted the paint.

My mother turned away from the hearth to collect the headless figure from the floor. She gazed at the broken neck for a moment, caressing the cerulean robe with touching gentleness before tossing what remained of our icon into the flames.

Stunned, I cried, "Mama!"

She shrugged, mumbling something about her prayers not being heard.

***

My mother remained sullen and preoccupied throughout the day. Although she baked the apple tarts as promised, I didn't feel consoled by them. I thanked her for the treats but I could only manage a few nibbles. The tart tasted like dirt to me, and bile rose in my throat every time I attempted to swallow it down. I knew that something important had happened earlier today, but I didn't know what it was, and not knowing frightened me.

Later that night I watched my mother kneel before the hearth in order to retrieve the burnt remains of the Virgin Mary. Taking a piece of charred wood from the ashes, she etched a cross over her heart. I stared at the smudged black lines upon her skin as penitent tears rolled down her cheeks. She came to me and drew a black cross on my forehead, too. Together, we begged God's forgiveness for our heinous sins.

CHAPTER 2
BOSTON, MA
NOVEMBER 1, PRESENT DAY

The United States of America...the *New World*.

The plane began its initial descent, so I leaned against the window to take in the view. I could see the Boston skyline clearly despite the cloudy New England day. Seventeen boats glided upon the surface of the liquid lead bay.

My college buddy, Josh, sent me an email offering to pick me up at the airport. We reconnected last year through Facebook after he had casually mentioned that one of his clients served as the Department Chair of Portuguese Studies at Brown University. He also informed me that a few of my art history articles had been featured in the Portuguese newspapers of New England, capturing the attention of some influential academicians. When I told Josh that the private school I worked for in Lisbon had run out of funding, he wasted no time pulling strings. Emails were exchanged, proposals were made, and I scored a research fellowship.

My breath fogged up the window, thus obscuring the view of the bay. Hopefully, this new position at Brown offered a bit more stability than my last job. At least it would look good on my CV. I was pushing thirty and didn't have time to mess around—professionally speaking.

As bravely as I tried to look ahead to the future, I knew I'd pine miserably for my European lifestyle. How could I not? Being surrounded on a daily basis by fine art and architecture, history, culture, excellent food and wine—I was spoiled.

"*Pah-dun* me," said the corpulent man beside me in a thick Bostonian accent.

It was the hundredth time he had bumped my arm during the transatlantic flight.

"No worries," I replied, inching away from his large bulk.

"Miss, please return your seat to the upright position," the flight attendant said while pacing down the narrow aisle.

I obediently complied before stuffing the latest issue of an underground graffiti magazine into the black laptop case resting across my knees. Despite my seemingly intellectual persona and academic prowess—AKA: nerd vibe—there were three secrets about me that challenged the stereotype often attributed to art historians.

My area of expertise focused on sixteenth century Western Europe, but that didn't stop me from nurturing a passion for gritty street art with social or political undercurrents—the more radical, the better.

I wasn't so vocal about my second secret since it could potentially harm both my professional and personal reputations. Not only was I completely fascinated by U.S. government conspiracies involving U.F.O. aircraft and extraterrestrials, I was an Ancient Alien Theorist. I certainly wasn't alone in my belief that aliens came to Earth thousands of years ago to share their technology with humans. Many fellow theorists were accomplished and well-respected historians who kept a low profile, while others foolishly showed their faces in dubious conferences—or even worse—the History Channel.

"Ladies and gentlemen, please make sure that your seatbelts are securely fastened. We'll be landing shortly. Thank you."

I checked my seat belt and gazed thoughtfully at the laptop case. Stored within the laptop, carefully protected with impenetrable security passcodes, existed the third and most dangerous secret in my life: my manifesto. I've been working on it for almost a decade, and harbored no regrets over the illegal means used in obtaining much of the damning evidence. Exposing the deliberate censorship of scientific data seriously endangering the public could easily destroy elitists around the globe—the type of people who would probably seek revenge. Regardless of the threat, I believed humanity had a right to know the truth.

"Sorry," said the big man beside me as he bumped me again

with his fleshy arm.

One hundred and one.

"It's okay," I assured him as Logan's tarmac loomed into view in the window.

I peeked into the cockpit to thank the pilots before deplaning, and immediately noticed that the air seemed modern, hollow. After a ten-minute wait at baggage claim, I pulled my luggage off the conveyor belt and headed for the exit. My eyes instantly picked out Josh in the crowd. A good-looking guy, despite the extra pounds and bald spot, he offered me a dazzling smile. Irish freckles and bright blue eyes only added to his charm. Josh never had a problem attracting girls in college, but he was the type who enjoyed chasing the ones who weren't interested.

"Welcome home, Veronica," he cried in a Massachusetts accent. "Oh my God, you look even better in person than on Facebook!" He crushed me to his chest in a bear hug. "It's been a while, huh?"

"Seven years…thanks for picking me up at the airport."

"Maybe I should be thanking you. It's not every day I get to leave work early to meet a beautiful woman in Boston."

"Where's Cindy?" I asked, hoping the mention of his current girlfriend would discourage any attempt at flirtation.

"Working. She couldn't get the night off. Oh—happy birthday, by the way. You look exactly the same as you did when we were in college." Lowering his voice and cocking his brow theatrically, he asked, "Did you make some kind of shady deal with the Devil?"

"Maybe," I replied, keeping my expression serious.

He chuckled. "Here, let me help you with your luggage. Hold on. That's it? Two bags?" When I nodded, he added, "You're the dream woman."

"Well, I gave a lot of stuff away to charity and shipped my books to my new address."

"That reminds me," he said while extracting a metallic green shamrock keychain from his pocket. "I picked up your keys from the landlord."

13

I dropped the keys in my purse. "That was nice of you."

The moment we stepped outside, I shivered. I'd forgotten how bitterly cold autumn could be in New England.

"You missed a kick-ass Halloween party last night," Josh said as he led me toward a glossy, new silver BMW sports car. "Everyone wore awesome costumes."

"Really? I love Halloween. Nice car, by the way."

"Glad you like it. I got promoted at the law firm recently, so I gave myself a little reward." He put my suitcases and laptop bag in the trunk, and we entered the vehicle. "I'm really happy you're back. You may not believe it, but I've thought of you so many times throughout the years."

Uh oh, Veronica...

I ignored his sappy comment by pretending to be keenly interested in the scenery outside the car window. "What was that, sorry?"

"Nothing," he mumbled irritably as he maneuvered the car onto the highway.

Feeling bad, I cheerfully inquired, "Hey, have you been hitting the gym? You look pretty fit."

His face lit up. "Actually, I started lifting weights a few months ago. Check it out." He removed his right hand from the steering wheel in order to flex his bicep.

Ah, male vanity. I dutifully poked his arm. "Wow."

He dove into his entire lifting regime, complete with recipes for the perfect protein shake to enhance muscle performance. Thankfully, we arrived at the pub in a short amount of time.

Josh glanced at his flashy Rolex. "Are you tired?"

"Nope. Took a nice long nap on the plane."

"Well, there it is—O'Malley's Pub. We sure had some fun times here," he said, cutting the engine after parking the car. "Ah, the awesome years at UMASS Boston."

"Juggling work and school, pulling all-nighters to cram for exams…I was tired most of the time, but I can't complain. I had lots of fun." As he opened his car door, I said, "Wait a sec— would you turn on the light, please? I'd like to freshen up a bit."

"You're gorgeous enough already."

I rolled my eyes at him as he turned on the light. I quickly applied a coat of black mascara to my lashes and some lip gloss to my lips. I finished off with a spritz of perfume.

"Such a diva," he teased.

"Let's not exaggerate."

"Okay, you revel in your femininity—is that better?"

"Actually, yes," I replied primly, tucking the makeup bag into my purse.

He pointed to the little swirl of birthmarks on the inside of my right wrist. "I see you still haven't gotten rid of the tat."

"How many times do I have to tell you? It's not a tattoo."

"It looks too contrived to be a random design of nature."

I traced the spiral of countless dots with my left fingertip before letting it rest on the tiny star in the hollow center. "I was born with this so I'm used to it."

We both got out of the car. The muffled sounds of a bass guitar and drums filtered through the rusty brick walls as we approached the pub's entrance. The poster on the door depicted a medieval Virgin Mary statue with golden eyes and the words "ICON: Live Tonight."

Seized by a powerful déjà-vu, I began to tremble.

Josh paused mid-step. "Hey, are you okay?"

I touched the poster. "This image..."

"Icon is the latest music sensation from Providence." Josh explained as he opened the door and urged me through it. "Come on, it's freezing out here."

The band was in the middle of a song as we headed for the bar. The music had a driving beat and the sound of the lead singer's voice brought to mind supple velvet and rich dark chocolate—all things decadent. I shook my head slightly to clear it of these bizarre thoughts.

The moment the stage came into full view, I couldn't tear my eyes from the lead singer's face. *Drop-dead gorgeous*. Tall and fit with short black hair and chiseled features, he stood out in stark contrast from the other men inside the pub.

Wow. Get a grip, Veronica.

I mentally chastised myself as I scanned the bar to see if

15

there was anyone I recognized. The sexy musician's presence could not be ignored, however, and he soon had my full attention once again. I wasn't the type to easily fall for a guy, so this inexplicable attraction made me feel a bit unsettled. I couldn't help admiring his sensuous mouth and the strong, elegant curve of his jaw. How would those lips feel against my skin? A sudden, powerful yearning stirred deep within me and my breath caught in my throat.

I really needed to get laid. *Soon.*

His unique golden eyes slid my way as I passed in front of him, making my heartbeat accelerate. Very cool contact lenses—did he wear other funky colors, too?

Chapter 3
Lisbon, Portugal
October 31, 1520

I stretched lazily before getting out of bed and throwing open the shutters. The pre-dawn sky flaunted the most delicate shades of violet and rose.

My mother stirred. "Veronica?"

I detected pain in her voice. "It's early yet, Mother."

She mumbled incoherently and went back to snoring. I prepared a draught to ease her discomfort. Her health had gone from bad to worse in a matter of months.

She won't be baking any birthday treats for you tomorrow...

Every year, I relived the bizarre events that had happened on the day I became physically and mentally branded. The mysterious golden-eyed stranger never visited me again, and I often wondered why he came in the first place.

My mother had eventually fashioned a bracelet by weaving leather straps together to form a thick band. Fastening it around my right wrist, she had admonished in a severe tone, "Never remove your bracelet or reveal your mark to anyone for it would be dangerous. You bear the kiss of Satan, the mark of a witch."

My mother sat up in bed. "Veronica, you're up early."

Her ashy pallor alarmed me. "It's a fine morning," I said with forced cheerfulness. "Would you like to sit in the sunshine for a bit? I could move your chair—"

"No," she cut me off, rubbing her legs while wincing.

"I have prepared a draught for you."

"I need my ointment. Would you go into the city and fetch me some?"

"Of course." I poured the hot draught into a cup and handed it to my mother. "Here, drink this. It will ease your pain."

I donned a wool cloak, placed a few coins into the pouch at

my waist, and walked down the hill. I passed the city gates and meandered through narrow streets, pausing briefly to admire the public statues on my way to the apothecary shop. After purchasing the ointment, I went to the market where vendors shouted to potential customers. The heady aromas of cloves, black pepper, and incense blended with pungent aged cheese, salted cod, blood sausages, and overly ripe fruits and vegetables. Dogs, cats, rats, and pigeons foraged for scraps between the crowded market stalls. Traders from the East displayed exotic silks dyed in shades of lilac and amber. One merchant offered silver bud vases etched with Arab curlicues.

Our widowed neighbor called out to me from a nearby donkey cart. "Veronica!"

"Good morning, Dona Maria," I said, shading my eyes from the brilliant morning sunshine.

"We're off to see the tower, my dear. Come with us."

"The Torre de Belem?" I inquired.

When she nodded, I climbed onto the cart and nodded at the familiar man holding the reins.

"You know my nephew, Norberto," Dona Maria said. "His wife is heavy with child and craves blood sausages. Pregnant women should not be deprived, is that not so?"

Norberto nodded. "Happy wife, happy life."

The Torre de Belem, strategically positioned at the mouth of the Tagus River, stood like a proud beacon to incoming ships. Constructed of pristine white stone, it glistened like dew in the sunlight. Inspired by various Portuguese colonies, the exotic design boasted stylistic elements from India and China, including an African rhinoceros.

Dona Maria crossed herself. "What an age we live in—God be praised! What say you, Veronica?"

I shook my head in awe. "It's magnificent."

Norberto eventually turned the cart around to head back.

My mother came outside to greet us. Leaning heavily on her walking stick, she said, "I wondered what was keeping you."

"It's our fault she's late," Dona Maria explained. "We took Veronica to see the new tower."

My mother invited everyone inside for a bit of refreshing ale. As soon as Norberto and Dona Maria took their leave, she regaled me with questions. I described the Torre de Belem as vividly as I could, knowing in my heart that she would not see it anytime soon.

"I think it quite fitting," my mother commented. "Your twentieth birthday is tomorrow and the splendid tower commemorates your second decade of life."

I chuckled at her grandiose thinking. She bent over in pain and I became alarmed. "Mother, are you all right?"

"A cramp, nothing more. Time to put your old mother to bed. Did you get the ointment?"

"Yes," I said, snatching it from the basket.

"You need to marry," she declared, settling into bed. I ignored her comment as I quietly applied the odiferous, greasy concoction to her legs. "I'm *serious*, Veronica."

I inquired sweetly, "Can I make you some dandelion tea to ease your stomach pains?"

"Do not ignore me!"

I set down the ointment, placed my hands on my hips, and sighed tiredly. "Are we having this conversation again?"

"You should spend more time searching for potential spouses and less time with those books of yours."

"So this week you're blaming the books. What will you come up with next week?"

"Mind your tongue, girl. You need to start behaving like the other young women in our parish. You never see them with their noses in books."

"Would you prefer an empty-headed ninny for a daughter instead of one that is dutiful, responsible, and possesses a bit of curious intellect?"

"That's not what I meant and you know it. What good is intelligence if you can't use it to find a husband?"

I sat down. "Whom would you have me marry?"

"There are plenty of eligible young men—like Tiago."

I crossed my arms. "The big buffoon with the axe?"

"He's a lumberjack. That's almost as good as a carpenter."

"Father was a carpenter," I corrected.

"Tiago could build you a house."

I imagined a lopsided house with sloping floors and shook my head. "He's far too oafish for my taste. Besides, I cannot tolerate his meddlesome sister."

"Sara can be difficult," she reluctantly agreed.

I scoffed at her. "Difficult? You're being too kind. Who else is on your marriage list?"

"Francisco."

I raised an eyebrow. "The little man who had me carry a basket of vegetables uphill to his mother's house because it was too heavy for him to do it himself? *That* Francisco?"

"He makes a decent living as an accountant in the city center." She paused with a twinkle in her eye and added matter-of-factly, "He knows how to read and write."

"I know how to read and write *and* I'm capable of physical labor. I won't marry a weakling who can be easily bullied; I would be tempted to boss him around. Next?"

"Well, I suppose that leaves Diego."

I placed my head in my hands. "He's deaf and mute."

"You are far too picky, Veronica. You do realize that you're on the brink of being called an old maid." I shrugged indifferently, which only served to further irritate my mother. "Every girl of marriageable age in our parish is already wed—except you."

"None of them seem to be living blissfully."

"Marriage is not easy, I'll give you that, but it's a blessing."

I went to the table and began chopping carrots. "Are there any turnips left? Perhaps I should gather some kale to make us a nice soup."

"This conversation is not over!" I stared at my mother as her eyes glistened with unshed tears. "Oh, Veronica, I won't be here much longer."

"You *will* get better," I said, trying to sound convincing.

"I desperately wanted to see you married and settled before..." She stopped abruptly, her face red with discomfort and—*something else.*

I became instantly suspicious when she refused to meet my eyes. "Before…?"

"Dear God, it's inevitable." I stared at her expectantly until she finally confessed, "He'll for you come tomorrow."

The golden-eyed stranger.

My heart raced uncontrollably. "How do you know? Did you have another dream?" She nodded, which made me angry. "Why didn't you tell me? Why all this ridiculous secrecy?"

"I believed if you got married and started a family he would leave you alone. Perhaps find someone else to curse. Too late for that now. He'll mark you again." My mother heaved a shuddering sigh, then sobbed. "In the dream, he warned me not to impede you from your destiny."

I paced around the room. "This explains so much. I feel as if I'm meant for something important in life; something more than being a wife and mother."

Eying me warily, she said, "You openly reject your God-given duty to wed and procreate?"

"I'm not afraid of my destiny. Actually, I must confess that I've been eagerly awaiting his return."

"What?!"

"I want to know why he came to me ten years ago." Holding up my wrist, I added, "Why do I bear this mark? What does it mean? I need answers."

"Are you mad? He's not human—he's an evil abomination of nature."

"Not being human doesn't make him evil," I reasoned. "Angels aren't human."

My mother banged her fist against the wall in frustration. "This creature is no angel. This is why I was against your father teaching you to read. It's made you a daft spinster."

"I'm sorry for being such a disappointment to you."

Despite the regret in her eyes, she remained silent.

I continued, "When he comes tomorrow, I'll face him as bravely as I can to find answers to my questions."

"You stupid, stubborn girl! He may be the Devil himself, for all we know."

"But we don't know. Who is he? What is he? How will we know if we're too afraid to ask?"

"No sane, God-fearing person speaks to a demon."

"What if he's not a demon but something else? Something beyond our limited understanding?" I paused, recalling my father's words before he died. "Remember: we are Portuguese. Father used to say that the world's greatest explorers were spawned from our bloodlines. Insatiably curious men who possess no fear are bravely sailing to places that our ancestors only dreamed of seeing. Surely, these noble traits—so common in men—can be present in women? Even in myself, perhaps?"

"Your words are clever, daughter, but extremely foolish. You're dealing with a being who is possibly far more powerful than all of our great men combined."

"Which is exactly why I wish to learn the purpose of his existence, and why he has chosen me."

My mother's lips clamped down to form a hard line and she shook her head in staunch disapproval.

The silence stretched between us until I picked up an empty basket and went to the door. "I'm going out into the garden. I'll be back shortly."

"We need more firewood," she said, not meeting my eyes.

CHAPTER 4
BOSTON, MA
NOVEMBER 1, PRESENT DAY

"Happy birthday, dear Veronica, happy birthday to you!"

My former classmates applauded, cueing me to blow out the twenty-seven candles glowing atop a chocolate cake. A wise-ass in the crowd called out for a fire extinguisher. *Masshole.*

Slices of cake were passed around while I tried to reconnect with my former classmates. Most of the women were stay-at-home moms, and it soon became painfully evident that we had little in common. The pub became stuffy as more Icon fans arrived. I wriggled my arm out of one coat sleeve before Josh helped me with the other.

"Wow." He looked me up and down. "Nice outfit."

"Thanks."

The wine red mini sheath complimented my black tights and Italian leather boots.

"You're looking pretty hot. I may have to fight somebody."

I took my seat. "Very funny."

He winked at me then turned around to talk to someone. I enjoyed my drink while listening to the conversations taking place around me. As the alcohol blurred the edges of my mind, I recalled my last psychotherapy session with Dr. Sousa. The intense memories, powerful déjà-vu, and recurring dreams that I had been experiencing on a regular basis began exactly one year ago today. Despite my psychologist's expertise and high credentials, I still had no idea what had triggered these manifestations, let alone their meaning.

"Another drink?" Josh asked, breaking my reverie.

He rested against the bar, placing his face close to mine. Icon finished their last set and, the minute the band vacated the stage, pre-recorded music poured from the speakers.

"Bartender, can we get another gin and tonic here?" Josh shouted over the noise. "Hey, are you having fun?" I nodded as he handed me the drink. "Better go easy on those, hon, you might take advantage of me when you're drunk."

The girl sitting beside me overheard his comment and rolled her eyes. Seeing this, Josh said something cocky to her and I'm pretty sure she retorted in like manner, but I only half-listened. The lead singer of Icon sauntered toward me with a feline stealth that made me squirm in my seat—in a good way. I was astonished by my sexual response to him. Wearing a snug black T-shirt and slim black pants that highlighted every asset of his magnificent body, he stopped directly in front of me. I noticed that his left bicep sported an intricate black ink tattoo. The medieval coat of arms flaunted the letter "V" surrounded by traditional Manuelino embellishments—nautical ropes, shells, and even a tiny armillary sphere. I almost gasped aloud in pure art historian delight.

It suddenly dawned on me that everyone around the bar had grown silent and still, especially the women. Without breaking eye contact, he reached for my right hand and turned it over. A tiny smile touched his lips when he caught sight of my strange birthmark. He ran his thumb gently over the delicate skin of my inner wrist, causing the mark to tingle. The simple, yet incredibly intimate, act sent a jolt of electricity throughout my entire body. Meeting my eyes once more, he turned my hand over and brought my knuckles to his lips. The gallant gesture took me off guard because it felt both natural and familiar.

"Happy birthday, Veronica," he said softly.

The way his tongue lingered on my name both thrilled and disturbed me. His strange accent triggered déjà-vu. He knew me—I was sure of it—but I had no recollection of him. My brain quickly went through a mental file. Had we shared a college class together? Did we meet at a party?

A giggling couple leaned against the bar to order drinks, thus placing their bodies between me and the golden-eyed Adonis. Before I had the chance to ask him anything, the ever-growing crowd of people swallowed him up.

"Well, *that* was weird," Josh said in a surly tone dripping with male envy. "Who does that? Walk up to a girl and kiss her hand like he's a knight in some medieval role-playing game. And what's with those strange yellow contacts? He may be a talented musician but he's a total freak."

"You're just jealous," said the girl who had had gotten sassy with Josh a few minutes earlier.

The two began to argue again so I slid off the stool. "I need to use the ladies room. Josh, would you please hold my seat and watch my drink?"

"Sure, the bathroom is—"

"I remember," I said over my shoulder.

I practically ran to the ladies room, scanning the crowd in search of my mystery man but he was nowhere in sight. I pulled out my phone and began dialing Dr. Sousa's number. "Yeah, right," I said aloud, hanging up immediately.

I couldn't tell him of yet another strange déjà-vu episode that led nowhere. Besides, Dr. Sousa had already washed his hands of me, so to speak. He had put me in contact with one of the best Past Life Regression therapists in New England and had already set up the first appointment for me.

I went into the ladies room and splashed some cold water on my cheeks. The mirror above the sink reflected an unusual brightness in my mossy green eyes and my fair skin flaunted a pink flush. Who wouldn't be in a state of heightened awareness after such a sexy encounter? I ran a hand through my long hair and took a deep breath before grabbing a paper towel to dry my hands. A blonde woman almost plowed into me as I exited the ladies room.

"Sorry," she offered. "Hey Ronnie!"

"It's Veronica," I corrected as politely as I could.

"Oops, I forgot." She cocked her head to the side. "Don't you remember me?"

I took in the fake blue contacts, overly bleached hair, heavy makeup, breast implants, and micro-mini denim skirt. How did I know this blonde bombshell? Then it hit me—the sorority girl who sat beside me in English Literature during my junior year of college. Cool girl, but not the brightest crayon in the box.

I smiled. "Long time no see, Stephanie."

"I knew you'd remember me. Go UMASS Alumni," she shrieked like a cheerleader. "Welcome home and happy birthday. How was Portugal?"

"Great."

"Did you live in *Lisboa*?" she asked, making an attempt to pronounce the city correctly.

"Yes, and nice pronunciation."

"Cool. I would love to visit Europe someday. I hear the guys are really cute. Is that true?"

I smiled at Josh when I saw him waving at me from the bar. Stephanie followed my gaze and smiled, too. "A lot of European men sport trendy haircuts and dress to impress," I replied with a shrug.

"Oh, I know. They're so ahead in fashion over there. Speaking of which, you look great." She took in my outfit with the appraising eye of a shopaholic. "I like your hair, too. It brings out your eye color. Is that reddish brown natural or from a box?"

"Thanks—oh, it's natural. You look good, too." I refrained from commenting on her overly processed hair. "Hey, I need to get back to Josh and my drink. Great seeing you."

"You, too!"

I took my seat at the bar and Josh said, "I saw you chatting with Slutty Steph. What words of wisdom did she impart?"

"She wished me a happy birthday. Why do you call her 'Slutty Steph'?"

Josh answered my question with a long look and a raised eyebrow. He took a sip of his beer and said, "She lives in Providence, you know."

"Maybe I'll see her around." I followed his example and took a sip of my watered-down gin and tonic. "Hey, after this drink I think I should call it a night. Would you give me a ride home? I know it's a long drive from Boston to Providence, but I'll pay for the gas and you can crash on the couch. The apartment did come furnished as advertised, right?"

26

"Yes, but there's no need for me to crash on your couch. I'm in Providence now."

This news surprised me. "You don't live in Boston anymore?"

"Nope. My firm opened an office in Providence for the convenience of our clients who live there, and that new branch is being headed by yours truly. They offered me the transfer as a promotion and it came with a decent raise. As much as I love my new car, commuting is a pain in the ass."

"I don't blame you. Boston traffic is atrocious."

"Anyway, I was saving the best surprise for last."

"What surprise?"

"We're neighbors!" Seeing my blank expression, he added, "My office is in College Hill. Your new apartment is upstairs from mine. Why do you think the people at Brown suggested that specific place to you?" When I shrugged, he said, "Because I suggested it to them, silly rabbit!"

"Oh."

"Seriously, it's the perfect location."

Being so close to Josh on a daily basis could lead to problems. I liked him a lot, but his constant flirting and attempts to date me in college grew so tiresome that we stopped hanging out for a few months until he agreed to knock it off. Maybe things would be different now that he had Cindy in his life.

He looked smug. "You're going to fall in love with the apartment, I just know it."

"I'm sure I will," I replied with forced enthusiasm.

27

CHAPTER 5
LISBON, PORTUGAL
OCTOBER 31, 1520

I exhaled a breath of relief as I stepped out into the afternoon sunshine. Worrying about my mother's health and dealing with her constant criticism sometimes took its toll on me. My irritation gradually melted away as I cut stalks of kale.

Nature had a way of calming me, healing me. The corners of my lips lifted as I admired the trees flaunting glorious autumnal foliage. I have always marveled at the changing seasons; how trees slept soundly in winter after bearing fruit throughout the summer, only to awaken and bloom again in the vibrancy of spring.

Sadly, people like me who nurtured a close bond with the earth were viewed with suspicion by the Church. Although I dutifully attended Holy Mass every Sunday alongside my mother, I cringed at the hypocrisy of the clergy, who said and did as they pleased beneath the cloak of divine authority, yet expected everyone else to abide by stern rules. Naturally, I kept these damning observations to myself, oftentimes biting back indignation so fierce that it tasted bitter as bile.

Well, that wasn't completely true.

My secret thoughts were meticulously documented in hand-bound journals, which were kept hidden along with my inheritance—a precious collection of six books that my late father had bequeathed to me. To my mother's disappointment, he had accepted them as payment from an old man in exchange for a finely crafted cabinet. Each book was sturdily bound in oiled brown leather: *Political Science*, *Astronomy and Astrology*, *Poetry*, *Natural Science*, *Roman Mythology*, and *Greek Philosophy*. The Church deemed pagan mythology, astrology, and philosophy spiritually dangerous topics.

Luckily, like most people, my mother was illiterate. Had she known—or even suspected—what lurked inside those pages, she would have destroyed the books a long time ago. My father, on the other hand, had been a clever, learned man who viewed books as small treasures. Sensing my natural aptitude for learning, he taught me to read and write—a gift that I appreciate until this day. Unfortunately, he succumbed to illness shortly after my ninth birthday.

The song of a nearby cardinal broke my reverie. Looking down at my hand, I removed my leather bracelet and gazed in wonder at my unusual mark. Ten years ago, my mother's superstitious fear had frightened me. Everyone knew the harsh trials and sadistic torture awaiting those suspected of witchcraft. The *Malleus Maleficarum*, the veritable handbook of the Holy Inquisition, clearly stated that those who consorted with Satan should be punished by fire.

Shivering with apprehension, I refastened my bracelet, walked over to the chopping block, and picked up the axe to chop the firewood.

Later in the day, when he twilight sky boasted fiery clouds against an indigo background, I prepared our evening meal. The anticipation of seeing *him* tomorrow weighed heavily on my mind. My mother and I ate without speaking since silence was her preferred method of chastisement. After clearing the dishes and tidying up the kitchen, I stared out the window and marveled at Venus, which sparkled like a diamond in a sky of black velvet.

"Veronica!"

I turned away from the view.

"Time for bed."

"Yes, Mother. Goodnight."

"Goodnight, Veronica. Don't forget to say your prayers. Be sure to ask God to grant you wisdom and good sense. You'll need it for tomorrow."

I got off at the designated bus stop and noted with relief that the professional office complex was around the corner. My appointment with Dr. Clarice Barnum made me so anxious that I bit the inside of my lip until it bled. In an attempt to calm my nerves, I remembered the last words Dr. Sousa said to me before my departure from Portugal:

"I've arrived at the conclusion that what you've been experiencing is possibly the residual imagery of a past life. Science has proven that energy never dies, so many in my field are rethinking reincarnation. Initially, I believed that you were suffering from a severe anxiety disorder, but I was mistaken. I encourage you to dig deeper into another form of therapy with someone who is better equipped to help you. Dr. Clarice Barnum is reputed to be the best therapist in Rhode Island, and I've taken the liberty of making an appointment for you. Do not be afraid to seek the truth, Veronica."

Do not be afraid…

I made my way into the sunlit lobby and walked up to a stunning Asian woman seated behind a desk.

"Good morning," she said in a melodic voice as her matte red lips curved into a smile. "Do you have an appointment?"

"Yes."

"Name, please?" she asked, her fingers hovering over a white computer keyboard.

"Veronica Cabral."

"Down the corridor, last door on the right."

Within minutes, I was standing face to face with a mature woman with piercing gray eyes and a kind smile.

"Veronica Cabral? It's a pleasure to meet you. Please, make

yourself comfortable," she said, indicating a plush cream sofa. "Dr. Sousa believes that you would benefit greatly from seeing me. Before we get into the reason why you're here, how do you feel about this kind of therapy?"

I settled into the corner of the sofa. "To be completely honest with you, Dr. Barnum, I've never believed in past lives. My parents were fervent Catholics and taught me that we either go to Heaven or Hell after death. Reincarnation is a foreign concept to me, but I do have an open mind."

"That's a fair answer and I appreciate your honesty." She sank into an armchair, facing me. "Why don't you tell me what's going on?"

Hesitating, I looked down at my fidgeting hands. "I really don't know where to begin..."

A tempting bowl of Italian Baci chocolates sat on the coffee table between us. She reached into the bowl and withdrew two chocolates, then handed one of them to me.

I smiled at the gesture. "Thank you, Dr. Barnum."

"I prefer Clarice, if that's okay. I know you're nervous, Veronica, maybe even a bit scared. It's normal. Everything you say in this room will be held in the strictest confidence. I don't make judgments."

"I don't want to appear, well...silly."

"I don't think any of my patients are silly. For example, I have one person who believes to be the reincarnation of Queen Marie Antoinette."

I chuckled softly. "Do you believe her?"

"Him," she corrected. "It's not my job to believe or not, it's my job to help people work through what science cannot easily explain."

I took a deep breath. She nodded, encouraging me to go on as she set her clipboard on her lap and took out a pen. "My recurring dreams began last year on the night of my twenty-sixth birthday. Since then, I've been experiencing powerful episodes of déjà-vu and having strange visions," I caught myself. "No, not visions. They're actually more like memories—impossible memories."

31

"Impossible in what sense?"

"I haven't lived through any of those moments."

"Not in this lifetime, but perhaps in another." She paused. "How many times have you had the recurring dream?"

"I've lost count."

"Would you like to share it with me?" Sensing my uneasiness, she added, "If you're uncomfortable doing it today we can wait until the next time."

I took a moment to gather my thoughts. "The dream always begins the same way: I'm in a vast field facing a man whom I love very much. We're both wearing sixteenth century outfits in matching shades of red. A storm is brewing and our hair is being whipped around wildly by the wind. Water stretches out before us and I see a galleon bobbing on the angry waves. The man is in danger and my anxiety mounts as I try desperately to tell him something…I always wake up at this point."

"What are you trying to tell him?"

"I don't know, but there's a sense of urgency, so I think it must be important."

Clarice studied my face. "How do you know you're dressed in sixteenth century clothing?"

"Historical fashion has always been a hobby of mine."

"Ah, of course. Dr. Sousa mentioned that you were an art historian. Tell me, why is the man in danger?"

I shook my head. "I don't know."

"What language are you speaking in the dream?"

My brow wrinkled in thought. "It's a cross between Italian—maybe Spanish—mixed with Portuguese."

"An old European dialect, perhaps." She wrote down some notes, then asked, "What does the man look like?"

"Long black hair and no face—well, he's got a goatee but his face is like a void."

She flipped the notebook to a new sheet of paper. "Any other dreams?"

"Only one other dream."

"Recurring?"

"No. I had it once, last Christmas Eve. I was dressed in a

gold brocade gown with a miniature jeweled starfish and shells. The embellishments were nautical—the kind commonly found in Manuelino architecture."

Clarice looked up from her notes. "What kind of architecture?"

"King Manuel I commissioned a lot of architecture flaunting the nautical spirit of Portugal's Golden Age. If you Google search Torre de Belem or the Convento de Cristo, you'll see what I mean."

"I'll have to look it up," she said, writing down the information.

"The thing is, I remember *wearing* this gown. Even now, sitting here, I can recall the heaviness of the fabric, the feel and smell of it, the constricting bodice…"

"An extraordinary memory," she whispered. "What else can you recall from the dream?"

"I danced in a candlelit ballroom while a man—the same one from my recurring dream—watched from the shadows."

Clarice's pen moved quickly across the paper. "Have you ever shared your dreams and memories with anyone else, like your parents?"

"My parents are deceased. They died a long time ago."

Her pen froze. "I'm sorry. When you were a child, did you foster any kind of connection with the distant past?"

"I've always been comfortable around old things and felt the U.S. to be too modern."

"In New England we have many buildings dating back to the seventeenth and eighteenth centuries," she pointed out.

"Not old enough for my taste."

"Not old enough," she repeated. "Interesting. What do you think that means?"

"I'm hoping that you can help me find out."

"Fair enough, Veronica. If you continue being as honest with me as you were today, I'll do everything within my power to help you," she said, standing up to let me know we had concluded the session.

I left the office feeling somewhat relieved to have finally

talked to someone who wouldn't judge me harshly or write me off as crazy. My mind raced as I rode the bus to College Hill. Josh exited the house as I ascended the porch steps.

"Hey, Veronica," he said, holding up the thank you card I had slipped under his door earlier. Inside was a gift certificate for a nice dinner for two at a swanky downtown restaurant. "This was not necessary, you know."

"I know, but it's my way of showing appreciation for all that you've done for me."

"Well, thank you. Cindy has been wanting to try this place out for a while." He paused. "So, what do you think of Providence and the new job?"

"So far, so good," I replied brightly.

"What are you doing tonight?"

"A couple of my boxes arrived. I need to sort through a ton of books and put them away."

"Do you need some help?" When I shook my head, he continued, "We could grab a bite when you're done."

"Thanks, but I've been running around all day and I'm really tired. I think I'll stay in tonight."

"Okay, cool," he said, obviously disappointed. "Let me know if you change your mind. We can grab a drink later."

"I'll let you know," I said, moving toward the door.

He took hold of my arm. "Look, those fancy boots and this coat are cute, but you're going to need something a lot more substantial for winter. Otherwise, you'll freeze your butt off."

I looked down at myself. "Yeah, you're right."

"You haven't forgotten what New England winters are like, have you?"

"I've tried hard to forget."

I let myself inside my apartment. Since the area housed transient university students, many properties were rented out fully furnished. My unit was no exception, and came decorated in neutral tones of beige and white. The house itself was a big old Georgian revival, split up into four separate apartments. There were other historical homes and plenty of mature trees on the street, which added extra charm to the neighborhood.

I went into the kitchen to make myself a cup of green tea before doing some serious online shopping. In addition to finding a fabulous pair of insulated weatherproof boots, I also ordered a goose down coat and a Russian faux-fur hat. Free delivery on all items, too.

I turned my attention to the scattered boxes in my living room and began methodically organizing my books before placing them on the bookshelf. Only one box remained when I had finished, and it contained old photo albums, a few tattered sketch journals, and other personal belongings. There was no more room on the bookshelf, so I carried the box to my bedroom closet and placed it beside my black laptop case, which was hidden beneath a comforter thanks to my paranoia.

Next, I took a shower and nestled into bed with a book. I fell asleep shortly afterward, only to wake up with a start. I had the uncanny sensation of being watched. The heavy, dark silence made me shiver so I forced myself to get up and make a soothing cup of chamomile tea. The street lights provided enough brightness so I didn't need to turn on a lamp.

I made the tea then walked to the large window in the living room. Rows of tall maples and oaks lined both sidewalks. A man dressed in black pants and a black hooded sweatshirt crossed the street. I took in his height and the broadness of his back as he tugged the rim of his hood forward to conceal half of his face. When he reached the other side of the street, he turned around and looked directly at the window where I stood.

"What the—" I heard myself say before spilling some of the hot tea on my foot. "Ow! Damn it!"

I looked down for a second and, by the time I turned my attention back to the window, he had vanished. The trees grew so close together that the branches touched, leaving no visible gaps of sidewalk for me to peer through. My imagination made the connection between the eerie presence in my bedroom and the man in black, but my common sense insisted it was impossible. There had to be a logical explanation.

I woke up to the roar of thunder and shivered from head to toe in anticipation of what the day would bring. Quietly, so as not to wake my mother, I slipped into my shoes and wrapped a woolen shawl around my shoulders. The rain fell with such ferocity that it prevented me from opening the shutters. Winter would come early this year.

The interior of the cottage was dark and chilly, so I lit a candle and added some kindling wood to the glowing embers within the hearth. Gradually, the flame spread. As I reached for the metal poker leaning against the wall, something behind me stirred. I looked to my mother who slept peacefully. I turned my attention back to the hearth and, this time, I heard the scraping of a stool.

The blood ran cold in my veins. The bravado I had displayed yesterday, the foolish resolve to face my strange visitor, dissolved completely as I trembled like a coward. What was wrong with me? I had waited ten years for this moment! I eventually willed myself to face him. A set of impossibly bright golden eyes met mine as I edged closer to the wall at my back. He looked exactly the same as he did ten years ago, only now he was much closer. Despite my fear, I found him extremely attractive. His shoulder-length black hair was neatly combed, his fair skin was unblemished, and a fashionable goatee framed his sensuous mouth.

"Vera Iconica," he said softly in a deep voice.

I was too stunned by his beauty to respond. Suddenly, I became keenly aware of a burning sensation on my right wrist. I hastily removed my bracelet only to discover that I had a new mark! Within the hollow of the spiral was a perfectly formed tiny star.

"Do you remember me?" I barely nodded in response to his question and he inquired, "Do I frighten you, Veronica?"

"Yes."

"Yet, you do not run away."

Every muscle in my body tensed. "If your intention was to hurt me, I believe you would have already done so."

"That's a very logical way of thinking, but please know that I would never harm you."

For some inexplicable reason, I knew he spoke the truth. I glanced at my mother, who was still asleep. "She knew you would come today."

"What about you?"

"It's been ten long years," I replied. "I admit, I've been waiting my entire life for something to happen."

"You have a destiny to fulfill."

"Are you here to tell me what it is?"

He moved for the first time by leaning forward and resting his elbows on the table. "In time." He paused, eyeing me intently. "Ask your questions. I know you must have many."

"What's so special about my tenth and twentieth birthdays?"

"You were destined to receive Our Mark on those years," he replied, pointing to my right wrist. "You received one on your tenth year and another one just now, did you not?"

I nodded. "Are you the one who marked me?"

"I do not have that kind of power."

Studying my wrist with newfound interest, I inquired, "What does it mean?"

"You're the one the prophecy speaks of. You are the Icon."

"What prophecy?"

His eyes glittered in the dimness of the cottage. "The Sacred Oracle foretold of your coming."

"Who is the Sacred Oracle?"

"I promise to answer your questions, but not today. Your human fragility requires that I reveal information to you slowly," he explained in a tone usually reserved for children.

He was right, of course. My head was already spinning.

Pointing to my wrist, he asked, "May I see it?"

I moved toward him and cautiously held out my right wrist. His hand darted forward and I instinctively flinched.

"Forgive me," he offered. "I didn't mean to frighten you."

Appeased, I took a step closer and offered my wrist to him again. His face took on an expression of awe. "Do you realize what you are?"

My face flushed under his scrutiny. "No."

"Someday, you will." A frown marred his perfect brow and he seemed distracted. "Before I depart, do you have any other question you wish to ask of me?"

"I have many. Must you depart so soon?"

He stood, towering over me. "Unfortunately, yes."

I needed to know more about the prophecy and the Sacred Oracle; the prospect of being kept in ignorance for much longer was utterly maddening. "Will you be visiting us again soon? Or will you wait another ten years?"

His face grew sad as he stole a glance at the reclining form of my mother. "There is only you now, Veronica."

"What?"

"Your mother passed from this world just now. I'm sorry."

I almost tripped as I ran to the bed. "Mother?"

Limp as a ragdoll, my mother was not breathing despite the fact that her skin was still warm to the touch. She had died in her sleep. I threw my arms around her and wept in sorrow. When I finally turned around, my visitor was gone.

My eyes stung with tears as I put on my heavy cloak and went out into the driving rain to fetch the priest. My mother didn't get the chance to receive her last rites, and I know she would have wanted prayers said on her behalf. I had spent a lifetime fooling my mother and everyone else in our parish into thinking that I was a devout Christian, and I would continue doing so for the sake of my own self-preservation.

Chapter 8
Providence, RI
November, Present Day

Dr. Nunes was Brown University's expert on Portuguese history and culture during the Manuelino period. His current academic project involved one of the tombs housed within the Mosteiro de Batalha. I spent the first three weeks of my fellowship aiding him in this endeavor, locating valuable cross references to support his theories. It wasn't easy deciphering the underlying meaning of sixteenth century Portuguese texts and translating them into modern English, but I relished the challenge.

Dr. Nunes and I hit it off immediately for two reasons: first, my passion for the Manuelino style matched his own and, second, my last name. His doctoral dissertation focused on the navigational exploits of the Portuguese navigator, Pedro Álvares Cabral, and the Brazilian colonies. After our initial introduction, he had playfully asked, "Any relation to Pedro?"

I also liked the two graduate students working in our department—Tara, a large-boned blonde from Nebraska, and Josie, a petite Hispanic brunette from New York.

Dr. Nunes asked me to go on a coffee run one cold morning and I readily agreed. I didn't mind doing such menial tasks, especially since I spent many hours in front of a computer.

He held up his finger. "Large, black—"

"Two sugars," I interjected as I stuck my hand in the coin jar labeled: Coffee Money.

"Thanksgiving is next week," he said. "That's a holiday not celebrated in Europe. I bet you missed eating turkey with stuffing—oh, and let's not forget scrumptious pumpkin pie."

"I admit, missing out on Thanksgiving was pretty tough."

"What are you doing for the holiday? Visiting family?"

"No family. I'm going to hang out here," I replied with shrug. I planned on spending the long weekend reading and watching movies. Maybe I'd even treat myself to a good bottle of red wine and some fine dark chocolates to compensate for the lack of a traditional feast.

"What? No turkey? No stuffing? No pie?" When I smiled wistfully, he added, "Why don't you come to my house? I live in Newport near the water and it's really pretty there."

"Thanks for the offer, but I don't want to be that weird single woman at the dinner table."

"The one I invited out of pity?"

I laughed. "Yeah, that one."

"Nonsense! Tara and Josie plan to remain in Providence so I've invited them as well. If you accept my invitation, then there will be three weird single women sitting at the table instead of only two. Does that make my offer more tempting?"

"It does, indeed. That's very nice of you, Dr. Nunes."

I grabbed my coat and made my way out into the misty morning. The coffee shop around the corner was packed with people buying hot beverages to ward off the chill. While I waited in line my eyes were drawn to the front window and I spotted him outside on the sidewalk.

Him...as in the lead singer of Icon! He stood less than fifteen feet from me looking mighty fine in a pair of designer jeans and a stylish black wool coat. He spoke animatedly with a group of people then, unexpectedly, he looked directly at me, as if he knew I'd been staring at him the entire time.

Mortified, I glanced away quickly. *Shit.*

"Next."

The plump barista behind the counter regarded me with a dull expression. Small silver hoops ran along the length of her right eyebrow, two hung from her left nostril, and a metal stud pierced her bottom lip. She also sported a black spider tattoo on her neck and a red rose in the center of her chest. Hair dyed cotton candy blue completed the ensemble. I smiled warmly and, in response to my polite gesture, the corners of her painted black lips lifted only a fraction of an inch.

"Good morning," I said. "A large black coffee with two sugars, please."

I peeked out the window as I waited. He was gone.

"Here you go," she said, placing a styrofoam cup the size of a thermos on the counter.

I paid for the coffee, turned around and stopped short. He had come inside and was standing directly behind me. His eyes were warm brown like smoky topaz. An inexplicably delicious tingle spread throughout my entire body.

"Veronica," he said, looking at me with an expression that made me blush.

His scent was an intoxicating blend of moist earth and newly cut grass, which I found irresistibly distracting. When did they start making colognes that smelled like a forest after rain? I usually handled most situations with a fair amount of confidence, but this man left me tongue-tied—and it wasn't only because of his good looks. "Oh, ah…hi. Yes?"

Damn it.

Graciously overlooking my total lack of poise, he continued, "I didn't have a chance to introduce myself properly the last time we met. My name is Victor."

"Victor," I repeated.

A pleasing light came into his eyes, as if the sound of his name coming from my lips made him happy. I was startled by the burning intimacy of his gaze. I immediately chastised myself for wishful thinking.

"Have we ever met?" He appeared hopeful until I added, "You seem to know who I am, but I don't know who you are."

His wistful expression almost made me feel guilty. He looked down at his well-shod feet, and I could see that he was struggling with something. "What makes you think that I know you?"

"Well, you knew my name when you wished me a happy birthday at the pub."

"Happy birthday dear Veronica," he sang softly. "Everyone in the pub knew your name that night."

Yes, but you knew it long before my friends sang the song.

41

The thought had crept into my head unbidden. I was sure it was a fact and not a mere speculation, either. Narrowing my eyes, I studied him for a few seconds. "There's something about you that's familiar," I insisted.

He held my gaze for what seemed like a small eternity. "Maybe it's just déjà-vu."

I was speechless.

His friends came to the door and gestured to him.

"Come on, man," said the guy I recognized as Icon's drummer.

"Yeah, we're already late for practice," said the bass guitarist.

Victor sighed. "I have to go."

I stood there like an idiot as the most interesting and gorgeous man I've ever met walked away. What could I do? Shout out my cell phone number at his retreating backside? That definitely wasn't my style.

As if reading my mind, he turned around and said, "See you soon." My face must have registered confusion because he added, "I know where to find you, Veronica."

Again with the intimate tone. He winked before donning his stylish sunglasses. Puzzled, I walked out of the coffee shop. How would he know where to find me? Did he mean he'd see me again here at the coffee shop? I looked down at my cell and saw that it was ten-o'clock. From now on I would try to do coffee runs for Dr. Nunes at around this same time. Hopefully, if I "casually" bumped into Victor enough times, he'd ask for my number—or better yet, a date.

CHAPTER 9
LISBON, PORTUGAL
CHRISTMAS, 1520

I forced myself to get out of bed and attend Holy Mass. I would have preferred to stay under the warm covers, but that would be inexcusable on Christmas. The weather outside was cold and damp, compelling me to don a warm gown over my linen shift. I combed the tangles from my long hair and studied my reflection in a polished looking glass. Deeply saddened by my mother's death, I had lost weight due to my lack of appetite. My high cheekbones stood out in stark contrast to my hollowed face. My eyes were almost the same moss green as my gown, but they looked tired. Sighing in resignation, I pinched my cheeks and bit my lips to give them a hint of color before throwing my wool cloak around my shoulders and pulling its hood low over my head.

The thick coat of frost on the grass crunched beneath the soles of my boots as I walked down the narrow path leading to the old church. A delicate veil of mist graced the silent morning as I picked my way carefully through the leafless brush. I had covered nearly a mile when the sound of a twig breaking underfoot made me stop in my tracks. The mist had thickened to fog, thus impeding my visibility. I heard the sound again and, trembling with fear, hid behind the wide girth of an oak's trunk. When a stag emerged from the fog, my body relaxed and I almost laughed aloud. I ventured out of my hiding place, scaring the poor animal in the process.

Chastising myself for being such a ninny, I continued my walk along the path. I still had the uncanny sensation of being watched and therefore quickened my pace. Relief washed over me when I finally spied the rustic bell tower. Since I was one of the last parishioners to arrive, I took my seat in the back row.

The nave stretched out before me and the cloying incense formed a hazy cloud. A few heads turned to look at me, but I stared at the priest with rapt attention and refused to meet anyone's gaze.

Dona Maria greeted me after the service and we exchanged pleasantries. When I admitted to missing my mother, she said, "The Lord took her so young. God bless her."

I changed the subject. "How are you feeling these days?"

"This weather makes me ache all over," she replied. "That poultice you made for me last time eased the swelling. Do you think you could stir up another batch?"

I nodded. "I'll bring it to you tomorrow."

The notorious gossip, Sara, approached us. "May the peace of our Lord be with you both on this most blessed of days," she said in a sticky-sweet tone.

"May His peace be with you and yours," I replied coolly.

"Yes, yes," Dona Maria mumbled, crossing herself and sighing in irritation at the younger woman's interruption.

"I would like to speak with you privately, Veronica," Sara said, looking pointedly at Dona Maria. When the old woman excused herself, she continued, "We are heartbroken over your dear mother's death. She was such a good Christian woman and a fine example for all of us." She took a step forward, closing the gap between us. "To think of you in that cottage alone— without the protection of a man—makes everyone in the congregation sick with worry."

"Thank you for the concern," I replied flatly.

She took my arm in a friendly gesture. "You may not be aware of this, but I think of you as a sister. My brother thinks highly of you, too."

Oh, no, not the lumberjack...

"Tiago is a good, God-fearing man who needs a suitable wife. In return, he could protect you."

"Protect me from what, exactly?"

She regarded me coolly. "Every woman needs a husband."

"There must be plenty of girls who would marry Tiago."

"That may be true, but he's fond of you."

I crossed my arms. "I have no intention of marrying your brother or anyone else for that matter."

"No intention to marry?" She repeated, placing her plump hand on her chest. "Marriage is God's holy institution. The sole purpose of a woman is to do His will and to procreate."

"May I remind you that I'm still in mourning? You cannot possibly expect me to behave in such a disrespectful manner toward my mother's memory!"

Sara's face flushed red when heads turned in our direction.

Tiago came over to where we stood and nodded clumsily, staring first at my face then at my chest. "May the peace of our Lord be with you, Veronica," he said to my breasts.

Disgusted, I stomped off toward the path and headed home. The fog had dissipated and the sunshine made the frosty branches sparkle like crystal. When I arrived home, I stood in the center of the room, unsure of what to do next. My mother and I usually celebrated Christmas by baking biscuits in fanciful shapes, sipping sweet wine, and telling stories by the fire. I didn't feel like celebrating or baking by myself.

In order to pass the time and not ponder on my loneliness, I decided to make a poultice for Dona Maria. I made my selection from the dried bunches of plants suspended from the rafters, then ground the herbs with a mortar and pestle, adding linseed oil to help with inflammation. Next, I placed the moist mass in a ceramic bowl and covered it with a damp cloth.

The sun was still high, so I tidied up before slipping on my cloak to go for a brief walk. Hearing footsteps outside the cottage, I ran to the window and saw Dona Maria. I hid my disappointment as I opened the door.

She held out a loaf of warm bread wrapped in a linen cloth. "I couldn't bear the thought of you being alone today."

I offered her a heartfelt smile. "Thank you."

"Were you about to go out?" she asked, noticing my cloak.

"Oh, no. I just…"

When I said nothing more, Dona Maria reached for my hand and gave it a squeeze. "No need to explain, my dear. I understand perfectly. Why not celebrate her memory today?"

I nodded, removing my cloak. "I don't have anything special to offer you…"

"At least we have bread."

"Oh, I made your poultice. We can apply some now."

"That would be kind of you." She rubbed her lower back and winced. "There's nothing as merciless as old age."

I applied the poultice to the painful area on her back then covered the skin with a clean linen bandage.

"Ah, your remedy is already taking effect," Dona Maria said, relieved. "Thank you."

I washed my hands, poured some wine, set out a small chunk of hard cheese, the bread, and a handful of roasted chestnuts. I also had a cauldron of broth inside the hearth and set it directly over the fire to boil.

"Have you been eating, Veronica?" Dona Maria asked, noticing my loose-fitting gown.

I stood up straight and self-consciously smoothed the folds of my skirt. "I have very little appetite, to be honest."

"This won't do, child," she said softly. "Your mother wouldn't want you wasting away on her behalf."

"No, she wouldn't," I admitted.

My impromptu dinner looked appetizing and, to my surprise, I was actually hungry. Dona Maria and I chatted as we chewed, and I was grateful for her pleasant company.

"Did Sara approach you on account of her halfwit brother?" Dona Maria asked of me when I rose to ladle the broth into two bowls.

"She did," I replied, amused by the fact that there was no filter between the old woman's thoughts and her tongue.

I set a bowl of broth before my guest and she inhaled the fragrant steam. "A good broth is like a poultice for the soul."

"In truth, Sara has been trying to match me with her brother for as long as I can remember," I said, also inhaling the steam from the broth and allowing it to warm my insides.

Dona Maria frowned and waved her hand as if swatting at an imaginary fly. "You can do so much better. I do think he needs to marry soon, however. That boy leers at all the women in church—married or not. Men are not like us, you know."

"Oh?" I asked, inviting her to elaborate.

She put on a face that made her look wise. "Men are carnal creatures. They have physical needs that must be met. Women, on the other hand, can easily live without the pleasures of the flesh. Remember: men are above beasts, women are below angels."

"Below angels," I repeated thoughtfully.

She held out her empty cup and I refilled it with wine. "Besides, you certainly don't want such an unpleasant and meddlesome creature such as Sara for your sister-in-law."

I shook my head emphatically. "I'm sure she gossips about me behind my back."

The old widow took a hearty gulp of wine, which was obviously loosening her lips. "Humph! Sara gossips about anyone who is better off than she is, and right now that person is you. She's an envious creature."

"Me? I have nothing to be envious of."

"Is that so?" she countered, cocking her head to one side. "Let's examine your situation objectively, shall we? You're pretty and clever, which are two strong motives for envy. Although your parents are both dead, you're not burdened by debt, and have even inherited a decent cottage with some fertile land. In addition to this, you are your own mistress with no husband to boss you around. Many women would enjoy being in your shoes right now, Veronica."

"Lately I've been lamenting the fact that I'm so alone. I never thought of it as freedom."

"Free as a bird—within certain limitations, of course."

"How sad it must be to live your life in constant comparison to someone else," I mused aloud.

"Tragic," she agreed. "People like Sara need to find fault with others in order to feel better about themselves. Ignore her and live your life as happily as you can."

"I'll drink to that," I said, lifting my cup to hers in a toast.

"Your prince will come someday," she assured confidently before peeling a chestnut and popping it into her mouth. "A girl

47

like you won't be alone for long."

My prince.

The conversation turned to harmless local gossip. For an old widow who claimed to not get out much, Dona Maria seemed to know everything about everyone. Where she obtained this information was a mystery.

There was still plenty of light in the sky when Dona Maria took her leave. A moment later, there was a knock at the door. I was in the middle of gathering plates and noticed the linen cloth in which she had wrapped the bread.

I snatched it off the table and opened the door. "Oh, you forgot—"

It wasn't Dona Maria standing in the threshold, however. I dropped the cloth and the golden eyed creature gracefully picked it up and handed it back to me.

"Greetings, Veronica. May I come inside?"

I stood aside and let him enter. "Where have you been? I still have many unanswered questions."

"I know you do." He paused. "I've been overcome with concern for you, but thought you needed time and privacy to honor your mother's memory." When I looked surprised, he added, "Just because I'm different doesn't mean that I lack emotion. I'm very familiar with the grief that accompanies the loss of a loved one."

I took a deep breath. "Oh…"

"Your mother died in her sleep. When her energy—her life force—left the room, it was peaceful. She felt no pain."

"You knew the exact moment when she died?"

"My kind always knows when death and life are near."

"I need to know who—or what—you are."

"Straight to the point, Veronica. You're a fine example of this modern era."

"What do you mean?"

"I'm referring to your desire to explore and uncover the truth; the curiosity to discover what lurks beneath the obvious. Had you been born a man, you would have been an exceptional navigator."

48

His words humbled me. I was suddenly aware of the height and breadth of him, and how his presence filled my home.

"May I?" he politely asked, indicating a stool.

I nodded and he sat down. He flung his black cloak over his shoulder, and I noticed that he wore the fine, costly garments favored by the Portuguese nobility.

"Are you here because I'm still unmarried and childless?"

"Where did you get such a notion?"

"My mother." He was confused for a moment then his face lit up with realization. I continued, "She believed that you would have sought someone else to take my place."

"She was wrong," he said. "You are the Icon—regardless of your marital status or if you had ten children. I would have still come on the tenth and twentieth years of your life to be sure you received Our Mark just as the Sacred Oracle had predicted. Besides, how could I possibly ignore your flame?"

"My flame?" I shook my head. "I don't understand."

"Please sit with me and allow me to explain how I see your kind." I obediently pulled up a stool and sat down. "I see humans as burning flames. Most of you are so beaten down by tedious labor, oppressive religion, and familial obligations that the flame burns very low, like those dying embers," he said, pointing at the hearth. "Some of you manage to overcome these obstacles and burn as brightly as beacons in the night. The majority of these people are teachers, artists, musicians, scientists, and philosophers—critical thinkers with the power to change the world they live in."

"Am I one of these people?"

"You are no mere beacon, Veronica, you are a shining star. You are the one we have been waiting for."

"What am I supposed to do? I'm neither rich, nor powerful, nor do I possess much life experience. I'm only a woman."

"From today onward I will instruct you and, in time, you'll come to understand what is expected of you. This is your destiny." Sensing my anxiety, he added, "You continue to look upon me with doubt."

"This may sound foolish, but are you a demon?"

His eyes registered surprise. "No, nor am I the Devil."

"Why is it that you never age? You look the same as you did on my tenth birthday."

"I do age, only much slower than you. My concept of time is different than yours."

I dragged my stool closer and leaned forward in order to better study his face. The dark pupils dilated within their golden irises as I drew near. "Are you a spirit?"

"Not in the sense that you're thinking."

I took a deep breath. "May I touch you?"

He barely nodded in consent as I pressed my palm against his cheek. His eyes shut briefly, his expression blissful. His skin was warm and smooth, but there was something else. I brought my hand up and examined my fingertips.

The corners of his mouth lifted. "They tingle, yes?"

"How did you know?" I asked, a smile playing upon my own lips. I'd never felt anything like this before!

"I know many things, Veronica," he said in a deep, low voice that insinuated...

Insinuated what? Something—a yearning—stirred deep within me. Most women my age were already married with children, yet for all of the knowledge I had gleaned from books, I was ignorant in matters involving the opposite sex. I was helplessly drawn to him as though I were floating down a river and forced to follow its current. My heart fluttered within my ribcage like a trapped bird, which caused my breathing to become shallow. Slowly, he reached out and placed his hand on my chest. My heart slowed down and a warm feeling of peace and tranquility washed over me.

"My little star," he whispered affectionately.

I flinched. "You practice witchcraft!"

"Do you honestly believe that, Veronica? I thought you were above such banal superstitions."

"How did you slow my heart if not with magic?" I countered, already feeling slightly foolish.

"I am capable of many things—none of them attributed to the supernatural."

"Please tell me what you are," I implored.

"If I tell you now, you won't understand, but the day will come when you'll be capable of understanding. I'll reveal my identity to you at that time. You have my word."

"Do you have a name?"

"My name cannot be pronounced by human tongues."

"What do I call you?"

"I have never taken a human name."

I thought for a moment. "I shall call you Victor since you can triumph over Death."

"I, too, shall die someday. Everything dies, even the stars." He paused. "I accept the name Victor. Any more questions?"

"Yes, hundreds of them, actually."

He chuckled slightly. "Walk with me, Veronica," he said as he rose from the stool and extended his hand in invitation.

I accepted his hand and we exited the cottage. Walking along the wooded path, we talked mostly of the natural world around us. Victor knew a great deal about plants and animals. Impressed by his vast knowledge, I listened to him like a student would a teacher. When the moon rose high in the sky and the night grew cold, we headed back to the cottage. I stoked the embers in the hearth back to life and made some hot mulled wine. We sat down to watch the flames and sipped the soporific drink.

I marveled at the way the firelight made his eyes shimmer like two precious jewels. "Your eyes..."

"What of them?"

"They glow like the eyes of a wolf. Why is that?"

"Unlike Earth, where light-eyed people live in cold regions and dark-eyed people live in hot jungles or deserts, there are no extreme temperatures in my world. All of my people share a similar eye color. Also, our nights are much longer than those here on Earth. Our nocturnal eyes allow us to see clearly in the blackest of shadows." He lowered his gaze. "Do you find them offensive?"

"On the contrary. They are unique."

He asked questions about my childhood, what I thought of

the Portuguese monarchy, and my opinion of the Church. I replied candidly, expressing intolerance for human injustice.

"You're highly perceptive," he commented. "A real credit to your kind."

"You don't have a high opinion of us, do you?"

"It isn't my place to judge, but it's obvious that the powerful treat the weak unfairly and unkindly."

How could anyone argue with that statement? What defense could I possibly make in favor of humanity? Even after the candles had burned down to their wicks and I could no longer keep my eyes open, I still asked questions and he tirelessly answered them. At some point, I drifted off to sleep.

The next day I awoke on my bed fully clothed with my cloak thrown over me for warmth. The morning sunshine permeated the wooden cracks of the window shutters and I could see flecks of dust dancing in a sunbeam.

Victor must have carried me to bed. The thought of him performing such a tender act made me smile. The memory of our encounter last night filled me with joy, and I felt truly alive for the first time in my life. We shared the same views, and it was a relief to speak my mind rather than hide the truth.

"Victor?" I called out as I leaned up on my elbows and looked around the cottage.

Silence.

I scrambled off the bed and threw open the shutters to see if he was outside. My hungry chickens were already pecking at the earth for worms. Throwing my cloak over my shoulders, I slipped on my shoes and went outside.

"Victor," I called out into the morning sunshine.

There was no sign of him anywhere. I sighed. Once again, I was alone.

CHAPTER 10
PROVIDENCE, RI
PRESENT DAY

"Tomorrow is turkey day!" Dr. Nunes announced when he walked into the office. Tara, Josie, and I glanced up at him and smiled. "Better bring your appetites tomorrow." He paused in front of the office window and peered outside. "I think we should start celebrating early. No breaks, no lunch, we'll just work straight through and leave at one o'clock. Deal?"

"Deal," we replied in unison.

I was disappointed by the fact that I wouldn't be doing a coffee run today. Since Tara and Josie lived downtown and none of us owned a car, Dr. Nunes graciously offered to pick everyone up at Brown the next day.

My colleagues and I put our noses to the grindstone and, as promised, we were allowed to leave early. I changed into warm athletic clothes when I got home, then darted back outside to take a nice, long walk. My sneakers rhythmically pounded against the sidewalk as I tried without success to ignore the constant, annoying stream of traffic.

A screeching ambulance siren made me wince and I turned up the volume on my iPhone to drown out the noise. I finally came to a decent-sized park with tall trees. Being in nature always made me feel better; more than that, it healed me.

What exactly do you need healing from?

The sobering thought caused me to slow my pace. I tried to concentrate on the lyrics of the current song blasting through my earphones, but the tiny voice inside my head forced me to face what I had been purposely ignoring for quite some time: The Truth.

The trees grew close enough together that some branches intertwined with those of their neighbor to create a canopy above my head. Protected by the trees, my breathing and my heart rate automatically slowed. Trees were good company.

My wayward thoughts inevitably led to my last boyfriend— a brilliant PhD student who was keenly observant. It didn't take him long to figure out that there was something wrong with me. More than once he had kindly invited me into his confidence, offering to help. I had refused him each time. That relationship ended as predictably as my previous ones. I had no problem attracting men but always ended up pushing them away. What was I so afraid of?

I needed to fix what was broken inside of me, but first I had to get to the bottom of my strange dreams and memories. Who was the faceless man? Could the answers I hoped to uncover in therapy be the key to finally solving my relationship problems? I certainly hoped so; otherwise, my love life would be doomed forever.

Clouds gathered in the sky, the temperature quickly dropped, and it started to drizzle. It was common for the weather to change drastically from one moment to the next in New England. Reluctantly, I left the secluded area and jogged the rest of the way home.

Once inside, I stripped and took a long hot shower. Wrapping myself in a thick terry robe afterward, I decided to do some research on reincarnation. I found several bizarre New Age sites that completely turned me off with their loony theories and spiritual gibberish. I was tempted to abandon the project, but my persistence paid off when I stumbled across some information researched by doctors and scientists. There were several examples of case studies, each one described in vivid detail. I was both surprised and relieved to know that I wasn't the only person experiencing bizarre déjà-vu and inexplicable dreams—and these people were ordinary professionals just like me.

Satisfied, I powered down the computer after an hour and went into the bedroom to fetch my hidden laptop. My manifesto was already organized cohesively with documentation properly formatted. All it needed was a bit of revision. I heard a knock at the door.

I set the laptop aside and adjusted my robe. "Who is it?"

"It's me—Josh." I opened the door and he eyed my attire. "Hope I'm not bothering you."

"Nope. What's up?"

"I need some help. Cindy's parents invited me over for Thanksgiving tomorrow."

"No pressure," I teased.

"Yeah, tell me about it. I was wondering if you'd take a ride with me to the liquor store. Help me pick out some nice wines— I'm a beer and whiskey drinker."

"Give me a minute," I said, going into my room and closing the door.

I dressed quickly, threw on my new winter coat, and followed Josh downstairs to his car.

"Nice coat, by the way," he commented.

"Thanks."

Josh had no idea if Cindy's parents drank red or white wine, so he opted to buy one of each. I suggested a nice Bolgheri Bianco and a Bolgheri Rosso. I took advantage of the occasion to buy a fine bottle of vintage port for Dr. Nunes.

As soon as I was back in my apartment, I placed the port wine in a gift bag and set it on the counter. I wasn't sleepy so I fired up my laptop and continued editing my manifesto. It was almost two in the morning when I finally stopped working and got ready for bed. I washed my face, applied night cream, and looked long and hard at my reflection. Two dark smudges stood out under my tired, bloodshot eyes. I turned off the bathroom light and got under the covers. My white goose-down duvet was soft and fluffy and I imagined being wrapped in a cloud as I closed my eyes.

I had the dream again—he and I dressed in crimson, the threatening storm, the desperation, the strange dialect. I awoke to the sound of my own sobbing.

***

Thanksgiving dawned clear and cold with a deep blue sky that reminded me of lapis lazuli. Josh called me as I was eating breakfast and offered me a ride to the university. I gladly accepted. I chose a warm outfit and applied a bit of makeup, being careful with the application of concealer. I grabbed the port and went downstairs. Josh emerged from his apartment in a pair of wool pants and a cashmere sweater.

"You look nice." I sniffed the air. "Smell good, too."

"Gotta impress the parents," he said, waggling his eyebrows. "Between you and me, I'd rather stay home in a pair of sweats and eat in front of the TV. Her whole family will be there, you know. My ass hurts just thinking about how many hours I'll be sitting at the dinner table." He groaned and added, "Hey, you look great. Ready to go?"

"Sure."

I was the first one to arrive at the meeting point. No big deal. Dr. Nunes would be pulling up in about ten minutes. "Enjoy yourself and thanks for the ride, Josh," I said as I got out of the car. "And happy Thanksgiving!"

"Yeah, happy Thanksgiving to you, too." He waved before pulling away from the curb.

I glanced down the street at the closed coffee shop and cursed myself for not having had the guts to give Victor my number when I had the chance.

"Veronica!"

I spun around and, to my surprise, Stephanie was running toward me. Despite the cold, she wore a purple suede mini skirt and high-heeled black boots. In her hand was a glass pie plate covered with aluminum foil.

"Are you waiting for Rodrigo?" she asked breathlessly, coming to stand beside me.

"You mean Dr. Nunes? Yes, how did you know?" I replied, puzzled.

"He's picking me up, too. I didn't feel like driving." She pointed in the direction she had just come from. "I live like five blocks from here."

I was dumbfounded that 'Slutty Steph' was on a first name basis with my employer. "Oh?"

"You drink one too many glasses of wine and get caught

driving above the speed limit and—bam! The staties are all over you! Revoked license, heavy fine, ruined driving record—the works."

She sounded as if she spoke from personal experience, but I refrained from verifying my theory. "How do you know Dr. Nunes?" My curiosity was killing me.

"Oh, Rodrigo and I have been dating for the last couple of months," she replied with a giggle. "He's such a sweetheart."

I almost dropped the bottle of port I held in my hands.

Oblivious of my shock, she continued, "I totally dig older men; they're so sexy." She smiled. "Yeah, we met at work. Rodrigo is one of my patients."

Another shocking revelation. "You're a doctor?" I tried not to sound too surprised. After all, I didn't want to offend her.

"Hmm-hmm. I'm a dentist," she replied, flashing her ultra-white, super-straight teeth.

I was beginning to realize that perhaps Stephanie was not as flaky as she appeared.

Tara and Josie waved from across the street. They already knew Stephanie because she had been to Brown a few times to see "Rodrigo." Dr. Nunes pulled up a minute later and everyone got into the shiny blue Audi sedan. Stephanie sat up front and kissed him full on the mouth in greeting while the rest of us crammed into the backseat.

"Hello ladies," Dr. Nunes said. "Everybody hungry?"

We assured him that we were.

"Will Charlie join us today?" Stephanie asked.

"This year was actually my ex's turn to host him, but she booked a last minute cruise to the Caribbean, so Charlie will be dining with us. He's invited a few of his friends, too." Dr. Nunes peered at me through the rear view mirror and added, "I think you'll like them, Veronica."

"Charlie and his friends are so cool," said Stephanie, glancing back at us as she spoke.

We enjoyed the scenic ride to Newport. Dr. Nunes lived in a prestigious neighborhood located only a few blocks away from the famous Newport Mansions. He led us from the tree-lined street to a charming, early twentieth century bungalow bursting with New England quaintness. Three fat pumpkins decorated the steps of the front porch.

Mouthwatering aromas emerged from the house and Dr. Nunes said, "My aunt is an excellent cook, which isn't surprising since she's straight off the boat."

"Does she speak English?" Tara asked worriedly.

"Fluently," he replied.

"Hello," said a cute little old lady wearing a black dress and white apron. "Welcome, everyone."

"She could be Mrs. Claus," Dr. Nunes teased as he put his arm around his aunt.

She laughed good-naturedly while patting her carefully styled white hair, which had been rolled into a neat bun. Her plump cheeks resembled two rosy apples, and her only piece of jewelry was the gold crucifix around her neck.

"Where's Charlie?" Dr. Nunes asked.

"Upstairs showing his friends around," she replied. "I have to make the gravy."

Refusing our offers of help, Aunt Sofia shuffled back into the kitchen with Dr. Nunes at her heels. Stephanie placed her pie on the table and we followed suit with our gifts.

"My favorite!" Dr. Nunes exclaimed, eyeing the port with satisfaction as he exited the kitchen with a bottle of wine and several glasses. "Wine, ladies?"

He poured the wine, doled out the glasses, then gave us a moment to look around. The walls of the living room were lined with bookcases and we gravitated toward them. Tara and Josie selected an art book from the shelf and were soon engrossed in conversation while Stephanie played kissy-face with Dr. Nunes in the corner. I browsed the titles while sipping my wine, and soon heard male voices and footsteps.

"Ah, here comes Charlie," Dr. Nunes said as he moved away from Stephanie. "Come give your old man a hug, son!"

A pair of red classic Chuck Taylor All-Stars came into view on the stairwell, followed by two slim legs in blue jeans, a cool vintage t-shirt, and finally, a face. A cute young man with sandy blonde hair waved his hand in greeting. I swayed a bit from shock—Icon's drummer! More feet came down the stairs and a riot of butterflies sprang to life inside my stomach.

"I don't think these boys need any introductions," Dr. Nunes said jovially.

I gripped the stem of my wine glass so tightly that I was afraid it would snap in half. Victor and I locked eyes, but no one seemed to notice until he walked right up to me.

"Hello Veronica," he said, his honey-brown eyes boring into mine and turning my legs to melted wax in the process.

I heard Dr. Nunes ask, "Victor, Veronica—you two know each other?"

Without breaking eye contact with me, Victor nodded.

Everyone began talking at the same time. Josie and Tara were Icon fans and began babbling about their upcoming New England tour.

Victor poured himself a glass of red wine from the bottle on the table and came back to where I stood. He placed his hand gently on my elbow and led me out onto the deck. "I told you I'd know where to find you."

There was an awkward silence as he studied my face. Under such close scrutiny, it was only natural for me to blush and look down into the contents of my wine glass. I was relieved that I had taken some time to improve my appearance with cosmetics before leaving the house.

Victor took a step closer to me. "Have I been haunting your thoughts, Veronica?"

I became wary. Did he expect me to stroke his ego like some lame groupie? There was no arrogance in his expression, however, only sincerity. I answered honestly, "You have."

"As you've been haunting mine for so long."

His words struck a chord deep inside of me. "We *have* met, I knew it!" I exclaimed in relief. "Please refresh my memory. Did you attend UMASS Boston?"

"We've never met face to face in this country prior to your birthday party." At my puzzled expression, he leaned forward and placed his lips to my ear. "We met in Portugal."

59

Dr. Nunes appeared at my elbow, offering us some appetizers. "Come inside, you two. Join us."

I felt Victor's hand on the small of my back as he led me into the living room. There was something oddly possessive and familiar about his touch.

Aunt Sofia had written place cards with our names on them. My seat was two chairs away from Victor, which made conversation between us virtually impossible. In addition to roasting the turkey to perfection, our hostess had prepared mashed potatoes, stuffing, and a variety of vegetables.

After dessert, everyone insisted that Aunt Sofia sit in an easy chair with a glass of port while we cleaned up.

Dr. Nunes eventually asked, "Who wants to take a stroll along the Cliff Walk?"

Aunt Sofia went upstairs to take a well-deserved nap while our host led the way. Victor and I lagged behind, admiring the sweeping ocean views. Waves crashed against the rocks, sending a foamy spray into the crisp air.

I glanced up at Victor to find him staring at me.

His eyes held mine with intensity as he whispered, "Veronica... *Vera Iconica*."

The moment he said my name in Latin, I experienced a powerful memory of a small wooden head with a serene face being consumed by flames. The head was from a statue—the same statue that I'd seen on Icon's poster.

"Do you know that your name means 'True Icon' in Latin?" He looked at me expectantly. "Rather ironic when you consider our band's name, isn't it?"

"Very."

We both fell into pensive silences but inwardly, I was screaming.

CHAPTER 11
LISBON, PORTUGAL
SPRING, 1521

Victor's frequent visits and limitless wisdom were a consolation during my period of mourning. As much as I enjoyed learning from him, I still had no idea what was expected of me. Whenever I broached the subject, he admonished me to be patient.

One afternoon, while we were out walking, I was unable to restrain myself any longer. "I think I'm ready to know."

"Very well," he said cautiously. "You are a powerful being, capable of doing many good things."

"Teach me how to access this power you speak of! The restlessness within me can no longer be contained."

"Tell me what you would do."

"You already know. I want to put my beliefs into action," I replied passionately.

"Go on."

"I want to make certain that everyone has access to food, a decent place to live, and, most importantly, knowledge. People should not be deprived of an education."

"Veronica..."

"Everyone is deserving of dignity and respect, not just the chosen few who have inherited titles and money."

"How do you intend to bring about social revolution without being labeled a raving heretic?"

He was right, of course. My emotional outburst seemed silly in the face of sobering reality. "I lack experience and wisdom. I need your help and guidance to make these things happen." His eyes glistened with unshed tears, which surprised me since he had never displayed such strong emotions in my presence. "Forgive me, if I've upset you."

He shook his head. "On the contrary, Veronica."

Then he did something that took my breath away. He gripped my shoulders and pulled me forward, embracing me within the circle of his arms. Victor smelled of grass, trees, moss, water—the forest. My arms slid up his strong back and we stood like that for a long time, breathing quietly.

Nature emitted its vitality around us; the insects buzzed, the birds sang sweetly, and we stood within its magnificence. I had the impression that we were exchanging energy. Our life forces were one and the same, flowing back and forth continuously. It was such an incredibly exhilarating sensation that I cried tears of joy. In that moment, I knew without a doubt that I would remain in Victor's arms forever if given the chance.

CHAPTER 12
PROVIDENCE, RI
THANKSGIVING, PRESENT DAY

The twilight sky turned a rosy hue as the red sun hovered above the horizon. Dr. Nunes stopped ahead to point out something to the group.

"Such a lovely sunset," I commented to Victor.

"Very," he agreed. "Did you enjoy being raised here?"

The question caught me off-guard. "New England?"

"This country—the good old USA."

"Oh. Funny you should ask me that."

"Why, Veronica?" The way he asked the question implied that he already knew the answer.

"Because I've always felt as if I didn't belong here."

My answer seemed to satisfy him. "Portugal felt right."

It wasn't a question, but a statement delivered with conviction. How odd. I nodded slowly, wondering how he could have guessed such an intimate fact about me.

Dr. Nunes announced that we had walked far enough, so we turned around and headed back to his house. The enticing aroma of freshly brewed coffee greeted us as we walked through the door.

Aunt Sofia said, "I've made some coffee. Does anyone want another slice of pie or cake?"

Every male in the room accepted the dessert offer, but the females wistfully declined. By the time Dr. Nunes was ready to give us a ride back to Providence, I was tired. After saying goodbye to Aunt Sofia and thanking her for such a wonderful meal, Victor took me aside privately and asked for my number.

Finally!

He remained in Newport with Charlie and the rest of the band to practice for their upcoming performance Saturday night in Providence. Everyone was invited to the show.

Later that night, I drifted off to sleep while thinking of Victor. I dreamed of his golden eyes as he sang upon a darkened stage. The band members who stood behind him were obscured; he stood alone, bathed in a pool of pale light. I was the only member in the audience and he sang just for me...

I woke up the next morning, remembered the dream, and the first thought to pop into my head was: *yeah, right.*

I decided to do some Christmas shopping after lunch. I usually didn't leave the house on 'Black Friday' because I hated large crowds, but I didn't feel like being stuck at home alone. I knew the big shopping malls would be packed, so I opted for the unique stores on Thayer Street.

Despite the mild weather yesterday, it was bitterly cold today, but I was toasty warm in my new winter gear as I admired the festive holiday lights decorating the shop windows.

I noticed a flyer flapping against a lamp post where other flyers and posters had been stapled. The wind tugged so hard that the sheet of paper came loose and whirled in the air, ending face up on the wet sidewalk. A couple of black-clad Goth kids walked over it, leaving a grimy Doc Martin boot-print on its surface. I crept toward the flyer and looked down. It was the Icon poster I had seen in Boston, only smaller, with tomorrow's performance date printed in red letters across the top. I looked around and noticed for the first time that Icon flyers were plastered up and down Thayer Street, even inside shop windows and on restaurant doors.

The locals obviously liked them, and this made me feel proud of Victor. It was foolish of me to feel this way, especially since he and I weren't a couple—at least not yet. The thought of him as a potential boyfriend made me giddy. I was really looking forward to tomorrow night.

Slipping into a quirky shop known for its novelty gifts, I forced Victor out of my mind in order to could concentrate on Christmas shopping. The first display to catch my eye contained several picture frames made of colorful plastic buttons. Amidst the frames were handmade scented candles, artisan bath soaps, and hand-painted keepsake boxes.

"Hi. How are you today?" asked a perky bleached blonde salesgirl with retro 1950's makeup.

The Marilyn Monroe wannabe flashed her pearly whites and I noticed a slight smudge of red lipstick on her front tooth. I motioned toward my own tooth and mouthed the word 'lipstick.'

"Oh! Thanks!" she cried, quickly running the pad of her forefinger over her front teeth. "How can I help you?"

"Do you have any cookie tins?" I didn't like the commercial consumerism associated with holidays, so I usually opted to give cookies or wine as obligatory gifts.

She smiled. "You're in luck."

'Marilyn' led me to the back of the shop where several cookie tins were neatly stacked on shelves. Another customer needed help and I was left alone to make my selections.

I turned to go, but stopped in my tracks when I saw a display of big plastic storage cubes. I had some odds and ends stored in cardboard boxes due to lack of space. These would be a perfect storage solution. I decided to treat myself and selected three of them: blue, green, and violet. They would complement the top of my stark white bookshelves and add some fun color to my drab apartment.

"Here, let me help you with those."

I looked up to see a brunette salesgirl approaching me with outstretched arms. Black liquid eyeliner ran across her eyelids to create a cat-eyes look and vibrant red lipstick covered her pouty lips. I assumed the retro look was a job requirement.

"These are pretty big for you to carry by yourself," the salesgirl said. "I'll help take them to your car. Is it parked nearby?"

"Um, I don't own a car. I live downtown."

Her blue eyes widened. "If you purchase over two hundred dollars of merchandise, we offer free delivery within a ten mile radius. It's a special service for the holidays."

I did some mental calculations, then grabbed one of the display picture frames, two sofa pillows fashioned from Indian silk, and a bar of artisan bath soap.

The salesgirl took down my address. "We can make the delivery today after four-o-clock if that's convenient for you."

"Great. Thanks."

Josh was getting into his car as I arrived home. "Hi Josh. How did it go with Cindy's parents yesterday?"

"Okay, I guess. They loved the wine." He heaved a frustrated sigh. "Cindy insists on shopping at the mall today. I tried to talk her out of it and promised to take her next week."

"Good idea."

"No, bad idea. She accused me of lacking Christmas spirit. Hey, want to come along and keep me company while my girlfriend shops?"

"Ugh, no thanks. I hate Black Friday."

"Me too. Okay, off I go to be tortured by masses of shopaholics, corny holiday music, and tacky decorations."

"Oh, where's your Christmas spirit?" I teased.

"Yeah, yeah," he mumbled as he got into the car.

My evening was dedicated to organizing my stuff. The storage cubes were so roomy that two would have sufficed. I was left with one extra—the green one—for matches, candles, a sewing kit, and other household items. The three colorful storage cubes looked great atop the white bookcase.

Later that night, I went online to check if any new U.F.O. videos had been posted to YouTube. One in particular stood out among the rest: a U.F.O. bursting through a cloud at unbelievable speed. It was caught on tape by someone filming a jet during take-off. If the clip was 'doctored up,' it could only have been done by a professional in a Hollywood studio with sophisticated equipment. Definitely not amateur quality.

"I know you're out there," I whispered to the video clip.

When I was a child, I wanted nothing more than to be caught up in a U.F.O. beam and transported to a better place. As much as I loved Earth, I detested man's arrogance in believing that monetary profits trumped a healthy planet. I thought of humanity as parasitical, much the same way Mr. Smith had described in the cult film, The Matrix.

In recent years, I had joined every cause and signed every petition imaginable to spread awareness and inspire other like-minded people to take action. Some of the movements I had been involved with while living in Europe were extremely radical. I had come close to getting arrested several times in protest rallies and raids, but I didn't care. The protection of our fragile and precious environment merited the risk.

My phone rang. Unfamiliar number. "Hello?"

"Hello Veronica. I hope I'm not disturbing you."

My knees went weak at the sound of his velvety voice. "Hi Victor. You're not bothering me at all."

"I wanted to confirm that you're coming to our show tomorrow night."

"The three of us will definitely be there."

"Great. I'm looking forward to seeing you."

"Same here."

There was a pause, and I had the feeling he wanted to say more but held back.

"Well, it's getting late and I should let you go. Goodnight."

"Goodnight, Victor."

I saved his number to my contact list and turned back to the computer, but I was too distracted to continue watching videos.

***

Saturday morning dawned clear and sunny. I spent the day catching up on work-related stuff and doing laundry. The weather continued to hold and—miraculously—the sun shone throughout the entire afternoon.

When evening came, I looked through my wardrobe. I decided to wear my hair loose over my shoulders and made my eyes look smoky with an extra bit of gray shadow and black liner. Josie had told me that Heat, the new club where Icon would be performing, was casual and trendy. I slipped on a pair of designer jeans, a hip-length loose-fitting sequined tank top in charcoal gray, and a pair of Italian leather pumps. The effect was sexy but not overly garish. The dark gray color of the tank top made the sequins shimmer subtly rather than shine like a Vaudeville costume. Josie and Tara arrived at my place at the same time.

"Damn, girl! Look at you," Josie exclaimed, eyeing me.

Tara smiled. "We're used to seeing you in daytime attire with your hair up in a clip."

"It's been a long time since I've had a girl's night out, so I thought I'd skip the clip. Anyone for a Bombay and tonic?"

"Yes, please," Josie replied. "I'll take my drink with lemon if you have it."

"Me, too," said Tara.

I went into the kitchen and walked out a moment later with the drinks.

Raising my glass, I said, "To our health!"

Josie and Tara touched their glasses to mine before plopping down on the sofa. We sipped our cocktails and chatted about the upcoming night.

"So, are you excited?" Josie asked me with a wicked gleam in her eye.

"About?" I countered, feigning innocence.

She cocked an eyebrow at me. "About seeing gorgeous Victor! He was all over you on Thanksgiving."

"It was pretty obvious to everyone that he has a thing for you," Tara added. "Do you like him?"

Josie answered for me. "Of course, she does. What's not to like? Ooooh! Look at how she's blushing."

I smirked. "What's next, ladies? Playground songs?"

They looked at each other and, as if on cue, began to sing the most famous of childish tunes: "Victor and Veronica sitting in a tree, K-I-S-S-I-N-G!"

I couldn't help but giggle. We finished our drinks, donned our coats, and made our way out the door. The club was across the river so we had a decent walk ahead of us, but we didn't mind. A large crowd was already gathered at Heat's door when we arrived. Two bouncers checked IDs so it didn't take long to get inside, secure a table, and order a round of drinks. The opening band was finishing their final song.

A moment later, Victor sauntered onto a darkened stage wearing black from head to toe. Our drinks arrived as he took the microphone in his hand. The lights were turned down so low that we could barely see inside the club. First we heard the drums, then the base, and finally the lead guitar. Victor's deep voice filled the club just as a spotlight came on to illuminate him on stage. The rest of the band remained in darkness.

The music was sensuous, with a slow beat and exotic notes. He sang about a woman he had loved and lost; a woman who had possessed his heart and soul so completely that he vowed to find her, even if it meant searching forever and crossing oceans of time. What was most extraordinary was that he looked directly at me as he sang this song, as if I was the only person in the room.

My dream serenade.

Tara and Josie followed Victor's gaze, as did many of the people at neighboring tables. I even overheard someone remark, "Maybe she's his girlfriend."

"Wow," Josie said, arching her eyebrows.

"Uh-huh," Tara agreed, slack-jawed.

Victor finished the song with his eyes closed and head low. Although the room exploded with applause, he stood on stage completely motionless. The lights came on and the band immediately went into another song with a faster, heavier beat.

The fact that so many people rushed the band after they finished the show was proof of their talent. The stacks of promo CDs available for sale were completely sold out in minutes. Tara, Josie, and I each bought one while a few hot girls in mini dresses began flirting with the band members.

Ugh, groupies…

I was happy when the band finally excused themselves from the little clan of willing sluts—not nice, I know. Charlie made plans to meet some friends, but the rest of the guys remained with us. A big man who looked like a thug approached our table. The members of Icon introduced him as Big T, and the scary factor disappeared when he grinned.

"That was an awesome show!" Big T said. "You guys can play here anytime you want. In fact, what's your schedule like for next month?"

Victor spoke for the band. "We'll have to get back to you on that, Big T. Can we talk next week?"

Big T put his hand on Victor's shoulder and handed him a fat envelope. "Sure thing, Vic. Here's your cut from tonight." He paused to admire the three women sitting at the table and added, "You boys got yourselves some lovely company tonight. Hello ladies."

Josie, Tara, and I smiled at him. Big T waved to get the bartender's attention then pointed at our table in a circular motion before pointing to himself. The bartender gave him a thumbs-up sign.

"Your next round is on me," Big T said.

Everyone thanked him before he walked away to greet the people at another table. A waitress came over immediately to take our order.

"Look at that wad," Seth said, eyeing the fat envelope.

Victor opened the envelope; it was full of cash. "Not bad, boys. So, who gets this?"

"Greenpeace," said Alex.

"No, we gave to them last time and to St. Jude's Hospital the time before that. How about the Zeitgeist Movement? I like their agenda," suggested Seth.

Victor nodded in agreement. "Zeitgeist it is."

"Wait a sec," said Josie. "You guys don't keep the money you make?"

"We can keep it if we want to, but we don't need it. We each have good jobs and we're doing well," Alex explained.

"So we give it to charities and movements that help people and protect the environment," Seth added.

"That's so cool!" Tara exclaimed.

Her comment brought a warm smile from Alex. Josie was nodding slowly, as if she also liked the concept. My heart fluttered wildly in my chest as I met Victor's eyes. Our drinks arrived and I took a sip as I gathered my thoughts. It was my third cocktail of the evening, and I was starting to feel tipsy.

Victor leaned closer to me and inquired, "Do you think we're a bunch of idealistic idiots?"

I looked at him squarely. "I admire you all the more for it. By the way, I've been supporting the Zeitgeist Movement ever since they became a movement. Their desire for a resource-based economy is well-received throughout the world."

Both girls turned to look at me in surprise, but it was Tara who asked, "What is that, exactly?"

I ignored her as Victor reached for my hand and kissed my fingertips gently, sending goose bumps up my arm. As my female colleagues gaped open-mouthed at the sexy gesture, Seth busily started jotting down the Zeitgeist website on napkins for them.

"Bravissima," Victor said softly.

"Don't tell me that you can speak Italian," I whispered disbelievingly.

"Not as well as I can speak Portuguese," he replied.

"I didn't know you spoke Portuguese," Alex interjected, looking at each of us in turn.

"Fluently," Victor replied, his gaze never wavering from mine.

"I guess you two have a lot in common," Alex said, playfully nudging Victor in the arm.

"Including saving the world," I said.

Victor held out his hand in invitation. "Walk with me."

I looked to my companions to see if they'd mind. Josie practically shoved me off my chair in response. Victor helped me with my coat and I said goodbye to everyone.

We stepped out into the chilly night air and he gallantly offered me his arm, which I gratefully accepted. We were almost at eye-level and he frowned. "You seem taller tonight."

"High heels."

He looked down. "Are you okay to walk in those impractical—yet incredibly sexy—shoes?"

"I live right across the river in College Hill. I'll be fine."

"I'll escort you home. I rode here with Seth, so now I'm on foot, but I can call a cab if you change your mind."

We headed toward South Main Street Park across the river. The night sky was clear and there was a crescent moon. A full minute of silence passed between us before I asked him what had been on my mind since Thanksgiving.

"May I ask you a question, Victor?"

"Yes."

"The image on your poster—the Virgin Mary—where did you find it?"

"Why do you ask?"

"I think I've seen it before."

His face lit up and he looked at me expectantly. "The image is computer generated from my memory. I saw that statue a long time ago in someone's home."

"It looks like an antique from the sixteenth century."

"That's right," he said, facing me fully.

A wave of uneasiness swept over me. "Wow, the owner must be a collector, huh?"

He continued to stare at me, willing me to say something else. When I said nothing, he looked away.

I experienced another déjà-vu episode and didn't wish to ruin the moment, so I tried to think of something to say.

Sensing my uneasiness, he tactfully changed the subject. "What did you think of our opening song?"

I pulled the promo CD out of my purse, grateful for the distraction. "I loved it. Is it on the CD?"

He laughed. "You actually bought one?"

"We all did. Will you sign mine?"

"You didn't have to do that. To answer your question—no, that song isn't on the CD. In fact, it was the first time I ever sang it in public," he said as he pulled out a black Sharpie from his pocket and signed the CD cover.

"What's the title?"

He looked down at me with a secret smile. "It's untitled."

I had my hand in the crook of his arm and he covered it with his other hand, giving it an appreciative squeeze. His touch was warm and...*tingly*? "You said you could speak Portuguese fluently. Are you originally from Portugal?"

He didn't meet my eyes as he nodded in response to my question. "On the Cliff Walk you told me it felt wrong to be in the U.S. Is that why you left for Europe after college? I know you remained there for a long time."

I wondered if he knew these details about me from Charlie, who'd heard them from Dr. Nunes. "Yes…seven years."

"You must miss Portugal very much."

"I do. It's an intriguing country full of rich history."

"Italians credit their Renaissance for dragging humanity into modernity, but it was really the Portuguese who led the world into the Age of Discoveries."

"Agreed," I said, looking up at his incredibly handsome face. "Unfortunately, people don't know much about Portugal's history—or Italy's, for that matter. No one cares about the past anymore."

"You're obviously passionate about history."

"Very."

"And totally unimpressed with today's society, I take it?"

"I don't mean to sound prissy, but have you watched TV lately? It's gone from educational and entertaining to downright stupid. It's as if the networks are trying to dumb down the nation." Victor's head swiveled toward me and he gave me such a surprised look that I stopped and sighed. "Forgive me, Victor. I don't mean to get on a soapbox."

"I totally understand what you mean."

"So much has changed from when I was a child—not just in the U.S. It's a global phenomenon. It's like I'm behind a glass wall watching the world and I'm no longer a part of it."

He frowned. "Because you can't or because you won't?"

"I think a little of both," I admitted.

We walked past RISD in silence. A flyer pasted on a door advertised an upcoming student art exhibition.

"There are so many things that can't be easily explained," he said suddenly, gazing up at the sky.

"True, but those who seek answers will find them."

Still looking up, he said, "Most people don't care about the truth; they only accept answers that suit them. Many even settle for outright lies out of fear, greed, or societal pressure."

I thought for a moment. "Why are you telling me this?"

He stopped looking up at the sky and turned to me with an apologetic smile. "I'm only voicing some random thoughts. Perhaps someday you'll find my words useful."

The expression on his face was serious and intent, as if he wanted to say more but didn't dare. Was I to blame for this sudden change of mood? *Damn it.*

We arrived at my house. "Well, this is my place."

He looked up at the big house. "Do you like living here?"

"My home is close to everything so I don't have to give up my former lifestyle, so that's good. Walk, walk, walk!" I shrugged. "It keeps me from getting soft."

He eyed me up and down with an appreciative smile. "I seriously doubt you have any reason to worry."

"Thanks," I said, melting under his gaze.

"I really appreciate you coming out to see us tonight," he said, taking a step closer.

"It was my pleasure," I said a little breathlessly.

He gently tucked a strand of my hair behind my ear then bent down to kiss my cheek. "I'll see you soon, Veronica," he whispered in my ear.

I shivered. "Okay, goodnight."

I climbed the porch steps and looked over my shoulder. I was about to invite him inside for a nightcap when he waved and turned his back on me. Disappointed, I let myself in. By the time I got into my apartment and looked out the window, he was gone.

Chapter 13
Lisbon, Portugal
Christmas, 1521

King Manuel I died on the thirteenth day of December in the Year of Our Lord 1521. The man who had brought so much glory to our great kingdom would be missed by all. Six days after his father's death, John III, nicknamed *Piedoso*, or Pious, was officially crowned King of Portugal.

Christmas Day dawned misty and cold that year. As I dressed to go to church, I thought about Victor. He had now been visiting me for exactly one year. Lately, our conversations revolved around the betterment of mankind and how to go about achieving such a lofty goal. I was fully committed to helping others through education, which I believed was the greatest liberating force in existence.

My biggest enemy was hypocrisy, which was exactly what the clergy and political rulers doled out to the people on a daily basis. In order to be better exploited by the rich, the poor were forced to remain ignorant and endure a miserable life in constant fear. Threatened by Hell or hanging, countless peasants submissively accepted their fate. For these desperate and defeated people, the heavenly reward offered by the Church was like a crumb of bread held out to a starving man. Such an abuse of power disgusted and angered me to no end. Despite this, I was obliged to go to church in order to avoid drawing suspicion to myself.

The sermon offered nothing new or inspiring, but I listened dutifully. When the service was over, I turned to see both Sara and Tiago standing behind me.

"May the Lord be with you, Veronica," Sara said.

"And with you," I replied.

Tiago cleared his throat and took a step toward me. "My

family is having a small feast in honor of the Lord's birth. We would be happy if you would grace us with your company," he said, his tongue stumbling over the words with some difficulty. Sara shot him a severe look and nudged her brother in the ribs before he added, "I would be particularly pleased if you said yes."

I put on my most polite smile. "Please thank your family for thinking of me, but I have already made plans for today."

"Plans?" Sara blurted out involuntarily. "You live alone! What *plans* can you possibly have?"

She must have regretted her words the moment she saw the icy expression on my face. "I bid you both a merry feast."

I turned to go and heard Tiago mumble something about doing as he was told. Sara admonished him to be quiet. I hurried home in the expectation that Victor would be there when I arrived, but he wasn't. Disappointed, I went about my day trying not to think of him. When the sun began to sink in the sky, I lit a candle and wrote in my journal. I heard his footsteps outside and smiled as I opened the door.

"Victor!"

"I'm taking you away." My eyes were drawn to the parcel in his hand and he added, "I want to celebrate with you."

"Celebrate? You taught me that Christmas is an ancient pagan celebration instituted by Rome to convert the populace and has nothing to do with Christ," I countered.

"I want to celebrate us, not Christmas. One year ago today you became my pupil—and my friend." Handing me the parcel, he added, "This is for you."

It felt soft in my hands. "It's not a book," I said, puzzled. Over the months, he had brought me many.

"No, this is something especially for you with no other purpose but to give you pleasure."

I opened the gift and gasped in surprise. "It's a gown!"

Fashioned from exquisite tawny gold brocade, the garment boasted delicate seed pearls on the bodice. A starfish and two seashells made of semi-precious stones adorned the neckline. I had never seen anything so fine in my entire life.

"Do you like it?" he asked, a note of anxiety in his tone.

I was at a loss for words as I gently picked up the gown and carefully held it against my body.

He continued, "I commissioned one of the best seamstresses in the city. She also sews for the royal family."

My mouth dropped open in absolute shock. "A royal seamstress created this?"

"It's time for you to see another side of life—a finer side, full of grace and elegance."

Was I dreaming?

Surely, this was too much; the sort of thing fairy tales were made of. Since I lived in a one-room cottage, Victor politely waited outside so I could put on the gown. Luckily, it was relatively easy to get into. I ran a comb through my hair and let it fall down around my shoulders. He came back inside a moment later and stared at me.

"Thank you, Victor."

"You are beautiful, Veronica," he said simply as he picked up my cloak. "Here, put this on. We need to go."

I noticed that he was also dressed in rich clothing—high boots of buttery leather and a patterned doublet of cut velvet.

He froze at the sight of the sheets I had been writing on before he arrived. "What is this?"

"My thoughts. Those are pages from my journal."

His look was almost accusatory. "You've been keeping a journal and never mentioned it to me?"

I shrugged. "I have a few journals, actually."

He glanced over the sheet in his hands with alarming speed. "May I read all of them?" When I hesitated, he added, "They may be linked to your destiny."

How could I refuse after his generosity toward me? I unlocked the chest where I kept my books and removed the journals. He accepted them from my hands with what I perceived as reverence.

"Thank you," he said, clutching the journals to his chest. "These will be well-guarded, I promise you."

"I trust you."

We walked outside into the night.

A large shadow moved in the distance and I paused mid-step. "You came on horseback?"

Victor's eyes glowed in the darkness. "Do you think I would make you walk to the city in a gown fit for a princess?" he asked, freeing the animal's reins from a thick branch.

He helped me into the saddle, then placed my journals in the leather saddle bag. He mounted the horse, and I was very aware of this firm chest against my back. His arms came around me to grip the reins, and I nestled against his embrace.

"Hold on tightly," he said softly in my ear.

The full moon rose in an early evening sky streaked with deep violet. We rode toward the river, then up a gently sloping hill where a cluster of grand houses stood facing the watery horizon of the Tagus River. Built far enough away from the bustle of the busy port, they allowed inhabitants to enjoy stunning water views and fresh breezes.

Victor urged the horse in the direction of the largest house and I asked, "This is yours?"

"It is now," he replied cryptically.

He helped me dismount and led the horse toward the back where I assumed there was a stable. I was amazed by the structure's size and grandeur. Its façade boasted windows made of expensive glass, and candlelight poured from them.

Victor returned and offered me his arm. "Come, Veronica."

I walked through the front door, taking in the rich furnishings and lovely paintings. I marveled at the sight of bookcases brimming with precious books and began skimming their titles. Victor stood quietly in the corner watching me.

I turned to face him. "You never told me that you were a member of the nobility."

"I'm not."

"Or that you were wealthy."

"One of my students has passed on from this life. Since he had no family, he generously bequeathed everything he owned to me out of appreciation for all that I have taught him. I neither asked for nor expected it, but he left me with this home, along with several acres of land and a few other properties in the city."

"One of your students?" I asked, puzzled. "I don't understand."

"Yes, a student. A pupil—like you," he explained. "I became his mentor shortly after becoming yours."

My heart sank and my eyes stung with unshed tears. I pretended to be keenly interested in a book so that Victor wouldn't notice my reaction. He wasn't fooled, however.

"Veronica, what's wrong?"

"Nothing."

"You cannot lie to me," he prompted gently.

I met his insistent gaze. "Is that all I am to you, Victor? A mere pupil?"

A strange light came into his eyes. "Ah, but you are that and so much more."

CHAPTER 14
PROVIDENCE, RI
DECEMBER, PRESENT DAY

My next appointment with Clarice was scheduled shortly before Christmas. I wondered where Victor could be as I got off the bus and walked to her office. The last time I had seen him was the Saturday night after Thanksgiving when he had walked me home. The following Monday, he called to let me know he'd be out of town for several weeks, but didn't tell me where he was going or with whom. There was something rather mysterious about this sudden departure. He had assured me, however, that the first thing he intended to do when he returned was to call me, and I have been waiting anxiously ever since.

Clarice seemed excited to see me as she welcomed me into her office. I reached into my tote bag and pulled out a cookie tin full of chocolate chip cookies that I had baked the previous night. "For you."

"This is so thoughtful of you," Clarice said as she opened the tin. She bit into a cookie without hesitation. "Mmm. These are delicious."

"I'm glad you like them."

"Thank you," she said, smiling cheerfully as she replaced the lid on the tin. "I've been doing a lot of research lately. Has anything new happened in your life since we last talked?"

"I met a guy. Does that count as something new?"

"Sure it does. Is he a new romantic interest?"

"I really like him and we've seen each other a few times, but only as friends. He..." She waited patiently for me to continue and I laughed nervously. "There's something strange about him—not in a bad way. I mean, in a familiar way. I get these weird feelings of déjà-vu when we're together."

"Can you give me an example?"

80

"Well, he's in an up and coming band called Icon."

A smile lit up her face. "I know the band. They're quite good. Which musician is he?"

"Lead singer. His name is Victor."

"A handsome young man if my memory serves me well."

"It does," I said, feeling my cheeks burn. "Have you ever seen the image that's on their posters?"

"The Virgin Mary statue with the wolf eyes?" Clarice asked, eyeing me curiously. "Sure, I've seen it. The posters are all over town."

"A *sixteenth century* Virgin Mary statue," I stressed. "And although I didn't recognize it the first time I saw the poster, I had a powerful memory when Victor said the Latin words Vera Iconica, meaning 'true icon,' which is where the name Veronica is derived from."

"Interesting. What do you remember?"

"I saw the statue's head being consumed by flames. The memory was so vivid, like it happened yesterday."

"That's a very powerful mental image. I don't know what to make of this," she confessed. "I need to do some more research. In the meantime, I found an article about a man in India who was suffering from recurring dreams. Like you, he saw himself in another time and place and would wake up in panic. Under hypnosis, this man discovered that he was trying to save his mother from death."

"His mother from his past life?"

"Yes. The fact that he failed to save her created many unresolved feelings, such as overwhelming sadness and guilt. This tragedy left such an indelible imprint on his soul that the memories followed him into the next life."

"Do you think that I may have some unresolved issues from a past life?"

"Perhaps. Here's another interesting point: this Indian man began having the dream at a certain age, and in the dream he appeared to be the same age." She paused. "How old are you, Veronica?"

"Twenty-seven."

"In your dream, do you look older or younger?"

"I look about the same age as I am now." A thought struck me. "Do you want to put under hypnosis, too?"

"We'll resort to that only if and when you feel comfortable. I've had great success using this method with other patients, but to force this kind of treatment before you're ready to accept the outcome would be unwise."

"I'm open to hypnosis, but it does frighten me," I admitted.

"Why? I only ask out of professional curiosity."

"I guess I'm afraid to know the truth."

She leaned forward in her chair. "So far, my patients have experienced great relief. I'm not saying that it's easy to accept the truth, but it's certainly liberating. I have a book for you."

"Okay," I said, watching her as she stood and went to the massive bookshelf against the wall. She selected a book and handed it to me. "This deals with hypnosis, reincarnation, and how people with tumultuous past lives can finally let go so that they can enjoy their present life."

"Thank you. I did a lot of research online after Dr. Sousa suggested that I had a past life. I don't know what's legitimate and what's not."

Clarice gave a little humorless laugh. "There's a lot of crazy, weird stuff out there. Being in my field isn't easy—especially since other mental health professionals don't always take me seriously. But as you said yourself, there are things that we simply can't explain with science or nature so we must keep an open mind." She paused. "I want to warn you that hypnosis is not a guaranteed cure. Some people can't even be put under, so I'm not promising you anything."

"I understand."

"By the way, have you had the dream since you've been here in the U.S?"

"Yes, once. The day before Thanksgiving."

"Hmm." She jotted down more notes.

"Is that significant?"

"Not sure, but I want to note it just in case. Did anything unusual happen to trigger the dream?"

"I had been walking in the park and thinking about my past relationships."

"What about them?"

I hesitated. Did I really want to go into my past? I was in therapy, after all.

Sensing my reluctance, Clarice said, "We don't have to talk about it today if you're not ready, but this is definitely a subject we'll have to tackle eventually."

"No time like the present," I said. "I have a habit of running away from people. Mainly men."

"Problem with commitment?"

"I don't think so. I mean, I'm a loyal person and once I'm committed to something I stay on course."

"Did any of your past boyfriends mistreat you?"

"Oh, no."

"Then why would you run from them?"

I sighed. "I knew that I wasn't meant to be with them."

"How do you mean?"

"It's not like I'm waiting for Prince Charming on a white horse or anything like that—it's something much deeper."

"That's okay, Veronica. Plenty of people hold out in the hope of finding their soul mates."

The term "soul mate" rang corny in my ears. It was too commercial, too banal. "No, it's more than that," I countered. "There's someone that I'm specifically supposed to be with."

"How long have you felt this way?"

"Since childhood, for as long as I can remember."

"Do you believe you'll eventually find this person?"

"No."

Clarice looked puzzled. "No?"

"I believe he'll find me."

CHAPTER 15
LISBON, PORTUGAL
CHRISTMAS, 1521

I was convinced that I was in an enchanted dream. I gazed down at my gown and gently ran my hands over the tight-fitting bodice full of elaborate silk thread, pearls, and jewels. So overwhelmed was I when I first entered the house that I hadn't noticed the music playing in the background.

"Where is that music coming from?" I asked, walking in the direction of the sound.

"I'm hosting a banquet tonight," Victor replied as his hand shot out to take hold of my arm. "Wait, there's something I must do before I go in to see my guests."

He slipped into a small antechamber and emerged a moment later with brown eyes.

I edged away from him. "How did you do that?"

"Don't be frightened. Come closer and I'll show you."

I approached warily and watched in fascination as he carefully put the tip of his index finger on the rim of his iris. When he gently moved his finger, I saw that there was a tiny brown lens in the shape of a perfect circle sitting on the surface of his eye.

He continued, "A colored lens to hide my real eyes. This allows me to move freely among humans."

"Does it hurt to wear them?"

"No. The lenses are soft and gelatinous, like the body of a jellyfish. Do you understand?"

"Yes, I think so."

He moved closer to me and nearness made my heart race. "You are the only living creature on Earth that knows my secret. Can you keep it?"

I swallowed hard. "Yes."

He smiled. "Now, we may proceed with the evening."

"I have one more question. You told me you have never taken a human name before I called you Victor."

"That is correct."

"Yet you've had other students."

"In many countries."

I frowned. "What did they call you?"

He smiled softly. "Maestro, Lehrer, Maître, Teacher…"

"They called you 'Teacher?'"

"Yes…only you call me Victor."

My mind reeled at this revelation. We followed the sweet melody of stringed instruments down a long, dimly lit corridor that led to a grand ballroom awash with the golden glow of many candles. There were people gathered in small groups with goblets of wine in their hands.

"Who are all these people?" I whispered from inside the shadowy doorway.

"Philosophers, scientists, artists, musicians…humanists who care about the betterment of mankind."

"Your students." He stood so close that I could feel the warmth of his breath. "Where do I fit into this group?"

He gently stroked my cheek. It wasn't often that he touched me, but when he did, it felt divine. His eyes scanned the room. "These people are beacons with flames that burn continuously." Then, bringing his eyes back to mine, he added, "But none of them burn as brightly as you do, Veronica. For the past year, I've come to know you more intimately than I have ever known any other living creature."

"I can say the same of you."

"Wealth and beauty are meant to be enjoyed, and I want to share them with you. Let's make this house a center of higher learning, a refuge for the oppressed, a home for those in need…Veronica, stay here with me. Let this be our home."

"I'm at a loss for words," I confessed.

"No need to answer me now," he said, pulling me into the shadows and kissing my forehead. "But you do have to enjoy the evening's festivities."

We emerged from the shadows into the candlelit ballroom. Several people eyed Victor as he brought me to the center of the highly polished parquet floor. The musicians began a new song and he gallantly bowed to me.

I whispered nervously, "I only know a few dances."

"Follow my lead and allow the music to enter you."

I did as I was told and, to my delight, my body responded naturally to the rhythm. The lightheadedness I experienced in that moment made me giggle. Throughout the dance, he came very close to me several times and even held me in his arms.

The music eventually stopped and he led me to a table laden with delicacies. A group of distinguished-looking gentlemen approached Victor, and I found myself being introduced to some of the brightest minds of our time, including some of the city's most popular artists and writers. The conversation was both stimulating and enlightening, and I listened quietly as I sipped the finest wine I had ever tasted.

A cold chill crept up my spine when I noticed an extremely pale man staring at me from across the room. Not only was his expression hostile, but his eyes were as black as coal, with irises indistinguishable from the pupils. The world around us came to a halt as he regarded me with unmasked contempt. I looked away for a moment in order to capture Victor's attention, but he was too engrossed in conversation. By the time I turned around again, the strange man was gone.

Someone near me laughed aloud. I dismissed the black-eyed man and mentally chastised myself for reading too much into the brief exchange. The flickering candlelight and my fertile imagination had played tricks on me. After all, if he was an invited guest of Victor's, why would he be hostile?

Victor caught my eye and came toward me, exchanging my empty wine goblet for a full one.

I took a sip. "This wine is delicious."

"The cellar came fully stocked."

Something occurred to me as I gazed into his brown eyes. "Why did you not hide your real eyes from me?"

"I trust you."

CHAPTER 16
PROVIDENCE, RI
CHRISTMAS EVE, PRESENT DAY

I devoured the book that Clarice had lent me in one sitting. The experiences of the patients were riveting. Those who claimed to have been reincarnated were not New Age loonies but highly respected professionals. Perhaps it was time for me to accept reincarnation as a plausible theory.

I stretched lazily and yawned as I placed the book on the bedside table. It was after two in the morning and I was tired.

The ominous sky above our heads signals the oncoming storm. The howling wind whips our hair into a frenzy. To my right is a great expanse of water. A white vein of lightning streaks across the sky, illuminating the galleon bobbing on angry waves. I begin to cry—I do not want to board the ship without him. The roar of thunder pierces our ears. The tempest will soon be upon us. We are both in such terrible danger...

He leans in and I fall under the spell of his golden gaze.

Victor!

My eyes flew open as I sat up in bed. I was covered in a sheen of perspiration, but the wetness on my face was due to tears. I went into the bathroom and splashed cold water on my face before studying my reflection in the mirror.

Who are you, Veronica?

My thoughts turned to Victor as I hung my head in an attempt to slow my breathing. A light shuffling sound came from within my bedroom, trailing icy fingers up my spine. Slowly, I tilted the bathroom mirror until it reflected the open door behind me. The dim moonlight revealed nothing except my rumpled bed. My nerves were on edge and my imagination was running wild.

Tea. That's what I needed; a calming cup of chamomile tea

to soothe my frazzled nerves. I shuffled into the kitchen to put the kettle on, then walked over to the big window in the living room. I almost dropped the cup when I saw the familiar, shadowy form of a man crossing the street. My first impulse was to chase him down, but I knew that would be unwise. He could be crazy or armed with a dangerous weapon.

The man stepped onto the sidewalk. This time, the trees were devoid of leaves and the bare winter branches allowed me an unobstructed view. He walked to the top of the street and, just before turning the corner, he peered up at my window. Could he see me?

My thoughts turned back to my dream. I had expected Victor to call me while he was away. After all, we lived in the age of satellites and hi-tech cell phones; couldn't he at least have sent me a text?

Perhaps my strong attraction to him caused my imagination to run amuck and produce a big fat dose of Wishful Thinking. What if he was only being nice? What if he had no romantic inclination toward me?

That would totally suck, Veronica.

I blew on my tea as I stared at the night sky. My mother had once mentioned that my great grandfather had "mental issues." Maybe madness was the only inheritance that went with my noble name. No land, no title, no money—just bat-shit craziness.

Although my apartment came furnished with a TV set, I barely ever turned it on. I found a news channel and listened to a reporter drone on until drowsiness overcame me.

CHAPTER 17
LISBON, PORTUGAL
CHRISTMAS, 1521

The guests eventually departed and the candles burned down to their wicks. The party came to an end, but the enchantment continued when Victor led me upstairs. We entered a spacious and elegantly furnished bedchamber with a big canopied bed draped in pea green velvet with gold patterns. A fire burned in the hearth; I wondered who had lit it.

He followed my gaze. "A few servants came with the house. I told them they were free to go if they wished. They remained because they had nowhere else to go."

"They cooked the food for tonight's feast?"

"Yes. Did you enjoy it?"

"Very much."

He sat on the bed, leaned back against the plush cushions, and stretched out his long legs. The flames of the fire created a reddish glow on one side of his face, while the other side remained in deep shadow. The effect was eerie.

Patting the spot beside him, he said, "I would hear your decision now."

Obviously, Victor had not considered the social repercussions of his unconventional invitation. I sat down on the edge of the bed and chose my words carefully. "I truly appreciate your generous offer. Unfortunately, I am not allotted the same freedom as men. It would be most unseemly for an unmarried woman like myself to simply take up residence with a man."

"I see."

"Perhaps we could think of a ruse," I suggested. "I could pretend to be one of your servants."

"A servant in fine clothing? Dining with me at a richly laid table? I think the ruse would be quickly exposed. Besides, you were not born into this life to serve anyone, least of all me."

"Well, I..."

"Veronica, pretend for a moment that there is no societal pressure, no moral implications. Pretend that humanity is not burdened with such nonsense. I have visited you regularly for exactly one year, and we have talked about many things—more than most married people talk of in a lifetime. What you and I have shared is akin to human courtship, is it not?"

I blinked. "Yes, I suppose it is."

"I'm no stranger to you, am I?" I shook my head. "What does your heart tell you to do?"

"You mean what would I do if I were completely free?"

He took firm hold of my chin. "You *are* free, little star."

I looked at him shyly. "There are still so many things about you that I do not know."

"Very well. Let's put your mind at ease. Ask away and if I can answer now, I shall."

"You never took a single bite of meat tonight."

"I do not eat flesh."

"Because you have no taste for it?"

"No, because I cannot digest it as efficiently as you can. I can eat anything that comes from a plant—nuts, fruits, vegetables, grains..."

"Wine."

He laughed softly and closed his eyes. "Yes, wine. I like that very much, and it affects me the same way it does you."

I watched him quietly. "Do you sleep?"

He kept his eyes closed as he smiled. "Yes, of course. Every living creature rests at some point."

"Do you sleep every day, like we do?"

"Not every day, but I do sleep often enough."

"Do you lie down when you sleep?"

The corners of his mouth lifted higher. "Yes."

"Are you tired now?"

"I am."

"Allow me to remove your boots," I offered.

90

He nodded with eyes closed. I tugged each boot off and removed the gray woolen hose that encased his well-shaped legs. The soft wool smelled of cedar wood and smoke. I noticed that his legs were remarkably smooth and hairless. There was a faint iridescent sheen to his skin that reminded me of the inside of a clam's shell.

Intrigued, I leaned forward and began unfastening the hooks of his doublet. He shrugged out of the garment and I set it aside. He wore a loose shirt of white linen underneath, and I pulled at the ties. His eyes flew open and he watched me warily. The shirt fell open enough to reveal his sculpted shoulder. I touched his clavicle and his skin vibrated beneath my fingertips. My eyes dropped to the hollow at the base of his throat, which turned from the subtlest green to pale lilac depending on the light.

"What are you, Victor?" I asked, mesmerized by the look and feel of his strange skin. "I've never seen skin like this on anyone—not even the foreign vendors at the market."

"My skin absorbs many nutrients directly from the sun. That's why my skin appears so unusual to you."

"The sun turns our skin dark," I commented.

"You have a different form of pigmentation on the surface of your skin known as melanin."

"Melanin," I repeated, examining the skin of my own hand.

"When melanin is exposed to the sun, it deepens in color in order to protect your skin from getting burned. My skin keeps me from absorbing—or rather eating—too much sunlight. When my body has had its fill of nutrients, my skin naturally deflects the sunlight, making it impossible to penetrate or burn me. Do you understand?"

"Yes. How do you know of this? Are you a scientist?"

"I know many things, and you already know more than most of the people of your time."

My time? I was too tired to ask what he meant by that. I held my hand to my mouth to stifle a yawn. I wanted to fight off sleep and talk to Victor all night long.

"Your bedroom is adjacent to mine through that door," he said, pointing. "Of course, I would prefer that you slept here."

"I've never lain with a man," I confessed.

"Nor I with a woman."

"Surely, you've mated with your kind before?" I regretted the question as soon as it left my lips. "Forgive my rudeness."

He regarded me silently, which only made me feel worse. I felt his hands at my back undoing the ties of my bodice. I stood up and took off the magnificent gown, setting it carefully on a chair. Still not speaking, he got under the coverlet and so did I, then he put his arms around me and we slept as chastely as brother and sister.

That night, my dreams were fantastic! I was a ball of pure white light, free from the restrictive limitations of a physical body. I raced across the sky at great speed, which filled me with exhilaration. I was so high that the sky was no longer blue but black, and I saw countless stars glittering like diamonds. I marveled at the mystery of our universe and felt as if I were a wonderful, living, breathing part of it!

Victor stared at me expectantly when I woke up the following morning. "Did you enjoy the journey?"

I woke up ridiculously early on Christmas Day. The sun was out briefly, but by mid-morning, there was an icy sleet that eventually turned into rain. I spent the entire morning editing my manifesto and doing research on the Internet, working straight through lunch. The sun finally graced us with its presence at almost three o'clock in the afternoon, so I went out for a walk.

Five minutes later my cell phone rang. It was Victor. "Hello Victor," I said, trying to keep my voice from sounding too eager.

"Hello Veronica. Are you busy?"

The mere sound of his voice thrilled me. "No, I'm enjoying a quick walk before the sun changes its mind. Are you back from your trip?"

"I arrived late last night. Would you like some company or do you prefer to walk alone?"

"I'd love some company. Where do you want to meet?"

"How about the coffee shop near Brown?"

"Okay."

"See you in a bit."

I hung up and couldn't help smiling as I walked to the coffee shop. Victor was already there by the time I arrived, looking like a fashion model.

He greeted me with a kiss on the cheek. "It's great to see you again."

"Great to see you, too. I figured you'd be with family and wouldn't be back in Providence until after the holidays."

"Actually, can I make a confession?"

"Sure."

"I really don't like Christmas."

I leaned in conspiratorially. "Neither do I."

"Ah, Humbug!"

We both said it at the same time and laughed in unison. There was a pause afterward, and I was tempted to ask him where he had been for the last few weeks.

What if he has a wife and kids hidden away somewhere?

I furiously crossed out the thought from my head with an imaginary black magic marker.

"All I've had was a cup of coffee this morning and I'm starved. Have you had lunch?" I shook my head and he smiled. "Would you grace me with your company and have lunch with me?"

"I'd love to but is anything open today?"

"Do you like Indian food?"

"Love it."

Victor led me to a little Indian restaurant that advertised a neon pink 'OPEN' sign in the window. Predictably, the place was empty. Victor ordered freshly baked naan, vegetable samosas with yogurt sauce, fragrant basmati rice, malie koptha, chana masala, and curried lentils.

"I'm a vegetarian, Veronica," he explained over the top of the menu. "If you'd like to order some meat, please do so. Charlie is a big fan of the lamb vindaloo."

The waitress looked at me expectantly, her pen hovering over the order slip. I shook my head. "No, what you've ordered is perfect. Thank you."

"You're very polite," he said when the waitress left.

"I eat vegetarian food several times a week to cut back on meat consumption for both health and environmental reasons."

"We seem to have much in common, you and I."

"That same thought has crossed my mind, too."

"Is that a good thing?"

I shrugged. "Is it?"

"So far, yes."

Being the only customers meant that we didn't have to wait long for our food to arrive. We inhaled the delicious aromas under the watchful gaze of the painted Ganesh on the wall. We ate slowly, thoroughly enjoying the exotic spices as we shared a bottle of good white wine.

He smiled at me from above the rim of his glass. "This was an excellent choice."

"Glad you approve."

"You love wine."

"How can I not? It's genetically coded into my Mediterranean DNA."

"The elixir of the gods. We should shop for a couple of nice reds, pick up some good dark chocolates, and make a night of it. What do you think?"

Yes!!! "I'd like that."

"Okay, it's settled. Wine and chocolate night. How about a dinner night?"

"On the same night?"

"It could be a different night." He laughed almost shyly, which surprised me. "I'm trying to squeeze as many dates as I can out of you."

"Why didn't you call or text me while you were away?" I blurted out the question and half-covered my mouth afterward in mortification. The wine had loosened my lips.

He looked away uneasily, the smile quickly fading from his face. "It's a bit complicated. Taking care of some business."

"As long as you don't have a wife and kids stashed away somewhere," I said lightly, trying to make it sound like a joke instead of a real concern.

His face broke into a grin. "You caught me! I'm really a Mormon with ten wives and thirty kids back in Utah."

I laughed aloud and let the matter drop. The waitress cleared the plates and Victor ordered Feni, a coconut liqueur from Goa. I offered to split the bill when it arrived.

Victor looked offended. "Do you doubt that I'm a gentleman?" When I shook my head, he added, "My invitation, my treat."

"I'm only trying to be polite. You know, the whole equality of women thing."

"Men and women are equals, but that doesn't mean that chivalry should die. Females should be protected, revered, and respected by men."

"Well, this female thanks you very much."

He left cash on the table and stood. "My pleasure."

We walked outside into the fading afternoon. We had completely lost track of time during our long, leisurely lunch.

"I didn't realize it was so late," I said.

"Do you have plans this evening?"

"No."

"I'm really enjoying your company, and I don't want you to go," he admitted. "It's been too long since I've seen you."

"I've got nowhere to go. It's Christmas, remember?"

We strolled through the park and, as we passed by some older buildings, I paused to check out a cool graffiti mural.

"Do you like graffiti?" he asked.

"Love it."

"So do I."

Another thing in common between us?

We continued walking and talking. In addition to being drop-dead gorgeous, Victor was incredibly intelligent, cultured, and a gentleman.

Too good to be true, Veronica. He probably keeps human heads in his freezer.

I crossed the negative thought from my head with the same imaginary black magic marker I'd used earlier. We were so deeply engrossed in conversation that we barely noticed the oncoming storm. A loud crack of thunder startled us both.

"We'd better get you home," Victor said, concerned.

We hastily doubled back toward College Hill. By the time we arrived at my house, it was already dark out and raining hard. Soaking wet and chilled to the bone, we ran onto the wide front porch and paused to catch our breaths.

"You can take a hot shower to warm up while I put your clothes in the dryer. I'm sure I can find something for you to wear," I told Victor as I unlocked the outside door.

"I appreciate it."

96

I turned on the hallway light, but the stairs remained in total darkness. "What's going on?" I asked, confused.

"The power's out," he replied. "The streetlights aren't illuminated."

I followed his gaze. Every window on my street was black. "Bummer. Okay, well, we should still have gas for the heat and hot water, and I've got plenty of candles."

We made it up the stairs with the light of my cell phone. Victor followed me into the apartment. I dropped my phone then accidentally kicked it under the sofa.

"Damn it," I cursed, moving to retrieve my phone.

"Maybe you should let me—"

"Ow!" I bumped my shin into the corner of the coffee table and immediately sat down on the sofa.

"Are you okay?" he asked.

Rubbing my stinging shin, I replied, "That really hurt."

"Here, let me get you some ice."

I heard Victor's retreating footsteps. "Be careful," I advised, squinting into the darkness. "Where are you?"

"In the kitchen."

I heard him open the freezer door to get the ice. He came back a moment later and handed me a handful of ice wrapped in a dishtowel.

"I know you're already cold, but this will keep the swelling down," he said. "Where are your candles and matches?"

"In the green storage cube above the bookshelf."

Realizing what I had just said, I gave an embarrassing little laugh. How would he know which one was green in the total darkness? I was about to apologize for my stupidity when I heard him strike a match. By the time the glow of the candle reached my face, I was staring at him in shock.

Amazed, I demanded, "How did you do that?"

He was already lighting a second candle. "Do what?"

"The room is pitch black. Even in the candlelight, I can't tell which cube is blue, green, or violet—are you wearing military grade night-vision contacts or something?"

He laughed a bit nervously. "Must be all those Vitamin A

vegetables I've been eating."

I was not convinced. "No, seriously, how did you do that?"

Ignoring my question, he lit several candles before getting on all fours to retrieve my cell phone from under the sofa.

"Here you go," he said, handing it to me.

"Thank you."

I stood and placed some candles in the bathroom, then got a freshly laundered towel. "Soap and shampoo are in the shower caddy. Please make yourself at home."

"Thanks." He took a few steps and stopped. "Assuming the power comes back on soon, what do I wear while my clothes are in the dryer?"

Nothing. My face burned at the naughty thought. "I have an oversized T-shirt and some baggy sweatpants. Is that okay?"

"Perfect," he said as he walked into the bathroom.

I heard him run the shower while I searched inside my closet. Since the bathroom was en-suite, I laid the clothes on the bed and closed the bedroom door so that he could have privacy. He emerged from the bedroom and into the living room a few minutes later towel-drying his hair.

"The shower's all yours," he said.

My big, shapeless black T-shirt stretched snugly across his chest and wide shoulders, showing off his great body. He filled out my baggy sweatpants, too, and I couldn't help peeking over my shoulder and checking out his perfect backside as I walked into the bathroom.

"I'll be right out," I said. "Make yourself comfortable."

I took a quick hot shower and washed my hair. After drying off, I slathered on scented body lotion and slipped into a plush navy blue hooded sweater and matching athletic pants. I ran a comb through my damp hair and slicked it back away from my face.

I exited the bathroom to find Victor sitting on the sofa, watching me. Offering him a little smile, I headed toward the kitchen. "Now that we've thawed out, how about something to drink? I have several teas and an unopened bottle of Chianti."

"I prefer the wine over the tea."

"I thought so."

While I got the wine glasses out of the cabinet, I became acutely aware of the intimacy of the situation. I was so comfortable in Victor's company that I hadn't even thought of it beforehand. How well did I really know this man?

"Can I help?"

I almost dropped one of the glasses.

"I didn't mean to startle you," he said as I reached for the corkscrew. Taking it from my hand, he added, "Here, let me help you." He then reached for the Chianti and opened the bottle, pouring the ruby liquid into the wine glasses. "To us."

"To us," I repeated.

In the candlelight his brown eyes gleamed like copper. Speaking of eyes...

"I can almost hear the wheels turning in your head," he teased. "Tell me, what are you thinking?"

"I'm still trying to figure out how you picked out the green box in the dark. Color doesn't exist in the absence of light. What's your trick?"

CHAPTER 19
LISBON, PORTUGAL
OCTOBER, 1522

On the eve of the New Year, I moved into Victor's fine home. Aside from that one night when we slept in the same bed, he had not touched me nor expressed any feelings toward me other than respect. As time passed, he became my master, my teacher, my friend, my brother—but not my lover.

I often tortured myself by wondering if his lack of interest in me was due to my inferiority. Regardless of the reason, I harbored no regrets about selling my cottage and making Victor's home my own. My life used to be lonely and empty, and now it was full of joy and purpose.

Victor persuaded me to transform my journals into a book, so I diligently started putting together a cohesive manuscript. My ultimate goal was to free the minds of individuals, instill a respect for nature, and foster a deep compassion for humanity. Although I did not mention religion, I made sure that my philosophies aligned with the altruistic teachings of Christ.

When I wasn't working on my book, I was busy teaching. Our home now served as a school for underprivileged children. I had twenty-three students ranging in age from seven to eighteen.

My youngest pupils were the least influenced by our society. They were never afraid to ask questions or think independently. In contrast, the older ones possessed the tendency to hold themselves back. Traditions, religious beliefs, and social expectations often acted as impenetrable barriers against some of my teachings. My oldest student, Rosa, was my greatest challenge. Raised in a convent by mean nuns and cast into the street when she refused to take the vows, she had been forced to work as a prostitute. To complicate matters, she had recently fostered an inappropriate interest in Victor.

Due to my love of nature, many of my lessons took place outdoors. Victor always accompanied me on these excursions. One fine October morning, I took the children into the woods near my old cottage. We approached the clearing where I had first encountered Victor as a child, and his eyes slid my way.

"I never meant to scare you that day," he whispered.

"I know."

The trees around us were literally ablaze with color. I watched the amazement on the children's faces as they took in their surroundings.

With Victor seated beside me, I focused my lesson on the healing properties of the natural world. I talked of flower lore and how it could be used to cure and prevent many ailments.

Rosa motioned to speak. I could see the mischief in her eyes as I acknowledged her with a nod.

"Are you suggesting that an illness is not God's will?"

"No," I replied. "There are certain ailments, however, that can be easily avoided."

"The convent taught us to pray to God if someone was sick, not seek out healers and potions."

I looked at Victor nervously.

"Mistress Veronica is attempting to educate you on natural science and the medicinal properties of certain plants," Victor explained. "Many convents and monasteries in the city also serve as apothecaries and hospitals for the poor."

"The convent never served as an apothecary or hospital," Rosa retorted.

"Caring for those in need is a godly trait," I pointed out.

Ignoring my comment, she continued to stare at Victor. "The nuns put their faith in God *only*."

Victor frowned. "Jesus healed the sick, remember?"

"Of course," she replied, gazing into his eyes in a way that made me uncomfortable. Then, fixing me with an angry glare, she said, "You often stress the importance of nature. If our world ceased to exist, would God provide for the faithful?"

I usually avoided speaking about God or religion.

Nevertheless, I said, "Our physical bodies require a natural world, Rosa. Since we are made of flesh and bone, we need food, air, and water to survive."

"You did not answer my question, Mistress Veronica."

"The answer is no," I replied.

There were hushed whispers among the students. Rosa frowned. "The Holy Scriptures points out that God protects his faithful servants. My faith in God should be enough to keep me alive under any circumstance. He's omnipotent, after all."

It was obvious that Rosa was trying to trap me into saying something in front of the others that could later be misconstrued as incorrect or, even worse—heretical.

Victor eyed Rosa steadily. "Are you planning to leave our world, Rosa? Take a journey to the moon, perhaps?"

Everyone laughed. It was meant as a joke to distract the students in order for me to continue my lesson, but Rosa was not laughing. "The point I'm trying to make is that faith keeps us alive, *not* nature. Christian martyrs of the past survived on practically nothing but air."

"Ah, but they still had air," he countered playfully.

Rosa sighed, unwilling to relent. "If I have faith in God, then I don't need anything else—like those martyrs."

"Are you comparing yourself to a martyr?" Victor demanded. "The bible warns against such vanity and lofty thinking. Didn't the nuns teach you that?"

I could see Rosa's cheeks burn red with shame, but she persisted. "I would never compare myself to a martyr, but I demand an answer to my question."

Victor looked at her incredulously. "You wish to put God to the test despite the warning in the twelfth chapter of Luke, verse twelve, where Jesus himself clearly admonishes us to not put the Lord to the test?"

"No, I was only—"

He cut her off. "I would be very careful if I were you, Rosa. Someone could misinterpret your questions as heretical. Mistress Veronica is neither a Church theologian nor is she a nun; therefore, she is unqualified to answer such questions."

Rosa was utterly miserable. "But—"

Victor lifted his index finger to silence her. "I encourage you to seek such answers from a priest or an abbess—not your secular teacher."

Rosa was on the verge of tears, so I decided to end the lesson early and gave the children some time to play.

"You were a bit harsh with Rosa," I said to Victor when we were alone in the clearing.

"I had no choice. That girl has been asking theological questions and challenging your teachings for too long. I'm tempted to expel her from our home."

"She's difficult, but we can't toss her out into the street."

"I'll find accommodations for Rosa, if it makes you feel better, but I won't risk our well-being and safety for her sake. These are dangerous times. The Holy Inquisition is merciless toward even the slightest perceived affront against the Church. We must teach these children what we can within the boundaries of Christianity, but those who do not wish to learn should be cast out."

"If I have attained this level of understanding, surely others can," I countered, still trying to see Rosa in a hopeful light. "I want to help everyone."

"Only those willing to open their minds and hearts can attain your level of understanding. There are people who prefer to trudge through life blindly. Standing up for your beliefs is no easy task."

"I want to be a good teacher."

He came closer to me. "You *are* a good teacher. But you must accept the fact that a few of these children will reject what you have to offer. Trust me, it will be much safer for us if you heed my advice."

I knew he was right. My eagerness to bring others to a new level of awareness was sometimes so overwhelming that it eclipsed practical wisdom. "I only want to share my joy."

His eyes took on a soft expression. "I know. It's one of the reasons why I love you."

I was stunned. He had never spoken those words to me.

"I love you, Veronica," he repeated quietly.

He caressed my face tenderly, his fingertips gently tracing the contours of my jaw and throat. His eyes moved to my mouth and he ran his forefinger along my bottom lip.

"May I kiss you?" he whispered.

I could barely breathe. "Yes."

Having never been kissed before, I stood as still as a statue, unsure of what to do. Since he was considerably taller than me, he inclined his head and closed the distance between us. He brought his lips gently to mine, and a pleasant warmth radiated from the center of my chest out to my limbs. He continued kissing me softly until I wound my arms around him and pulled him closer. At that point, his kiss deepened and became more intense, his mouth slanting against mine.

I reluctantly pulled away. "Victor?"

"Forgive me. I didn't mean to—"

"I love you, too."

His smile shone first from his eyes before reaching his lips.

I interlocked my fingers around his neck. "Kiss me again."

Pulling me close, he obliged me. Our kiss was cut short by a rustling sound in the nearby bushes. We turned around to see movement amid the greenery, then we heard the sound of retreating footsteps.

"There's no trick. I really do eat a lot of vegetables rich in Vitamin A," Victor replied in answer to my question as we settled comfortably on the sofa.

"I'm serious, Victor. I want to know how you're able to see color in the dark," I insisted. My attention was abruptly diverted by the sound of a door slamming shut, stumbling, and a male voice cursing. "That has to be Josh," I said as I got up from the sofa to open the door.

Sure enough, Josh stood in my hallway using his cell phone light like a mini flashlight. "Hi Veronica and Merry Christmas," he said while offering me a hug.

"Merry Christmas. Hey, I heard you stumble on the stairs. Are you okay?"

"I'm fine, hon. I just got back from Cindy's and noticed the glow coming from your window." He shook his head, adding, "Blackout on Christmas. Do you have any extra candles?"

"Sure, come in."

Josh took a step and froze. "Sorry. I didn't know you had company."

I made introductions and the men shook hands.

Josh snapped his fingers and pointed at Victor. "Hey, you look familiar. Hang on, don't tell me...got it. You look a lot like the lead singer of Icon."

"He *is* the lead singer of Icon," I whispered. "Join us."

Josh held up both hands in protest. "Only if I'm not interrupting anything."

"Not at all. We're waiting for the power to come back on so that I can dry Victor's clothes," I explained. "We got caught in the rain."

"Maybe there was an accident and someone hit a pole, you know; downed some power lines or something," Josh said.

"Given the amount of drunk drivers on the road tonight, I'm not surprised," I said, pouring some wine for him.

"Thanks, hon," he said after I handed him the glass. "I see you've unpacked your books. Wow, you've got a lot of them." He pointed to the storage cube containing my DVD collection. "Mind if I take a look?"

"Go ahead. Feel free to borrow whatever you want."

"Dangerous Liaisons, Elizabeth, 1492, Underworld, Amelie—do you have anything recent?" Josh teased. "Any action-adventure or war flicks?"

"I own a few seasons of Game of Thrones."

"Cool. Hey, what are these?" he asked, holding up a couple of DVDs with handwritten labels. "Our True History: Pyramids and Sun Gods by Nassim Haramein and The Lion Sleeps No More by David Icke."

"Lecture videos," I replied. "Nassim Haramein is a physicist and David Icke is...well, he's a bit strange but has some very interesting theories."

"Theories on what?" Josh asked.

Victor took it upon himself to reply, "Controversial theories regarding Reptilians and their presence among us."

Surprised, I asked, "You've heard of him?"

Victor nodded. "David believes that Reptilians are manipulating perception, thus controlling humans by limiting their potential."

"Makes you think, doesn't it?" I said. "He also claims that humans enjoyed a much higher level of consciousness in the past, but now we're disconnected from that energy."

"And he believes it's because of Reptilians?" Josh scoffed. "What a wanker! I didn't know you were into this New Age stuff, Veronica."

"I'm not," I said defensively. "His lectures are thought-provoking. I don't agree with everything he says, but he does make some compelling arguments. He also brings in scientific viewpoints, like the moon being an intelligent creation and not a natural occurrence."

Josh burst out laughing and Victor said, "It's a theory among scientists and astrophysicists. There's a book——*Who Built the Moon?*—that suggests the moon was created."

Josh scowled. "Of course it was created. *By God.*"

"No," Victor countered calmly. "Not God, but rather an advanced civilization of aliens."

Josh chuckled, setting the David Icke DVD where he'd found it. "Is this Nassim guy also full of weird ideas?"

Once again, Victor surprised me when he said, "Nassim Haramein has dedicated his life to the study of physics, challenging many of the outdated views within his field. He's the Galileo of our time."

"His proposed theories offer such a fresh perspective on everything from ancient earthly sites to the universe," I added.

"Okay, would you two fill me in?" Josh asked, bringing the Nassim DVD with him as he sat back down on the sofa.

"Haramein proposes that the pyramids were built with the help of extraterrestrials." When Josh appeared skeptical, I added, "He's got several valid reasons for making this claim."

"Such as?"

"First of all, out of the thousands of hieroglyphs describing everything the Egyptians did—from what they ate to how they made love or went to the bathroom—there is not a single reference to the creation of the pyramids. In fact, the Egyptians never claimed to have built them."

"That's because the slaves built them," Josh said.

"Not according to the Egyptians. They give all the credit to the gods that came from the sky. They refer to these beings as the sun gods."

"Are you kidding me?" Josh countered.

"No, she's not," Victor said. "It's not feasible to think that a bunch of slaves with primitive tools could have built a structure of that magnitude in a relatively short amount of time—and end up with perfect mathematical precision."

I turned to look at Victor. "We're still clinging to foolish theories formulated in the early twentieth century. I think

Nassim has many other interesting points, too. Like the mysterious pillar inside the ten thousand year old Osirion Temple in Abydos, Egypt."

"The solid granite pillar with the symbols laser-burned into the stone with accurate precision? The one you never see in books because no archeologist or historian knows how to explain where such technology came from without venturing out of the accepted theories?" Victor asked casually. "I've been to Egypt and I've seen that pillar."

My mouth dropped. "Seriously?" Victor nodded and I continued, "I hope to see that pillar someday. My professor at UMASS told me about Haramein when I approached him after class one day and proposed the theory of extraterrestrials being involved in the building of the pyramids. He informed me that I was not the first person to arrive at that conclusion, then he warned me to be discreet."

Victor's eyebrow shot upward. "You came up with that theory all by yourself?"

I caught Josh's disbelieving look as he glanced first to me then to Victor.

I nodded. "All one has to do is compare the pyramids of Egypt to the Mesoamerican pyramids of the Mayans and Aztecs—not only are they similar massive triangular structures built thousands of miles apart, but their placement on earth corresponds to stellar constellations."

"Wait a sec," Josh said, holding up his hand. "I saw something about this stuff on the History Channel. Are you one of those—hang on, what are those people called…Ancient Alien Theorists?"

"Yes, I am," I proudly admitted. "By the way, did you know that most of the world's ancient civilizations claimed to have had contact with flying sky gods?"

Victor nodded. "I did."

I was on a roll. "Scientists have discovered several planets in the Goldilocks Zone and—"

Josh cut me off. "The Goldi—what?"

"The Goldilocks Zone. Remember the fairy tale? Well,

that's what scientists call the regions in space hosting planets that may be conducive to life. Not too hot, not too cold."

"Okay, I get it," Josh said.

I continued, "We've got a number of these planets just outside our own galaxy. A few decades ago scientists believed that the universe was lifeless and now they think the exact opposite."

"You realize Carl Sagan had a lot to do with that change of opinion," Victor interjected.

"My parents used to talk about him all the time," Josh added.

I placed my hand on Josh's arm. "What if we're the result of an alien slash homo-erectus mating experience? I don't know about you, but that theory is easier for me to swallow than the whole Adam and Eve fairytale."

Victor and Josh were now staring at me with wide eyes. I smiled sheepishly. "Did I offend you guys?"

Josh shook his head. "I can't believe we're talking about this stuff on Christ's birthday."

"The twenty-fifth of December was actually an ancient pagan celebration turned Christian to appease the Romans during Constantine's empire," I said, covering my mouth afterward. *Oops.*

"Agnostic or Atheist?" Victor asked simply.

"Agnostic. I like to keep my options open," I replied.

"You're both going to Hell, you know," Josh said, half teasing. Having been raised Irish-Catholic, he didn't like to joke when it came to Jesus.

"Sorry if I've offended your religious sensibilities," I said to Josh, patting his shoulder.

Victor's eyes narrowed. "Veronica, have you ever heard of Sergeant Clifford Stone?"

"I may have watched a few YouTube videos, but that's about it," I replied. "I don't know if I believe him when he claims the government has catalogued fifty-seven different alien species, but it sure takes a lot of guts to go public with that sort of statement."

Josh's eyebrows shot upward. "So, you two really believe in

aliens? You're not just joking around here?" he asked, setting the Nassim DVD down on the coffee table.

I settled more comfortably into the sofa cushions with my glass of wine. "Do you want to know what I honestly think?"

"Yeah," Josh replied uneasily.

Victor regarded me expectantly and I said, "The universe is incredibly awesome and so unimaginably vast—we can't even begin to grasp the concept. It would be extremely arrogant of us to believe that all of this exists merely for the human species. We cannot possibly be alone."

After a long silence, Josh said, "Interesting."

"Don't you feel the same way?"

"I've never given it much thought, but when you put it that way, it does seem weird that we'd be the only intelligent life in the universe," he admitted reluctantly. I noticed that Victor raised his eyebrow. Josh continued, "What do you think aliens look like? Little green men with big black bug-eyes, like the kind we see on T-shirts?"

I thought for a moment. "I don't know. I guess it would depend on their environment, wouldn't it? Hollywood likes to portray aliens as ugly monsters, but what if they're not like that? What if they're not aggressive or hostile? What if they're peaceful and beautiful or even divine?"

"Like angels?" Victor prompted with an unreadable expression.

"Exactly!" I cried.

Josh frowned. "Angels? Really?"

I nodded. "Okay, don't laugh, but I've always thought that angels are actually aliens."

"What?!" Josh protested, turning around in his seat to face me squarely.

"Angels are described in several historical accounts and holy books as heavenly creatures composed of light with the ability to fly. Obviously, they're referring to aliens!"

"Are you for real?" Josh demanded, almost angrily. "I think it's pretty safe to assume that you didn't have a very religious upbringing."

"On the contrary. I came from a religious family, but I firmly believe that what cannot be explained with science or nature must be left with a big question mark."

Victor smiled. "I must say, Veronica, you're a very unusual woman. There may be a few people out there who think and feel as you do, but they normally don't express it out loud."

"Well, I don't go around saying this stuff to everyone."

"So, you're saying that I'm special?" Victor asked, placing his hand on his chest in a gesture of being flattered.

Josh also asked, "Yeah, am I special, too?"

"I guess I feel comfortable around you for some reason," I confessed to Victor, ignoring Josh. "You're easy to talk to and have an open mind."

"You can tell me anything. I won't judge you," Victor said.

"Whereas I will now think of you as a freak," Josh teased.

We laughed heartily and, a minute later, the power came back on. I put Victor's clothing in the dryer. "Your clothes will be dry in a few minutes."

"Thank you," Victor said.

I turned my attention to Josh. "More wine?"

He shook his head. "I'm going to leave you two alone so you can compare U.F.O. notes. Thanks for the wine. It was great meeting you, Victor. I look forward to your next show."

"We'll be at Heat on New Year's Eve. If you don't have any other plans, I'll put you and your date on the VIP list."

"Cindy will love that. Thanks, man. Goodnight you two."

"Bye Josh," I said before closing the door behind him. Smiling at Victor, I added, "Okay, so now the word is out that I'm a total nerd."

"Wondrous strange is a more accurate description," Victor said, eyeing me in a way that made my face hot. "Turn off the lights, Veronica, I like the candlelight much better. I've never been one for electric lights."

Never been one for electric lights? His comment struck me as odd, but I said nothing as I turned off the lights. I was glad to be alone again with Victor. We continued discussing the theories of Haramein and the possibility of aliens having landed

111

on our planet. The buzzer on the dryer sounded way too soon, and I got up to retrieve his clothing.

"Here you go," I said, handing him the warm bundle.

"Do you mind?" he asked, indicating my bedroom.

"Not at all."

I watched him walk into my bedroom and partially close the door. I'd dropped one of his socks in the middle of the living room floor. Victor was outside my line of vision but when I heard the zipping of pants, I assumed he'd already put on the dry jeans.

I picked up the sock and went to the door, pushing it open. "Sorry, I dropped one of your—"

I froze. He was in the process of pulling his shirt over his head, his chest fully exposed. Unlike the skin of his face, neck and arms, his torso was pale, which in itself was no big deal since most men had the 'farmer's tan.' What was really strange was the subtle opalescent sheen of his skin, like the green-lilac iridescence of an opal.

"Thanks," I heard him mumble as he took the sock. I avoided his eyes and hastily ducked out of the doorway.

A few moments later, he emerged from the room eyeing me with a knowing look. The guilt of having seen his strange skin was plain on my face. I averted my gaze as he took his seat beside me and reached for his glass of wine.

"What's wrong?" he asked crisply.

"I'm thinking about our conversation tonight," I lied. "I hope Josh isn't offended."

"I'm sure he's fine. What are you doing for New Year's Eve?" he asked, playing my game.

"If I can get on Heat's VIP list, I'll be jamming to Icon," I replied, relieved that he changed the subject.

"Done. Big T made us an offer we couldn't refuse. Fifty percent of the admission, which will be one hundred dollars at the door."

I boldly placed my hand on his shoulder, relishing the feel of his hard muscles. "I'm really impressed that you donate the proceeds to good causes. I speak for Tara and Josie, too."

He surprised me by covering my hand with his. The warmth of his touch brought a wave of pleasure throughout my body. Victor leaned forward and kissed my cheek, holding his face close to mine for an instant before pulling away.

"Thanks for the wine, the shower, and for kindly drying my clothes, but most of all, thank you for your company." He stood. "I'll call you soon.

Disappointed, I walked him to the door. He hovered a moment and I thought for sure he was going to kiss me—on the lips this time. He didn't. "Good night, Veronica."

I forced myself to smile because I didn't want him to go. "Good night, Victor."

"I want to give you something special for your twenty-second birthday," Victor whispered in my ear.

"Mmm...sounds lovely," I said sleepily, relishing the feel of his warm breath on my skin. Was he finally going to claim my virginity?

Stretching as lazily as a cat, I waited for him to join me in bed. When he didn't, I turned over to look at him. He was fully dressed in a smart riding habit, holding a few apples in his hand. Disappointment washed over me.

"I've cancelled your lessons today." I sat up and reached for an apple, but he tapped my hand. "These aren't for you."

Rubbing my eyes, I sighed. "Where are we going?"

He grinned mischievously then headed for the door. "It's a surprise. Hurry and get dressed, we're going riding."

I washed my face and donned my riding clothes before meeting him at the bottom of the stairs. Loud footsteps approached, compelling us to turn our heads.

"Is it true that class has been cancelled?" Rosa demanded, storming into the hallway. She looked directly at Victor.

"Yes," he replied. "I thought I made that clear when I addressed the students yesterday."

"But you promised to teach me how to ride today," she whined, still not acknowledging my presence.

"I promised to teach the entire class how to ride sometime this week," he patiently corrected. "I have to discuss with Mistress Veronica which day would be best."

Rosa glared at me. "Instead of being here with the students you plan to spend the day with her? Alone?"

"Rosa, let me make something clear: I am the master of this

house and free to come and go as I please. As for Mistress Veronica, she tirelessly devotes her time and energy to you and the other students on a daily basis. Today is her birthday, and she deserves to rest and enjoy the day."

Rosa glared at me. If she could have emitted fire from her eyes, I would have been reduced to a pile of ashes. She stomped away with a loud huff.

"She's in love with you," I said quietly.

"You already know my feelings on this matter. I will throw her out of this house right now if you wish it."

"I still have hope that she'll come around in due time."

"I'll continue to respect your decision—even if I don't agree with it. Let's enjoy the day, shall we?"

We walked out into the morning sunshine and I saw the horses tethered to a post. Victor handed me the reins of the gentle mare. I patted her sweet face. "Good morning, Venus."

Predictably, Victor's horse was named Mars. We fed the apples to the horses, save one, which Victor tossed to me with a wink. I bit into the sweet, juicy fruit hungrily.

"Up you go," he said as he helped me into the saddle.

We exited the city gates and entered the surrounding woods. The trees above our heads grew so densely that their branches blocked out the sun.

We rode for the better part of an hour before I asked, "Where are we? I've never ventured out this far."

"Almost there, my love."

I sniffed the air and grimaced. "What's that awful smell?"

He urged his horse toward a spacious clearing and we dismounted under the shade of trees. Taking my hand, he led me to a free-flowing waterfall that fell at least twenty feet into a crystal clear hot spring emitting a sulfuric odor and steam.

"The ice cold water drops into the boiling water, creating the perfect temperature," he explained.

He reached into his saddlebag, pulled out a blanket and spread it out on the grass. Next, he produced a generous chunk of aged cheese, a handful of small pears, a fresh loaf of bread, dried figs, walnuts, and two bottles of excellent red wine.

Throwing my arms around his neck, I kissed his cheek.

My sudden burst of emotion, coupled with the unexpected physical contact, prompted his mouth to come down on mine. My knees weakened as he gently brought us down onto the blanket, never breaking the kiss. Eventually, he pulled away.

Propping himself up on his elbow, he said, "I knew you'd love it here."

I sighed blissfully. "How could I not? It's perfect."

"This is a very special place—our special place." He kissed me again. "You mean everything to me, and there's so much I want to share with you."

"I want to know what you know, and be wise like you."

"Perhaps someday you will."

"Why not now?"

He chuckled. "All in good time."

Uncorking a bottle of wine, he poured the fragrant red liquid into two silver chalices and handed one to me. "To you, Veronica," he said. "To your beauty, your inquisitive mind, and your pure heart."

Blushing from his lavish praise, I took a sip. We talked and laughed, drinking wine and nibbling on the delicious food.

Victor leaned back on his arms and inhaled the sweet, fresh air. After a moment, he stood. "Come, let's swim."

"You're certain the water is not too hot?"

"It's perfect, I promise you," he assured, removing his clothes. At my surprised expression, he stopped. "There are things about me you have yet to discover."

"What are you doing?"

"Don't be afraid."

He pulled off his shirt and I couldn't tear my eyes from his torso. The only other time I had seen his bare skin was last Christmas in a dimly lit room. In the natural light of day, the iridescence was glaringly obvious.

"Turn around," I said. He slowly turned his back to me. I studied the broad shoulders, the lean muscle and the strange, wondrous skin. "How do you hide them?"

"Hide what?" he demanded, peering down at me over his

116

shoulder.

"Your wings. It's clear to me what you are…an angel."

He grew serious. "That's one of the many names your kind has given mine. I'm not an angel—at least not in the sense humans would imagine."

"What other names have we given you?"

He removed the remainder of his clothing and stood before me completely naked. "Too many to mention; humans once worshipped us as gods."

I wasn't surprised. He was awe-inspiring and otherworldly, glorious from head to foot. Whatever notion I once fostered about Victor being an androgynous angel dissolved instantly. I had seen plenty of classical artwork depicting the male body—and Victor was unmistakably male.

"You are exquisite," I whispered.

"You would be surprised how much you and I have in common on a cellular level."

"A what level?"

"Never mind. It's too complicated for me to explain. Just know that we are very much alike. I'm of flesh and blood and take in nourishment as you do." He paused, his eyes boring into mine. "Our kind also reproduces much the same way as yours does."

"Yet, you are not like a man," I countered.

He offered me his hand and helped me up to my feet. We stood facing each other, and rather than respond to my comment, he slowly helped me to undress.

I was excited and fearful as my gown fell to my feet. As I stood there baring both my body and soul to him, I became aware of my physical inferiority and my fragile mortality.

He circled me slowly, taking in every inch of my flesh. "Your outer shell—your body—matches the beauty within."

He had grown physically excited. I had seen enough rutting animals to know when the male member was aroused.

Following my gaze he asked, "Do you still think I'm not like a man?"

Nervously, I shook my head. The apprehension I felt must

117

have been visible because he took a step forward and held me closely. When my skin came into contact with his, a vibrating heat pierced my body. He looked down at my hand as I touched his skin. The colors rippled ever so slightly beneath the surface.

"Your skin is like a living, breathing thing," I said.

"As is yours."

He led me down to the base of the waterfall and glided into the water. "Wonderful," he assured me with a smile.

My muscles relaxed almost instantly when I entered the warm water. I immersed myself completely, then slicked my wet hair back from my face when I broke the water's surface. Victor splashed me playfully and I splashed back. We laughed like children and forgot ourselves in the magic of the moment. We swam toward an outcrop of rocks where the waterfall met the spring. An ancient elm tree reached its branches out over the water and we faced each other underneath the leafy shade.

Victor's face held serious intensity and his eyes shone brightly. Taking hold of my shoulders, he pushed me against a smooth stone and brought his lips to mine in a deep, passionate kiss. His hands caressed my body until I literally trembled with desire, aching to be filled by him.

He pulled away and whispered, "I want you as I have never wanted another. Say you'll be mine, Veronica."

"I'm already yours," I confessed.

I felt both pain and pleasure as he gently entered me. He held me closely without moving until my need for him grew. It became so great that it was I who began to move against him. My wantonness ignited his passion, causing him to thrust harder. My hips met his demand until we both exploded with pleasure. Waves of energy and light passed between us.

Not even in my wildest dreams could I have imagined that making love with Victor could be so incredible. We were breathless and panting in each other's arms for several minutes before he tilted his head back to look into my eyes. My entire body tingled, and I was grateful that we were in the water because my legs were like jelly.

"I had no idea," I whispered.

"Nor I," he admitted, kissing my forehead. "My little star."

We remained in the deliciously warm water for quite a long time until the need for each other rose again. We made love once more before getting out and slipping into our clothes.

Reaching into the saddlebag, he withdrew a thin rectangular mechanism that looked like liquid silver. There was a perfectly round glass on one end and a little red light that blinked at intervals.

"What is that?" I asked, approaching the strange thing with trepidation.

"This is a…" he paused, no doubt searching for a word that I would understand. "A device that captures images so I can keep visual records."

"May I touch it?" He nodded and I gently touched its smooth surface. "This seems too perfect to have been fashioned by human hands."

"It was created in my world, not yours."

He pressed a tiny button that made a strange humming sound. I took a few steps back, fearful of what it might do. When Victor had finished, he placed the foreign contraption back in the bag.

"After being here with you today, I want to record this place," he explained.

"I wish to return here soon," I said.

"We will, my love. I promise." Looking up at the sky, he added, "We should go."

The sun's golden rays pierced through the trees, glittering on the water's surface. The sun would be setting in a couple of hours and we needed to get back to the city before dark. We left the remainder of the food for the forest animals and mounted our horses. I found myself smiling both inwardly and outwardly; it was a day I would never forget.

CHAPTER 22
PROVIDENCE, RI
NEW YEAR'S EVE, PRESENT DAY

True to his word, Victor called and we went out a few times. I learned a great deal more about him on these dates. In addition to being multilingual, he owned several properties in Lisbon, which had been passed down by a family ancestor. Sadly, some of the historical edifices were destroyed in the great earthquake of 1755, including a sixteenth century mansion that had once stood on a hill facing the Tagus River.

I have always thought of myself as a socially conscious person and an environmentalist, but compared to him, I was nothing. In addition to Icon's monetary donations, I was impressed to learn that Victor had volunteered in many countries throughout the world.

Needless to say, the more I got to know Victor, the more my respect and admiration for him grew. I was disappointed that he had not made any romantic moves toward me—not even a kiss. While I appreciated his respect, I was beginning to think that maybe he found me unattractive.

Since Tara and Josie had gone home for the holidays, I would be accompanying Cindy and Josh to the New Year's Eve party at Heat. I wanted to look my best, so I broke down and headed for the shopping mall. Most of my clothes were professional or casual, and I wanted to buy something sexy and black. Strolling past various shop windows, I mentally labeled the party dresses I saw on display: too young, too old, or way too trampy.

Then I saw it—the perfect dress: V-backed, knee-length, and cut from lustrous, black Duchess Satin. Paired with the dress were exotic emerald green snakeskin high heels with an open toe and sexy ankle strap. A small matching clutch dangled prettily from the mannequin's delicate wrist. The high-fashion ensemble was pricey, but worth every penny due to its quality and timeless style. Besides, it wasn't often that I splurged on a new outfit.

I went inside and was lucky to find my size in both the dress and the shoes. The neckline of the fitted dress created a straight line from shoulder to shoulder, but the back plunged into a deep "V" that exposed lots of skin. Since one could not wear a bra with the dress, the front panel was heavily lined. I thanked Fate for having blessed me with a set of firm B-cup breasts. Also, the deep plum nail polish I had applied to my toes last night looked great against the emerald green snakeskin.

I had a couple of hours to relax before getting ready for the party so made myself a cocktail when I got home. I had just squeezed some lemon into my gin and tonic when my cell phone rang. It was Victor's number.

"Hey, aren't you supposed to be rehearsing?" I teased.

"We are rehearsing—I'm taking a break. I called to let you know that you've been haunting my thoughts."

"As you've been haunting mine," I replied in a voice so sexy that I surprised even myself.

"I'm really looking forward to seeing you tonight."

"You're so sweet. I'm looking forward to seeing you tonight, too. Josh and Cindy are really excited. It was nice of you to invite them."

"My pleasure. See you later, Veronica."

I hung up the phone and took a sip of my drink. I sat on the sofa and my eyes were instantly drawn to the big colorful storage boxes above my bookshelf. How the heck had Victor known which box was green in a totally black room? Now that I think of it, how had he known where my kitchen was located or where I kept my dishtowels? His evasion of this issue bothered me whenever I've tried to bring it up. As I mulled over these thoughts, my phone rang again. Only this time, I didn't recognize the number.

"Hello?"

"Veronica?"

"Yes?"

"It's me, Stephanie!"

"Oh. Hi, Stephanie. How are you?"

"Fine, thanks. Hope you don't mind that Rodrigo gave me your number. I wanted to know if you're going to the show tonight."

"You mean Icon's show? Yes, I'll be there."

"Great! Charlie invited us, too. I thought it would be cool if we sat together."

"Victor already reserved a table. I'm sure they'll have no problem adding two more seats."

"Yay! Rodrigo will be so happy." She paused. "So...you and Victor are getting pretty close, huh?"

"Er..." She caught me completely off guard.

"Sorry, sweetie, I didn't mean to pry. It's just that, well, Charlie said a few things."

My heart skipped. "Oh? What did Charlie say?"

"That Victor's been spending a lot of time with you and talks about you often. I think he really likes you."

"I guess you could say we've been seeing each other."

"That's awesome! Okay, we'll talk later. Rodrigo is yelling from the shower—he forgot his towel again. Gotta go!"

Stephanie hung up and I stared out into space. So Victor was talking about me to his friends. That was a good sign. I finished my cocktail and took a warm bath. After slathering on scented body cream, I applied some makeup and got dressed. I tossed my hair into a chignon and fished out a pair of slinky earrings from my jewelry box. Josh knocked at my door just as I was spraying a bit of perfume to the nape of my neck.

"Hi Josh," I said, holding the door open.

Looking me up and down, he mouthed the word 'wow' while pointing downstairs. Loudly, he asked, "Ready to go?"

"Sure." I grabbed my keys and threw on my winter coat.

Cindy came into view as I descended the stairs. She looked as Irish as Josh with pale skin and long red hair.

"This is my girlfriend, Cindy," Josh said.

I shook her hand. "It's so nice to finally meet you."

"Same here," she replied in a surprisingly deep voice that implied years of smoking.

Josh jingled his car keys. "Shall we?"

Cindy began chatting animatedly the minute the car pulled out of its parking space and she didn't stop until we reached the club. I noticed that Josh had perfected the art of saying things like 'uh-huh,' 'cool,' 'yeah,' 'wow,' and 'really' at the appropriate intervals without actually listening to a word Cindy said. I had to resist laughing.

There was already a long line at Heat's door. Two massive bouncers in black suits stood behind the red velvet ropes as a buxom blonde in a white satin dress checked off names on a guest list. Big T had spared no expense for tonight's party. I walked up to the woman and gave her my name, and she immediately called for someone on her walkie-talkie. A good-looking young man in a dashing tuxedo arrived immediately, and she instructed him to lead us to our seats.

"We're really getting the VIP treatment," Cindy commented as we simply cut in front of everyone in line to be let through the velvet ropes.

The young man led us to a table positioned in front of the stage. Big T came over to greet us personally as Dr. Nunes and Stephanie arrived.

Dr. Nunes cut a dignified figure in a black suit while Stephanie flaunted a silver sequined tank dress with red heels.

"Hi Josh. Long time, no see," Stephanie said.

"Hey Steph. How's it going?" he replied.

I noticed how Josh's eyes widened as he stared at Stephanie's big breasts. Unfortunately, Cindy also noticed her boyfriend's open admiration and gave him a swift kick to the shin under the table.

Victor and Charlie came out to greet us.

Dr. Nunes placed his arm around Stephanie. "It was nice of you boys to get us a VIP table. We feel like royalty, isn't that right, baby?"

Stephanie practically purred as she nodded in agreement.

Victor took my hand and kissed it. "You look amazing."

123

"Thank you, so do you."

A waitress arrived with two buckets of chilled champagne.

"I'm happy you're here," he said. "I'll join you after the show. Enjoy the champagne—I told Big T to give you the best."

Dr. Nunes stood. "I need to use the men's room, so please excuse me."

"I need to pee, too," Stephanie said. "The ladies room can't be far from the men's, right? You girls want to join me?"

Cindy and I declined politely.

"What is it about women going to the bathroom together?" Josh mumbled.

"I can't believe your boyfriend is the lead singer of Icon!" Cindy exclaimed, ignoring her boyfriend's comment. "He's so cute—sorry Josh—and he's going to be famous someday."

I blushed and sipped some of the delicious champagne. If I drank enough, maybe that nagging feeling about the green storage cube would be drowned out.

Josh leaned toward me and said, "Hey, um, remember your birthday in Boston when I called Victor a freak? I totally take that back. He's a really cool guy."

"Do you honestly think that? Even after our weird Christmas conversation about aliens?" I teased.

Cindy cleared her throat and looked at us. "What are you two whispering over there?"

"I was apologizing for having called Victor a freak the night of Veronica's birthday party in Boston," Josh explained.

"You did what?" she exclaimed loudly.

They ended up getting into a little tiff. I didn't pay any attention to them because I was too busy taking in the tasteful décor. There were candles set in votive holders at every table, along with an elegant orchid arrangement. Dr. Nunes and Stephanie returned to the table hand in hand.

"So, you're Veronica's boss?" Josh asked of Dr. Nunes.

"Oh, don't call Rodrigo that," Stephanie whined. "At least not tonight. No talking shop."

"Yes, I'm her employer," Dr. Nunes said, smiling at me.

Josh and Dr. Nunes were soon engrossed in conversation

124

with Cindy listening attentively. Stephanie took the opportunity to lean over to me.

"Victor is totally into you," she said with a knowing smile.

"You think so?"

"Oh, yeah, it's obvious! That outfit is to die for, by the way. Very sexy—you'll have him eating out of the palm of your hand later on."

"Thanks, Stephanie."

"Do you know what Charlie told us?" I shook my head and she continued, "He said 'Victor isn't joining us for the after-party because he wants to hang out with his 'girlfriend'—in those exact words."

"I wasn't aware of an after-party."

"*Exactly*."

"What are you two girls up to?" Dr. Nunes asked playfully.

Stephanie pulled her chair closer to him. "Just girlie talk."

Icon came on stage and soon the club was filled to maximum capacity. As expected, they put on a great show and even performed a couple of encore songs.

A trendy guest DJ from Ibiza performed after the Icon show. Within minutes, the dance floor was full of writhing bodies pumping to the hypnotic beat. Meanwhile, Icon's musicians came to our table. We enjoyed some champagne before hugs were exchanged. Everyone had after-party plans except for Josh, Cindy, Victor and me.

The DJ possessed serious talent and we couldn't resist the music. Cindy seemed to be having a hard time with her mega heels, so she ditched the shoes and opted to go barefoot.

I wasn't surprised that Victor was a great dancer. I honestly couldn't remember the last time I had so much fun.

The New Year's Eve countdown was soon announced over the sound system. Servers doled out complimentary flutes of champagne. I was already tipsy, but that didn't deter me.

Ten, Nine, Eight...

The giant video screen in the club displayed Times Square in New York City. The New Yorkers out on the streets were bundled up in heavy coats, cheering and waving flags.

125

Seven, Six, Five…

The screen displayed people in Boston sporting glittery tricorn hats, throwing colorful streamers and shiny confetti.

Four, Three, Two…

The entire dance floor appeared on the screen and people screamed, 'Providence!'

One…HAPPY NEW YEAR!!!

People laughed and cried, hugging and kissing one another, including Josh and Cindy. I noticed that Victor was the calmest person in the club.

Closing the gap between us, he smiled and said, "Happy New Year, Veronica."

"Happy New Year, Victor."

Then, he kissed me. I reached for his shoulders and pulled him closer to me. I felt the pressure of his strong hands at my waist and the warmth of his fingertips as they touched the bare skin of my back.

Although I could have easily pretended that we were the only two people in the club, I gently pulled away. We stared at one another and I realized something strange. My lips were vibrating slightly, as if there was a low electric current running through them. I put my fingers to my mouth.

The corners of his eyes crinkled with humor. "Let me guess—tingling sensation?"

"Are you wearing some kind of peppery lip balm?"

"No," he replied quietly.

"How do you know my lips are tingling?" I challenged.

"I know many things."

Josh interrupted us by slapping Victor on the back and shaking his hand. "Happy New Year, man."

Cindy wrapped her arms around me, crushing me against her voluptuous frame. "How cool is it that I met you tonight?" she said, slurring slightly from her happy buzz.

The DJ started up again, and we continued dancing for a few more minutes before deciding to go home. Josh and Cindy were heavy drinkers, while Victor and I had reached our limit of alcohol for one night.

I placed my hand on Josh's shoulder and said in his ear, "I think we're going to call it a night, but you two look like you're having fun, so stay. I'm taking your keys, okay? I want you and Cindy to take a cab home."

"Right," he agreed as he patted his pockets and fished out his keys. He handed them to me. "Remember to leave the hallway door unlocked and hide my keys under the doormat."

Reassured that Josh and Cindy would be fine, Victor and I said our goodbyes and left. Once we got outside, the sudden drop in temperature made me shiver from head to toe. Victor put his arm around my shoulders and drew me close to his side as we walked down the sidewalk. It didn't take long to find a taxi since they were out in full force tonight.

"Happy New Year, folks," said the driver.

I gave him my address and within minutes we were cruising through downtown Providence. A few people were still outside in crazy party hats, and there was confetti scattered on the sidewalks. Neither of us spoke during the short ride to my house. Victor paid the driver and told him to wait while he walked me to my door to say goodnight.

Before I realized what I was doing, I blurted out, "Why don't you come upstairs?"

His expression was unreadable. "Are you sure?"

"Yes, I could make us some tea or a nightcap…"

He motioned for the driver to go. As I watched the taxi pull away from the curb, I felt tremendously foolish and wondered what was going through Victor's mind. Was I coming across as too forward—or even worse—desperate?

Maybe you should have said goodnight and let him go home, Veronica. Now he'll think you're a slut.

Well, it was too late. I left the hallway door unlocked and hid Josh's key under the rubber doormat before going upstairs. Victor followed me in silence. I was so nervous that I fumbled with the keys and dropped them.

"Allow me," he said after picking them up off the floor. He unlocked my door and opened it, then stepped aside as I entered the apartment. He followed me, then closed the door.

127

"Make yourself comfortable," I said, feeling terribly awkward. "What can I get you?"

He sat down and crossed his long legs. He was so masculine and elegant that I felt slightly intimidated. "Tea would be good."

"Green tea okay?"

"Perfect."

Although my feet were sore from dancing, I didn't take off my new shoes. I went into the kitchen and filled my teapot with water. "Are you hungry? I may have some snacks."

"No, thank you."

A moment of complete silence passed and I didn't know what to make of it. Inviting him up had been a mistake. The last time he was here was due to his soaked clothing after we had been caught in the rain—I had a perfectly good excuse to invite him up then. I didn't have any reason whatsoever now. It was nearly two in the morning, and women who invited men into their homes at such an hour usually had only one thing in mind. I heard my mother's voice in my head uttering the advice she gave me as a teenager: 'Sleep with a man too soon and you'll lose him.'

Oh, no! You're going to ruin a relationship that hasn't even started yet!

"Need some help?" Victor asked, inches from my ear.

I yelped and dropped a spoon.

He picked up the spoon and put it in the sink. "Looks like I have a knack for sneaking up on you. You must be pretty deep in thought."

"Forgive me," I said, pouring the steaming hot water into a ceramic tea pot. I placed plenty of loose green tea into a silver tea ball and let it steep.

I reached for the mugs and he shifted close to me. "Here, let me help you."

His nearness made my heart beat faster. I poured the tea into the mugs. "Sugar?" I asked, my voice trembling.

"No, thank you."

We took our tea into the living room and sat on the sofa.

"You're awfully quiet," he observed.

"Sorry, I'm a bit pensive."

"Did you have a good time tonight?"

"I had a lot of fun. Everyone loved the show."

"Did you love the show?"

"I'm a huge fan of Icon."

He laughed a bit and the seductive sound made the butterflies in my stomach fly around wildly. "Thanks, but I want you to be a huge fan of me."

With those words he put down his mug, took the mug out of my hand, and placed it beside his own. Then, he leaned forward to kiss me. My eyes closed as our lips touched; I drowned in a sea of emotions and sensations that both fascinated and frightened me. I pulled away and heard myself mumble 'No' against his mouth.

Upon hearing my protest, Victor stopped immediately and leaned back on the sofa. "Forgive me, Veronica."

"Oh, no! I didn't mean to...what I'm trying to say is—"

"You don't have to explain anything. It's my responsibility to be a gentleman in your home. I meant no disrespect."

His words were so sincere and formal, that I laughed. He looked at me oddly. "May I be honest?"

"Always."

"I didn't want our night to end just because we got tired of the club, so I invited you up. I'm so nervous right now because I don't want you to think that I...I don't want you to get the wrong idea about me."

"You're the classiest woman I know. When you asked me up for a drink, I took the offer at face value." Staring at me intently, he added, "Besides, I know who you are."

I know who you are...

"What do you mean by that?" I demanded warily.

"Someday I'll explain it to you. For now, suffice it to say that I know your personality traits and your character."

As absurd as this statement sounded to my ears, I knew it to be true in my heart. How I knew this was beyond me, but I was so sure of it that I became suddenly frightened.

"Don't be alarmed," he said, as if sensing my fear.

"How can I not be? I don't know you that well, yet you claim to know me—perhaps even better than I know myself."

"I *do* know you better than you know yourself."

Then, he reached out for my hands and slowly brought them to his lips, kissing the top of each one softly. My skin vibrated, and the sensation brought back vague recollections. He gazed deeply into my eyes, and the look was intimate; familiar. I was on the verge of a memory, but it was heavily shadowed and refused to break through the surface.

"Who are you, Victor?" I whispered.

"Are you having a memory?" he asked hopefully. He turned my right wrist over and kissed my strange birthmark, still holding my gaze. The feel of his lips on the sensitive skin made me melt.

"There's something stirring beneath the fog's surface," I confessed, barely breathing. "I wish you'd tell me instead of playing this mind game."

His face grew serious. "I'm not playing any games with you. *Think*, Veronica. Think hard."

Then it struck me. "Stand up," I said, the anxiety mounting.

Victor stood. I tried to imagine what he'd look like with long hair and a crimson doublet. My face must have registered something significant in that moment because he began to speak to me in the same strange dialect from my dream. Upon hearing the words from his mouth, I was instantly filled with sorrow so deep that I began to cry.

"How is this possible?" I demanded tearfully.

"Veronica, please calm down," he said, putting his arms around me and rubbing my bare back. The touch of his warm hands on my naked skin sent fire up my spine.

He let go of me and went into the kitchen to fetch a glass of water. Putting the glass to my lips, he urged, "Here, drink this. I didn't mean to upset you. I won't say another word until you're ready, I promise."

"Until I'm ready?" I repeated. "Ready for what?"

"I'm trying to go slow...this isn't easy for me, either," he admitted, setting the glass down on the coffee table.

"You're him!"

"Veronica…"

"You're the man in my dream!"

My head swam. Was I hyperventilating? I was vaguely aware of someone in the kitchen opening drawers. A moment later, a paper bag was placed over my mouth.

"Breathe," Victor instructed.

Slowly, my eyes and my head returned to focus. He told me to keep breathing into the bag while he went back into the kitchen.

"Drink," he said, handing me a glass with a splash of gin.

I drank it like a shot and closed my eyes as the liquid heat radiated through my body. I sat back against the sofa cushions.

"Better?" he asked gently.

I nodded, but when I met his gaze my eyes filled with tears. He wiped them away with his fingertip. "Don't cry, little star."

Little star…"Who are you?"

"It's better if you remember by yourself."

"Why? Why can't you just tell me? This is torture!"

"I don't want you to have another panic attack." I covered my face with my hands and he asked, "Do you trust me?"

His eyes gleamed like a pair of topaz in the dimness of my living room. They reflected truth, friendship, hope, faith, and even love. The corners of his lips turned up slightly. Something inside me told me to trust him.

"I do," I admitted shakily.

"Then believe me. You should remember on your own."

"At least tell me this: what language were you speaking?"

"If you listen carefully, you'll recognize it as Portuguese."

"I've never heard that accent or that dialect before. Which remote part of Portugal is it from?"

He hesitated. "Lisbon."

"I'm serious, Victor."

He didn't crack a smile. "So am I."

"You know what? I was being sincere when I asked for some help," I said a bit testily.

His hand locked around my wrist as I stood. "It's sixteenth century Portuguese from Lisbon."

"I don't know about you, but the tea isn't cutting it for this conversation. I'm making us a couple of gin and tonics." I went into the kitchen and voiced my thoughts aloud as I got some ice from the freezer. "There's a fishing village in Malaysia that still speaks Old Portuguese, but it's quite different from what you've just spoken. Did you work as a historical tour guide in Portugal or something?" When he said nothing, I continued, "We know how people wrote back then, but how they pronounced things is an entirely different story; the cadence of each word, where the accents are placed—language evolves throughout time."

He began speaking once again in that strange dialect. Only this time, I paid close attention. To my astonishment, I understood every word. I had no idea how I understood, but I did. I'd never heard sixteenth century Portuguese spoken before, but I knew that he told me to 'Go light on the gin.'

"It's authentic," he assured, returning to English.

"There were no recording devices in existence back then so how can you be sure?" I demanded, splashing a bit of gin into his glass but being generous when it came to mine.

"Thank you," he said, accepting the drink from my hand.

"You weren't around back then to hear it with your own ears," I chided. "So how can you know?"

Watching me expectantly, he said nothing.

"Victor?" Every hair on the back of my neck stood on end. "That's impossible," I whispered without conviction.

He remained as still as a statue, which was not only disturbingly unnatural, but downright scary.

I took a big gulp of my drink and placed the glass down on the coffee table. "Are you trying to tell me that...that you..?"

I couldn't finish my sentence because his serious expression turned to one of pity. "Maybe I should go now," he said, placing his untouched drink beside mine. "I'm upsetting you, and that's the last thing in the world I ever want to do, especially after such a wonderful evening."

"No, you can't go. I need some answers."

"I think I've given you more than enough material to talk over with your therapist."

"How do you know I'm in therapy?"

"We've talked about many things—"

"Not once did I ever mention to you that I was in therapy. I'm extremely private about that."

"I know a lot about you…"

"How?"

"Veronica, please. You're getting worked up again."

"Are you spying on me or something?"

He put both hands up in a defensive gesture. "No, it's nothing like that, I swear."

I didn't care if he was gorgeous or talented—he was starting to freak me out. "This is getting too weird for me."

He stood and said, "I really should go."

"No."

"No?" he repeated, confused. "It's obvious that my presence here is upsetting you."

"Not your presence, your words. My gut instinct tells me to trust you…I know you don't mean to hurt me."

He appeared wounded. "Hurt you? I would die for you."

I stared at him askance. "But you've only just met me." The way he stared back at me made me believe that he really would die for me. "Stay, Victor. Please. I don't want to be alone tonight. I'm not suggesting that we…you know."

He nodded. "Very well. I can sleep on the sofa."

I shook my head. "Would it be okay if you held me for a little bit? Until I fell asleep? My head is full and I don't want to talk about this stuff anymore. At least not now."

Victor's expression in that moment was akin to that of a father about to indulge a child. He allowed me to lead him by the hand into my bedroom. I kicked off my heels and stretched out on the bed, pulling him down beside me. He wrapped his arms around me and we spooned together, fully clothed. There were several questions that I wanted to ask him, but I refrained. I needed quiet now. The minutes ticked past and the longer I remained in his embrace, the calmer I became. It felt as if energy was radiating out of his entire body and entering mine. Before I realized it, my eyes grew so heavy that I had no choice but to shut them.

I dreamed of stars—millions of them. They twinkled and reflected the light in a rainbow of colors. Suddenly they began to spin; slowly at first, then with increasing speed. I grew dizzy as my eyes tried to follow their frenzied dance. They came to an abrupt stop. I blinked and saw they had formed a swirl with a tiny star in its hollow—my birthmark!

***

The bright morning sun shone through the open blinds. I blinked against the light, realizing that I was still in my party clothes. The dried mascara stuck to my lashes in thick clumps and my white pillow case was smeared with lipstick.

Last night's events came rushing into my head like a mini tidal wave. I sat up in bed. "Victor?"

No response. I looked down at my badly wrinkled black satin dress. My new green heels and clutch were thrown in the corner of my bedroom. I scrambled out of bed quickly, almost stumbling in my haste. I caught a glimpse of my disheveled hair and smudgy eyes in the bathroom mirror as I made my way into the living room. It was empty.

"Victor?" I called out again. I saw a note on the refrigerator.

Dearest Veronica, I had to leave early this morning and didn't want to wake you. I promise to get in touch with you as soon as I can. We still have much to talk about. Thank you again for last night. Yours, Victor.

Victor didn't believe in the human marriage ceremony, and neither did I after discovering that ancient Romans invented it as a business contract for the transference of property. Roman women were not considered citizens, but rather goods—like brooding mares.

We pledged ourselves to one another privately with our own vows. To celebrate, we decided to hold a New Year's Eve banquet and invited a small number of distinguished guests.

The last day of the year dawned cold with heavy fog rolling in from the Tagus. Victor and I lounged in bed for a bit longer than usual, enjoying the warmth of our naked bodies under the covers.

"I think we should go to the market to get some extra treats for the children," he suggested.

"A fine idea," I agreed, throwing back the coverlet and sitting up in bed. "Let me dress and fetch my basket."

Victor growled and pulled me toward him. "Not yet," he said, nuzzling my neck. "I'm hungry for you."

We made love quickly and passionately before he released me to get dressed. Smiling, I brushed my hair, washed my face, and put on a warm gown. Although I slept in his bed, we kept separate chambers for the sake of appearances.

I returned to his room and saw that he had something in his hand. "What's that?"

Victor held a thin white oval disk with several buttons. Green lights blinked on each side. It was quite different from the silver device he used to document the waterfall.

"This is used for communication. Sometimes my people want a report and I must oblige them."

"May I see it?" I asked, drawing closer.

He held it out to me and placed it in my palm. I marveled at how smooth and weightless it felt. "Do you talk about us?"

"Yes."

Carefully, I handed it back to him. "What would happen if you made these objects known to our rulers?"

"Wipe the thought from your head, Veronica," he said, his face so serious that it frightened me. He put the strange oval device away in a small trunk and locked it.

We threw on our cloaks and descended the stairs. Two adolescent students accompanied us, each one carrying a big empty basket. We walked briskly to the outdoor market, and Victor purchased rounds of fine cheeses, smoked meats and fish, honeyed figs, and sweetmeats. When the baskets were full, we sent the students back to the house and remained to shop for other items. I was admiring a bolt of fine wool when I felt the weight of someone's stare. It was Sara. Beside her stood Tiago, holding a basket of pig's feet.

Victor stood silently at my side as Sara eyed him with great curiosity. "We have not seen you at church in such a long time, Veronica," she said, her smile sticky sweet. "You must have joined a different parish."

"I did," I lied.

"Have you sold your cottage?"

"Yes. It's common knowledge in the parish, so I'm surprised you didn't know. I sent Dona Maria a letter several months ago."

She seemed embarrassed. "People have been asking…"

Before she could ask any more questions, I said, "Give my kindest regards to all those who have been asking about me."

There was an awkward pause as Sara smiled at Victor, waiting to be introduced. I refused to oblige her.

"Come Tiago," she snapped irritably. "Let's not keep Veronica from her friend any longer."

"That was unusually rude of you," Victor commented after they had stormed off.

"Sara is a notorious gossip who holds a grudge against me

for rejecting her brother," I explained.

"The oafish fellow?" When I nodded, he continued, "You do realize that you've given her plenty of fodder for gossip."

Grinning mischievously, I said, "Because I'm in the company of a mysterious, handsome stranger?"

"Veronica, this is serious."

"Does her wagging tongue worry you?"

"I worry for you. These are dangerous times. We don't attend church."

"We live in sin, too."

He looked around to make sure no one was eavesdropping. "You lied about moving to another parish. What if she discovers the truth? We need to keep a low profile and make no enemies."

"I don't consider Sara my enemy."

"That may be true on your part…Envy is a powerful and destructive emotion. It breeds hatred."

No sooner were the words out of his mouth, I spotted Sara staring at me from across a market stall with a mixture of curiosity and contempt.

Victor followed my gaze. "Let's go."

Sara's contemptuous face remained in my mind as we left the market. I had never spoken ill of her, never argued with her, never tried to deceive her, yet she disliked me intensely. Was it solely because I was not interested in marrying Tiago? Or was there more to it?

Sara was relegated to the very bottom of my thoughts when we arrived home. The students and servants were scurrying about to get everything ready for the party. I went into the ballroom and decided to dust the plates and give our silver a quick polishing. When I was done, I went upstairs to bathe and prepare for the festivities. Victor's bedroom door was slightly ajar so I went inside. I was drawn to the small trunk where he had locked the white oval device. What other wonderful things lurked inside? To my surprise, it was unlocked.

The white oval device and the silver image recorder were on top of a stack of stiff paper. Every sheet flaunted a realistic image. The surface of the paper itself was smooth and shiny, without any brushstrokes. There were images of our lovely home, the center of Lisbon, several of the city's monuments, and the waterfall.

"What are you doing?"

I whipped around to see Victor standing in the doorway. He seemed displeased as he took the images from my hand.

"Forgive me, Victor," I said, faltering. "I was curious…"

He glanced up and down the corridor before closing the door and placing the images in the trunk. "If you want to see something, ask me. Never go through my things—it can be dangerous." Seeing my quivering lip, he added, "I didn't mean to be harsh with you, I'm only trying to protect you."

"They look so lifelike; how were they made?"

"The students and guests are waiting for us downstairs, my love. We'll talk later."

"Do you promise?"

"Yes," he replied while leading me toward the door. "It would please me if you wore the gown I gave you last year."

I bathed and put on the exquisite tawny gold gown. Rather than wear my hair loose, I parted it down the center and coiled each half into two buns above my ears. The effect was charming, especially since the style flaunted my slender neck.

I greeted our guests and played the part of hostess, catching Victor's appraising eye. Everyone seemed to be having a good time at the party except for Rosa, who sulked in a corner. I approached her with the intention of making peace.

"Rosa, you should be enjoying yourself with the others."

Her eyes were hard and accusatory. "Leave me alone, you hypocrite. I know about you and Victor."

I was completely taken aback by the viciousness of her tone. "What?"

"You heard me."

Rosa's infatuation with Victor had not yet dissipated. In fact, she grew more aggressive toward me every day. I took a deep breath. "I don't appreciate your tone, and it's neither the time nor the place for this conversation. You can tell me your troubles in the morning, but right now you should try to have some fun with your fellow students."

"Do you think I can have a good time in a place where immorality is shamelessly flaunted under my nose?"

"I'm not going to listen to this nonsense any longer."

As I turned to walk away, she whispered, "Whore."

I whipped around and she ran off. From across the room I saw Victor discreetly chase after her. They reentered the ballroom a moment later and walked to where I stood.

"Forgive me for what I said earlier," Rosa said contritely.

She was on the brink of tears. I didn't have a chance to respond because Victor led her away. He returned alone.

I leaned close to him and whispered, "She called me a—"

He placed his finger on my lip to silence me. "I know."

"How do you know?"

"I witnessed the entire scene from across the room. I used mind control to calm her down."

"What did you say?"

Victor looked guilty. "She's calm now."

"You said that you used "mind control" on her? What do you mean by that?"

"I can control the thoughts of people who are close to me."

I was instantly jealous. "And Rosa is close to you?"

"What I mean is that it doesn't work with strangers."

"Oh. Did you ever use it on me?"

He gave me a wry smile. "Never."

"How do you do it?"

"You won't understand, but it has to do with physical aspects of the human brain and electromagnetic energy."

Would Victor ever cease to amaze me? "Where is Rosa?"

"Fast asleep in her bed."

I wrung my hands together. "What are we going to do?"

"You already know what I think should be done."

"Perhaps if you continued to use mind control on her, she could change for the better."

He frowned. "Mind control works for a short period of time and is only to be used in extreme circumstances. Humans possess free will and should be allowed to choose how they

139

think." Picking up two goblets from a buffet table, he handed one to me before holding his up to make a toast.

"What are we toasting?" I asked.

"It's almost midnight."

The guests gathered around the big fireplace and gazed up at the mantle where our expensive Nuremburg clock was proudly displayed. A ripple of excitement went through the room as the single hand of the spring-driven clock pointed to the Roman numeral twelve.

Victor gently brought his goblet to mine and smiled. "To a happy and prosperous new year, little star."

The festivities continued well into the wee hours, and only the oldest students managed to stay awake. Later that night as Victor and I climbed the stairs leading to our bedchambers, I wondered how Rosa could have discovered our secret romance. The upper level of the house was strictly off-limits to the students, and we cautiously displayed chaste respect toward one another in public.

As if reading my thoughts, Victor said, "Don't worry about Rosa. Dogs that bark loudly are usually harmless."

I relaxed a bit as we entered his bedchamber. "I believe you have a promise to fulfill."

"Ah, yes," he said. "Come."

Victor led me to a tall painted screen that hid a secret door. He motioned for me to follow him. "Do not be frightened of anything you see in this room. Remember: everything can be easily explained with science. Are you ready?"

I nodded. He snapped his fingers and it was as if the sun itself had penetrated through the walls. The illumination came from a small orb suspended from the ceiling...strangely, there was no fire. The room was filled with fantastic objects and blinking lights that mimicked tiny colorful flames. A mixture of terror and fascination washed over me as he indicated a flat metal rectangle.

"Watch," he said, pushing a series of buttons.

The metal rectangle spit out a glossy sheet of paper.

"Take it," he said.

I did as I was told. The image was of me—my frozen reflection in the mirror. Every detail was shockingly accurate.

It struck me that I was trapped in a world with many limitations, and I suddenly envied Victor's freedom.

"May I have this image?"

"Yes," he replied, "But you must always keep it hidden. It must never be left out in the open where someone else can find it. You and I are the only two people who know about the existence of this room and its contents. Do you understand?"

"I do," I assured, meeting his intense gaze.

"Would you like to see something else? You must promise to stay calm." I nodded and he walked over to another machine. "If I push this button here, this machine will create a lifelike image of you called a hologram."

"Push the button," I prompted.

He did so and a cobweb of lightning appeared for an instant before my twin materialized right before my eyes. I was too stunned to say a word. She looked like me, moved like me, and when I reached out to touch her, I discovered that she was made of thin air.

"A hologram projects an illusion of reality," he explained.

"Are you using mind control on me right now?"

"No, nothing like that. This machine emits..." He stopped, perceiving the completely blank look upon my face. "It's complicated."

"Your science is needed here in Lisbon. It could be used to help many people."

He pushed a button and the image disappeared. "My science would be mishandled and abused in your world."

He led me out of the room and locked up. We undressed quietly, got under the covers, and held each other until we both fell asleep.

That night, my dreams consisted of incredibly shiny machines and bright blinking lights.

CHAPTER 24
PROVIDENCE, RI
JANUARY, PRESENT DAY

Victor called me on the second day of January while I was doing some research at home, and we agreed to meet in the late afternoon at the park. It was awkward seeing him face to face after the episode in my apartment.

He kissed my cheek in greeting. "How are you?"

"I'm good. Thanks. I'm sorry about the other night."

"Why? You've done nothing wrong."

"It was so...weird."

"No worries. Hey, are you hungry? I'd like to have dinner with you."

"I'm not hungry now, but I will be in about an hour or so."

"What can we do in the meantime?"

"I've been cooped up inside all day in front of my computer. How about a nice walk?"

He nodded in approval. "Sounds good."

We strolled through the barren trees, our breath forming white vapor in the icy air. "Do you live nearby?"

"I live about a fifteen minute walk from here."

"I'm curious to see your home."

"Really?"

"They say you can tell a lot about a person from their environment."

"Is that so? What do you expect to find at my place?"

Answers to my questions. "Ultra-modern designer furniture and sophisticated gray walls with tons of glossy black and white photos. Maybe a few modern art paintings."

He laughed. "Wow, you've given this some thought."

"Art historians like to analyze architectural spaces. Is my description accurate?"

"Nothing could be farther from the truth."

"So...you've got a man-cave? Big reclining easy chairs, bookshelves made from concrete cinder blocks, serious speakers, huge flat screen TV, and video games?"

"Whoa! That's too far in the opposite direction."

"Okay...describe your place to me."

"I'll do better. Not only will I take you there, I'll cook you dinner myself. I have some pasta and fresh tomatoes in my kitchen. Sound tempting?"

"Fresh tomatoes in January?"

"I grow them myself, inside my home."

"In that case, I can't turn down such a fabulous offer."

He looked at me closely. "Besides, I'm pretty sure you'll bring up the topic of New Year's Eve again, and I think it's best to discuss such matters privately. Don't you agree?"

"Definitely," I said, blushing slightly.

We crossed the river and walked toward the old factory district of Providence where former mills and warehouses had been converted into upscale lofts.

"You live in one of those?" I asked, pointing to an early nineteenth century faded brick building that had been refitted with expensive floor-to-ceiling studio windows.

"Yes. The district of the Urban Renaissance. Come on."

Taking my hand in his, he led me into the main entrance and up the stairwell. "These are the original wooden stairs that have been reinforced with steel," he explained. "There's an elevator, but I thought you'd appreciate going up the old-fashioned way."

We reached the fourth and final floor, then walked down a brick corridor and stopped at the last door. Victor unlocked it and allowed me to enter into his home. I stepped into a huge loft with incredibly high ceilings. The space was completely bathed in soft golden light from the late afternoon sun.

"Wow," I whispered, walking straight to the floor-to-ceiling windows overlooking downtown Providence.

He stood directly behind me. "Let me show you around."

The first thing I noticed after the view were the plants. There were dozens of potted plants everywhere; lined up along the walls, hanging from the windows, and on the tables and countertops. A few potted trees were even taller than Victor.

"You like plants, huh?" I asked sarcastically.

"I love them. And so do you."

It was a strange thing for him to say, but it was true. "You're right. I haven't had a chance to buy many plants yet, but in Portugal my apartment was full of them."

There were healthy tomato plants, yellow bell peppers, parsley, basil, cilantro, ferns, orchids, and countless other house plants. There was an entire garden in his loft and their collective fragrance was divine. I looked down at the highly polished, acid-washed concrete floors and the exposed brick walls. Oriental and Turkish rugs were scattered throughout the enormous space, which boasted eclectic décor.

"Your home is nothing like I imagined," I commented.

"I hope you're not disappointed."

"On the contrary. We seem to share the same tastes."

"In that case, you may appreciate this piece here." He indicated a small writing desk that looked at least four hundred years old.

"Where did you get this?" I asked, touching the carved wooden legs with reverence.

"Vienna. I also purchased a small lute during my visit." My eyes were drawn to an antique lute displayed on the mantle above the fireplace. "It's too old and fragile for me to play, I'm afraid."

An antique clock stood beside the lute, evoking a strong déjà-vu. "Isn't that a Nuremburg clock?"

"Yes it is," he replied excitedly. "It used to be in my house in Lisbon."

I had only seen photos of the spring-driven clock in books and knew they dated to the early sixteenth century. Having only one hand to keep track of hours, they were extremely expensive and displayed in the wealthiest of noble homes. For some inexplicable reason, I knew this clock well. I moved to stand directly in front of it.

"Are you okay?" he asked.

"I'm fine," I lied.

Victor eyed me with an expression of concern. He opened his mouth to say something then changed his mind.

"Show me the rest of your place," I prompted.

A medieval tapestry depicting members of the nobility seated in a garden hung on the far wall. I stared at it for several minutes. "Your loft is better than a museum!"

My eyes darted around the apartment as I stood in sheer amazement of the high quality pieces he owned. A flat screen TV, ultra-modern speakers, and a stainless steel kitchen stood out in stark contrast to the antique furnishings. It was like the Old World clashing with the New World.

Next, he showed me the guest bathroom, which came complete with a porcelain claw foot tub and gleaming white subway tiles on the walls. Finally, he showed me his bedroom.

I became immediately aware of his scent. The big bed was covered with a plush duvet and pillows. The exposed brick walls were bare, and there were delicate white orchids growing on the window sills. I imagined him sleeping in the nude, and the intimate thought made my heart race.

He led me out of his room and we passed a closed door. "What's in here?" I asked.

"Oh, just my messy office."

He steered me away from the door into the living room where he sat me down on the oversized cordovan leather sofa facing the city view. I found it odd that his office would be "messy" when the rest of his home was clean and orderly.

That's the S&M room...

I really had to do something about that annoying little voice inside my head. I also had to stop finding fault with Victor. He sat down beside me and took my hand.

"Twilight is my favorite time of day," I said.

"Mine, too," he said. "You're thinking about the other night again, aren't you?"

I looked at him guiltily. "I am."

"Out with it. Say what you have to say."

"You were right about me going to therapy," I admitted. "I

was seeing a psychologist in Portugal and was referred to another therapist here. I'm only trying to get some answers, that's all. I'm not crazy or anything."

"I never thought you were."

"I've been having these strange memories and dreams."

A spark of light came into his eyes; he appeared almost gleeful. I don't know why I was so comfortable with Victor, but the words poured out of me like water from a pitcher. I confessed everything. He listened quietly with his eyes focused on the horizon. When I had finished speaking, he stood and walked into the kitchen without a single word. I remained on the sofa, dumbfounded. Did I make a big mistake? Did he think I was a freak?

I watched as he began chopping onions and garlic on a cutting board. He didn't look at me. After a few awkward minutes, I stood up. "Maybe I should go home."

"Nonsense! You've only just arrived. Would you like a drink?" He opened a bottle of wine, and set it on the counter to breathe. "I have a nice bottle of Brunello di Montalcino and I've been waiting for an occasion to open it. Now seems like the right time."

"You're acting as if what I've told you is the most normal thing in the world."

He stopped what he was doing and regarded me calmly. "Would it surprise you if I said that I do think it's the most normal thing in the world?"

"Then maybe you're as crazy as I am."

"Or maybe I know things that you don't."

I heard the sizzle of onions being tossed in a hot skillet and went into the kitchen. "Let me help you," I offered.

Using the wooden spoon in his hand, he indicated a big metal pot on the counter. "Fill that pot with water and set it to boil for the pasta, please."

I did as he requested then watched him chop some ripe tomatoes. He smiled when he felt the weight of my stare. "You've made it pretty clear that you put your faith in science." I nodded and he continued, "Well, just because you can't explain the inexplicable doesn't mean that there isn't a logical, scientific answer for what's happening to you."

"True, but—"

"Have patience, the answers will come. You need to trust me when I tell you to go slow. It's for your own good."

His words had such conviction and authority that I had no choice but to agree with him. "You're right, but I might go insane while I'm waiting for the answers."

"Okay," he relented. "Go back into the living room. On the coffee table is a pile of books. Grab the black leather photo album at the bottom of the pile. Tell me if you see anything that looks familiar."

I followed his instructions and placed the black leather photo album on my lap. I leafed through it haphazardly, starting in the middle. "These are old photos of Lisbon," I said, confused.

"Close the book and start again from the beginning. Look at each image carefully in sequential order and compare it to the next one," he instructed from the kitchen.

I closed the book and started over. The beginning of the photo album contained color photos that were taken recently, followed by a set of photos taken a few decades ago, followed by another set that was older still. The photos were going back in time. When I arrived at the 1940s, the photos became black and white, each one becoming more yellowed and damaged from age. I flipped through the late nineteenth century photos, then a few blank pages.

I placed the photo album back on the coffee table. "Very interesting, but I don't see how this solves my problem."

Wiping his hands on a dishcloth, he left the kitchen and walked to an old armoire where he extracted another photo album with the same dimensions as the first, only it was bound in red leather. Hesitating, he held it out and said, "The continuation of the black photo album."

He watched me like a hawk as I opened the book. The first photograph portrayed a colorful Lisbon landscape with the date 1859 stamped in the lower right corner. It was perfectly crisp, as if it had been shot with a high-tech digital camera.

Fascinated, I turned the pages. Each glossy image revealed an earlier depiction of the city, going back in time.

"Where did you get these?" I demanded. "Did you have them custom-made from old photos?"

"Keep going," he instructed in a tight voice.

Did I detect a note of worry? I turned the page and stopped. The date on the photograph was 1805. Up until that point, the images had been created within the era of photography; this one couldn't have been created from an old photo. I continued to turn the pages and my mouth dropped open. I was looking at images of Lisbon in the late eighteenth century after the earthquake of 1755, then images depicting the city before the earthquake. There were also a few images from the seventeenth century and finally, the sixteenth century.

"How can this be possible?" I whispered.

Victor knelt before me and took both of my trembling hands in his own as he searched my face. "Did you feel anything when you looked at the last images?"

I chose my words carefully for his sake as well as mine. "These computer-generated images are incredibly realistic. Did you use old maps and drawings as a reference guide to recreate Old Lisbon?"

He stared fixedly at me, then stood. "Why don't we have some wine while I finish up dinner?"

"I don't understand why you're upset, Victor."

"I'm not upset," he corrected. "I only hoped…"

"What?" I prompted.

Pointing to the red album in my hand, he asked, "None of them mean anything? Not even the last two? Look again."

I took a closer look at the last two images. One depicted a grand house on a hill facing the Tagus River, and the other was a spectacular waterfall in a secluded forest glen. Something began to stir inside of me. My forehead creased in concentration. "Yes, I…"

He looked at me expectantly. "Do you remember?"

"Remember?" I repeated, looking up at him in confusion.

"Oh, Veronica, please remember," he pleaded, barely hiding

the desperation in his voice.

My mind suddenly went blank. "I'm sorry, Victor."

Visibly upset, he turned his face to the side. He said shakily, "Don't be sorry; it's not your fault."

"I feel bad that I can't remember whatever it is you want me to remember," I said, fighting back my own rush of emotion. What the hell was going on?

He held his hand out to me. "Don't upset yourself. Come on, let's eat. I'm famished and I'm sure you must be, too."

I placed the red photo album on the coffee table and took his hand. He led me back into the kitchen and told me to drain the pasta in the sink. He added the pasta to the tomato sauce simmering in a large skillet and tossed everything together.

I set the plates and forks on the table along with two wine glasses before taking a seat at the dining table. He placed a generous portion of steaming pasta onto each plate, then sat across from me and poured the wine.

Lifting his glass, he said, "Saúde."

We each took a sip and began eating.

"Delicious," I said. "Thank you for making dinner."

"Ah, Veronica?"

I looked up to see him smirking. "Yes?" I asked.

He reached across the table and wiped the side of my mouth with his napkin. "Tomato sauce."

"Oh!" I blotted my mouth with my napkin.

"Has anyone ever told you that you're adorable?"

"Not recently."

"Oh, so you hear it often?" he teased.

"What if I said yes?"

The conversation became light and playful. Victor's witty comments throughout the meal made me laugh. The wine was absolutely divine and quickly went to my head.

"I don't have any sweets to offer you for dessert, but I do have some good port and aged cheese if you'd like."

Victor's palate was as refined as his taste in antiquities. "Cheese and port are perfect."

"The view of Providence at night is pretty impressive. Go

149

have a seat and enjoy it while I get everything ready."

"Okay."

I took a seat on the sofa. The red tail lights of cars stuck in traffic created patterns on the streets below. My eyes wandered from the windows to the red photo album, and I began leafing through it again. There was a pocket in the back cover, so I slipped my finger inside and pulled out a hidden photograph. My mind reeled as I studied the image of myself in a tawny gold gown with Manuelino embellishments—the same one from my dream! My dark hair was parted in the center and wound into two coils over my ears. My cheeks were rosy and my eyes were bright, but I wore no cosmetics. I looked at Victor and shook my head in disbelief.

"Where did you get this?" I demanded angrily.

He set the tray with cheese and port on the coffee table. His face paled when he noticed the image in my hand. "Veronica, listen to me. I recorded that image a long time ago."

"You took this photograph yourself?" I asked, my voice shrill. "This isn't a computer-generated image?"

Gripping my shoulders, he said, "Calm down. That night was very special for me and I wanted to record it forever."

"There must be a rational explanation...they say everyone has a twin, right? Okay, so here's what I think. You were at a Shakespeare play—yes, that's it. And she...she..."

"Veronica..."

My eyes stung from unshed tears. "The fact that I've dreamed about this dress is only an uncanny coincidence."

Victor's face lit up with joy. "Wait a second—you had a dream about this dress?"

"More than that, I remember wearing it. I remember the weight of it, the feel of it, the smell of it..."

Victor heaved a sigh of relief. His eyes fluttered closed in a moment of pure bliss. I took the opportunity to flee the loft, leaving the door swinging wide open behind me.

CHAPTER 25
LISBON, PORTUGAL
APRIL, 1523

Victor went out to handle the publication and distribution of my book on a fine spring morning while I stayed behind to help take inventory of the kitchen's stock. I was in the middle of checking the flour supply when one of my youngest students, Carlos, came running into the kitchen.

"Mistress Veronica! There are people here to see you."

"What people?"

"Rosa is here with a priest. There is another woman with them," the boy replied breathlessly.

I felt the color drain from my face. Rosa ran away after the New Year's fiasco, and we hadn't seen her since.

I placed my hand on the boy's shoulder. "Run along now."

I took a deep breath and made my way to the main part of the house with head held high. Rosa appeared smug as our eyes met. To my surprise, she was accompanied by my former parish priest and Sara.

"Good day, Veronica," the priest said.

"What an unexpected surprise, Father," I said politely. "Greetings, Sara. Rosa, we were very worried about you after you left the school without so much as bidding us farewell."

Rosa only glared at me.

The priest cleared his throat. "These godly women have come to me recently with some disturbing information."

Godly women? I tossed a skeptical glance at them.

He continued, "I have come here today out of concern for your spiritual health and your immortal soul. I understand that you are working as a teacher."

"I am."

"What exactly do you teach?"

"Arithmetic, reading, writing, history..."

"Do you have theological discussions with your students?"

"I'm neither trained nor authorized to teach such things."

"I see. What about your living situation here?"

"What of it?" I challenged in a gentle tone.

"You live with a man and act as mistress of his house, yet you are an unmarried woman."

"My master, Victor, has taken me in along with many orphaned children. I'm in charge of running his school. Rosa is one of the many young people who have benefitted from his generous Christian charity." I paused and the priest frowned at Rosa. I added, "I earn my keep through honest hard work, Father. I am breaking no secular or religious laws."

"You may not have broken God's law *yet* but you may be in danger of doing so."

Sara turned to the priest. "I saw her at the market with this man, and they appeared to be quite intimate with one another."

The priest's face turned red. "Are you saying they were behaving indecently in public? Are they guilty of lewd and lascivious conduct?"

Mortified, Sara replied, "No, not exactly, but the man is exceptionally handsome—a temptation for any woman to fall into sin." The priest frowned at her imprudent words, so she hastily added, "They were standing side by side and—"

"We are standing side by side. Tell me you didn't drag me to the center of Lisbon on a false accusation, woman!"

"There's more, Father. Veronica cruelly enticed my brother, then rejected his offers of marriage. You know that Tiago is a decent, God-fearing man. He has suffered greatly because of this woman."

I crossed my arms and scoffed. "Refusing to marry a man is not a violation of God's law."

"I'm here to see with my own eyes that God's laws are not being broken," the priest declared. "Immorality is not the only charge made against you."

"What else have these two liars accused me of?"

"Is it true that you're teaching spells to children?"

"I teach a bit of flower lore," I admitted. "The children learn how to heal common sicknesses using herbs and roots; there's no trickery or magic involved. You can find my healing remedies in any apothecary shop or in some of the city's monasteries."

Sara's malicious gaze slid in my direction. "Father do not believe her. I know in my heart that Veronica has cast a love spell on poor Tiago."

Rosa interjected, "She has also bewitched Victor and lives here as his whore. I've witnessed her treachery and wickedness with my own eyes."

"You dare call me a whore, Rosa?" I demanded angrily.

The priest cleared his throat and frowned. "Let me remind you that witchcraft is a very serious charge, Veronica."

My knees went weak. To my relief, I heard the sound of Victor's approaching footsteps.

"What is the meaning of this? What are you doing in my house?" he demanded of the three uninvited guests.

Rosa flushed to the roots of her hair and stared at the floor.

The priest swallowed hard. "We are here to protect Veronica from falling into serious sin and possible heresy. She has been accused of immorality and witchcraft."

"We are concerned for her immortal soul," Sara added, her face one of mock concern.

"I remember you," Victor said, staring hard at Sara. "You're that insolent girl who accosted us in the market." To the priest, he said, "If you want to worry about someone's immortal soul, you need not look further than the bitter and envious creature before you."

Sara gasped, her hand flying to her chest in outrage.

"As for you, Rosa, this is a fine way to repay us. We took you off the streets when you were nothing more than a prostitute. And now, because I have rejected your indecent advances toward me, you have taken it upon yourself to persecute someone innocent—Mistress Veronica!"

"Sir, you are in the presence of a holy man," the priest reminded him.

153

"All the more reason why you should know the truth about the two vipers at your side," Victor retorted.

Looking at me, he added, "Mistress Veronica is a woman of excellent character and generous spirit who wants nothing more than to help others. Rosa is a silly lovesick girl who is acting out of pure jealousy."

Rosa whimpered and Sara patted her back, eyeing us with contempt.

Undeterred, Victor placed his arm around me. I stiffened nervously at the intimate gesture. What was he thinking?

"Father, Veronica will soon be my lawfully wedded wife," he announced proudly. "How dare these women come here and make such heinous accusations against my betrothed."

Rosa's head snapped up and she stared at me.

The priest held out his hands in supplication. "It is my duty to investigate any serious charge that would threaten other faithful Christians."

Victor's nostrils flared. "I'm a respectable member of society and would never concede to immorality or heresy under my roof, much less witchcraft!"

The priest frowned at Rosa and Sara. "Perhaps I have been lured into a vicious web of women's lies and gossip. They are, after all, the weaker sex and prone to such lowly practices."

Sara looked beseechingly at the priest. "Father, I only wanted to protect Veronica from the machinations of Satan. I would never have approached you if Rosa had not come knocking on my door."

Rosa's eyes narrowed into slits. "You're the one who called her an uppity shrew for not wanting to marry your brother! This whole thing was your idea!"

The priest looked at me. "Do you swear that you are not invoking spells or holding theological discussions?"

Victor pushed me behind him and demanded, "Is that what these liars have told you?" Pointing to Rosa, he added, "Last October, in the presence of the other children, this ingrate talked of putting God to the test. She even compared herself to saintly martyrs. I advised her repeatedly to cast aside such dangerous thoughts."

The priest's face became grim with concern as he eyed Rosa. "I expect that you have much to confess, girl. Need I remind you that dishonesty is detestable to God?" To me, he asked, "Are you still attending church?"

"Yes," I lied.

"Do you need to confess anything to me?" At my blank expression, he added in a very low whisper, "I am referring to fornication."

I shook my head, hoping he would not detect the dishonesty in my face. The priest was satisfied with my response. "My work here is done." To Sara and Rosa he said, "The two of you must stop this spiteful gossip. Remember, the bible says that envy is like 'rottenness to the bones.' I expect to hear both of your remorseful confessions soon."

Sara and Rosa lowered their heads in humility before the priest, but their shifty eyes fell upon me when he wasn't looking. I tried not to appear too smug in my triumph. Relief washed over me as they left the house.

"You are in no condition to teach classes today. I'll dismiss the children," he said, gathering me in his arms.

"They are waiting for me."

"You're shaking from head to toe! I insist that you come upstairs with me and rest a bit."

Later, when we were alone in his bedchamber, he said, "Why would Rosa align herself with Sara to speak against you? This worries me."

"I am your betrothed?" I asked, ignoring his question.

"If marrying you with a silly earthly ceremony will secure your safety, then we shall be wed as soon as possible."

There was a bottle of brandy wine on the mantle and two dainty goblets. Victor poured some for the both of us.

"Dona Maria believes Sara is a wicked, cunning creature and I agree with her. The nerve! Coming here with Rosa."

Victor rubbed his chin in thought. "We should pay Dona Maria a visit. Perhaps she knows something that can help us defend ourselves against these scheming women in case they

make another false accusation in the future. Put on your cloak."
Seeing my expression of disbelief he added, "You've been accused of invoking spells and committing the sin of immorality—a priest has just visited our home and questioned you. We do not want the authorities knocking on our door next. The sooner we get to the bottom of this farce, the better."

We saddled our horses and left the city.

***

Dona Maria, who had heard our approach, was already standing at the door when we arrived at her cottage. I dismounted and ran to her with open arms.

"Veronica, what a surprise," she said, hugging me tightly. At the sight of Victor, her face paled. "Who have you brought with you, my child?"

"This is Victor, my betrothed."

I thought I caught a flicker of fear in Dona Maria's eyes as she waved us inside. She had aged considerably since the last time I saw her. Indicating two stools, she urged us to sit, then poured hot broth it into three ceramic cups.

"Here, drink this. It will warm you," she said.

"Thank you," I said before taking a sip.

Victor accepted the broth with a grateful nod but didn't touch it.

Dona Maria held her ceramic cup in both hands and sat down beside me. "Where did you meet Victor?"

"In Lisbon," I lied. "I'm a teacher at his school."

"When will your marriage take place?"

"Tomorrow," Victor replied, shocking me in the process.

Oddly, Dona Maria's eyes shifted in his direction but she did not turn her head to face him.

"We are having a private ceremony," I added quickly. Then, changing the subject, I asked, "How is your family?"

She scratched her head. "Norberto doesn't come here as often anymore. His wife has recently given birth to their fifth child. Oh, how time flies…"

"Dona Maria, I actually came to talk to you about Sara."

"What about her?" the old woman asked, suddenly alert.

156

"Have you seen her in church lately?"

"I have. She always sits by her new friend, Rosa."

"Rosa, has caused us some trouble, I'm afraid."

"Oh?" Her wrinkled brow furrowed into a frown. "She showed up at our church several weeks ago seated beside Sara. At first I thought Tiago had finally landed himself a bride, but I was wrong. Sara told everyone that Rosa had escaped from a home that practiced immorality and witchcraft."

"The parish priest went to Victor's home this morning to investigate these claims," I said. "He was accompanied by Rosa and Sara."

Dona Maria crossed herself. "Wicked creatures."

"Please, Dona Maria, try to keep your eyes and ears open. Find out what you can," I pleaded. "For my sake."

"I will," she assured with a wince.

"You're in pain." When she nodded, I said, "I'll make a poultice as soon as we get back and have one of the students deliver it to you."

She smiled tiredly. "I would be grateful for that kindness."

"We should go," Victor said.

He had never taken his eyes off of our hostess, and Dona Maria had not looked at him once. I followed him to where our horses were tethered.

"I almost forgot," Dona Maria said from the doorway. "I baked some tarts yesterday and would like to give you a few. You can eat them on your ride back to the city."

Victor's head snapped up and he locked eyes with the old woman as I doubled back toward the cottage. Dona Maria disappeared inside and came back a few moments later with a small bundle wrapped in a cloth.

Placing it into my hands, she whispered, "You are in grave danger."

After uttering that dire warning, she shut the door and left me standing on the doorstep, bewildered. I felt Victor's eyes burning into my back.

Clarice had taken an extended holiday break that lasted until mid-January. Sporting a deep tan, she was in high spirits when I entered her office. "Hello. I trust you've had a wonderful holiday season, Veronica," she said cheerfully before inviting me to take a seat.

"Yes, but you look like you've had a better one. Nice tan."

"My husband and I have dreamed of taking a Caribbean cruise for years. It was the ultimate Christmas gift to ourselves. But enough about me, let's talk about what's been going on since your last visit." She picked up her clipboard. "Any progress on the relationship with that young musician you mentioned?"

"I found a photograph in his apartment that's been bothering me for the last couple of weeks. I didn't want to tell you about it, but if I don't get this off my chest, I'll go nuts."

Clarice's face grew serious. "What happened?"

"Victor and I started dating, and we were doing great until I decided to confide in him. I told him I was in therapy and the reasons why. I even shared some of my strange memories and dreams with him. He was very receptive and supportive."

"Sounds like a good guy," she interjected.

"He is," I agreed. "One night he invited me over for dinner and showed me some old photographs of Lisbon. Most of them were actual historical images and some were computer generated to portray what the city looked like long before the invention of the camera."

At least you're trying to make yourself believe that to be the case.

"Interesting," Clarice said, jotting down notes.

"It was interesting until I found this," I said, handing her the photograph I had stolen from Victor's loft.

She smiled. "Oh, you look beautiful—-love the costume. Why would this upset you?"

I didn't return the smile. "That's not me."

She studied the image closely. "Looks like you."

I shook my head. "Victor took that photo and, according to him, it was taken a long time ago."

"You have a twin," she said. "Someone once stopped me in New Hampshire thinking I was someone else. It's not uncommon."

"Yes, I know. He's obviously dating me because I remind him of this other woman," I said, fighting back tears of anger and humiliation.

"You've given this much thought, I see."

"He claims that I have it all wrong."

"You don't believe him?"

"He's been trying to contact me. I've been avoiding him." I could hear the hurt in my voice. "But I haven't told you the strangest part yet."

"What would that be?"

"Remember the dream I told you about? The one with the music and the candles?"

She flipped through several sheets attached to the clipboard and stopped. "The dream where you wore a gold gown with the Manuelino embellishments...that one?" she asked, looking up from her notes.

Pointing to the photograph she held in her hand, I said, "*That* is the dress from my dream."

Clarice's face paled. I could almost hear the wheels spinning furiously inside her brain as she tried to offer me a reasonable explanation.

"Well? What do you make of this?" I asked.

"I honestly don't know." She paused in thought. "I think the best thing we can do at this point is to put you under."

"Hypnosis?"

"Yes." Seeing my apprehension, she added, "Only if you're

ready."

"I'm ready right now. Let's do it."

"There are no guarantees, and you may discover things that will upset you," she warned.

"I need to find some answers before I lose my mind."

"You do understand that the sole purpose of hypnosis is to help you overcome the obstacles you're facing in your life right now." She waited for me to nod, then added, "What happened in your past—even what happened with Victor a couple of weeks ago—-is no longer considered reality. What is real is what's taking place now, in this moment."

"I want to get to the bottom of this. I want to know why I feel restless. I can deal with the whole Victor thing later."

"You do realize that he's involved in this, too."

"How?"

She replied by simply holding up the photograph.

I nodded in agreement. "Okay, but first let's figure out what's going on with me before trying to solve that mystery."

Clarice pulled her chair closer to mine. "Very well. Clear your mind, breathe deeply, and close your eyes." She lowered her voice and spoke soothingly. "My intention is to put you into a deep trancelike state conducive to evoking memories. If you feel a strong emotion, think of a word or a phrase linked to this emotion. Keep on repeating this word or phrase in your head until images emerge with the memory. If it becomes too painful or frightening, just say the word 'stop' out loud and I'll bring you out of the trance. Can you do that?"

"I can do that."

"Let's begin. I want you to picture yourself in a place that you feel safe and comfortable. It can be in a room within a house or outside in a quiet garden. Clear all the thoughts from your mind and close your eyes..."

For some strange reason, the first thing that came to my mind was the image of the waterfall I'd seen in Victor's red photo album. I pictured myself in the center of the clearing, listening to the sound of the water. I recalled a strange sulfuric smell, too.

"Try to imagine that you're floating..."

Clarice's voice gradually sounded like it was coming from the other room. I allowed my body to become weightless; I was no longer anchored to the ground. I floated around the forest, gazing down on the green treetops and listening to the sing-song of birds. My body was bathed in pure sunshine, and a comforting warmth radiated throughout my limbs.

"Let yourself remember..."

I heard Victor's voice. *Remember, Veronica.*

I floated higher into the azure sky, marveling at the fluffiness of the cumulous clouds as I headed toward my home in sixteenth century Lisbon. Somewhere in the far recesses of my brain, I was aware that I'd never been there before, yet I knew the old city well. I smiled inwardly at the familiar landmarks, the magnificent churches, and the Tagus River full of merchant vessels. I even spotted a far-off spice ship heading out to sea.

Without warning, I landed in front of a gracious noble home that stood on a hill facing the water. It was the same house I'd seen in the red photo album, but it was so much lovelier in real life. I knelt before the roses that grew in the front yard...flowers that I had planted with my own hands.

"Breathe, Veronica..."

Closing my eyes, I took several deep breaths and inhaled the sweet fragrance of the roses. I opened my eyes and the house was cast in deep shadow. Dark clouds gathered in the ominous sky. Where was the sun? I felt cold and empty.

A storm brewed and I became filled with foreboding. I heard a noise coming from inside the house. A pair of golden wolf eyes watched me from behind the glass window panes. Terrified, I took off running through the field. A galleon tossed haphazardly on the river's roiling waves.

Suddenly, there was nothing but pain; an excruciating pain unlike anything I've ever experienced before. I couldn't breathe, my throat and eyes burned. Something clutched my neck and choked me. I looked down and noticed that my skin was gone...Oh, my God! Oh, my God! The pain was more than

I could bear. A blood-curdling scream filled my ears.

My body shook from head to toe. I saw a faint light in the distance that gradually expanded. Someone called my name.

"Veronica! Wake up! Wake up!"

I opened my eyes. It was Clarice. Her face was only inches from mine, and she had a vice-like grip on my shoulders.

"Veronica, can you hear me?"

I nodded but didn't speak. My face was wet from tears.

She thrust a handful of tissues at me and fetched me a glass of water, then sat down and gave me a moment to compose myself. Finally, she asked, "What did you remember that made you react like that?"

I took a sip of water before replying, "Pain."

"Are you okay? We can take a break or end the session."

I shook my head to clear it. "I saw Lisbon, not as it is today, but how it was in the sixteenth century. There was a big house, the same one I saw in Victor's red photo album. I saw a pair of yellow eyes, then terrible pain."

"What kind of pain? Physical? Emotional? Mental?"

"All three." I heaved a shuddering breath as I rubbed my temples. "I'm overwhelmed right now. Maybe the next time I go under—"

Clarice held up her hand in protest. "I don't suggest that my patients go under hypnosis again after a traumatic episode like the one that happened here. Maybe it's best for us to work through your issues with therapy alone."

"I'm not afraid to face my past or my problems. Please, Clarice, give me another chance."

She regarded me dubiously. "Are you sure? This session was intense and you're pretty upset right now. I'm worried. I've never had anyone react the way you did."

"I can handle it." *I think*.

"Very well," she conceded, albeit skeptically. "Make an appointment to see me next week. Take notes on any new memories or thoughts, okay?"

"Thank you, Clarice."

"Remember what I said about reality being *now*, okay?"

"I understand."

She lent me another book about the pros and cons of past life regression hypnosis. I promised to read it, zipped up my coat, and left the office. My mind inevitably thought of Victor as I walked toward home. He had tried to call me countless times, but I was too embarrassed and angry to speak with him. I don't know what the woman in the photograph meant to him, but she must have left quite an impression. Why else would he seek out her lookalike? The mere thought of it brought tears to my eyes. How the gown in the photograph managed to creep into my dream was still an unexplained mystery.

I experienced an inexplicable, all-consuming urge to see Victor. Before I knew it, I was on a bus.

What are you doing?

Several minutes later, I was in the old factory district. The winter sun was beginning its descent in a pale pink sky, and long gray shadows stretched across the concrete sidewalk. Something was pushing me forward; a force too great to resist. Upon entering the building, I paused at the foot of the stairwell.

What can you possibly say after avoiding him for weeks?

I practically ran up the stairs. Victor's door was slightly ajar. Shocked by my own impertinence, I pushed it open and stepped inside. None of the lights were turned on and the loft was dim, almost spooky. Victor sat quietly on the sofa and his head snapped up the minute I walked in. I took a few steps back when I saw a pair of yellow glowing eyes staring at me—the same eyes I'd seen peering out the window while under hypnosis.

He stood up and came toward me, his eyes shifting from glowing yellow to amber gold as he moved from the darkness into the light. "Veronica…"

Did I just imagine that? I wanted to run, but my legs refused to obey. Taking hold of my arms, he held me steadily. As much as I wanted to look away from him, I couldn't. A warm vibration spread throughout my body.

"Who are you?" I asked, unable to hide the fear in my voice.

"You already know who I am." He paused. "I know about your session today with Dr. Clarice Barnum."

163

"How do you know? Did you follow me?"

"I know many things."

"Stop saying that!" I snapped. Was there an unseen power, a force that led me here against my better judgement?

His face reflected pain. "Why did you run away from me the other night? Why won't you pick up the phone and speak with me? At least tell me what I've done to offend you."

"You're right," I agreed, stepping back and crossing my arms in front of my chest. "I didn't expect to see a photo of another woman—much less someone who could be my twin. Is that why you like me? Because I remind of you her?"

His pained expression was replaced by one of disbelief. "You're behaving this way because you're jealous?"

"I'm not jealous!"

"Oh, no?" he challenged, amused.

"I want to be with someone who likes me for me, not because I look like one of his old girlfriends," I retorted defensively. "Here, I believe this belongs to you," I added primly, removing the photo in question from my pocket.

"I want to be with you, I swear."

I believe you…I trust you…

Yet, I could not say the words aloud. I turned my attention to the spectacular view outside the windows. The loft was bathed in the reddish light of sunset. The moon and stars were already visible in the salmon colored sky.

He took hold of my chin. "Go home and ponder on the memories you experienced in therapy today, then come back when you're ready to talk."

"How do you know what happened today?"

"As I said before—"

"Yeah, you know many things. I get it."

"Please trust me, Veronica. I know you tend to be skeptical. All I'm asking is that you give me the benefit of the doubt."

"Why should I?"

"Because I can help you find the answers you seek." I nodded and he added, "Let me escort you home."

"Thanks, but no," I replied. "I prefer to be alone with my

164

thoughts right now and a brisk walk will clear my head."

His brow creased slightly with worry. "As you wish."

I raced down the stairs and went outside before he could dissuade me. I navigated the streets like a zombie and, when I got home, I performed mundane tasks. By the time night fell I was at my computer doing some serious research on reincarnation. Two hours later, I was still no closer to finding the answers that I desperately needed. I stood up and stretched my legs. My eyes skimmed over the storage cubes above the bookcase and settled upon the green one.

Suddenly, I remembered something.

I sat back down at my computer and did a search on "Sergeant Clifford Stone." There were several articles, videos, and book titles, but what I was looking for was a specific news conference I had seen a while back on You Tube.

I finally found the video and stared with rapt attention at the screen. Sergeant Stone, seated with other government officials, in a room full of journalists, countless cameras, and video recorders, stated that the U.S. government currently has fifty-seven documented species of aliens. While a few of these beings were commonly known as *Grays*—those with big heads and large black eyes—several boasted a humanoid appearance. This meant they could blend in somewhat easily with humans. Stone offered detailed accounts regarding the technology these extraterrestrials have bestowed upon mankind, and he also mentioned that many aliens have special skills. *'Some can manipulate the mind, while others are able to see color in the dark...'*

CHAPTER 27
LISBON, PORTUGAL
AUTUMN, 1523

Victor and I were married the day after our visit to Dona Maria's cottage. My book was published soon afterward. Three months after its publication, people in Lisbon were openly citing the phrases I had penned—my words. I cannot even begin to describe the satisfaction that I drew from this.

I had chosen *Human Injustice* as the title for my powerful manuscript, which exposed religion and corrupt governments as the primary cause of mankind's woes. Due to its controversial nature, Victor insisted that I remain as far removed as possible from my book. I was not even allowed to keep a copy in the house.

Lisbon had suffered through an unbearably hot summer in the year 1523, so it was a relief when temperatures dropped at the end of September. I received a message from Dona Maria's nephew, Norberto, stating that his aunt was seriously ill and wished to see me. Since I had not received any news from Dona Maria throughout the summer, I assumed that Sara and Rosa had abandoned their malicious schemes against me. Perhaps the humiliation they suffered in Victor's presence was enough for them to mend their petty ways. I sought out Victor to let him know I'd be leaving immediately for the old widow's cottage.

I found him in the stable brushing our horses. "Victor, Dona Maria is ill and has requested to see me. I wish to leave at once."

"I shall accompany you," he offered.

"I think it best if I go alone. This could possibly be the last time I see her, and she may want to speak with me privately."

He reluctantly conceded to my wishes and saddled my mare. I made it to Dona Maria's home in good time.

"Thank you for coming," Norberto said after he opened the

door. "Her illness has taken a turn for the worse and she does not have much time. I have just sent for the priest."

Sitting up in her bed, Dona Maria appeared pitifully frail and her skin resembled parchment. A single candle sputtered on a nearby table.

"Veronica," she croaked in a hoarse whisper.

I sat on the edge of the bed. "Dona Maria, what can I do to ease your suffering? Shall I whip up a draught for the pain?"

"No pain, thank God, just weak...so weak. Not much time."

Her labored words ended with a coughing fit. She put a dingy handkerchief to her mouth and, to my dismay, it was bloodstained. I poured water into a cup and held it to her lips.

"I wanted to warn you about him before I die..."

"You mean Victor, my husband."

"You married him?" When I nodded, she crossed herself with a shaky hand. "Oh, my poor child. You have put yourself in league with Satan."

It dawned on me why she thought so harshly of Victor. Making sure Norberto was out of earshot, I whispered, "Did he show himself to you?"

"Yes, many years ago when I was a girl. He's a demon."

"No, Dona Maria, you are mistaken. Victor is an angel. He is kind, generous, and wise."

"Foolish Veronica...he'll lead you to your death."

Shocked by her words, I asked, "What do you mean?"

"Satan can disguise himself as an angel of light," she said before being seized by another violent coughing fit. I offered her more water, but she slapped my hand away as her eyes rolled into the back of her head.

"Dona Maria!"

Lack of air caused her face to turn blue. Terrified, she stared at me and I reached for her hand, giving it a squeeze. The parish priest arrived and Norberto ushered him inside to perform the last rites. The old widow heaved her last breath with her knowing eyes locked on mine.

Norberto kissed his aunt's forehead then retrieved a folded piece of parchment from his coat. "My aunt wanted me to give

167

you this upon her death."

I took the letter as my eyes filled with tears. "Thank you."

I stayed a bit longer to help clean and dress the body. When my assistance was no longer needed, I mounted my horse and headed back for the city with a heavy heart.

"How is Dona Maria?" Victor asked when I got home.

"She died shortly after my arrival."

"Do not cry, my love. She has led a full life and died at a ripe old age. Go upstairs and rest. I'll have a tray sent up from the kitchen and we can enjoy a quiet dinner together."

I went upstairs and retrieved the letter from my pocket. It was written hastily with ink blots scattered throughout the sentences.

My Dearest Veronica,

I have always thought of you as the daughter I never had, so it pains me to tell you that the man you claim to love is an abomination of nature; an evil being not of this world. Many years ago while I was in the woods, he appeared before me with his unholy eyes. I cursed him and cried out to our beloved Lord for help. The creature left me in peace, only to show himself to you several years later. I know this because your mother confided in me shortly before her death. Now that my own demise is near at hand, I feel compelled to warn you. May the Lord watch and keep over you.——Maria

I reread the letter before tossing it into the flames of the hearth in my bedroom. A servant brought up a tray laden with food and Victor came in afterward. We ate our dinner in relative silence and I caught him looking at me several times.

"You're unusually quiet," I said.

"I'm giving you space to grieve."

"Dona Maria told me a few things before she died," I said, nibbling on a crust of bread.

"I showed myself to her when she was young."

His confession caught me off guard. "Why?"

"She had an open mind and a free spirit."

"Her flame burned brightly?"

"It did at first, but she chose a different path and it sputtered out. Wasted potential."

"She warned me about you."

"Of course, she did."

There was a heavy silence as we stared at each other. "Something doesn't feel right, Victor, I can sense it."

"There is something wrong, terribly wrong…but it has nothing to do with Dona Maria," he said with a grave expression.

"What is it?"

"Your book."

His expression chilled me to the core. "What about it?"

"I've received a letter from an Italian friend. A new book entitled *l'Ingiustiza Umana* is the talk of Venice. Copies are in high demand."

"My book has reached Venice?" I asked incredulously.

"And Germany, too, since it was a German merchant who introduced the book to the Italian man who penned the letter."

I shook my head in disbelief.

He continued, "People are outraged and have started questioning authority. Some have gathered together to openly protest against injustice, while a few brave men have made a case against the Catholic Church. They're accusing the clergy of ignoring Christ's true teachings."

My smile stretched from ear to ear, whereas Victor appeared grim. My forehead creased into a deep frown of confusion and slight irritation. "What's the matter with you?" When he looked at me sadly, I added, "This is excellent news, Victor! People are finally opening their eyes and thinking for themselves!"

"The Holy Inquisition has banned the book and is seeking out its author."

PART II

THE PHOENIX

The Phoenix will rise from the ashes…
Her Word will shake the fragile foundation of Humanity to its
core, and she will ultimately save them from Gehenna.

—Second Prophecy of the Sacred Oracle

Chapter 28
Providence, RI
January, Present Day

After watching the video of Sergeant Stone, I made myself a potent gin and tonic. What was the probability of figuring out this mess before having to attend AA meetings? I knew that self-medicating with alcohol was wrong, but right now I didn't give a damn.

I paced around my apartment reliving the stormy Christmas night and the power outage. A normal human being who found himself in a unknown environment without any light source would be groping the walls, walking carefully with hands outstretched, and going slowly so as not to stumble. Victor acted as if he could see perfectly in the pitch blackness.

Maybe it's a freak coincidence.

What's the alternative theory? Vampire?

"Don't be ridiculous," I said aloud in response to that irritating little voice. "Oh, God," I murmured, gulping down some of my drink and letting the alcohol take its soothing effect.

I glanced at the computer with apprehension. Part of me wanted to continue researching, but the other part was afraid of what I'd find. What if the images in the red photo album weren't computer generated, but actual hi-tech prints taken in the sixteenth century? Did he have access to time travel?

The sensible part of me pushed its way to the front of my frazzled mind. I was, after all, an Ancient Alien Theorist. Why was I having a hard time dealing with this? I should be jumping for joy at the prospect of confirming my theories. Instead, I panicked. What kind of mess had I gotten myself into? Like Alice in Wonderland, I had fallen into the rabbit hole and I had no idea how deep it went.

"Fuck!"

I wasn't one for cussing—-much less dropping the F-bomb—-but I firmly believed there was a time and place for every word in the English vocabulary.

What to do? What to do?

I needed to confront Victor. It was almost midnight. No time like the present. I donned my coat, grabbed my purse, and left my apartment. I practically flew down the stairs with the cell phone plastered to my ear as I called for a taxi.

I arrived at Victor's place a moment later. I was about to press the intercom button at the main entrance, then I noticed that the door was unlocked. I ran upstairs with purpose and froze outside his door.

Are you going to barge in and accuse him of being an alien?

I took a deep breath, gathered together every shred of courage and determination that I possessed, and lifted my trembling hand. Beads of perspiration broke through the skin of my brow. The door swung open, causing me to jump. Victor stood in the doorway.

"Come in, Veronica."

There was only one small lamp on in the loft, which left most of the huge space in shadow. His strange golden eyes glimmered in the dimness.

"You seem tense," he said. "May I fix you a drink?"

I've just had a drink. A stiff one. "I'll have some water, please." I watched as he entered the kitchen and filled a tall glass with water. "Why are you still wearing those contacts? Do you have a late gig tonight?"

He handed me the glass and regarded me levelly. "There's no gig, these are my real eyes."

My chuckle failed to alter his stony expression. I pushed him aside and ran into his en-suite bathroom. I knew it was rude, but I had to know the truth. He made no attempt to stop me as I went through his medicine cabinet.

Aha! I quickly found what I was looking for: a contact lens case. Carefully, I unscrewed the cap of the lens marked "R" and lifted it up. Immersed in saline solution was a brown contact lens. With shaking hands I unscrewed the cap marked "L," revealing yet another brown lens.

"I wouldn't lie to you," he said from the bathroom doorway.

Startled, I dropped the case. The two brown lenses fell out and appeared to be staring up at me from the tile floor. "What are you?" I demanded, inching away from him.

"I'm someone who cares greatly for you," he replied gently, closing the gap between us. "Veronica, please remember."

I closed my eyes as tightly as I could in order to avoid looking into those strange eyes, which were hauntingly familiar.

"Look at me," he prompted.

Reluctantly, I obeyed. Slowly, he pulled me into an embrace and held me. Waves of tranquility washed over me and, before I realized it, we were breathing in unison. I felt completely safe and secure. "Victor," I whispered.

He kissed my forehead and I pulled his head down toward my face. My mouth sought his and he crushed me against his chest, kissing me fiercely. My hands ran down the length of his muscular back, slipping beneath his shirt to feel his bare skin. When I tried to pull off his shirt, he stopped kissing me and tugged it back down to his waist.

"Don't," he warned. "Not yet."

"Why not? What have you got to hide?"

"I think you've had enough surprises for one day. Your behavior lately has been a bit...erratic. I don't want you to feel overwhelmed."

"Too late. Take off your shirt."

He cocked an eyebrow at me. "Let me get this straight—you ran out of here after I cooked dinner for you, then refused to speak with me for two weeks. You finally decided to see me today, but only to accuse me of being in love with another woman. You come back here late at night to destroy my contact lenses, and now you want me to strip for you?"

"That's right."

His expression was a cross between sternness and amusement. "If I remove my shirt you must promise to not to freak out or run away."

173

"I promise."

Victor pulled the black knit shirt over his head and waited for my reaction. I didn't notice anything out of the ordinary. Until he moved. The shift in light revealed a subtle iridescent sheen on the surface of his skin.

"Your skin reminds me of an opal," I commented, placing my hand on his chest. "What's going on beneath the surface? There's a faint vibration, as if a low electric current is making my hand tingle. How is it possible?"

He shrugged. "This is my natural skin. I was born with it."

"Okay, I promised that I wouldn't freak or run, but I want you to explain why your eyes and skin are unlike anything I've ever seen. What are you?"

"I think you already know the answer."

He's right, Veronica, you already know.

"Tell me anyway."

"I'm not human."

I shifted nervously. "I needed to hear that confirmation from your lips. So I ask again, what are you?"

"I'm from a planet that's fairly close to yours, at least by our standards. I'd tell you its name—and mine for that matter—-but you wouldn't be able to pronounce either one. Your scientists would refer to me as a humanoid extraterrestrial."

"You're an alien."

"Nowadays, that's the term widely used by humans. In the past, people called me god, angel, demon, even monster." He paused. "Well, are you satisfied now?"

"I knew we weren't alone in the universe, I just...I never thought I'd meet an E.T. face to face."

He put his shirt back on. "There are more of us around than you think."

"Really?"

"Yes," he assured, taking my hand and leading me back into the living room. "I promised myself that I wasn't going to do this, but I can't wait any longer."

"Do what?"

"Tell you everything. I was hoping you'd remember on your

own—much better for your sake that way—but I've waited long enough. You'd better sit down. Let me begin by telling you that my planet still has not been picked up by Earth's telescopes or satellites due to our manipulation of them."

"You said I wasn't capable of pronouncing your planet or your name."

"You're not, which is why you named me Victor."

"I named you? When?"

"I'll answer your question, but not yet. Let's get back to the topic of my planet, which has been inhabited for several million human years."

My mouth hung open. "Your species is that old?"

"Yes."

"How old are you?"

"In my years or human years?"

"Both."

"I'm thirty years old on my planet, but on yours I'm approximately fifteen hundred," he replied nonchalantly.

"What? That's impossible!"

"Oh, it's very possible, I assure you. Time is relative."

I quickly did some math in my head. "So you're telling me that one of your years is equal to about fifty of ours."

"Correct."

"You're an immortal!"

"That's what you said last time," he mused aloud.

"Huh?"

"Never mind. I'm not immortal, Veronica. Every living, breathing creature dies eventually. The only thing that doesn't die is energy."

I shook my head. "Unbelievable."

"Why do you find it so hard to believe? Doesn't the mayfly live for only one day? To a mayfly, you're an immortal."

"Yes, but humans are superior to mayflies."

Victor's eyebrow shot upward. "As my species is superior to yours."

Wow. "Point taken," I said, defeated.

"As you've said yourself, Earth's scientists now know that

the universe is an organic wonder filled with the ingredients needed to create life. Humans are finally beginning to realize the potential for limitless energy. What you refer to as the "soul" is actually the energy residing within the flesh. When your body dies the energy travels back into the universe where it originally came from and gets recycled into another form."

"Enter the theory of reincarnation."

"Exactly."

"Does God exist?"

"Sentient energies exists in the universe, but they are nothing like the gods created by man." He reached out for my hand. "And now, let me fill you in on a few facts. The first time we met was in Lisbon in the year 1510. I thought you remembered because you asked me about the wooden statue on the Icon poster."

I was dumbstruck. "1510?"

"On your tenth birthday, to be exact. In a fit of anger your mother threw the Virgin Mary statue into the fire." I stared at him open-mouthed and he asked quickly, "Shall I stop?"

"Don't stop."

"I came to your mother in a dream, informing her that you would be chosen for a great destiny and would be physically marked. Rather than be happy for you, your mother believed that I was a demon. Given the era, I can't blame her. The second time we spoke was on your twentieth birthday in the year 1520. You received your second mark that day—-the star in the center of the spiral."

I turned my right wrist over and stared at the birthmark. "It was the same mark back then, too?"

Victor traced the swirl pattern on the delicate skin with his fingertip. "Exactly the same. This shape represents my galaxy," he explained. Then, he touched the tiny star. "This is our sun."

"Your sun," I repeated.

Lifting my wrist to his lips, he kissed my birthmark. "You named me Victor because you believed I could triumph victoriously over death."

Suppressing the distracting sexual arousal he had just

evoked in me, I asked, "What was her—my- name back then?"

"Veronica." At my surprised expression he added, "I'll explain in a minute, I promise."

"I know you're the man in my recurring dream. What were we to each other?"

His expression became wistful. "You used to tell me that I was your lover—"

"—my friend, my brother, my master and my teacher," I said, finishing his sentence. The words had left my mouth of their own accord, as if my subconscious forced them out.

His eyes filled with joy. "Yes. I was devastated when you..." He hesitated. "When you died." The memory must have been extremely painful because I could see his eyes glisten and the muscle in his jaw tighten. "I knew you'd eventually come back. We can track specific life energies, especially the powerful ones like yours. You can't imagine how happy I was when you finally showed up on the radar, so to speak. I was in the hospital the night you were born, and I should confess to you that I used mind control on your mother."

"Mind control? You can do that?"

"We have that ability, yes. Your name was supposed to be Elizabeth," he said with a smirk. "I hope you don't mind."

"Not at all," I mumbled.

"I got this to celebrate your second birth on Earth," he said, pointing to the tattoo I had noticed when I saw Victor for the first time in Boston. "It's a V for Veronica."

I smiled, touched by the gesture. "How did I die?"

He looked at me long and hard. "You don't remember anything at all?" I shook my head. "Your dreams and visions, when did they start?"

"The night of my twenty-sixth birthday."

"Let me show you something."

I followed him across the living room to the locked door near his bedroom. There was a tiny keypad by the door that I hadn't noticed before. He punched in a code and the lock clicked open.

"That's some heavy security," I commented.

"I have important things in here."

Several lights came on as we entered the big space, revealing ultra-modern equipment resembling nothing I'd seen on Earth."

"Wow," I said. "What is this stuff?"

"Technology that your government would kill for," he said under his breath as he closed the door and locked it.

The stark white room didn't have any windows and the walls were so thick it blocked all sound. "It's like a bunker."

"Pretty close. The bulletproof door requires a code, and it's programmed to work only if the keys are pressed with my fingertips. There are sensors that recognize every single detail of my DNA." He walked over to a large gilded frame partially covered with white fabric. "Does this stir any memories?" he asked, pulling off the fabric to reveal my blown-up twin in the tawny gold gown. "If you still have any doubts about what I've told you, this should put you at ease. Look into her eyes."

It was odd to see a historical figure portrayed in such a modern manner. Up until now the only original sixteenth century images I had ever seen were rendered in paint or ink, not an astonishingly crisp laser print. What would happen if the museums around the world were to discover the existence of these incredible visual documents?

"Are you okay?" he asked.

Staring fixedly at my "reflection," I replied, "I'm fine."

He walked to a silver tower. "I'm going to show you a series of images. Hopefully, they'll help you remember other things.

After a few seconds, a holographic image was projected in the room. It was the same beautiful house I'd seen in the red leather photo album.

"This was our home," he said.

"I planted the roses in the spring." I remembered!

He showed me several images of the interior of the house, room by room. I shook my head at each one, not recognizing anything. Then I saw something that triggered a memory.

"Wait," I cried out.

Victor tapped the top of the device with his fingertip and the picture froze. "Do you remember this room?" he asked, barely keeping the excitement from his voice.

"It's your room. I've had visions of being in this room with you and sleeping on that bed."

"We did much more than just sleep on that bed," he said in a very sexy voice.

I had the sudden urge to sit down and cross my legs. "My room was next to yours."

From that moment onward, I recognized the rooms in the house. I also remembered the lively outdoor market in the main square, and the merchant ships docked in the busy port.

By now, Victor was ecstatic. Finally, he showed me an image of the clearing in the woods with the waterfall, the one I visited under hypnosis.

I nodded. "That's a magical place—our place."

He took me into his arms and I knew I had once loved him fiercely, and I was falling in love with him again.

"My little star," he said huskily before kissing me in such an intimate way; a way that I had never been kissed before.

His mouth and hands were devouring every inch of me. Without breaking physical contact, Victor unlocked the door, and led me out of the room.

"I want you," he said. "I've waited so long for you, wife."

Wife? My head snapped up. "We were married?"

He nodded slowly and a sexy smile stretched across his lips. With one quick move, he pulled my sweater off and removed my bra. He cupped each of my breasts in his hands and desire flooded through me, making me ache and yearn for him. I heard myself moan and made no move to stop him from stripping off the rest of my clothes.

"Beautiful," he whispered as his eyes looked up and down my naked body with admiration. He placed both hands on either side of my head. "Let me join with you."

I nodded in consent. He slowly ran his palms all over my bare skin and I experienced a pleasant relaxation, as if I'd just had a fabulous massage. I was vaguely aware that he was edging me toward his bed and easing me onto my back. I had never felt so warm within, so completely alive, and so eagerly excited to be with a man. He took off his clothes while kissing me and resumed touching me until I became delirious.

Then he entered me.

It was unlike anything I had ever felt. This was more than phenomenally hot sex, it was like the binding of our minds and spirits; we were one big mass of pulsating energy. It didn't take long to reach climax and when it happened, I wondered if hardcore drug addicts ever achieved such a high. My body was as light as a feather, and the radiating pleasure of my powerful orgasm lasted for several minutes.

Oh. My. God.

After my mind, body, and soul returned to the room, and I was in full control of my mental faculties, I finally took the time to study his naked body beside me. I already knew he was lean and muscular, but seeing him in his naked glory was quite a sight—like a perfect Roman statue.

Propping himself on one elbow, he asked in a sultry voice, "Did *that* bring back any memories?"

"*That* was unlike anything I have ever experienced in my entire life," I said. "But don't let it get to your head, okay?"

He laughed aloud. "It was wonderful for me, too. I can't tell you how good it feels to join with you again."

"Is that what you call it where you're from? Joining?"

"Yes, because we join not only our bodies but also our energy forces. It's much more intense than mere physical, animal mating."

How the hell could I not have remembered something that felt this awesome? "You know, Victor, aside from your eyes and your skin, you look like us," I pointed out, admiring the subtle opalescence of his skin in the silvery moonlight.

"Actually, my love, it is your species that resembles us," he corrected. "We created humans and made you in our image."

I sat up. "Are you serious? You mean my whole theory about humans being an alien experiment isn't crazy?"

"Not crazy at all. Aside from the differences of skin and eyes, which has to do with our different environments, we are virtually alike. Oh, and the only other genetic difference is that we're hairless."

My eyes were drawn to his head. "So what's that? A wig?"

"I've been genetically altered to blend in here on Earth. That's why I wear the brown contact lenses and apply a special cream to my exposed skin to suppress its iridescence."

"Why does it glow in the first place?"

"On my planet, the days are short and the nights are long. Our moon is dominant, making our nights more luminous than here on Earth. Our sun, on the other hand, is somewhat feeble, so we absorb its life-giving vitamins through our skin."

"Like a plant?"

"Very much like a plant."

"Does this have anything to do with you being a vegetarian?"

"Sort of. Humans are able eat and digest flesh because they're technically animals. You have the proper teeth and stomach acids for eating and processing meat; we don't. It's not that we can't, we just prefer not to because the end result is unpleasant. Imagine if you ate a plate full of tree bark and grass. It wouldn't kill you, but it might make you sick."

"I see. I assume your eyes are well equipped to see in the dark because your nights are longer."

"Correct. That's how I could clearly see the green cube in your living room during the blackout. I've been so apprehensive; torn between wanting to tell you everything, and allowing you to remember on your own, which is less shocking to your system."

"Are you here to gather data on us in order to see how we're adapting and evolving?" I asked, believing that I was drawing a logical conclusion.

"We only created a species, not life itself," he corrected. "The only reason we did that was because Earth is so unique. But there's much more to my mission than gathering data. You're part of an important prophecy."

"Woah, wait a sec. I'm part of a prophecy?"

"An important one."

"I'm only an ordinary human woman with no wealth, no connections, and no super powers. I'm nobody."

"Funny, you told me the same thing five hundred years ago. There are two prophecies. The first has already been fulfilled."

"Are you saying I fulfilled it back in the sixteenth century?"

"Yes, and you're here again to fulfill the second one." He paused. "When we first found your special planet, we believed it should be populated with intelligent life. We also believed that you could preserve and protect it."

"Are you kidding me?" I shook my head disdainfully. "What a bitter disappointment we must be to you."

"While you have historically proven yourselves to be violent, destructive, and greedy beings, you are also capable of great love and kindness. Humans are full of contradictions." He smiled tenderly. "It's late. You should get some rest. We'll talk more tomorrow."

I snuggled beside him in the big bed. My breathing fell in synch with his and I drifted off to sleep. I dreamed that I was flying through space. Billions of stars glittered against the black backdrop. The planets were awe-inspiring in their serene and timeless beauty, and I was at one with them. When I caught sight of the giant burning sun, I was gripped by a paralyzing fear and woke up with a start. Gasping for air, I sat up in bed unable to breathe. The mere thought of getting too close to those hellish flames almost pushed me into a full blown panic attack.

Victor sat up and put his arm around me "Are you okay?"

"I'm fine," I lied. "Sorry I woke you." I placed my hand on my chest and felt my racing heart. "I was dreaming of space and saw the sun. The flames terrified me."

He pulled me close. The feel and warmth of him excited me and it wasn't long before we were making love again, or rather, 'joining.' I didn't think it was possible to have such mind-blowing sex twice in the same night, but Victor proved me wrong. Satiated, we both fell into a deep, dreamless sleep.

***

The next morning, Victor called in sick for me. While he made coffee, I took a hot shower and put on the same jeans and sweater I wore yesterday. My host had thoughtfully left a new toothbrush on the sink. I walked into the living room and inhaled the enticing scent of freshly brewed coffee.

"Espresso?" he asked.

"Oh, you know me so well," I replied with a grateful smile. I took a sip. "Thank you for calling the university and making breakfast."

"Josie answered the phone. She hopes you feel better soon."

I sat on the sofa and picked up the red leather photo album from the coffee table to see if there was anything else I could remember. I finally came across a photo of several people in fine clothing. In the background stood a pale man with ash blonde hair and demonic black eyes. Something about him made my skin crawl.

"I remember this man," I said, taking the photo album over to Victor.

He frowned. "What do you remember about him?"

"His eyes were weird. They creeped me out," I replied. "It's strange how there are huge gaps in my memory, yet some things are so clear." I noticed Victor's grim expression. "Hey, you seem upset, who was he?"

"An enemy."

"An enemy?" I repeated, confused. "If that's the case, why did you invite him into your home and take his picture?"

"I didn't invite him. He tagged along with another guest. There were tiny image-recording devices hidden throughout the house. I collected the data after every event I hosted. I didn't know what he was until this image was recorded."

"You mean *who* he was."

"Let's have breakfast first. I have a long story to tell, and you should be on a full stomach to hear it."

CHAPTER 29
LISBON, PORTUGAL
OCTOBER, 1526

I loved being Victor's wife. There was always something to learn from him and our joinings were sublime. I often wondered if human men were capable of giving their women the pleasure that my husband consistently gave me.

The last three years had been full of peace, happiness, and meaningful accomplishments. I became involved with local charities and spearheaded various educational programs for children and adults.

The highly controversial book *Human Injustice* was still in circulation despite being banned by the Church. Try as they might, the servants of the Holy Inquisition had failed to apprehend the author. Unfortunately, people were tortured and even killed for possessing a copy of my book.

Needless to say, Victor and I prudently kept to ourselves.

We were at the market one morning when Victor said, "Your birthday is only three days away. What shall I buy for you?"

"I have everything I could possibly want or need, my love."

"Perhaps you'll be tempted by a lovely trinket."

We walked hand-in-hand admiring the merchandise. I spotted an extremely pale man heading our way and, as he got closer, I recognized him as the strange man at Victor's Christmas celebration years ago.

The pale man blocked our path and his frightening black eyes looked me up and down.

Victor's eyes widened in shock and he immediately let go of my hand. "What are you doing here?"

"I'm visiting Lisbon, what else?" Grinning at me, he added, "She may be lovely, but she's only human."

Victor shoved the man aside, took hold of my arm, and urged

me forward. We had only walked a few steps when I peeked over my shoulder. The pale man caught my eye and licked his thin lips. His nostrils were small and several vertical lines framed his wide mouth. They weren't the kind of lines one sees on the elderly, but the kind one sees on a snake.

"Who is that?" I asked.

"Someone I hope never to meet again."

"But you invited him to your home."

He stopped in his tracks. "What? When?"

"The first time you brought me to the house. He was there at the Christmas party."

"I'll have to go through my visual recordings to see if he was alone. He couldn't have been tracking me all this time…" Realization dawned on him and the expression on his face worried me. "Something made him return to Lisbon."

"Victor, you're scaring me."

Gripping my shoulders, he said, *"He knows."*

"What does he know?"

Ignoring my question, he continued to muse aloud. "If he doesn't know, then he suspects. Why would he confront us?"

I sobered instantly. "Who is he?"

"An enemy." He pinched the bridge of his nose with his thumb and forefinger. "It's no longer safe for us to stay in Lisbon."

"What? Victor——"

"We must leave the city as soon as possible. You're in danger. Forgive me, little star."

"I don't want to leave Lisbon. What about our life here? The school? Our special waterfall in the forest?"

"We're leaving now."

"No—at least let me see our special place one last time."

He glanced around frantically then took a deep breath. "Very well. We can go while our servants pack our belongings, but we can't stay long. I'll send one of the students to purchase two passages on the first ship leaving tomorrow morning."

"What about my work here?"

"None of that matters anymore. Don't you see? If he hasn't

185

already figured out that you're the Chosen One, he surely suspects. We can't stay here."

On the way home from the market, Victor said very little. His mouth was set in a hard line. We ate a quiet meal before mounting our horses and setting off. Once we were out of Lisbon, our anxiety began to melt away. We urged our horses through the trees letting nature fill our spirits with its healing presence. Upon reaching the clearing, we stripped off our clothing and eased into the crystal clear spring. I watched the ice cold curtain of the waterfall create a cloud of steam as it hit the hot, sulfuric water. I ducked my head underwater for several seconds then broke through the surface, slicking my hair back from my head. I pulled the crisp autumn air into my lungs and saw that Victor's eyes were on me.

"You are exquisite," he said softly.

I swam over to him and snaked my arms around his neck. There was worry and fear in his expression—-two things that I had never before seen on my husband's face. I kissed him gently, stroking his hair. "I hate having to say goodbye to this special place."

"Me, too, but there will be other special places, my love."

"Please tell me who that man is."

"That thing is not a man," he replied between clenched teeth.

CHAPTER 30
PROVIDENCE, RI
JANUARY, PRESENT DAY

"Planets are constantly being formed," Victor explained as I sipped my second espresso. "Depending on the distance from their galaxy's sun, some of these planets remain in a hostile state for billions of years, while others become temperate. Whenever a new planet is formed, it automatically attracts the attention of nearby civilizations."

"Is that what happened with Earth?"

"Yes. When Earth began sustaining life, it was visited by a warmonger species known as Reptilians."

"You mean to tell me that Reptilians really exist? I thought they were the mere inventions of creative sci-fi authors and Hollywood scriptwriters."

"How I wish that were true. Reptilians are very real."

Victor explained how the Reptilians experimented with artificial insemination between themselves and Earth's reptiles, which were the most highly evolved creatures at that time. Through trial and error they eventually created a hybrid species that was physically powerful, but not highly intellectual. What surprised the Reptilians was their enormous size.

I held up my hand. "Wait—you're talking about dinosaurs."

He nodded. "The Reptilians tried to genetically alter the dinosaurs to get them to stand upright and speak, but they failed. Frustrated, they abandoned their project and their creations, and returned to their home planet. Dinosaurs inhabited the Earth for millions of years until a colossal meteor shower caused their extinction. Very few creatures survived the severe change in climate. Those that did slowly evolved into various kinds of animals. It was at this point that we arrived."

"Wow. I know that I can't pronounce your name or the name

of your people, but would you at least tell me so I can hear what it sounds like."

He proceeded to utter sounds that were unlike anything I had ever heard—human or otherwise.

"You're right, I could never repeat that," I said. "Can you give me a name that's a human equivalent so that I can at least have a pronounceable reference for your species?" When he was at a loss for words, I suggested, "How's this: what are you? You told me the Reptilians are warmongers. What are your people known for?"

"We're universally known for observing other species. We travel throughout galaxies seeking to impart wisdom, knowledge, and to help wherever there's a need. You could say that we're always on the watch."

Something clicked. "The Watchers. That's what I'll call your kind. The name fits, doesn't it?"

"I suppose it does."

Victor informed me that the Watchers were aware of the Reptilian failure with the dinosaurs, but that didn't deter them from trying their own experiments. Not only were the life forms on Earth far more evolved than before, but the Watchers themselves were genetically superior to the Reptilians. They artificially inseminated the most intelligent creature they could find on Earth at the time, which was the ape. The ape's offspring was artificially inseminated, and natural selection and evolution eventually gave way to other species such as Homo-Sapiens, until the world became dominated by Humans.

"So I guess unwanted body hair is a result of our ancestors, the apes," I interjected, trying to add a bit of humor.

He laughed apologetically. "I'm afraid so."

"Why not continue breeding scientifically instead of relying on nature and evolution?"

"Risk of deleterious recessive genes."

"Right. What about space travel? Wormholes?"

"Wormholes are useful, but our technology allows us to travel at the speed of light."

I sat back and stared at him in disbelief. What I wouldn't

give to have a glimpse of all the wonders he had seen in his lifetime. "What happened after the first human came into existence? You didn't name him Adam, did you?"

"No," he replied. "Besides, it was not the male who first stood erect, it was the female. She was genetically superior."

He went on to explain how the Watchers had remained close to the first humans in order to teach them vital things, like a parent would. The clever humans procreated and evolved, developing useful skills for making tools, creating social boundaries, and so on. They were taught how to use their environment to the fullest advantage, and to always respect nature as the source of life.

Gradually, under the guidance of the Watchers, humans became more advanced and began to travel to different parts of their planet. They built magnificent structures, like the Egyptian and Mesoamerican pyramids. These massive creations aligned perfectly with the constellations used by the Watchers whenever they traveled through space. I was not the least bit surprised when Victor confirmed that the Nazca Lines in Peru were indeed landing strips for their spaceships.

The Watchers regularly visited the humans to carefully observe their behavior and collect important data. For the most part humans were good, intelligent, and capable of reason. Unfortunately, their ancestry to the apes gave them animal qualities like territorial possessiveness and the propensity for violence. Apes possessed something else, too—the need for social hierarchy.

The Watchers believed that humans would eventually evolve beyond their bestial tendencies, and someday bring honor and glory to the universe. Things were going relatively well until the Reptilians came back to Earth to reclaim their right as the planet's first explorers. Now that intelligent beings inhabited the Earth, the Reptilians wanted to seize it as a colony for themselves and turn the humans into slaves.

The Watchers would not allow it, and a terrible war ensued between them. Most of the fighting took place in the sky with hi-tech spaceships, while terrified humans watched from far

189

below. The humans later wrote about this war in many forms, and these accounts appeared in various ancient accounts and sacred books throughout the world. It later became known as the Great Battle in ancient Sanskrit texts.

The Watchers defeated the Reptilians, but their victory was bittersweet. During the Great Battle, a giant meteor had penetrated the force fields of their beloved planet and crashed into the atmosphere, causing massive destruction. Millions of lives were lost, and several major cities destroyed. When news of this tragedy reached the victorious Watchers here on Earth, they left for home immediately, thus abandoning the humans.

Armed with little technology and bestial instincts, mankind was left to their own inexperience and naiveté. Being such a young species, they were practically as helpless as newborns. It was shortly after their mentors' departure that humankind entered the Time of Lost Knowledge, or as humans coined it: the Dark Ages.

During this period of vast ignorance and superstition, the Reptilians had managed to sneak back to Earth and abduct humans for experimental insemination. They finally succeeded in creating a hybrid life form that resembled a human and could tolerate Earth's temperatures, but its mental capacity was rudimentary. These hybrids are known to the Watchers as Repticlones.

"Wow, what a story," I exclaimed when Victor stopped speaking. "I'm glad you weren't around when that devastating meteor struck."

"It was the worst natural disaster ever to happen to my planet. Had we not advanced to the point of being able to create powerful force fields, the meteor would have completely annihilated my world."

I thought about his words for a moment. "Earth would never survive such an impact, would it?"

"No."

My stomach turned at the mere thought. "What happened to the Repticlones? Are they still around?"

"Yes."

An icy chill ran down my spine. "You're telling me that these creatures walk among us?"

"I've detected quite a few since my return to Earth, which was on the day you were born. Prior to that, the only other time I came in contact with a Repticlone was in Lisbon."

Something in my memory was triggered. "The pale blonde man with creepy black eyes in the photo."

"Yes. The humans knew him as a priest by the name of Dario, but his real name was Nebuzak."

Another powerful memory hit me. "You had words with him in the street," I said, staring off into space while seeing the scene unfold in my mind's eye.

"Your memory is improving," he said, his eyes glittering with anticipation.

CHAPTER 31
LISBON, PORTUGAL
OCTOBER 1526

Victor pulled me toward the waterfall and we slipped through the curtain of icy water. My husband usually made love to me in a sensuous manner, but today he performed with an intensity that bordered on roughness. His mouth was hungrily devouring me as he literally crushed me against his body. After our passionate joining, I had a terrible sense of foreboding.

He caressed my cheek. "There are so many things about me that you still do not know, my love. The time has come for you to learn the truth."

Victor described his world, which was farther away than the moon. He told me there were many worlds in our universe, and many kinds of life forms. Some of these beings were peaceful and lived in advanced societies, while others were violent savages. A few could easily blend in with humans and others could not. Victor was one of the life forms that walked among us. The strange, pale man with coal black eyes was an enemy of my husband's people, and his real name was as strange as his reptilian appearance.

"Do you truly believe this—Nebuzak—knows about the Sacred Oracle and the prophecy?"

Victor nodded and took hold of my chin. "It's time to go."

I knew better than to question his wisdom. We mounted our horses and headed home. The full moon hung close to the horizon, suspended like a glowing pearl in the night sky.

Victor dismounted when we arrived home, but I remained in the saddle basking in the celestial queen's glory. "It saddens me to leave Lisbon. We have so many wonderful memories here."

Victor followed my gaze and stared up at the moon. "I'm tempted to leave the city right now."

"I'm so tired...one more night won't make a difference."

He was troubled as we climbed the stairs. I bathed in my room and changed into a linen shift. I found Victor in his room with a small bellows in his hand. A lively flame sprang to life inside the hearth. He picked up two delicate glass goblets filled with sweet wine and handed one to me.

"To us," he said, holding up his goblet.

I touched the rim of my vessel to his, then we sat on the bed quietly watching the fire as we sipped the wine.

"I love our life," I said softly into the silence.

Victor met my gaze. "Me too. Thank you for showing me how truly special human love can be."

"Being by your side has taught me so much, Victor. You're everything to me...my lover, my friend, my teacher, my master. You're my world and I can't imagine my life without you in it."

"I know you're worried. I'll do everything to keep you out of harm's way. I love you, Veronica."

"I love you, too."

Without another word he took my glass and eased me onto my back. As tired as we were, we still had the energy to join before going to sleep.

I dreamed of pleasant things: the forest after the rain in the springtime, and how the Tagus River gleamed like polished silver on a sunny day. These delightful images were soon interrupted by a jarring noise. Was someone beating a drum? The persistent pounding grew more intense and I tried not to let it bother me as I snuggled into the warm pillow.

"Veronica, wake up!"

My hand instantly flew to my brow to protect my eyes against the early morning sunshine pouring from the windows.

Victor threw back the coverlet. "Get dressed. Hurry!"

I sat up in bed. "What is it?"

Someone pounded on our front door. Scrambling out of bed, I ran to the window and saw several men on horseback. Nebuzak was with them and, to my horror, so was Rosa. She stood beside him clutching a book to her chest. My knees buckled, but Victor caught me before I hit the floor.

"They have come for me," I said.

"I'm sure this is only a misunderstanding," he assured me in a voice that implied otherwise.

"Rosa is holding a book—what if it's mine?"

The hinges finally broke on the door downstairs and it fell to the floor with a thud. The sound of heavy boots running up the stairs filled the bedchamber.

"Oh, God, Victor," I sobbed.

Victor placed me behind him as the bedroom door swung open. Two armed men invaded the room. The royal coat of arms was sewn onto the breasts of their uniforms, making their identities unmistakable.

One of the men stepped forward with a sword in his hand. "Mistress Veronica, we arrest you in the name of the king and the Holy Inquisition."

Victor was indignant. "I am her lawful husband and I demand to know on what charges you are arresting my wife!"

"Witchcraft and heresy," the man replied curtly.

Victor turned to me and whispered, "It's too soon. I can't control their minds yet—I will come for you, I swear."

The two men came forward and took hold of each of my arms. I looked over my shoulder at my husband as they led me out of the room.

CHAPTER 32
PROVIDENCE, RI
JANUARY, PRESENT DAY

"So, your first visit to Earth was in 1510?"

"No," Victor replied. "The Sacred Oracle's prophecy foretold that the Icon would—"

"The Icon? Is that supposed to be me?"

"Yes. The prophecy foretold that you would come after Dark Times, which we believed to be soon after the Age of Lost Knowledge, or as you would call it—the Dark Ages. We miscalculated, and I ended up coming here two hundred years earlier than I should have. My first trip to Earth was in the late thirteenth century." He smiled smugly. "It ended up not being such a bad thing for humankind, however. One of the first humans I spoke with was Giotto di Bondone."

"You spoke to the Father of the Italian Renaissance?!"

"Incredible man, talented artist. He knew me as 'Maestro.'"

My mouth hung open in awe. "Are you insinuating that *you* sparked the humanistic movement in Italy?"

"Well, yes, at least part of it. I reminded Giotto and other great men of their glorious ancient past when philosophy, nature, and humanity were celebrated. I spoke to them of classical Greece and ancient Rome—the world before Christianity."

"When you say 'other great men,' who exactly are you referring to?" I asked, already excitedly anticipating his answer.

"I met and spoke with philosophers, writers, and many artists such as Donatello, Brunelleschi, Michelangelo, Botticelli, Leonardo da Vinci," he said casually. "These gifted souls began to create visual celebrations of the humanistic spirit that had been tragically lost shortly after the fall of Rome."

"Amazing!"

He rubbed his nails against his chest and blew on them in the familiar gesture of great accomplishment. "All they needed was a little push."

"I love you!" I blurted out happily, not thinking.

Victor's eyes grew soft and he looked away. "The last time you said that to me was almost five hundred years ago."

"Oh, Victor," I whispered.

"There's so much more to tell you, but I don't want to complicate matters by adding emotional drama." He paused. "I don't expect you to love me—at least not right now."

"I'm pretty sure I've loved you from the moment I first saw you in Boston," I confessed shyly.

He smiled. "You need to know something: as much as I love you, you're not the only reason I'm here on Earth."

"You came back for the fulfillment of the second prophecy."

"Yes."

He looked at his cell, then went into the kitchen. "Almost noon; a respectable time for prosecco."

I shrugged. "I'm on the verge of becoming an alcoholic anyway, so why not?"

I heard the 'pop' of the cork and the fizz of the pale gold nectar being poured into two flutes.

"Thank you," I said, accepting my glass.

He sat down beside me. "We deserve these. It's been quite a morning, wouldn't you say?"

"Delicious," I said after taking a sip. "Yes, it has. Tell me about Nebuzak and why he's our enemy. Is he still alive?"

"He's dead," he replied in a low, steely voice.

I hesitated. "Did you kill him?"

"Yes," he replied curtly, offering no other details.

There was a tense pause. "Would he still be alive if—"

"No, Repticlones only live a few hundred human years."

In an attempt to lighten the mood, I said, "We humans really got screwed over in the longevity department."

"Unfortunately, that's the ape in you," he said with a wink. "Nebuzak was casing the joint, so to speak, when we encountered him in Lisbon. Repticlones still send scouts to important cities that are making an impact on the world."

"Casing the joint?" I repeated.

"Checking out what was happening on Earth so that he could report back to his superiors."

"The expression 'casing the joint' makes it sound like he was gathering information in order to commit a crime."

"Based on the information Nebuzak provided regarding the Age of Discoveries and mankind's new way of thinking, the Reptilians managed to almost single-handedly bring about the Age of Enlightenment, which eventually gave birth to the Industrial Revolution."

I frowned, confused. "How?"

"By using other Repticlones as they had used Nebuzak—gather Intel and influence humans in power to act in accordance with their agenda."

"I thought you said there weren't many of them."

"There aren't, but the few that do exist are highly efficient, just as Nebuzak was in the sixteenth century. They've influenced monarchs, popes, and anyone else who possessed the power to dictate change."

"Okay, but how? How are these Repticlones so influential? Do they use mind control or something?"

"No, they aren't as advanced as we are."

"So what do they use? Drugs?"

"In a way. They employ the most powerful drug of all: human vanity and greed. Whisper a few promises into the ears of greedy men and they will stop at nothing to achieve money and power."

He was right, of course. "But the Age of Enlightenment and the Industrial Revolution were good, weren't they?" I countered, referring to the political, social, and technological advancements made between the eighteenth and nineteenth centuries.

"Were they?" he challenged calmly. "Peasants starved in France while the hedonistic aristocracy held lavish feasts and ignored their plight. It led to a revolution that overturned the monarchy via gratuitous violence. Many innocent people

197

suffered bloody and gruesome deaths...so much for Enlightenment. The Industrial Age was no better. Young children worked in factories under deplorable conditions, and countless immigrants were forced to live like rats in crumbling tenement buildings. They led horrible lives to make a few pennies and keep starvation at bay. All this to support an ever-growing consumerist society that would eventually exploit humans and cause environmental damage on a global scale."

His words brought to mind a photograph I'd seen of a young Chinese child inside a famous American sneaker factory. The dejected little boy sat at a sewing machine instead of being in school. The image was disturbing and tragic.

"You're right," I agreed. "I was only trying to point out the positive aspects of these movements."

"That's expected. Being so highly adaptable, your species has a propensity for looking on the bright side. It's in your genes," he explained.

"Did we get that from the apes, too?"

"No, you got that from us," he replied, lightly touching his flute against mine.

I fished my cell phone from my purse. "Now that the pieces of the puzzle are finally fitting together, there's no need to continue my therapy."

"You're going to call your doctor right now?"

I shrugged. "Why not?"

I dialed Clarice's number and got her voicemail. I kindly explained that I didn't want to see her as a patient anymore. I blamed the hypnosis session, claiming that it had totally freaked me out. I ended the message by thanking her for all she had done for me. I felt guilty lying to Clarice, especially after she had been so nice to me, but I couldn't tell her the truth. If I did, she would most likely have me institutionalized.

I hung up the phone and my stomach growled.

Victor grinned. "Hungry?"

"I am, but there's one more thing I really wish you'd tell me before we eat lunch."

"Let me guess. You want to know how you died."

CHAPTER 33
LISBON, PORTUGAL
OCTOBER 1526

Thanks to my husband's wealth and social status, my captors refrained from putting me in shackles. The smugness on Rosa's face confirmed my suspicions. Victor's eyes expressed desperate determination as he watched me being hoisted up onto a saddle. I knew he would get me out of this mess.

The alternative would be unthinkable.

The guard adjusted himself in the saddle behind me and steered the horse away from the house. I caught Rosa looking at Victor with the eyes of a woman who has finally achieved her goal. Now that I was out of her way, she would try to claim my husband's love.

I was taken to the city's prison where I would be held for questioning. My head swam as I stepped into the damp, grimy interior of the building. The stench was so horrible, it took great effort not to vomit. I hesitated inside the threshold. The guard gave me a light shove, but my feet refused to cooperate.

"This is a terrible mistake," I cried, fighting against hysteria. "I'm no witch! I'm a teacher! I'm known in the city for my charity work. Please!"

The guard shoved me again, only harder this time.

I forced myself to put one foot in front of the other, trying hard not to stumble against the slimy stone walls on either side of me. He led me to a small cell at the end of a narrow hallway, opened the door, and pointed. An involuntary cry escaped my lips when I entered the dirty space. I turned my back and he locked me inside.

I put my face up to the small barred window cut into the door. "I beseech you," I said. "Have mercy! I'm innocent!"

He laughed, but it sounded like a pig's snort. "Once a witch is brought in here there's only one outcome."

"But I'm not—"

His cruel laughter cut me off. He was joking at my expense. Outraged, I temporarily forgot my predicament and turned my back to him. As his footsteps retreated from the door, the last shred of my composure simply dissolved. I proceeded to weep quietly for several minutes. When I finally regained some control, I wiped my eyes and assessed my surroundings.

In one corner there was a pile of straw and a wooden bucket reeking of excrement. It was no doubt left behind from the last prisoner, and the thought made me cringe in disgust. In the opposite corner was another wooden bucket. A crude ladle rested within, which meant that it was drinking water—and most likely foul. I was at least grateful for the tiny window above my head because it allowed some light into the cell.

Placing my head in my hands, I resisted surrendering to sheer desperation. Every hour that passed seemed like an eternity, and each sound, each footstep, made me run to the door in the anticipation of Victor's arrival and rescue. At midday, a guard came and slid a chipped ceramic plate through the dugout space under the door. To my horror, a big rat shuffled out of a hole in the wall and began to consume the mysterious brown mush and moldy bread on the plate. I had to cover my mouth tightly with my hands to keep from screaming.

The light of the afternoon began to fade and the temperature dropped inside the cell. The linen shift in which I had slept in last night offered little warmth. I was also hungry and thirsty.

Where are you, Victor?

An hour must have passed before I heard footsteps in the hallway and a knock on the door. I ran to the small opening expecting to see my husband, and almost burst into tears when I saw the same guard who had escorted me to my cell.

"Your husband paid dearly for this," he said, unlocking the door just enough to toss a wrapped bundle at me.

He left, locking the door and leaving me alone once again. I was comforted that Victor had tried to come and see me, even though he had not been allowed access. I wondered why he had not yet manipulated the guards with mind control as I untied the rope that kept the bundle together. Nestled inside was one of my best gowns. Cut from the finest crimson velvet, it was not only warm, but the expensive color and elaborate adornments would remind the guards of my social status. It was a clever choice on Victor's part. Within the folds of the gown was another bundle containing a generous chunk of cheese, some fresh bread, and two flasks—one with water, one with wine.

I drank the water first, then devoured the food. I tried to eat slowly, but I was too hungry. I saved the wine for later. Next, I donned the gown over my shift, glad to have my dignity and warmth restored. I stayed awake for as long as I could, and when my eyes became too heavy, I curled up into a fetal position on the straw and slept.

I awoke the next day with the pale dawn light on my face. Gingerly, I sat up in my makeshift bed and rubbed my stiff back. My bladder ached and I eyed the bucket dubiously as I walked over to it. Squatting with concentrated balance, I relieved myself, then smoothed the folds of my gown when I was done. I also removed any strands of straw sticking to the fabric. Next, I carefully combed out the tangles in my hair with my fingers. Footsteps approached, so I ran to the door. It was the guard holding a ceramic cup and a loaf of brown bread.

"The water's clean," he said, regarding my improved countenance with an appraising eye. "You should thank your husband for this special treatment." Before locking the door, he patted the pouch at his waist, making the coins inside jingle.

"Wait!" I cried through the small grate in the door. "Please let me see my husband."

The guard shook his head. "Not allowed. Besides, you're going to receive a visitor this morning."

"Who?" I demanded, but my question went unanswered.

I drank the water and ate the bread without tasting it. Soon afterward, I heard footsteps again, then a key turning in the lock. The tall man who entered my cell had black hair and brown eyes, and a rather flamboyant mustache. His clerical robe was violet brocade lined with expensive ermine, eluding to his high

201

status within the Church. A matching bishop's hat sat snugly on his head, and an opulent jeweled cross hung from a gold chain around his neck. On the middle finger of his right hand sat a ruby the size of a quail's egg. He made the sign of the cross at me, sending a chill up my spine.

The Holy Inquisition had found me.

His dark gaze lingered on the generous amount of gold thread and silver beads embellishing the hem and bodice of my gown. I gathered myself up to my fullest height, lifted my chin, and set my shoulders firmly against his inspection.

"I am Bishop Mendoza. Do you know why you have been brought here?" he asked in a deceptively gentle voice. His accent was unmistakably Spanish.

"There has been a terrible mistake, Your Eminence," I said, addressing him with the title reserved for such clergymen. "My husband can clear my name and prove to you that I am innocent. We have a school for orphans. I'm a teacher."

"I have heard of your husband and his so-called school where young people learn about everything except the ways of God," he retorted sourly. "Your husband chooses to surround himself with scholars, philosophers, and men of science, and none of them are affiliated with the Holy Church."

"I swear to you—"

He lifted his hand abruptly to silence me. "By whom do you swear?" he mocked. "Surely not our Lord Jesus Christ or you would not be here in this predicament."

"Please, my lord, will you not listen to reason?"

The corners of his mouth lifted in a condescending smile. Reaching into the folds of his robe, he extracted a book and held it out to me so that I could read its title: *Human Injustice.*

"Did you write this book?" he asked, peering into my eyes knowingly. When I refused to answer, he continued, "We already know you did. One of your former students can quote word for word what you taught in your lessons. Those same words can be found within this text."

"A mere coincidence, Your Eminence," I countered, hoping to sound convincing. "That proves nothing."

How could I have been so careless? It didn't matter that Victor and I had worked so hard to keep our alternative beliefs a secret; the truth always has a way of leaking out.

And Rosa was that leak.

Bishop Mendoza stared at me in reproof, as if I were an errant child caught in a lie. "Your former student, Rosa, is a true Catholic and a lover of God. She was approached by one of Holy Mother Church's most zealous champions. Perhaps you have heard of our beloved Father Dario?"

My forehead creased in confusion. "Father Dario..?"

Yesterday morning I had seen Nebuzak atop a horse, and now that I think about it, he wore a black priestly robe. Realization hit me and my stomach did a complete revolution. The sound of several approaching footsteps made me wonder if Victor had finally come to save me. I was devastated when a handful of guards stood and waited outside my door.

"Your Eminence, please—"

Again, he raised his hand to silence me. "Do you still insist upon your innocence?"

"Yes!"

"Very well," he conceded. "I will grant you the opportunity to clear your name."

Relieved, I allowed a tiny smile of gratitude to stretch across my lips. "Thank you."

He held out his hand in invitation. "You may come with me now and perform an *auto de fé* and—"

"No!"

Anyone accused of witchcraft was expected to perform an auto de fé—act of faith—to prove their innocence. If the accused survived, he or she was in league with the Satan. If the accused died, the innocent soul would go straight to Heaven. Of course, no one ever survived the cruel acts; the most common being dunked and held under water.

The Spaniard eyed me coldly. "As you wish."

Reaching into the pocket of his robe, he pulled out a small metal device that I recognized at once—the dreaded pear of anguish. The mere sight of it made the blood rush from my face.

Victor and I had once discussed the vile deeds inflicted by the Church, which included the employment of torture. Of the many cruel ways to inflict pain, the pear of anguish was perhaps the most sinister. Constructed from razor sharp sections, when tightly closed it resembled an elongated pear with a corkscrew mechanism on one end. It could be inserted orally, vaginally, or anally. When the torturer turned the handle on the corkscrew, the pear's sections opened, slashing away at the surrounding flesh. The pain was unimaginable.

Seeing the shock on my face, the bishop smiled. Turning to the guards, he stated calmly, "The time has come to make the witch confess her sins."

I swayed unsteadily. I was already promised the pear of anguish, but they wouldn't stop at that. What other atrocities awaited me? Would I be stretched upon the rack until my ligaments were savagely torn, and my arms and legs popped out of their sockets? Perhaps they would pull out my fingernails and toenails one by one, or shove a burning hot poker up my anus. And when they were done with their sadistic games, they would take turns violating me, satisfying their bestial appetites to the fullest. I wanted to vomit.

Oh, the pain! The humiliation!

My eyes slid toward the guards. The thought of their groping hands on my body made me burn with indignation. A new energy shot through me like a jolt of lightning. I would not allow anyone to strip me of my dignity, put me through unspeakable pain, only to be presented before a corrupt court that would find me guilty anyway! The outcome would be the same regardless if I confessed now or under torture. I would not serve as perverse amusement for this fanatical Spaniard—or anyone else for that matter.

Slowing my breath and clearing my mind, I went deep inside myself until I found that private, special place that belonged to no one else but me. Like an impenetrable womb, it protected me from the outside world and filled me with serenity. My mind became totally lucid; free of fear and worry. In my mind's eye, I saw only the color green. Above my head was a canopy of twisting tree branches and each sunlit leaf bent to caress my face. Even the wind whispered soothingly in my ear. Once I had regained control of myself, I knew exactly what to do.

The guards advanced, their hands gripping my arms and wrists in anticipation of a struggle. To their surprise, I stood completely still. I stared directly at the bishop and in my loudest, most authoritative voice, I cried, "IN THE NAME OF SATAN, I DEMAND MY RELEASE!"

Every hand immediately released its grip on me. Some of the men actually staggered backward and fearfully crossed themselves. The intense weight of my words reverberated throughout the walls of the tiny cell and hung heavily in the air like a poisonous cloud. No one moved.

When the bishop finally spoke, his voice held the unmistakable note of fear. "You confess to being the heretical author of this evil book and teaching witchcraft in your school?" he asked while fingering of the gold crucifix that hung from his neck as if it were a talisman against evil.

I knew I had to be extremely careful of my answer in order not to implicate others. "Do you think me daft, bishop?" I challenged, tossing my head back for effect. "My students are devout Christians. If they ever discovered my secret, I wouldn't have any students to teach, now would I? I needed the school as a ruse; I refuse to share my knowledge or my powers with anyone—not even my husband."

"You want the Devil's powers for yourself," the bishop stated, shocked.

"Of course, I do!" I lowered my voice and added, "I practice the Dark Arts alone at night when everyone is asleep, including my gullible husband."

By now the guards had recoiled from me. They stood with their backs against the wall, staring at me with terrified eyes. They were well accustomed to accused witches desperately whimpering and begging for mercy. I, on the other hand, proudly confessed my crime.

The Spaniard's eyes were wide and glassy. "In the name of Jesus Christ I command you to repent!" Bishop Mendoza said with false bravado for the benefit of the cowering guards.

I hissed furiously at him in response, which caused one guard to cry out to the Virgin Mary and flee the cell. I took a step toward the crucifix, thus proving that it couldn't deter my power. The bishop continued to brandish the holy relic in my face as he retreated. My guttural laughter was wild as I began to chant unintelligible words, raising my arms above my head for dramatic effect. The bishop took hold of a sword from a nearby guard and brandished it before me.

Staring into his eyes, I took a small step forward so that the sharp tip of the blade actually pierced the skin of my collar bone and drew a drop of blood. My boldness surprised him. "If you think to kill me before allowing me to stand trial, my faithful demons will visit you and your loved ones in the middle of the night to avenge the death of their sacred High Priestess."

Without another word, the Spaniard turned on his heel and left the cell. The guards quickly followed in his wake and locked the door, leaving me alone. Only then did I realize how hard my heart hammered against my chest, and how badly my hands shook. I ran to the bucket and heaved several times until the bread and water I had consumed earlier came out in a torrent of acidic vomit. Exhausted by the incredible performance I had just given, I sat on the floor, completely oblivious to the filth around me, and wept.

Veronica.

Closing my eyes, I was instantly transported to a lovely forest glen full of trees ablaze with the colors of autumn. In my hand was a perfectly formed chestnut.

Veronica...

This time, I saw a beautiful man with ebony hair and golden eyes. My angel, my demon, my husband.

"Veronica!"

My eyes snapped open. I must have been dreaming. My body was stiff and sore.

"Veronica, are you there?"

"Victor!" I scrambled to my feet, ignoring the sharp pain in my back. "Victor, I'm here," I cried up at the tiny window.

"Be brave, my little star. I've come to free you."

A moment later, I heard a key in the lock. The glassy-eyed guard opened the door and stood aside to let me pass. I ran down the narrow hallway, relieved to see the prison door wide open. I paused at the doorway to make sure no one was around, then stepped into the deliciously cold night. The air outside was sweet in comparison to the putrid air inside my cell, and I greedily pulled it into my lungs. Heavy clouds, pregnant with rain, signaled an oncoming storm.

Victor's arm went around my shoulders as he urged me away from the prison. Once we were safely within the maze of cobblestoned streets, he led me into an alley. The wind played with his shoulder-length hair, which he normally kept neatly tied at the nape of his neck. He wore a crimson doublet.

"You used mind control on my guard," I said.

"I would have done it earlier if I could. Luckily, I bribed the same guard twice and managed to get inside his head."

"Rosa told Nebuzak about my book. He's working with the Holy Inquisition as Father Dario!"

Victor looked furtively over his shoulder. "I know, my love. Listen to me carefully. I've purchased a passage for you on a ship sailing tonight."

We ducked out of the alley and ran toward the field leading down to the docks. A white vein of lightning lit up the sky followed by loud thunder.

"Aren't you coming with me?" I asked breathlessly.

"It's safer if you go alone. I need to deal with Nebuzak."

"I can't go without you!"

"I'll join you as soon as I can—as soon as it's safe."

"No! Come with me, Victor! If he finds us, we'll face him together. This time, we'll be ready."

The wind pulled at our hair, tossing it wildly. Icy rain fell.

Victor shook his head. "You must go alone," he insisted. "I don't care what happens to me, all that matters is getting you to safety. Besides, I'm more powerful than Nebuzak. The only advantage he had over us was the element of surprise."

Another blinding flash of lightning revealed a galleon

bobbing up and down on the turbulent waves of the Tagus. It was a mighty caravela, our kingdom's fastest vessel.

He followed my gaze. "That's your ship," he cried above the howl of the wind. "It leaves within the hour. We must get you on board at once!"

I was overcome by deep sadness as I feared for my beloved husband's safety. We were both in danger, and it was so close that I could almost taste it. I began to cry copious tears as he urged me across the field.

He stopped and took hold of my shoulders. "Veronica, please! I swear we'll be together again soon," he said before kissing me on the mouth.

There was such passion, such desperation in his kiss. Deep down inside I knew something bad was going to happen. He clasped my hand and started to pull me toward the docks again, then he stopped.

"Nebuzak," Victor said between clenched teeth.

My husband felt the enemy creature before he saw it. We both turned around at the same time, only to discover that we were surrounded by royal guards. The howling wind had masked the sound of their approach. Leading them on horseback was Nebuzak in the role of Father Dario.

Rough hands grabbed me and dragged me away. My last image of Victor was of him standing in the field with a dozen sword blades pointed at his throat.

***

A hasty mock trial was held the following day. Normally, an accused witch is presented before the court in soiled clothing and shorn hair, yet there I stood with my fine red gown and loose locks falling down my back. The scary threats to Bishop Mendoza yesterday, coupled with the ominous promise to the guards earlier that day—I told them their hands would fall off if they cut my hair—kept everyone at arm's length.

Those present at the hearing were unusually quiet as they took in my expensive clothing and proud bearing. My eyes searched among the faces of the spectators, but my husband was nowhere to be found. I assumed he was being held prisoner. The judge tried to incriminate Victor because of last night's attempted escape, so I let out a growl so fierce that it surprised even myself.

I stood up to my full height and pointed a finger at the judge. "Should any harm come to my husband, I swear by Satan that a horde of demons shall wreak my vengeance upon you and yours! Prepare yourself for a bloody reckoning."

Everyone began crying out to God. Some made the sign of the cross, while other kissed the wooden crucifixes around their necks. In their eyes, I was a powerful witch to be feared.

"Silence!" the terrified judge commanded as he pounded his gavel to establish order. "Silence! Silence!"

When everyone had quieted down, he addressed me in a most civil tone. "Madam, there can only be one outcome for you in this lawful court. Based on your own admission of guilt, I hereby declare that you are to be executed tomorrow on All Saints Day." He turned his head to the spectators and added, "I pray that Our Lord and all His saints keep and protect us from this wicked creature."

The guards cautiously escorted me out of the eerily silent courtroom. No one dared to throw rotten vegetables at me for fear that I would bestow a curse upon them.

Poor, ignorant people.

Back in my cell, I focused my thoughts on Victor. Rather than cry over the time I would no longer have with him, I chose to celebrate the years we spent together. I remembered the laughter and tears we had shared, and all of our passionate joinings….I thought of his sweet kisses and how easily I melted under his golden gaze.

Later, as I slept, my husband and his handsome face crept into my dreams. He took me into his arms and together we flew up into the sky. We were so high that I could see the Earth far below and the twinkling stars. We continued our journey past planets large and small, and I was filled with wonder and awe. Rays of blinding light flashed around us and I saw the familiar swirl of my mark, only it shimmered like diamonds on black velvet in the distance. I held up my wrist to compare, and knew they were one in the same.

Home.

I heard the sound of church bells. I was a little girl again celebrating my birthday. All Saints Day...a day for special treats; roasted chestnuts and sweet apple tarts.

I opened my eyes as one of the sun's rays broke through the tiny window in my cell. There were footsteps outside my door. I sat up and prepared myself for what was to come.

Six armed men led me to the large courtyard within the prison. At least I was spared the humiliation of being killed in a public square surrounded by a jeering crowd. Only a few people came to witness the execution. Nebuzak and Rosa were among them. Rosa didn't look so smug now that she realized that she was directly responsible for my death.

I was led to a wooden stake with a small platform. My wrists and ankles were bound and my body was firmly tied to the stake. The guard who bound me discreetly reached into his pocket and leaned very close to me.

"This is a gift from me to you," he whispered, quickly tying a fat leather pouch around my neck and hiding it within the tangled mass of my hair. "This will ease your suffering and give you a quick death."

"Gunpowder?" I whispered.

He nodded with eyes full of worry. "Please remember my face, mistress, and do not send your demons to my home."

"Thank you," I said, truly grateful for his kindness. "You and yours may sleep soundly."

I watched him join the other guards who were arranging the kindling wood beneath my feet. My eyes searched frantically for Victor, but he was nowhere in sight. They didn't even allow my husband to say a last farewell to his wife. When the kindling was packed neatly against the stake, one of the guards approached with a lit torch and touched it to the dried wood. The flame caught instantly and the instinctive panic rose within me. My whole body trembled with terror as I watched the fire spread, and I lost control of my bladder. The smoke curled its way past my feet and stung my eyes, its cloying thickness

210

choking me.

"Victor!" I screamed with all my might.

I was overcome by an irresistible urge to look to my left. I saw my husband's golden eyes staring at me from behind iron bars—he must have removed his brown lens discs for my benefit. Victor was being held in the prison cell farthest from the courtyard. The lower half of his face was hidden.

"I'm so sorry," I said, hoping that he could read my lips. "I love you…I love you so much!"

His eyes glistened with tears and I could see all the love in the world reflected in them.

The black smoke was everywhere. The intense heat beneath my toes made me struggle helplessly against the ropes that bound me, but it was no use, of course. I was tied too tightly; there was no escape. I began to cough as my oxygen-deprived lungs struggled to breathe. I was sure the smoke would kill me before the flames actually reached my flesh.

I was wrong.

The flames licked my feet, searing the skin and cooking the flesh. I tore my eyes away from my beloved husband and screamed. The primal sound was unfamiliar to my own ears. Never in my life had I experienced such agonizing pain. I was on the brink of unconsciousness when the flames caught the hem of my gown and raced up to the bodice. My hair caught on fire and I knew my agony would end soon. Using the last bit of strength I had in my body, I cried out to Victor one last time.

***

The Official Public Records from the Judicial Court of Lisbon:

31 October, 1526, A.D.:

The teacher known as Mistress Veronica, author of the heretical book Human Injustice, openly confessed to being in league with Satan the Devil. Bishop Mendoza, faithful servant of the Church and authorized agent of the Holy Inquisition, has proclaimed her a witch. The prisoner is sentenced to die tomorrow on All Saints Day in the hope that God will protect those faithful Christians who are trying to rid the world of such wickedness.

Addendum: 1 November, 1526, A.D.:

During today's execution several people witnessed the convicted witch call out to her husband before being consumed by the flames. Her death was quickened by a hidden pouch of gunpowder that exploded and took off her head. The guard who had provided the gunpowder was sentenced to receive thirty lashes as punishment for displaying mercy toward a convicted heretic and witch. May the Lord protect us all from the machinations of Satan and keep us safe within His realm.

CHAPTER 34
PROVIDENCE, RI
JANUARY, PRESENT DAY

"Please, Victor. I have a right to know."

He went into the bunker and returned with a manila envelope. "I took these when I was released from prison, the day after your death. First, I want you to read this," he said, handing me a sheet of paper.

I read the words aloud. "After Dark Times the Icon shall come. She will walk the Earth as a Sage, but will only provoke rage. Our Mark she will bear on the Tenth and Twentieth year. First Prophecy of the Sacred Oracle." I paused. "The Phoenix will rise again from the ashes. Her Word will shake the fragile foundation of Humanity to its core and she will save them from Gehenna. Second Prophecy of the Sacred Oracle."

"You, Veronica, are the Icon and the Phoenix."

I let that sink in. "This second prophecy is pretty heavy. If my memory serves me well, Gehenna is the Lake of Fire mentioned in the bible. It's a place of second death or final destruction."

"That's correct. This prophecy is very old, so Gehenna was a modern human term back when it was written."

"I'm supposed to save mankind form total destruction? Are you kidding me? How?"

He pointed to the second prophecy written on the sheet. "It states clearly that you'll accomplish this through your Word. Think, Veronica. What have you been working on for the last several years?"

There was only one plausible answer. "My manifesto."

"It's a socio- political manuscript, is it not?"

"Yes."

"Well, that's what the prophecy is referring to."

"How do you know about it?"

"It's stored in a laptop that you keep well hidden." Seeing the shock on my face, he added, "I've told you before—"

"Yeah, I know what you're going to say."

Still holding my gaze, he handed me the manila envelope. Inside were two photos. The first was of a crude stone compound with barred windows that looked like an old prison. The other depicted blackened wooden stake with a small platform. The ring of dirt surrounding the stake was sooty.

"Looks like a stake once used to burn witches and heretics."

Victor's face was tight. "Correct."

I remembered everything.

A thin wail escaped my lips as I relived the horror of being burned alive while Victor, unable to help me, watched from behind metal bars.

"Oh God," I sobbed, dropping the photograph. My body shook violently from head to toe. "I am the Phoenix, arisen from the ashes..." Victor had been right—reliving the agony of my death was too much to bear.

"You remember now," he said gently, stroking my hair as he held me tightly in his arms. "It was as the first prophecy had foretold, your goodness only provoked rage. You died because of your pure spirit, and you did it with a dignity that surprised everyone, even my superiors."

I wiped my eyes and sniffed. "Who the hell became provoked to the point of wanting me dead?"

I wanted to know partly out of curiosity, partly because there were still some blind spots in my memory, but mostly out of self-preservation. I didn't want to repeat the mistake of pissing off the wrong people.

"Nebuzak, the Holy Inquisition, the Kingdom of Portugal...remember, this all happened in the sixteenth century. Anyone who deviated from the teachings of the Church was in danger of being labeled a heretic. You were so ahead of your time; so independent in an age when women were expected to be godly and blindly obedient. You wrote a powerful book exposing the many sins and injustices of the Church and the

214

secular rulers it supported. You championed the poor and the ignorant. Your words sparked much debate and heated revolts throughout Europe."

The memories flooded into my brain, and I began to speak incessantly. I told Victor about pretending to be in league with Satan, thus escaping torture and rape.

"My brave little star," he said softly. I know this is hard to deal with, but it's over, okay?"

I stood up. "Give me a minute."

"Take all the time you need."

I walked into the guest bathroom and splashed cold water on my face. Then, I took some deep, calming breaths.

"Better?" Victor asked when I came out of the bathroom.

"Yes."

"Are you still hungry? We can go out to lunch."

"I've lost my appetite" I paused. "I think I should go home."

"Good idea. Being in your own environment will help you focus on the present. Let me get my coat."

"You don't have to come with me." He looked a bit hurt, so I added, "I'll feel better in a few hours. You can come by later and we'll have dinner. What I need right now is a stroll through the city. I think the cold air will do wonders for me."

"I respect your independence, I always have. Call me if you change your mind and want some company."

I turned to fetch my coat and stopped. "I love you."

He looked worried. "I love you, too."

I left the building and stepped into the icy January sunshine. Within ten minutes of walking, I allowed the familiar sights and sounds of Providence to distract me. I even paused to admire some cool graffiti stencils. My cell phone rang. It was Josie.

"Hey, how are you feeling?" she asked. "Any better?"

"Yeah. I think it was something I ate last night," I lied.

"Bummer. Did Victor take you out to dinner?"

I was forced to lie once more. "Yes, we went to an Italian place in Federal Hill. I ordered the mushroom risotto."

"Ew, maybe the mushrooms weren't fresh. They can make you sick, you know." Her voice went from concerned co-

215

worker to friend. "If Victor called in for you this morning, does that mean you two spent the night?"

"Um..."

She giggled. "Say no more. Will you be in tomorrow?"

"I should be. See you then."

She hung up the phone. I crossed the street and became aware of footsteps behind me. I turned down another street and the footsteps continued at a steady pace.

It's only your paranoid imagination, Veronica.

I rounded a corner and cut down an alley. The footsteps followed me! I walked faster and the footsteps also quickened their pace. Peeking over my shoulder, I saw a broad-shouldered man in a black coat with a hat pulled low over his face. There was something familiar about him, then I remembered the man I had seen from my window crossing the street in the middle of the night. I took a sharp right out of the alley and ducked into a crowded student hangout called Java. Once inside, I noticed two big guys waiting in line to order. Each man stood well over six feet tall and probably weighed close to two hundred fifty pounds—muscle heads.

My pursuer ducked out of the alley and peered in through the coffee shop window. Thankfully, he didn't see me hiding behind the bulk of the two body builders. The moment he walked away, I dialed Victor's number on my cell phone.

He picked up on the first ring. "Veronica?"

"I've been followed."

"Are you sure?"

"Yes."

"Where are you?"

"Sitting inside Java."

"Don't move."

Victor entered the coffee shop a minute later. His golden eyes scanned the room behind a pair of mirrored sunglasses.

Before I could question how he had arrived so quickly, he asked, "Are you okay?"

"Yeah, I'm a little freaked out because—"

"Male or female?"

"Male."

He sat down across from me. "What did he look like?"

"Broad shoulders; he wore a hat pulled down over his face."

"Any other details?"

"Black coat—I was too scared to really notice much."

"Are you absolutely sure he was following you?"

"I'm positive.

"We need to go."

"What? Why?"

Victor's serious expression silenced me. "Not here."

He clasped my wrist in a vice-like grip and led me outside. Placing me protectively behind him, he scanned the street before urging me toward a black Mercedes sports coupe with tinted windows.

"Is this yours?" I asked, finally realizing how he had gotten to the coffee shop so quickly.

He glanced nervously over his shoulder. "Get in."

Victor merged into the traffic. I noticed that his jaw was set and his mouth formed an angry line. Every few seconds, he'd look at the rearview mirror.

"Are you angry?" I asked.

"Very."

"At me?" I asked, barely keeping the worry out of my voice.

His expression softened immediately. "Of course, not, sweetheart. Forgive me, but I want to be sure you're not in any danger before I fill you in on what's going on." To emphasize this, he reached over and gave my hand a reassuring squeeze.

I sat back in the tan leather bucket seat. The luxury car was fast and smooth with a very quiet interior that muffled outside noise. "Where are we going?"

"I'm going to drive around for a bit until I'm sure that no one is tailing us, then I'm taking you to your place so you can get your things."

"Get my things?" I repeated.

He glanced at me before checking the rearview mirror again. "Your apartment is no longer safe. You're staying with me."

It wasn't a question, it was a command. "I can't stay with

217

you, Victor. This is going too fast—"

"This isn't about us—it's about saving your life."

I stared at him open-mouthed. "What?"

"Someone is on to you. Where's the laptop?"

"You think the man who's been following me—"

"What do you mean 'been following?' This isn't the first time? Why didn't you tell me?"

"It's the first time he's actually followed me, but I think I've seen him on my street."

He looked straight ahead at the road and frowned. "He knows where you live?"

I told Victor about the two instances when I woke up in the middle of the night and saw the same man in black on the street. I added, "He stared up at my window on both occasions."

Victor was now visibly upset.

I continued, "I didn't think it mattered. Besides, I had no idea I was in any danger."

"You're being stalked and you don't think it matters?"

"Please stop. You're scaring me."

"I'm sorry, it's my fault. I should have answered your questions when you asked them. Better yet, I should have told you the truth the night you arrived in Boston."

"Why didn't you?"

"As I've explained before, it's better for you to remember certain things on your own." He took a sharp turn. "We have to get that laptop. Do you have the information saved elsewhere?"

"Yes."

Satisfied that no one was following us, Victor steered the car toward College Hill. He slowly drove up the street past my place before looping around and parking several houses down from where I lived. His eyes probed the sidewalks and the spaces between each house. What struck me as odd about his paranoid behavior was that it appeared to be automatic and instinctive.

"You aren't with the CIA or anything, are you?" I asked.

He snorted softly. "They wish."

"You've dealt with this sort of situation before?"

218

"Yes."

I didn't like his curt replies, but I attributed them to his total concentration. Before unlocking the car doors and getting out, he reached into the glove compartment and pulled out what appeared to be a futuristic gun.

"That's not ours," I said, implying that the lethal-looking weapon was not from Earth.

"No."

"Is it a gun?"

"Works much the same way: aim and shoot."

We got out of the car and walked cautiously toward the house. I unlocked the door with trembling hands and was about to race up the stairs when Victor stopped me. He motioned for me to be silent. He opened the door of my apartment, forcing me to walk behind him. I covered my mouth with my hand when I caught sight of my living room. Someone had ransacked my apartment. Several books and folders were strewn across the floor, and my desktop computer was missing. A few of the kitchen cabinets were open, too. Victor went into the bedroom and checked the bathroom and closets before tucking the gun into the waist of his pants.

Relief swept through me when I opened the bedroom closet and saw the black laptop case. I handed it to Victor.

"The Word of the Phoenix," he said softly. "Pack a few things. Only take what's important; documents, passports."

I fished around my storage box for my document folder. Inside were medical records, my birth certificate, and my U.S. and EU passports.

Victor was going from window to window, monitoring the street below. "Better hurry," he said.

Grabbing a big duffle bag, I tossed in the folder, clean clothing, shoes, and underwear. I'd have to be presentable for work, so I went into my bathroom and grabbed my cosmetic bag and several hygiene products.

I came out of the bedroom lugging the bag. "Done," I said.

"You may not get a chance to come back here again, better take a second look to make sure."

219

As upset as I was to hear this advisory, I wasted no time going back into my bedroom and getting the silver charm bracelet my mother had given me on my sixteenth birthday, and a couple of greeting cards from friends. I also took a few of my best quality silk scarves.

"All set," I said.

Victor took the duffle bag and silently motioned for me to exit the apartment. I took one last peek over my shoulder. He made a visual sweep of the street before jogging toward the Mercedes. He threw the duffle bag in the backseat and got in. After handing me the black laptop case, he turned the key in the ignition. We cruised down the street in the direction of his loft. Not a word passed between us. The silence continued as he parked in the underground garage beneath his building. Only after he cut the engine did he turn to me.

Removing the sunglasses so that I could look into his eyes, he said, "Veronica, I want you to know that I really didn't want our reunion to be tainted like this. I was truly looking forward to courting you properly and enjoying our time together before..." He hesitated. "Before the fulfillment of the second prophecy began. I believe that I—that we—deserved at least that much after having waited so long to be reunited."

"You could have made your presence known to me sooner," I said. "Perhaps even as a child."

He shook his head. "I was strictly advised not to contact you until you arrived at the age of your last death."

"Why?"

"In order to not interfere with the flow of the prophecy," he replied. "You died on the first of November, 1526, on your twenty-sixth birthday. The prophecy states that you would rise from the ashes and we believed it to be on the anniversary of that fateful day. Although I could have contacted you when you turned twenty-six, I wanted your memories to return naturally. It's far less mentally and emotionally taxing when you remember on your own."

"That's when all my dreams and visions began."

"I promised myself I'd give you an entire year to remember

without any added pressure on my part. If your memories didn't come, then I would be present for your following birthday and give you a little push."

"Thus, your presence at my twenty-seventh birthday in Boston."

"Precisely."

"I wish you had come to me earlier instead of having wasted a year."

He hung his head and let out a long breath. "Had I known your safety would be in jeopardy so soon after your memory returned, I wouldn't have waited a single minute, let alone an entire year. Unfortunately, I can't predict the future. Whatever happens, I'm grateful for the moments we've had together. The time spent with you has been short, but precious, and well worth the wait."

My eyes grew misty and his words touched my heart. We left the car and he looked around before ushering me into the service elevator. The metal doors opened to a small entryway leading to the kitchen door, the loft's second entrance.

He opened the door and I heard the thin wail of a tripped alarm. With gun drawn, Victor's shadowy figure entered the kitchen and silently went from room to room. He only reentered the kitchen when the coast was clear. Reaching behind me, he punched a code into the alarm key pad.

"I'll teach you how to arm and disarm the alarm."

I rubbed my arms. "Okay."

"Don't look so glum, Veronica. It's for your protection."

"I'm sorry to cause you so much trouble."

He looked surprised. "What? No! I knew this day would come eventually. My mission here on Earth is to protect you while you fulfill the prophecy. Believe me, I've been preparing for this for a long time."

Chapter 35

Victor placed my duffle bag and laptop case by the sofa then beckoned me to sit beside him.

"I really can't go back to my place?"

"Not until it's safe to do so. We need to figure out our next move. Meanwhile, this is your home—everything that's mine is yours. My hope was that our relationship would progress to the point that you would want to move in with me. We no longer have that luxury."

A thought struck me. "Is Josh in any kind of danger?"

"It's possible that he's being monitored, especially if he's been seen with you, but I don't think he's in any actual danger."

"Who are we running from? Who wants my manifesto?"

"Repticlones."

I rubbed my temples to alleviate the headache that was coming on with impressive force. "You have more things to tell me, don't you?"

"I wanted to space this information out to allow you some time to process everything." He stood and went into the kitchen. "Now I have no choice but to give it to you all at once."

I followed him into the kitchen and watched as he filled a bowl with meaty green olives. He also cut up aged cheese and opened a bag of thin Italian breadsticks.

"What are you doing?" I inquired.

"I don't know about you, but I'm hungry."

My stomach growled. "Me too."

He retrieved the remainder of the prosecco from the refrigerator and poured it into two flutes. We set our drinks and snacks on the coffee table.

I reached for an olive. "I have a question. If you have such advanced technology and you're so superior to us, why would you need me to fulfill a prophecy, anyway? Can't you force humans into submission?"

He stared at me until I became uncomfortable. "Typical human thinking. On Earth, the strong easily force their will upon the weak."

Embarrassed, I averted his gaze. "I suppose that's not how the rest of the universe thinks."

"On the contrary. Less evolved civilizations tend to be violent. Advanced species don't need to resort to such base means. There are strict laws to keep the delicate balance of peace within the known universe. The strong cannot simply conquer the weak. There are repercussions and consequences for that kind of tyrannical behavior."

"Much like the nations of Earth," I offered.

"Yes, but on a grander scale. Every planet is allowed to govern itself how they see fit as long as universal laws are not broken. This applies to colonies, too. For example, Earth is technically our colony, but we must grant the species we've created free will to do as they please."

"Even if the planet's occupants are on the verge of self-destruction due to their own stupidity?"

"Unfortunately, yes, and that's where the Sacred Oracle and the prophecies come in. We're not allowed to interfere directly, but rather within the realm of the law. Here on Earth you humans refer to this as a legal loophole."

My cell phone rang. It was Josh. "Excuse me, Victor. I should take this call. Hello?"

"Veronica," Josh cried. "Thank God you're all right!"

"What's going on?"

"Where are you?"

Victor held up his hands and shook his head, so I replied, "At a friend's house. Why?"

"Our house is on fire!"

I almost dropped the phone. "What?!"

"Flames are shooting out of your windows right now. The firemen are trying to get it under control. The police are here looking for you. Want me to pick you up?"

Victor shook his head again. "Um, no..."

"Veronica, you sound like you're in shock. I'm coming to

223

get you right now. Tell me where you are."

I looked to Victor, who placed a finger to his lips to silence me before closing his eyes in concentration.

Seconds later, a much calmer Josh said, "You know what? I'll just tell the cops that you're out of town and can't be reached. Call me when you can, okay?"

"Okay." I looked at Victor in wide-eyed amazement. Josh hung up and I cried, "You used mind control!"

"It took me over two human centuries to be able to perfect that technique long distance. Sorry, but I had to do it."

Realization hit me. "You suspected this would happen, didn't you? That's why we retrieved the laptop."

He nodded. "The local authorities will be looking for you."

"I can't believe they torched my apartment," I said, my voice betraying my outrage. "They must have just missed us."

Victor stood and extracted a plush white towel from the linen closet in the guest bathroom, then ran the hot water in the tub. "I'm afraid I don't have any girlie bubble bath or fragrant oils, but I do have Epsom salt. It'll soothe your muscles. There's a robe behind the door."

"What are you doing?"

"Running a nice bath for you. I think it would do you good to soak and relax. Oh, there's one more thing you need." He left and came back with my flute of prosecco filled to the top.

I accepted the glass. "Thank you."

"Take your time," he said before closing the bathroom door.

I stripped and eased myself into the big claw-foot tub. Yes, I definitely needed a nice, hot soak.

Your life has never been so exciting...

Or dangerous, I reminded myself. I wondered if my manifesto would really make a difference to mankind as I closed my eyes and breathed in the steam. Could my words actually have a role in saving the planet? Victor believed they would, and the Repticlones obviously believed that, too. Why else would they follow me and torch my place?

I took a sip from the heavily steamed flute, then set it on the floor. I lowered myself into the tub, totally immersing my body in the hot water. Shortly after moving to Europe, I joined several movements for the betterment of humankind. I began ignoring the media and researching the cold, hard facts on my own. Much of the damning evidence in my arsenal came from hackers and political terrorists who stopped at nothing to find truth. I had managed to procure written statements from brave, ethical scientists exposing the outright lies made by various corporations regarding hidden perils to human health and damage to the environment. Armed with so much information, I decided to create a manifesto against the elitists destroying our planet—and the politicians supporting their agendas. I also disclosed the names of the guilty parties, which was a dangerous thing to do.

Most would argue that my methods of procuring incriminating evidence were unethical—even illegal—but my reasons were always noble. My manifesto would be more than a mere wake-up call, it would be a slap in the face.

Along with that slap, however, I offered hope. Throughout history, those who possessed knowledge, possessed power. Rich countries refused to share technology with developing nations. Without money to pay for patented information, the poor remained vulnerable for exploitation by the rich. I wanted that to change, which is why the last chapter of my book contained a list of altruistic doctors and scientists who happily agreed to share their knowledge. I listed many organizations and websites that also fostered this view. Open source, non-patented technology for all—it was a glorious thing.

There was a knock on the bathroom door. "Are you okay in there?" Victor inquired. "Can I get you anything?"

"No, thank you. I'll be out in a minute."

I got out, combed my hair, and slipped into the robe.

"Your bag is in the bedroom," Victor said when I exited the bathroom. "The first three drawers of my dresser have been emptied for you, and there's some space in the closet, too."

"Oh, you didn't have to do that, I can—"

"I insist. I know we've been intimate, but I don't expect you to share my bed until you're ready. This sofa is very

225

comfortable and I've fallen asleep on it many times."

It was indeed an awkward situation.

He continued, "I know this isn't easy for you—being caught between two worlds. Take your time to sort things out. I'd offer to leave and give you some space, but my mission must take precedence over your emotional comfort in this case."

"I don't want you to go, Victor," I assured him. "I'm overwhelmed, it's true, but I definitely want you here. When I told you that I fell in love with you the moment I saw you, I wasn't kidding."

Victor gathered me to his chest and I gazed into his exquisite eyes. With his forefinger, he gently traced a line from the curve of my cheek down to the hollow at the base of my throat. I pulled him closer to me, which evoked a moan of pleasure from him. His mouth sought mine and he kissed me hungrily while his hands caressed my back, molding my body against his own. I felt his hands at the sash around my waist. The terry robe opened in the front and he took a step back to admire my body.

"Take it off," he said huskily.

I obeyed. Without another word, he pressed my back against the nearest wall and devoured my throat while cupping my breasts. I was immediately aroused. Encouraged by my moan of pleasure, his hands began to explore other, more intimate regions of my body.

The delicious torture was too much. "Take me to bed."

Victor carried me into his bedroom. Our joining was as passionate as the night before, only now there was urgency to our lovemaking. Since our last time together, I had been followed, my house had been burned down, and I was in danger. Feeling languid and satiated, we lay in the muted glow of the late afternoon sun.

"It gets better with you every time," he said, lazily tracing the curve of my hip with his finger while I admired the intricate details of his tattoo.

"I've never felt like this before," I admitted. "It's wonderful and frightening at the same time."

"Frightening?" he asked.

"Well, I don't want to get hurt," I said hesitantly.

He laughed softly. "I've waited five centuries for you. Do you honestly think I'd leave you for the next cute blonde who walks my way?"

The question made me feel silly. "No, I guess not. But you'll have to excuse my frail human tendencies. I am, after all, a woman."

"Quite a woman, might I add." He hesitated. "May I look at what's in that laptop? It would be an honor to read your words."

"Yes."

Victor got out of bed and started getting dressed. "Great, I can start when we get back from dinner."

I reached out and took hold of his wrist. "Would you be upset if we stayed in? I don't feel like going out after everything that's happened."

"Are you sure?" When I nodded, he said, "I'll take you out to dinner another night."

We each put on comfortable athletic clothes, and he still managed to look amazingly sexy in a pair of black Adidas pants and a simple white cotton t-shirt. I grabbed my laptop and typed all the necessary security-enabled pass codes to open the document. Victor took the laptop from me and sat down on the sofa. His eyes scanned each page with fast precision.

My eyes narrowed. "You can speed-read?"

"Yes, of course," he replied, never taking his eyes off the screen. "Help yourself to anything you'd like in the kitchen."

Yes, of course? I was quickly developing a species inferiority complex. "How about I make dinner tonight?"

He looked up. "That's sweet, but we can order take out."

"I insist."

"I'd love for you to make dinner."

He resumed reading as I headed for the kitchen. "Victor?"

"Yes, my love?"

"You're not going to let me out of your sight, are you? Will you be accompanying me to work, too?"

"You don't need to work. You're my wife, Veronica. I'm capable of providing you with all the comfort and security you

227

could ever want."

"I *was* your wife." He looked offended by my thoughtless statement, so I hastily amended, "Forgive me. Let me correct that. What I mean is: I'm not used to the idea of someone supporting me after struggling on my own for so many years."

"I know how much you enjoy your job, but it's not important in the face of this greater work," he said, indicating the laptop. "This manifesto should be the number one priority in your life, especially now that the Repticlones are on to you."

"The people at Brown have been very good to me."

"I realize that, but they don't matter. I don't mean for that to sound harsh, but it's true. Anyone can do what you do at Brown, but only *you* can do the work that you've been destined for."

I couldn't argue with that. "So how do I handle this?"

"Don't go to work anymore."

"I'm not accustomed to blowing people off. Besides, it's unprofessional."

"Tell them you have a family emergency and need to take a leave of absence if it makes you feel better."

I called Dr. Nunes and informed him that I had a family emergency and needed to leave town immediately. I refrained from offering too many details in order not to lie more than what was necessary. Naturally, he was very concerned and kindly offered his help. He also assured me that he would handle things with the Human Resources department.

Victor nodded in approval when I hung up the phone.

Chapter 36

Victor came up behind me in the kitchen. "Mmm, smells good. What's in the big pot?"

"Vegetable and tofu curry. Have you finished reading?"

"Yes, it's even better than I anticipated," he replied while setting plates on the dinner table. "Your way of writing is both poetic and powerful."

I added olive oil to a fresh tomato, corn, and cilantro salad as he uncorked a bottle of chilled Müller-Thurgau. "Dinner is ready," I said, taking the lid off the basmati rice.

We sat down and he tasted the food. "This is delicious."

"I'm glad you like it."

"As far as your manifesto is concerned, even the most self-absorbed individual will be forced into feeling some kind of emotion after reading your words."

"I want people to wake up and take action."

"They will," he assured me. "Your book is going to piss off some powerful people, too."

"Do you think they'll try to hurt me?"

"I won't let anyone touch you. Not this time."

Victor washed the dishes while I went back to work. Editing made the time fly quickly.

A while later, he placed his hands on my shoulders and rubbed them. "You should get some sleep, it's late."

I pinched the bridge of my nose and squeezed my eyes shut. "What time is it?"

"Almost two."

"Oh my goodness! Already?" He picked up the laptop and walked away. "Hey, where are you going with that?"

"I'm locking it inside the bunker, as you call it."

He emerged a moment later. "You didn't think I'd leave something that precious unprotected while we went to sleep, did you? You look tired."

I went into the guest bathroom to wash my face and brush my teeth. I found Victor stretched out on the sofa with a pillow under his head.

I kissed him on the lips. "Goodnight, Victor."

"Goodnight, my little star."

I went into the bedroom and climbed into his bed, but it didn't feel right, so I got up and returned to the living room.

"I can't sleep in the bed without you in it," I said.

I saw his smile in the glow of the moonlight.

***

I worked non-stop for two days. Victor kept me well-fed by either cooking or ordering take-out. My manifesto was ready to be released by the end of the third day. To celebrate, he suggested we go out for dinner and I readily agreed.

I donned a pair of black boots, black skirt, and a blue V-neck sweater before wrapping a silk scarf around my neck.

"I'm ready," I said, tossing my hair up into a casual style.

Victor waited in the living room dressed in a pair of slim black pants, expensive suede loafers, and a green sweater.

I walked up to him. "I haven't applied any lip gloss *yet*."

His lips curved into a smile before his mouth came down on mine. He pulled away and warned, "If we continue like this we won't leave the house." He let go of me. "Wait here, I need to get something out of the bunker before we go."

He emerged with an ultra-thin vest made of otherworldly material and an alien gun.

"Is that supposed to be a bullet-proof vest?"

"Yes."

"That flimsy thing can deflect bullets?"

"It can deflect more than that." He pressed a button on the top of the gun and a flashing red light came on. "Here, hold the gun in each hand." I did as I was told and the light turned blue. "There. The gun will only work if you're the one holding it. Your fingerprints, as well as every detail of your DNA, are recorded on its memory chip."

"Incredible!"

"Please put this vest on under your sweater."

Like liquid metal, it molded itself to my body like a second skin. "Are you wearing one of these, too?" I asked, wriggling back into my sweater.

"I am," he replied. He tucked the gun into the waist of my skirt. "All set to go. Shall we?"

"Do you think we'll actually have to use these?"

"It's better to be safe than sorry."

I looked down at the sleek little gun. "This thing won't go off, will it?"

"The gun will immediately activate once you hold it in your hand. It will only shoot if your finger is on the trigger, it can't go off accidentally."

"I'm amazed by the technology of your planet."

"As you should be," he teased.

My cell phone rang as we walked out the door. It was Josh.

"Veronica?"

"Hey Josh."

"I wanted to check up on you. Sorry I didn't call sooner, but I've been busy moving. Our building was declared unsafe by the fire marshal."

Guilt washed over me. It was my fault that Josh and the other tenants were forced to relocate.

He continued, "I heard you had to leave town."

Victor mouthed the word 'who' while pointing to the phone, so I asked, "Who told you that?"

"I was picking up an order of Chinese food from that place around the corner from Brown—you know the one. Green Dragon or something. Anyway, Stephanie was there and she told me that you had a family emergency."

Relief swept over Victor's face and I replied, "That's right. I'm not sure when I'll be back in Providence.

"I didn't realize you had any family left."

Josh knew that I had lost both of my parents as a child, so I was forced to lie. "My grandmother is ill."

"Hope it's not too serious. Okay, well, I guess I'll see you around…I'm sad that we're no longer neighbors."

The forlorn tone of his voice made me feel bad. "I'm sad,

too. Thanks again and say hi to Cindy for me."

"I will." He hesitated. "Are you sure you're all right? I get the feeling that there's something wrong."

"I'm fine."

"Look if there's anything you need, let me know. I don't want to get off the phone until I'm sure you're really okay."

He was started to act clingy, which never failed to irritate me. "I'm really okay."

"Right. Take care, hon."

"You, too. Bye," I said, then hung up. Victor shook his head with a knowing smile on his face, so I added, "What? He's only trying to be a good friend."

"Josh is in love with you."

"No, he's not."

"Oh, yes, he is," he assured me while summoning the elevator. "Just because I'm not human doesn't mean I don't know how males think."

The elevator doors opened and we stepped inside. My cell phone rang again. Assuming it was Josh, I didn't bother to look at the screen as I picked up. "Look Josh, I appreciate your—"

"Veronica?" asked a woman's voice.

I pulled the phone from my ear to look at the screen. *Unknown number.* "Who is this?"

"It's Clarice Barnum. I'm calling you from my private cell." In a voice laden with urgency, she asked, "Are you okay?"

"I'm fine, Clarice, why do you ask?"

"Someone broke into my office today and went through my patient files. I don't know how to tell you this—your file was the only one stolen."

Victor took the phone from my hand and hung up on Clarice. "Did you tell your therapist anything about me?" When I nodded, he frowned. "They'll assume you're with me."

The elevator stopped. Victor placed me behind him, aiming his gun at the doors. I held my breath. Thankfully, there was no one in the parking garage. He pushed the button to go back up to his apartment.

"What do we do now?"

"We have to leave. Tonight."

"Are you serious?"

"Totally serious. The last time I hesitated getting you to safety, you were apprehended and killed. I'm not taking any chances this time. If you mentioned me to your therapist, she most certainly made note of it. The Repticlones will come here looking for you sooner or later."

"You still haven't told me why they don't want the prophecy fulfilled."

The elevator stopped. "I'm waiting for the right moment."

"Is it that bad?"

"Yes."

Victor instructed me to grab my passports and pack a change of clothing. Meanwhile, he went into the bunker to fetch my laptop.

"Ready?" he asked, heading for the door.

"Where exactly are we going?"

"Lisbon."

Chapter 37

Victor drove me to a nearby deserted parking lot and taught me how to use the gun. The ultra-sophisticated weapon had two options: temporarily paralyze or kill. We then raced to Logan Airport in his Mercedes where he purchased two business class seats on the evening flight to Lisbon. Our concealed weapons mysteriously failed to register on the X-ray machines, so we passed through security without incident and boarded the aircraft. We settled into the oversized seats at the front of the plane, and a flight attendant came by with a tray of drinks.

"Mimosa?" she inquired before handing us dinner menus.

We sipped our cocktails and Victor said, "Do you remember what I told you about the Repticlones being under the power of the Reptilians?"

"You said they were here to spy on us."

"There's more." He glanced down at the menu in his hand. "Are you sure you want to hear this before you eat?"

"Positive," I replied, reaching into the small dish of warmed mix nuts the flight attendant had placed on my tray table.

"The Reptilians send Repticlones here to influence humans, but they also have an established colony on a small planet near your moon."

"Why hasn't NASA picked up on it?"

"The only planets humans are allowed to know about are the ones that no longer sustain life. This decision was made by the Universal Council since humans are still considered primitive."

"I see. Why send cloned envoys? Why don't the Reptilians come here themselves?"

"They *can't*. Reptilians are unable to tolerate the vibrational patterns of Earth, and the temperature is too cold for them."

"You told me they were the first aliens to arrive on Earth; they created the dinosaurs."

"They did, but your planet was much hotter back then," he

explained. "When the meteor that caused the extinction of the dinosaurs hit the Earth, the force of impact knocked the planet off its original axis, causing the Ice Age. That's when the structure you know as the moon arrived."

"I knew it! Was it created by the Reptilians?"

"They don't have that kind of advanced technology," he replied. "We created the moon for two reasons: first, as a mass transport vehicle for the first exploration team and second, to save your planet."

"Otherwise, it would be uninhabitable."

"Correct. The moon controls the gravitational pull, keeping the planet as stable as possible. The abrupt climactic change dropped the Earth's temperature considerably, especially at the northern and southern poles. Without the moon the temperatures at the Polar Regions would drop further, and the ice would spread toward the center of the planet."

"This is mind-blowing," I said, excited that the theories I've nurtured for so long were finally being confirmed. "You said Earth wasn't hot enough for Reptilians. Tropical islands are very hot."

"As are the Earth's deserts, which Reptilians actually prefer. But those hot regions aren't large enough."

"Large enough for what?"

"Large enough to accommodate all the Reptilians," he replied cautiously, gauging my reaction.

I shook my head. "I don't think I understand."

"Their sun is dying and will soon become a white dwarf. They need to relocate to another planet..."

A shard of ice settled in my belly. "Are you telling me the Reptilians are planning to invade our planet?"

"Not exactly. That would go against the universal laws. An act of aggression of that magnitude would bring dire consequences to their species. The Universal Council is aware of their plight and has already assigned another planet, but the Reptilians don't like that particular quadrant of the galaxy."

My head spun. "The galaxies are divided into quadrants like neighborhoods?"

"Yes."

"And the Reptilians don't like the neighborhood—sorry, *quadrant*—they've been assigned, so they want to take over Earth, instead?"

"That's right."

"Are you kidding me?" I asked, feeling furious now that the initial shock had passed.

"They've been sending Repticlones to find and destroy the Phoenix, while at the same time influencing humans to do the unthinkable."

"Destroy our own habitat so that when we become extinct, the Reptilians can move in," I deduced.

Victor nodded slowly. "The Reptilians are ready to take over when the Earth finally reaches its breaking point and can no longer sustain life."

I silently stared out the window as I processed this information. Our greedy consumerist society with its constant need to have more was putting an enormous strain on the planet. The strategy of the Reptilians was nothing short of brilliant.

Flight attendants began taking dinner orders from the passengers in our compartment. Victor ordered for us both.

I turned to look at him. "What about the Repticlones? What happens to them once their overlords claim the Earth?"

"The Reptilians promised them independence."

The flight attendant arrived with dinner trays containing vegetarian meals: cream of leek and potato soup followed by spinach soufflé, butternut squash, and saffron rice pilaf. We quietly abated our hunger for a few minutes.

We continued our conversation between mouthfuls, only this time Victor steered it toward positive topics. After a dessert of rich chocolate cake and surprisingly decent coffee, we drifted off to sleep. I slept until the rays of the rising sun kissed my face through the airplane window.

"Hi sleepy-head," Victor said, already wide-awake.

Rubbing my neck, I inquired, "How soon before we land?"

"Another couple of hours."

We watched BBC news on the monitor attached to our arm

rests. More riots in Moscow, more violence in the Middle East, more protests against high unemployment rates within the European Union, more terrorists attacks, more devastating earthquakes...Was there ever any positive news?

I looked out the window and saw the European coastline. The sight of it brought a smile to my face.

We hopped into a taxi after landing in Lisbon, and zipped through the old city to the top of the hill where the shell of the Igreja do Carmo stood as a proud testament to the glory of Gothic architecture. The majority of the church had been destroyed during the earthquake of 1755.

The taxi let us off at the square in front of the church, and I followed Victor down a winding lane to an elegant nineteenth century building. The street level housed a charming bookshop.

"You own this bookshop?" I asked.

He unlocked the door and waved me inside. "I own this entire building. My living quarters are upstairs."

"This is lovely," I said, impressed.

I noticed a shelf behind the counter with several first-edition volumes kept prudently out of reach. I gravitated toward them as Victor's cell phone rang. He took the call outside.

"Who was that?" I asked casually when he returned.

"Charlie," he replied. "He wanted to know if I was going to miss practice. I told him I had to leave town for a while."

"I'm sure he'll put two and two together and figure out that you're with me. What about the band's New England tour?"

Victor shrugged. "I was only making music to keep myself entertained. Same with the bookshop. I've been waiting for you, Veronica. Now, nothing else matters. Icon will eventually find another talented singer and they'll become successful. More importantly, they'll continue doing humanitarian work and inciting fans to follow their example."

"You do have an incredible voice," I said, walking up to him and wrapping my arms around his waist.

He pulled me close. "What are you, a groupie?"

I nodded, looking down at his mouth. "I'm your biggest fan and the only groupie," I replied before kissing him.

Victor responded by sweeping his hands down my back and pulling me against his body. He eventually pulled away. "There's time for this later. Let me take you upstairs." He locked the shop door and led me up a white staircase. A single window allowed sunshine to fill the space with light.

"Welcome home," he said, opening a white door.

I walked into an elegant room with gleaming dark wood floors and peacock blue walls. The wainscoting, crown molding, and trim were painted crisp white. A huge copper Moroccan lamp with cutouts of blue and green glass hung from the middle of the ceiling. An oversized cream colored sofa and two matching chairs were arranged around an antique marble fireplace. An enormous Turkish carpet in shades of red, green and blue sectioned off the sitting area. One wall boasted three antique Oriental tapestries. The opposite wall had three big windows offering a stunning view of the Igreja do Carmo.

"This is gorgeous!" I cried.

"I'm glad you like it. Everything in this house has been chosen with you in mind. I remembered the colors and textures you liked. I hope your tastes haven't changed too much."

As I looked around, I realized that I would have decorated in a similar manner if I had Victor's big budget. A Tang Dynasty horse graced the mantle above the fireplace, and a large Buddha head sat atop the rustic wooden coffee table.

"How old is this?" I asked, pointing to the Buddha head.

"Mid-seventeenth century," he replied. "The Chinese tapestries on the walls are two centuries older."

I spun around to study them. "They should be in a museum."

"Is that art historian Veronica speaking or my Veronica speaking?" he asked with a twinkle in his eye.

"Art historian Veronica," I replied. "Your Veronica enjoys seeing such exquisite pieces scattered around the house."

"I thought so. Come," he said, extending his hand.

We toured the house and every few moments I was compelled to stop and closely examine some antique piece of furniture or an ancient artifact. The kitchen still had its original hearth, but several modern updates were made, including stainless steel appliances. Gracing the middle of the kitchen's marble-topped island sat a large Galo de Barcelos painted in the traditional Portuguese fashion.

I touched the charming black rooster. "I had to leave mine behind because it was too heavy to carry on the plane."

"Well, now you have this one."

The top floor of the building housed Victor's study, which had an entire wall full of books. The opposite wall was covered with antique, hand-painted blue and white *azulejos*—traditional Portuguese tiles—depicting an eighteenth century landscape.

The last room Victor showed me was the bedroom. A king-sized bed covered with a white duvet dominated the space. The walls were warm white, except for the wall behind the bed. Rather than a headboard, the entire wall was done in bas-relief plaster the color and texture of ancient stone, depicting a smaller, yet impressively accurate, replica of the most famous Manuelino window in Portugal.

"The window of Tomar!" I exclaimed.

"I noticed how much you liked it the first time you visited the Convento de Cristo, so I hired a sculptor to recreate it. I knew that one day you'd be standing right where you are now."

It took a moment for his words to make me realize something. I looked at the bottom corner of the wall; it was dated and signed seven years ago by the artist. "You followed me around the entire time that I lived here?"

"Why, yes, of course," he replied matter-of-factly.

"You said you were in the hospital the day I was born, but it never occurred to me that you stuck around. I assumed you went off to do your own thing and waited until I came of age," I said, flustered. *Why hadn't I thought of this sooner?*

"Don't think I've been stalking you constantly. Remember, I've been traveling around the world doing several humanitarian projects, but I did check up on you a lot. I was also present to witness certain milestones like the day you got your driver's license, your high-school graduation, and when your parents died."

I didn't know whether to be freaked out or flattered. Victor

239

had seen me as a geeky teenager and witnessed all of my awkward moments. He knew of the painful ones, too, such as the night a drunk driver claimed the lives of both my parents. As a child, I often experienced the uncanny notion that I was being watched. This sensation continued well into adulthood. It was a relief to discover that my paranoia was justified.

Upon reading my expression, he asked, "Does that bother you? I was only watching over you to protect you."

"I know. You were being what you are, a Watcher. You were my guardian angel."

"And I still am."

I noticed that the bed faced a wall made almost totally of tinted glass. A wide pair of floor-to-ceiling sliding doors led to a small terrace full of potted plants. The view from the terrace was charming; red tiled rooftops and the azure water of the Tagus River in the distance. Victor opened one of the doors and I stepped out into the fresh air.

"You really know what I like," I said, leaning against the iron railing.

He circled my waist from behind, pressing his warm, muscular chest against my shoulder blades. "Yes, I do," he said softly into my hair before kissing my earlobe.

He pulled my body closer to his and I felt him harden. It was enough to drive me wild. As the wintry midday sun warmed the city of Lisbon, Victor and I made love atop the king-sized bed.

Afterward, we talked while I marveled at the cleverly contrived Manuelino window above our heads. The blue and white tiled bathroom adjacent to the bedroom was big enough to allow us to shower together, and I was also glad to see a bidet again. I thoroughly enjoyed lathering Victor's body, letting my hands run over his chest muscles and the elegant line of his clavicle. He also relished the act of soaping me down with his hands, paying particular attention to my breasts and hips.

"There's one more thing I want to show you," Victor said while we dried ourselves.

"Are we going into the city?"

"Not yet."

I slipped into a pair of dark blue jeans, leather boots, and a wool sweater before running a comb through my damp hair. I grabbed my purse out of habit, then followed him down to the bookshop, only this time we went to the back of the room where a series of bookcases took up an entire wall. I watched as he pulled out a big leather encyclopedia and inserted his hand into the vacated space. I heard a beeping sound, then the bookshelves slid backward into the wall, allowing enough space for a person to walk through.

Victor winked. "I bet you didn't expect that, did you?"

"Woah…"

"Follow me," he said, stepping into the dark space.

The moment his foot touched the floor, the lights came on. I walked through the space and the massive bookshelves returned to their original location, concealing our point of entry.

"A secret passageway? Really?" I asked, stunned.

The long white corridor sloped downward. At the end was a set of stairs and a steel door with a keypad on the outside. I assumed we were several feet underground. This was so James Bond.

"Victor, you're the coolest guy I've ever met."

He grinned at me over his shoulder. "That's good to hear. By the way, welcome to my Lisbon bunker."

"This bunker is much older and better equipped than the one in Providence," Victor explained.

What an understatement! "How did you...who...when?" I stuttered. "Did you do this yourself or did you hire someone?"

"No humans were involved in its creation," he replied cryptically. Then, upon reading the question in my eyes, he said, "I have my ways."

The 'bunker' was almost half the size of a football field with high ceilings. Ultra-sophisticated pieces of equipment and giant holographic screens were grouped together in various areas.

The long sides of the enormous rectangular space, along with the short wall behind us, were composed of gleaming stainless steel. The opposite end of the rectangle was a cavernous mouth leading into a subterranean cave. A two-seater spacecraft was parked twenty feet from the edge.

Intrigued, I asked, "Is that your spaceship?"

"One of them."

"I feel like I'm in the alien version of the Bat Cave looking at the alien Bat Mobile."

He smirked. "You're quite funny, did you know that?"

"Can that thing fly at the speed of light?"

"It can."

"But it's so small," I pointed out.

"It's actually bigger than an eighteen wheeler, but it's dwarfed by the enormous space. It packs a powerful punch."

"How did you get it in here?"

"That opening leads directly into a sub-aquatic cave beneath the Tagus. My ship is amphibious, so I landed in the Atlantic and traveled underwater."

"That is beyond cool. Will you take me for a ride?"

He hesitated. "It's not a car, sweetheart."

"Is that a no?"

"It's a not yet. Let me show you something."

Taking me by the hand, he led me to the huge holographic screen that displayed Earth. The gauzy white cloud patterns swirling over the massive expanses of sapphire blue water and emerald green continents took my breath away.

Noticing my rapt expression, he said, "Earth is truly special. It's one of the most beautiful planets in the universe, in fact."

"And yet, so many people fail to see it for the paradise it is," I said, feeling suddenly sad.

"You're right—unfortunately. Humans are so consumed with silly, synthetic gadgets that they rarely appreciate the natural world around them. Come see the planet where I come from," he said, leading me to another gigantic screen.

"It looks like Earth except there's no blue," I observed.

"My home is covered in lush vegetation. Although we have some lakes and rivers, we don't have oceans. Most of our water supply is beneath the soil, which feeds the roots of the plants. It also rains daily for a short period, providing us with plenty of drinking water."

"Tell me more about your home," I prompted.

"My planet is much like Earth in the sense that it's a living, breathing organism. The food comes from trees and plants that grow out of the soil. Our fruits and vegetables look and taste a bit differently than anything you have here."

"Do you miss home?"

"Yes."

"Aside from family and friends, what do you miss most?"

"The peacefulness and the cleanliness. Unlike humans, we don't pollute our habitat, nor do we poison our food and water supplies. There are no wars. Our Sacred Oracle and our Elders are chosen for their wisdom, insight, and life experience. They are sworn to lead by example, and to always put the interest of our planet and our species before personal gain or desires."

"Sounds like Utopia."

"Oh, we have problems," he countered. "Only they're not as destructive as the ones here on Earth."

"Still, it sounds like a wonderful place to live." I noticed the screen over his shoulder and asked, "What's that?"

He turned his head. "Let's call that Planet Reptile."

I studied the sand colored orb streaked with brown and black. "So this is where the Reptilians live?"

"Yes, that's their dying planet. If you notice, this part is darker than the rest," he said, pointing to an area that appeared to be charred. "It's an uninhabitable zone due to a solar flare. As their sun starts to burn more hotly and expand, we expect to see more of these destructive flares."

"That's tragic."

"It is, which is why the Reptilians were given the option to move to another planet. They aren't the most popular species or the most pleasant to deal with, but they don't deserve to be sentenced to death, either."

He looked at the purse slung over my shoulder. "Do you have one of your pen-drives in there?"

I reached into my purse and pulled out a pen-drive. "As a matter of fact, I do. Why do you want it?"

"Is your edited manifesto on this?" I nodded and he continued, "I'm going to plug it into this device right here, which converts archaic technology into something we can decipher."

"Archaic?" I repeated. "Is our technology really so backward compared to yours?"

"I was being nice. What's the title of your work?"

"I don't have a title."

"Don't you think it merits one?"

I thought for a moment. "Human Injustice seems fitting. It worked then, why not now?"

"I agree. Human Injustice it is." He pushed a button and the words of my manifesto turned into strange symbols unlike anything I've ever seen. "What are you doing?"

"Your book is now translated into our mother-tongue," he explained. "May I upload it to our planet's database so that our

Sacred Oracle can read the words of the Phoenix?"

"Yes," I said, honored and humbled at the same time.

"There, now your book will be a bestseller on my planet," he teased. "How's that for recognition of talent?"

I blushed. "What are you doing now?"

"I've translated it into every known language on Earth."

"I've already got some people working on translation..." I trailed off.

"No need. It's been done uniformly and accurately, without sacrificing any of the nuances that can be easily lost in translation. Besides, your translators have limits, my technology does not. There are many indigenous groups who don't have written language, so it will be available in audio form. Even the most distant tribe member can listen to your words in his or her own dialect." He typed in a strange code. "I have set it up so that your manifesto can go viral instantaneously, all you have to do is push this button. Oh, there's one more thing—if you push that button the worldwide web will crash and freeze for hours, maybe even a day or two, displaying nothing but your manifesto."

Holy Hell! My finger hovered over the raised metal circle for a fraction of a second before applying pressure. In that instant, the culmination of all of my years of hard work was now accessible to everyone in the world.

Victor walked over to a small metal fridge, opened it, and extracted a bottle of French champagne. I hadn't noticed the crystal flutes sitting on top until he scooped them up in his hand.

I chuckled. "You had this whole scenario planned."

"For a very long time," he said, popping the cork. He filled each flute and held up his glass. "To you and your planet."

"Thank you, Victor."

"No, Veronica, thank you. We care about our creation and the health of this planet. Someday, humans may save a lesser evolved species that finds itself in similar danger."

"Pay it forward?" I asked before taking another sip.

"Exactly."

***

Later that night, in order to celebrate properly, Victor offered to take me out to dinner. He reserved a table at a revered Casa de Fado in the old neighborhood of Alfama. Although the neighborhood of Bairro Alto was now the trendy place to hear the fado while eating a good meal, the art historian in me preferred to stick with tradition.

We sat a candlelit table and enjoyed a wonderful seafood dinner followed by sweet rice pudding and coffee. The lights were dimmed and the musicians entered the dining room. The fadista, an attractive woman in her early forties with dark doe-eyes, sported a sheath of black satin with a traditional black lace shawl around her shoulders. The red rose in her hair matched the red hue on her lips and fingernails. She also flaunted a large Coração de Viana pendant on a chain around her neck and the intricate filigree sparkled in the candlelight. The two male guitarists were tastefully dressed in black suits, their dark hair slicked back into ponytails.

According to Portuguese etiquette, everyone must be silent for the fadista to perform. This meant no giggling or whispering, and no clinking silverware. In a true Casa de Fado, this was the moment when you could hear a pin drop. The instant her voice filled the room, I became lost in the haunting music. The fado had the power to evoke strong emotions and *saudades*, so it was without shame that I dabbed at my eyes.

It was well after midnight when we made our way home through the twisted cobblestoned streets of the Alfama. The full moon played peekaboo with sooty clouds. We both admired the Castelo de São Jorge, which was dramatically lit by electric lights.

Victor smiled wistfully and said, "I remember when the fortress was lit only by torches."

"Me, too," I admitted, surprised. "Were you still here during the earthquake of 1755?" I asked, eyeing the Igreja do Carmo in the distance as we headed up the hill.

He followed my gaze. "Yes."

"What was it like? I mean, I've read the historical accounts, but you're the only living survivor."

"There were two epic catastrophes on that fateful first of November—All Saint's Day. The initial tremor occurred early in the morning while I was grooming my horse. It was followed by two more devastating jolts. The churches in the city were offering candlelit services in honor of the holy day, and many of those candles were knocked off their perches. The cooking fires were also lit at that hour...it was disastrous. Some fires were put out, but the majority of people abandoned their burning homes. The flames spread throughout the city with alarming speed."

I shuddered. "I read that people threw themselves into the river to avoid the fire."

Victor nodded, his eyes distant. "An earthquake of that magnitude inevitably caused a tsunami. The animals had the good sense to run in the opposite direction of the river. If people had followed their example and sought higher ground, more lives would have been spared. I knew Lisbon's fate was sealed when I saw that massive wave looming on the horizon. Witnessing the devastation of our home was heartbreaking." He paused. "Rebuilding the city was a top priority, so able-bodied survivors remained to establish order. I stayed in Lisbon for several more decades, then I left Earth. I needed to go home and think."

"Think about...?"

"About what I had endured, about your expected return, about my mission, about Earth's impending doom—about everything. I needed to regroup."

"I didn't mean to bring up unpleasant memories."

"It's okay. It happened a long time ago. You're here now and the city is once again glorious."

"I didn't realize aliens get depressed."

"We most certainly do. In fact, my family and friends couldn't bear to see me hurting inside. They eventually introduced me to unattached females." He paused to gauge my reaction, then added, "I met several potential mates, but none of them compared to you."

Relief washed over me. "Is that how you normally refer to

women? 'Females' and 'potential mates?'"

"No, that's how I'm translating them for your benefit. We call them…" He then proceeded to make a strange sound.

"Have you ever fathered a child?" The question popped into my head and escaped my lips before I could stop it. "Sorry. You don't have to answer that—it's none of my business."

"I've never fathered a child, and it is indeed your business."

We both fell silent and got lost in our own thoughts as we made our way home.

The next few days passed uneventfully, allowing us time to enjoy Lisbon and each other without any drama.

One morning, while I sat leafing through books from Victor's amazing collection, he called me into his study and pointed to his computer monitor.

"Check this out," he said.

He pulled up several pages from the Internet, and each one featured a headline about the controversial manifesto entitled *Human Injustice*. News forums, social media networks, blogs, online magazines—my manifesto was everywhere! Most of the publicity was positive and encouraging, calling 'the unknown author' 'insightful' and 'brave.' Other articles painted me as a 'whistleblower.' I was already labeled a 'terrorist' in the United States for the crime of international computer hacking.

"It has begun," Victor said.

"Why does that sound so ominous?"

"Because you watch too many Hollywood movies," he teased, widening his eyes for effect. In a more serious tone he added, "We have to be extra-cautious now."

"We already wear protective vests and carry space-guns every day, what else can we do?"

"Growing eyes in the backs of our heads would be helpful."

"Very funny."

"I've been tracking the book since its launch. Everyone started posting information and articles only hours after its release—it's being called a global phenomenon."

"I hope it shakes people out of their complacency."

Later, the early evening news hinted that the identity of the

248

book's author had been discovered.

"Do you think he's serious?" I asked worriedly as Victor helped me with my coat before we headed out to dinner.

"I doubt it. The press would have already identified you. Besides, no one knows you're here, so you're safe—*for now.* We can't stay in Lisbon indefinitely."

The thought of being on the run saddened me. "I feel like going somewhere quiet tonight, if that's okay."

"Your wish is my command," he said, opening the door.

The wet sidewalks gleamed beneath the yellow light of street lamps while rain drops created tiny rings in golden puddles. We ducked into a narrow alley to avoid getting wet. A broad-shouldered man in a black coat and hat turned into the alley from the opposite direction and walked toward us. When he passed under a lit window, I froze in my tracks.

Victor stopped, too. "Veronica, what's wrong?"

"That's *him*—my stalker in Providence!"

The man lifted his hand and Victor pushed me to the ground. All I saw was a flash of white light.

Rain pelted my body as I peered up at Victor. He stood with gun lowered, staring down the alley. My mysterious stalker lay in a crumpled heap on the cobblestones.

"Sorry," he said, helping me to my feet. "Are you okay?"

"I'm fine," I replied shakily. "Did you kill that man?"

"That thing isn't a man, it's a Repticlone. It's only paralyzed. Let's make it look like he's drunk," he said, propping up the unconscious creature. "Get on the other side and pretend to help me carry him."

An upturned hat sat on the wet cobblestones, revealing the Repticlone's white-blonde buzzed haircut. I placed his heavy arm around my neck and tried to keep pace with Victor as we half-dragged the creature into the bunker.

Victor stripped off the creature's coat, revealing a fitted black cotton t-shirt and designer black pants. A weapon—not as sophisticated as Victor's gun, but still not as crude as a human gun—was tucked into the holster at his shoulder. He removed the weapon and bound our captive in metal chains.

The chains were rigged to a pulley that hung from the ceiling so that the Repticlone was standing with arms stretched upward. I wondered if the pulley and chains had been added to the bunker for this very reason.

"Sit over there," Victor instructed, pointing to a metal chair several feet away. "Set your gun to kill mode."

He extracted a glass vial from a nearby drawer, then waved it beneath the Repticlone's nose. The creature's black eyes snapped open and he began struggling wildly.

Victor watched him for a few seconds, his lip curled in disgust. "If you cooperate willingly I may consider giving you a quick, painless death."

Icy fingers crawled up my spine; I wasn't accustomed to seeing this side of Victor. The creature's eyes were so black and glassy they reminded me of something right out of a horror movie. When the Repticlone pinned me with his terrifying stare, my heart jumped.

Victor stood in the creature's line of vision so that his view of me was blocked. "What's your name?"

"You're making a mistake," the Repticlone growled.

Victor hit the creature so hard that it groaned and spat. I cringed when a slimy wad of saliva mixed with blood landed on the floor.

"Wrong answer," Victor said. "Let's try this again."

"Sebastian," the Repticlone replied in a gravelly voice.

Victor let out an irritated sigh. "Your real name."

"Reznik"

"How many of you are stationed in Lisbon?"

There was a moment of silence, but it ended quickly when Victor raised his fist again. "I'm the only one."

"Liar! How many of you are here?"

"I'm the only one—I'm not here to harm her, I swear."

Victor punched the creature once more, causing him to grunt with pain. "I'm only going to ask you one more time: how many of you are here?"

"Hear me out, will you?"

Victor knocked the thing out cold.

I stood. "Victor—"

"I'm so sorry you have to witness this, Veronica."

"What if he's not like the rest of them?" I asked quietly. "What if he's not here to harm me?"

"Why else would he be here?"

"Maybe you should listen to what he has to say."

The Repticlone moaned. "Hear me out."

"Why the hell should I?" Victor snapped. "Your kind killed her the last time she walked the Earth."

"I'm a rebel…I want to stop the Reptilians."

Hearing this, I moved toward the creature.

Victor motioned for me to stay where I was, then demanded, "Go on. Speak."

"I've been watching over the Phoenix ever since I was sent here to Earth two years ago," he explained. "I followed her from Lisbon to Providence and back again. I flew in on the same plane as you did from Boston."

I shifted my stance in order to get a better look at the Repticlone. He was about as tall and as muscular as Victor. His full mouth was a bit too wide and his unusually pale skin looked dry, almost scaly. He met my gaze.

"He's telling the truth," I said, never breaking eye contact with the Repticlone.

Victor looked at me. "How do you know?"

"Call it intuition. Besides, if he's been following me the entire time, he's surely had plenty of chances to kill me."

The Repticlone nodded at my words. "I could have killed you more times than you can—"

Victor's fist struck the creature in the mouth.

I put my hand on my lover's arm. "Calm yourself, please. Let's at least hear what he has to say."

Victor nodded. "Very well. Convince me, Repticlone. Your life depends on it."

The creature swallowed hard. "The Reptilians have a long list of women who can potentially be the Phoenix. There are many Repticlones throughout the planet, and each of us is assigned to one woman. Our job is to monitor her every move

251

until the true Phoenix reveals herself."

"What then?" I asked.

"Our mission is to destroy her." To me, he added, "Veronica, I suspected that you were the Phoenix when I followed you to several underground political rallies here in Europe. My suspicions were confirmed when Victor made contact with you in Boston."

Victor's face registered shock. "You know my name?"

"Yes," the creature said. "I know who and what you are."

Victor crossed his arms. "How? Ever since my unfortunate run-in with Nebuzak, I've learned how to exist undetected by scum like you."

"I would never have suspected anything of you either, if I hadn't believed her to be the Phoenix. I made it my business to find out what happened in 1526." He turned to me and added, "I know all about Nebuzak and your execution. The Reptilians have destroyed most of the historical records, but a few are still in existence."

"Why didn't you make yourself known to me?" I asked.

"If I had done that, who knows how you would have reacted or what kind of negative attention you would have drawn to yourself? If I continue to report nothing out of the ordinary to my superiors, they have no reason to believe that you're the Phoenix. I'm sworn to protect you, so I can't take any risks."

"If you're here to protect me, then who ransacked and torched my apartment?" I demanded.

"Another Repticlone did that—one who suspects that you're the Phoenix. He's even tried to convince me of it."

"I take it he's not a rebel like you," Victor commented.

"Not at all. Amuk is a loyal soldier."

Victor began to pace back and forth. "Reznik—"

"Please call me Sebastian."

Victor stared at him in disbelief. "Very well, *Sebastian*, how can you prove to us that you're not lying?"

Sebastian looked at me and said, "In addition to having been present at your birthday party in Boston, I know that you leave your house every morning at half past seven to be at Brown

University on time for work. You normally take a late morning break to get coffee for your boss, Dr. Nunes. I was there the day you met Victor at the coffee shop. I was also at the New Year's Eve party and enjoyed the Icon show." At this point, he turned to Victor and said, "You've got a good voice."

Victor and I stared at Sebastian in utter disbelief.

"He doesn't fit your description of Repticlones," I whispered to Victor, who shook his head, stunned. "Tell me, Sebastian, why are you rebelling against your kind?"

"I'll tell you both everything as soon as you untie me and let me rinse the blood out of my mouth." When neither of us moved, Sebastian added, "Please."

"Veronica, keep your gun aimed at him," Victor instructed while releasing our captive.

"Thanks," Sebastian said, rubbing his reddened wrists.

Victor pointed toward the wall. "There's a sink over there and paper cups in the cabinet."

Sebastian rinsed his mouth of blood, then took a seat. "Like every other Repticlone who walks the Earth, I was trained to find the Phoenix and prevent the prophecy from being fulfilled. Our overlords, the Reptilians, want this planet for themselves. In exchange for our support—as if we even have a choice in the matter—we will be allowed our independence."

"Freedom from tyrannical rule sounds like a good incentive to me," Victor pointed out.

Sebastian shook his head. "According to our rebel spies, the Reptilians plan to annihilate us the moment we're no longer useful, then take over our planet."

"I thought such acts of aggression were against the laws of the universe," I interjected.

"Oh, there are ways to go around that law," Sebastian explained. "Maybe they'll release a deadly virus or try to artificially induce a natural disaster. What you need to know is this: once they have Earth under their control, they plan on conquering other planets in order to expand their territories. Their ultimate goal is to create an empire."

"If what you say is true, why haven't you reported it to the

Universal Council?" Victor challenged.

"We don't have any concrete proof," Sebastian replied. "There aren't many rebels, but we're doing all we can to make sure that humans succeed in saving their planet. That way, the Reptilians will have no choice but to move to the quadrant designated by the Universal Council."

"You won't gain your independence," I pointed out.

Sebastian's coal black eyes locked on mine and he smiled at me, revealing a set of surprisingly perfect teeth. "No, we won't, but the designated planet would put a greater distance between them and us. It's surrounded by Universal Council outposts. The Reptilians would be watched and monitored much more closely than they are now, which is something our overlords don't want."

Victor added, "The Reptilians don't have the same level of technology that we do, therefore a greater distance means a greater burden of travel."

"They can't travel at the speed of light?" I asked.

Sebastian shook his head. "Our colony was established close to Earth for this reason—so that we can get here quickly."

The Repticlone then lifted his shirt to reveal a muscular torso. He touched his ribs gingerly and winced in pain. Two nasty bruises were blossoming on his skin. Oddly, I was somewhat relieved to see his navel because it meant that he had been born in a conventional manner and not hatched from an egg like a reptile. To my chagrin, he caught me staring at his body. I instantly averted my gaze.

Victor said, "Let me get some ice for that."

"I didn't mean to frighten you, Phoenix," Sebastian offered quietly. "I was only trying to protect you."

"Please call me Veronica, and I'm sorry about...*that*," I said apologetically, indicating his wounds.

Victor returned with an ice pack and looked from me to Sebastian, then back to me again. Frowning slightly, he handed the ice to the Repticlone.

"She's in danger," Sebastian said, gripping Victor's wrist. "You must take her somewhere safe. She needs to get the Word

254

out to the humans."

"We've already done that," I blurted out.

Victor gave me a look of disapproval while Sebastian's face registered surprise. "Part of the prophecy has already been fulfilled?"

"Veronica's manifesto has gone viral," Victor explained.

"This is great news!" Sebastian said happily.

Victor seemed surprised. "You didn't know? I'd think the Repticlones would be on the watch for something like that."

"Since our every move is monitored and can be easily intercepted by the Reptilians, I abstain from computers and rarely use a cell phone," Sebastian explained. "The reason for this is due to my close proximity to the Phoenix. I don't wish to draw attention to myself. The loyal soldiers will have already sent a report to our overlords. If you sent the Word from here, Lisbon will soon be crawling with Repticlones."

"They may suspect my whereabouts, but not my identity," I pointed out.

Sebastian's eyes sought mine. "Amuk is coming for you, Veronica. He arrived this morning in Lisbon." To Victor, he added, "I was on my way to your house to warn you when you shot me."

PART III

THE SACRED ORACLE

The contemplation of celestial things will make a man both speak and think more sublimely and magnificently when he descends to human affairs.

—Marcus Tullius Cicero, c. 30 BCE

CHAPTER 39

Victor and I retreated to the corner of the room to speak privately while Sebastian nursed his wounds.

"What do we do now?" I whispered.

"We need to get you out of the city." He opened various Internet pages on his cell phone. "There are no flights out of Lisbon at this late hour. Let me check morning flights...Okay, the only one that isn't sold out goes to Mozambique."

"No," I said. "I prefer to stay within the EU."

He continued searching. "I can get two seats on the afternoon flight to Paris." He waited for me to nod. "Done."

I sighed. "What about Sebastian?"

"I'm completely unprepared for this situation," Victor confessed. "I've always believed the Repticlones were stupid, mindless beings programmed to stop the prophecy from being fulfilled."

"I'm neither stupid nor mindless," Sebastian cried. "I can hear every word you're saying over there, you know."

Victor sighed and pinched the bridge of his nose. "Let me take care of those bruises." Reaching into a sleek metal box by the sink, he extracted a hypodermic needle and a small jar. Handing me the latter, he said, "I'm going to inject Sebastian's wounds. When the needle comes out of the skin, apply one of these."

The clear glass jar contained a moistened stack of circular pads. "What's this?"

Victor smiled. "You'll see. Lift your shirt, Sebastian."

I knelt beside the chair and waited as Victor injected both bruises. I felt the heat of Sebastian's stare as my fingertips pressed the pads onto the rock hard muscles of his torso. Miraculously, the bruises vanished in seconds.

"Are you going to inject his lip, too?" I asked. "It's cracked and bleeding where you punched him."

Victor was already heading toward the sink. "No need, just apply one of the pads," he replied over his shoulder.

Sebastian's eyes held mine as I placed the circular pad against the open skin of his lip.

Victor returned and extended a hand to the Repticlone. "Your injuries have been healed. I'm sorry for hurting you."

Sebastian stood and I noticed that both aliens were at eye-level. He took Victor's proffered hand and shook it. "You were only trying to protect the Phoenix; I would have reacted the same way."

"We have much to talk about, you and I," Victor said.

"Yes, we do," Sebastian agreed.

"How many rebels are on Earth right now?"

"Less than a hundred, but our numbers are growing quickly. We've begun to evolve."

"What do you mean by evolve?" Victor demanded, puzzled. "The Reptilians were careful to only use the human genes that pertained to physical appearance and climactic tolerance so that you could blend in here on Earth. The rest was discarded."

Sebastian looked smug. "So they thought. Recently, some Repticlones have begun openly exhibiting human traits like independent thinking, compassion, guilt—even love."

Victor appeared surprised. "Do the Reptilians know?"

"Unfortunately, yes. Rebels who display human traits are destroyed immediately, which is why some of us have developed the ability to deceive. Our survival now relies totally on secrecy and lies."

"Deception; a most human trait," I commented.

Sebastian nodded. "It's another reason why the Reptilians want us dead once we've completed our mission. They know we'll continue to evolve intellectually and emotionally, making it difficult to control us."

"You've given us much to ponder over," Victor said.

"Maybe it would be a good idea if we sat down and talked like civilized people," I said. "Victor and I feel terrible for this misunderstanding. Since we're not going anywhere tonight, would you like to have dinner with us?"

Sebastian's face registered disbelief. "I would be honored."

I handed him his coat. "Your hat may still be in the alley."

"Thank you." Patting his empty holster, he asked, "Ah, Victor, are you going to return my gun?"

"No," Victor replied. "I'll do better—I'll give you one of mine. You may need it if you run into Amuk."

The three of us left the house and retraced our steps to the alley where Sebastian retrieved his soggy hat. Victor positioned himself between me and the Repticlone as we walked to a cozy little restaurant. Candles flickered on each table and patrons conversed in hushed tones. We requested a table toward the back, settled into our seats, and ordered dinner along with wine.

Victor asked, "Does Amok know I'm here in Lisbon?"

"He believes Veronica is alone," Sebastian replied while staring at me over the candle flame. The light failed to separate the Repticlone's pupil from its iris.

I quietly sipped my wine as Victor practically interrogated Sebastian with questions about his home planet and their most recent technology. They also discussed tactics and strategies for defeating the Reptilians. I tried to keep up with the conversation, but every once in a while they would veer off onto subjects that simply didn't exist in my realm of understanding. I was relieved when the food finally arrived.

Unlike Victor, Sebastian was a carnivore. His thick, bloody steak was practically raw and he tore into it hungrily. When he eyed Victor's cooked vegetables he made no comment, but I could see the question in his eyes. I ordered the traditional bacalhau, consisting of boiled codfish and potatoes drizzled with olive oil. Thankfully, the conversation during dinner was a bit more palatable. We discussed the evolution of the Repticlones and the possibility of their future liberation.

"I would sacrifice my life if it guaranteed the freedom of my people," Sebastian said after swallowing the last bite of steak.

"That's very noble of you," I commented. "Hopefully, it won't come to that."

We nibbled on cheese and sipped white port for dessert. Sebastian inquired about my manifesto.

"What's the title?" he asked after I'd given him a brief description of its contents.

"Human Injustice," I replied.

"Same title as last time." He stared into his port, hesitated, then asked, "May I read it, please?"

"You can borrow one of my pen-drives."

Victor caught my eye and said nothing. After dinner we walked back to the house and invited Sebastian upstairs. His sharp black eyes took in every detail.

I extracted a pen drive from the desk drawer in Victor's study. "Here you go, Sebastian."

"Thank you," he said, tucking it safely away in his pocket. "I'll read it as soon as I get home and return it tomorrow."

Another speed reader.

Victor walked to the sideboard and poured brandy for the three of us. "To aid in digestion."

We accepted the crystal snifters and sipped slowly.

"What reaction do you anticipate from the humans?" Sebastian asked of Victor.

"Let's hope they assume responsibility for their survival and take action to save their planet."

"Our fates are intertwined." Sebastian finished his brandy and set down the glass. "Thank you for a memorable evening. It's very late and I should go."

We were about to show him out when Victor's cell phone rang. "It's Charlie. He's tried calling me twice today. I should take this call."

Victor retreated to the study, leaving Sebastian and I alone.

"To have finally met you face to face is an honor; breaking bread with you was a privilege," Sebastian said.

I smiled. "I'll escort you out."

I led Sebastian downstairs and he followed me as silently as a serpent. I reached the door and when I turned around, his face was only inches from my own. His eyes were so black and intense that I couldn't tear my gaze away; I was completely mesmerized. The more I stared into those fathomless obsidian pools, the deeper their magnetic pull.

Long black tentacles, smooth and dry as snakeskin, gently coiled around my ankles. Gradually, more of these sinuous creatures began slithering up my legs, curling themselves around my wrists and creeping up my arms. Ever so gently, they pulled me beneath the surface, urging me toward a downward spiral. I fell into infinity, the tentacles coiling around me, caressing my skin, filling me completely with nothing but obliterating blackness. One of them slowly circled my navel and started inching its way between my legs. I was consumed by the sweet torture, and an aching, urgent need began to grow from deep within me.

To my horror, I realized that Sebastian was hypnotizing me; rendering me motionless much the same way a snake would its prey. He squeezed his eyes shut and shook his head violently from side to side, breaking the spell.

"Forgive me," he whispered in a ragged voice while averting his gaze. "It's instinctive and I can't always control it."

"What was that?" I demanded breathlessly. "I couldn't move and..." I stopped, not wanting to describe the darkly erotic experience any further.

"I was pulling you in," he explained, still not meeting my eyes. "Again, I'm so sorry…it wasn't my intention. That was pure animal instinct. We're still evolving."

"Is that something you do to your prey before eating it?"

"No," he replied, stepping through the doorway.

The rain was coming down hard now. He placed the damp hat on his head, pulling the rim low over his eyes. I gripped the doorframe for support as I continued to look at him askance.

He finally raised his troubled eyes to mine. "It's what male Repticlones do to their females before mating."

Without another word he turned and ran, melting into the wet night. I stood in the doorway staring after him. Victor's tall silhouette appeared in the doorway as I climbed the stairs.

"Everything okay?" he asked.

"Fine," I replied with forced cheerfulness.

Liar.

Victor kissed my lips. How could I possibly explain what

261

occurred downstairs with Sebastian? The Repticlone was obviously mortified and repentant. Telling Victor would only create an unpleasant situation. Perhaps it would be better to simply forget the whole matter and pretend it never happened.

A giant black snake slithered into my dreams, each of its ebony scales reflecting a color of the rainbow. The serpent slithered toward me, raising itself until it stood completely on end like the feared Black Mamba of Africa. It coiled around my body, caressing every inch of my naked flesh. Its forked tongue came out to hiss at me and entered my mouth, swirling around my tongue. Several slithering tentacles forced my legs apart— each one teasing me, delighting me. My eyes flew open. Victor was coaxing me awake with his caresses.

"I need you," he whispered.

Our joining was hot and urgent. I came to know a side of Victor he had not yet revealed; a bestial side that excited me. It was just before dawn when I finally fell asleep again. I dreamed of brilliant stars floating in space, swirling into patterns that were mysteriously familiar to me.

***

The first thought to pop into my head when I woke up the following morning was the giant black snake in my dream.

"Good morning, beautiful," Victor said, kissing my temple.

I snuggled close to him. "Good morning."

"Coffee?"

"Please."

I watched him get out of bed, marveling at his feline grace. "We have a lot of time to kill before our flight."

"How about a long walk along the river?"

I peered out the window. "Sounds great."

We walked along the coast after breakfast, stopping at various shops to admire the local handicrafts, then we enjoyed a nice lunch. Victor glanced at his watch and announced that we should head back in order to not miss our flight. It was a relief to forget about our worries and act like a normal couple— even if only for a moment. I bade Lisbon a silent farewell as I followed him out of the restaurant.

Chapter 40

To our mutual shock, the bookshop's door had been forced open while we were out having lunch.

Experiencing the familiar chill of anxiety, I placed my lips to Victor's ear. "Do you think it's Amuk?"

He peered through the crack of the partially opened door and whispered, "If it is, he could still be inside."

I placed my hand on his arm. "Let's get out of here."

"What if he finds the bunker? There's sensitive information stored in there. I'm going to confront him. Get this over with once and for all so we don't have to keep looking over our shoulders." He scanned the street, eyes darting everywhere. "Go into the first shop you see—the more people inside, the better. Stay out of sight."

"Are you crazy? I'm not leaving you!"

"Veronica, this is no time to argue," he admonished while reaching for his gun.

"The last time you pulled this stunt, it ended badly."

He placed me behind him, mumbling something about my innate stubbornness. "Set your gun to kill mode. Stay close to me and be silent."

Silently, we crept into the bookshop. Fortunately, the giant bookcase leading to the bunker was untouched.

Thump!

We both looked up at the ceiling.

Thump, thump!

"Stay here," Victor said, heading toward the staircase.

"Wait, you can't go up there alone."

"Don't argue with me!" He frowned, his expression anxious. "Should something happen to me—"

"Victor, I swear if you—"

He clamped his hand over my mouth. "Listen carefully, my love. Go into the bunker and lock the door behind you. The cabinet closest to the door contains a communication device. Push the green button and follow the directions *precisely*. Do you understand?"

I nodded and he lifted his hand from my mouth. "Victor, I love you."

"I love you, too, but you have to be brave and do exactly as I've told you."

A big Repticlone appeared unexpectedly on the stairs. Victor lifted his gun and pulled the trigger. The creature ducked and fired his own weapon.

"No!" I cried as I watched Victor's shoulder jerk backward. The gun fell from his hand and he hit the floor.

The Repticlone took aim for another shot. I fired a white laser beam directly at the creature's chest. It fell instantly. I shot the intruder in the head for good measure.

"Veronica, you've already killed it," Victor said hoarsely, clutching his shoulder and wincing in pain.

I knelt beside him to determine the extent of the damage. "The bullet went straight through the flesh."

"Bunker," he said faintly.

Although he was much bigger and heavier than me, the adrenaline shooting through my body gave me enough strength to prop him up. He leaned against me as I led him into the bunker.

"Where do you keep that healing stuff you injected Sebastian with?" I demanded, urging him toward a chair.

He groaned. "That was the last of it."

I froze. "What?"

"I don't have any more. Besides, it's useless." He grimaced. "The venom is already in my veins..."

"What venom?"

"Must get anti-venom," he slurred, his eyes rolling into the back of his head. "The bullets...damn Repticlones."

Tears stung my eyes, blurring my vision. "Damn it! There's no way I'm going to let you die on me, Victor!"

"Sebastian will know what to do," he whispered.

Repticlone bullets were laced with venom?! WTF???

264

Sebastian mentioned that he would return the pen-drive today. Had he already come by while we were out? Instinctively, I reached for my cell phone.

"Damn it," I said, jamming it back in my pocket. Assuming he even had a cell phone, I didn't have the number.

I stumbled out of the bunker blindly, not knowing what to do. My helplessness only made me angry as I headed toward the front of the bookshop. Seized by overwhelming hatred, I kicked the dead Repticlone repeatedly.

The door creaked open. "Hello?"

My knees went weak with relief at the sight of Sebastian. "I need anti-venom right now!"

One look at the dead Repticlone and no more words were needed. I led him into the bunker where Victor was now on the floor, shaking and drenched with sweat.

Sebastian removed a tiny vial from around his neck and unscrewed the cap. "Injection would be quicker than ingestion."

A glass beaker containing several individually wrapped hypodermic needles caught my eye. I ran over, grabbed one, and handed it to Sebastian. "Here, you do it."

Inserting the tip into the clear liquid, he carefully filled the small tube. Victor let out a moan and writhed in pain the moment the anti-venom was injected into his body.

"What's happening to him?" I demanded. "I thought the anti-venom was supposed to help him!"

There was pity in Sebastian's eyes. "It does," he assured me. "The problem is that it burns up the venom in the bloodstream much the same way that acid would."

"Oh my God," I cried, horrified.

Sebastian's strong arms came around me, pressing me to his hard chest. "It'll be over soon."

Victor became still and silent.

I pushed the Repticlone away from me and knelt beside Victor to take his pulse. "Is he okay?"

Sebastian also knelt beside Victor and lifted one of his eyelids in order to check the pupil. "He should be fine in a few hours. He needs rest now."

We looked around the enormous space for a cot or anything Victor could recline upon, but there was nothing except a few chairs.

"We can take him upstairs," he suggested. "Have you been up there since Amuk broke in?"

So that was Amuk. My eyes narrowed. "How do you know he broke in?"

"Tampered lock, splintered doorframe, but what really gave it away was the dead Repticlone at the foot of the stairs with two holes in him."

I felt guilty for doubting him. "No, I haven't."

"Best if I go up first to make sure it's safe."

"Safe?"

He paused in the bunker's doorway. "Who knows what kind of trap he could have set for you. Good thing Victor was here to protect you."

"Victor didn't kill him…I did."

Sebastian's eyes lit up. "Gorgeous and deadly."

Realizing what he said, he blushed and turned to go. I stroked Victor's brow and spoke soothingly as I waited for Sebastian's return. He came back several minutes later and assured me there was no danger.

Sebastian lifted Victor effortlessly. "As soon as we put him to bed, I'll fix the outside lock and dispose of Amuk's body. No one must know he was here."

"Why?" I asked, following him down the corridor.

"If the Reptilians find out that a Repticlone came here and disappeared, it would look suspicious. They'd want to investigate," he explained as he stepped over the dead body and ascended the stairs.

Sebastian placed Victor on the bed. "I'm going to fix the lock now. Stay here with him."

"Okay."

Were it not for Sebastian's timely arrival, Victor would most certainly be dead. The thought of losing him made my heart ache. "Sleep, my love. You'll be better soon."

Exhausted, I went into the bathroom and splashed cold water

on my face. I checked the time and cursed under my breath. The flight to Paris would take off in an hour.

I went downstairs to check on Sebastian and asked, "Do Repticlones normally lace their bullets with venom?"

Glancing up at me while fixing the lock, he replied, "Yes, most of the time."

"Why?"

He stopped what he was doing. "We produce venom in abundance and our bite is deadly, so it's prudent to keep a vile of anti-venom on hand. Accidents happen sometimes."

"Or shootings."

Sebastian closed the repaired door with satisfaction, then heaved Amuk's corpse over his shoulder with apparent ease. "I need to get rid of this body at once."

I followed him back to the bunker. "How?"

The corpse was unceremoniously dumped on the floor where it landed with a dull thud.

Sebastian shrugged. "Dismemberment. Acid or fire."

"Oh, God." I covered my mouth.

"You don't have to stick around, you know," he said, sensing my revulsion. "I've been trained to endure worse."

A rush of pity went through me. What kind of life did this poor creature lead? "Thank you, Sebastian. Were it not for you, Victor would be dead."

"I debated grabbing a coffee before coming here," he confessed. "Glad I didn't."

Resisting the tug of his hypnotic black eyes, I said, "May I offer you something to drink before you..?" I couldn't finish the sentence; it was simply too grisly for words. "I don't know about you, but I'm badly shaken and need to take a break."

"All right."

"I can make coffee, otherwise there's water, tea, wine..."

"Whatever you're having is fine."

"I think a cup of soothing tea is in order."

He followed me upstairs into the kitchen. The simple ceremony of making tea had a therapeutic effect on me.

Sebastian looked around the kitchen, then suddenly asked,

"Do you really want me here?"

The direct question caught me off guard. "Why wouldn't I? You've just saved the man I love."

"Because of what I did to you last night."

The darkly erotic experience was hard to ignore. "Please don't beat yourself up over that."

"It's something we really can't control—at least not yet."

"I understand and I forgive you," I assured him. It seemed as if he was going to say something then stopped. "What is it?"

"Ever since I learned of your existence, my only desire has been to find you and keep you safe. Imagine my joy and utter surprise when I was assigned to you! The rebels were relieved, too. I can't imagine what would have happened if another Repticlone had been assigned to track you." He paused. "I pledged a vow to you."

His spontaneous confession left me flabbergasted. "A vow?"

His face lit up eagerly, like that of a little boy. "May I offer it to you right now?"

"Yes, of course."

Sinking down on one knee and taking hold of my hand, he reminded me of a medieval knight. "Precious Phoenix, you are my only salvation. I vow to protect you from harm with my body and every ounce of strength that I possess."

I was touched by his declaration. "Your loyalty is deeply appreciated, Sebastian. Thank you."

He threw his arms around my waist, pressing his cheek against the flatness of my stomach. "Do you have any idea what it's like?"

Stunned and moved by pity, I stroked his hair in an attempt to comfort him. "I cannot imagine."

He pulled back to look up at me, his eyes pained. "I've been walking in your footsteps every day for the last two years," he said. "I'd follow you to work and wait outside for hours only to get a glimpse of you again. The sight of you fills me with hope; your beauty and grace fill me with awe."

"Sebastian, I..." I didn't know what to say to this declaration of..? Of admiration? Of loyalty? Of stalking?

"Veronica," he whispered.

His black eyes glittered with unshed tears. I felt the familiar caress of a smooth tentacle on the base of my spine. It slid up each vertebra with feathery softness, making me shiver in delight.

"Veronica."

I drowned in soothing blackness as strong hands gripped my shoulders and pulled me forward. The clever tentacles became fingers as they stroked my hair. Warm lips kissed my neck, my temples, and finally, my mouth.

A piercing whistle escaped the tea kettle, breaking the hypnotic spell. Sebastian and I stood in the kitchen, wrapped in each other's arms. I took a step back, unsure of what exactly had transpired. Did he really kiss me or had I imagined it?

"If we're to become friends, Sebastian, you must promise never to do that again," I warned.

He hung his head in shame. "I couldn't help myself."

"That's what you said last time. I love Victor, do you understand?"

"Yes."

I reminded myself that the Repticlones were only beginning to evolve. Despite being a full grown male, Sebastian's emotions were as immature and fragile as those of an adolescent. I wanted to reprimand him for what he had done, but I didn't want to be responsible for scarring him emotionally.

I busied myself by making tea. "Sugar or honey?"

He looked up guiltily. "Neither."

"Here," I said, handing him the cup.

"Thank you."

"Why don't we sit on the balcony off the bedroom so that I can keep an eye on Victor?" I suggested crisply.

He agreed and followed me upstairs. Victor was still sleeping soundly. We sat down on the black metal café chairs and admired the view.

He looked miserable. "I really am sorry."

"I really do forgive you—*again*—but I may not forgive you a third time. Take note; it's unfair to lure a woman like that.

Good thing human males don't have that power, although I'm sure they would love it."

We sipped our tea quietly for a few minutes. I glanced over my shoulder at Victor. "How long will he be out?"

"Shouldn't be much longer. Lucky it was his shoulder and not a major organ."

A whizzing noise made me flinch. Something burned my cheek and exploded directly behind my head. Bits of plaster splashed into my teacup. Sebastian shoved me off the chair and I landed on my back with a jarring thud. He fell on top of me, smothering my body.

I could barely breathe. "What the—"

His hand clamped down over my mouth. I felt his arm grip me tightly against his muscular frame as he moved us into the bedroom. Another explosion hit the doorframe of the terrace and a shower of plaster littered the floor.

"Stay low! Get Victor off the bed and take cover in the bathroom," he ordered, pushing me in the direction of the bed.

Crouching low, I dragged Victor into the bathroom then peered through the door crack. Sebastian aimed his gun and shot at the unseen assassin outside.

"Amuk wasn't alone in Lisbon," he said, ducking out of range. "Stay back, Veronica!"

A ripple of pure terror went through me. If other Repticlones knew that Victor and I were here...

I saw movement on one of the terracotta roofs. A black figure aimed a gun at Victor's terrace. The bullet hit the carved Manuelino window above the bed and stone colored plaster fell in tiny bits over the white duvet.

Sebastian took cover behind the wall, then cautiously fired another shot. Nothing happened after that. In fact, the sniper was nowhere to be seen. After waiting a few minutes, he walked toward me with a grin. "Got him."

No sooner had he said the words than a bullet burst through his forehead.

Sebastian!

I gripped the sink as my knees buckled from shock. A

scream boiled in my lungs, but I bit my tongue in order not to give away the fact that I was still alive. I raised my eyes to the mirror. My cheek had been grazed by the first bullet—Repticlones laced their bullets with venom!

I glimpsed the sniper through the door crack. Dressed in black, he stared at Victor's apartment a long time before moving toward the roof elevator.

I needed anti-venom—fast! Since Sebastian had the habit of wearing a vial around his neck, maybe Amuk did, too. The sniper was most likely on his way to Victor's house right now. How many others were with him? I had to get to the bunker immediately.

I cast a sad glance at Sebastian's dead body, then gritted my teeth and dragged Victor across the smooth wooden floors. I paused for breath and wiped the sweat off my forehead. The venom was already working its way through my bloodstream.

It took the last bit of willpower and strength I possessed to drag him downstairs into the bunker. At least I had the good sense to lock the door behind me before dropping to my knees beside Amuk's body. Rigor mortis had already set in, and I cringed at the thought of touching the alien corpse. I tried to smother my rising panic as my trembling hands fumbled with his shirt buttons.

"Yes!" I cried, seeing vial around his neck.

I unscrewed the cap and drank the contents. It tasted bittersweet. Another wave of dizziness hit me as searing pain cut across my face.

Grabbing onto whatever I could, I made it to the cabinet closest to the door. Inside was a sleek silver device with a blank screen. I pressed the green button as Victor had instructed earlier and the screen turned blue. Propping it on the floor, I fell into a fetal position. Victor's handsome face appeared on the screen.

'If you're watching this video, I'm most likely dead. I'm sorry, Veronica. Please know that I would have given my life over and over again to protect you. You're too important to me, my little star—important to all of us. I love you and I'm counting on you to be brave. Now, you must follow my instructions carefully.

'What I'm about to tell you may be hard to accept, but it's the truth. The spaceship in the bunker was built especially for you, in anticipation of this moment. Your place is not Earth, but rather my planet—our planet. Everything will soon be explained to you, and my words will make sense. All in good time.

'You must go inside the ship and carefully enter the exact coordinates that I'm about to give you. I'll resume speaking in fifteen minutes. Take this time to enter the spacecraft.'

I stared at the screen in horror. The thought of entering the alien spaceship and traveling at the speed of light to another planet was terrifying. Of course, it definitely had its allure, too. Could humans safely travel at that speed? What about oxygen?

Victor would never put you in harm's way.

For once, the little voice inside my head was right. I looked over at Victor, who was still sleeping soundly. What if the anti-venom didn't heal him completely? What if there were side-effects? Human technology wasn't sophisticated enough to deal with this sort of thing. He needed Watcher technology.

The need to secure Victor's health and safety trumped my fear. I stood and picked up the silver device. Running to the ship, I opened the door and placed it on what looked like a hi-tech dashboard. Three minutes had elapsed. I had twelve minutes to get Victor into the passenger seat.

Dragging him across the floor was relatively easy. Lifting him up was a different story. It took most of the twelve minutes to get him into the seat. By the time I sat down behind the control panel, I was panting from exertion. The screen lit up again.

'By now you should be inside the spacecraft. There is a metal arm to your left with a blue lever. Flip the lever until you hear a hum and sit back in the seat with your hands above your head. Hold very still.'

I maneuvered my body so that I could flip the blue lever and hold up Victor's hands. Two silver straps came out of the sides of the seat. They went from the shoulders to the hip and crossed over the torso. I dropped Victor's arms and repeated the procedure to secure myself into the seat. A loud noise made me turn my head. Someone was outside the door, shooting at the bunker's lock.

Repticlones!

'Next, flip the green lever beneath the blue one so that your helmet can provide you with oxygen.'

I did as I was told and a semi-clear helmet made of a material not found on Earth lowered itself onto Victor's head. The clear, pliable breathing apparatus adjusted itself over his nose and mouth. I repeated the same for myself.

'There are two blue rectangular keys on the control panel. One will securely lock the spacecraft and the other controls cabin pressure. Press them both now.'

It sounded like someone was trying to break down the bunker door. I hadn't bothered to activate the secret bookcase in my haste. The corridor leading to the bunker was clearly exposed. I may as well have left neon signs for the Repticlones to follow me.

How could you be so careless, Veronica?

How many of them had traced Amuk to Victor's house? I pushed the keys while mentally willing the instructions to just hurry up!

'There is a key pad with seventeen symbols you will not recognize. I will visually show you each symbol and you will press the corresponding key. Do it now.'

I paid close attention to the images on the screen and pushed the correct keys on the first try. Go, girl!

'The autopilot switch is directly above your head. Turn it on now.'

I turned it on and the spacecraft came to life.

'Bon Voyage, my love. You will see space briefly when we exit Earth's atmosphere, and I will tell you when to place the ship in light-speed mode. Enjoy the view.'

The small ship levitated smoothly and made its way into the dark cave. The sound of bullets bouncing off the stainless steel

273

walls made me look over my shoulder. Three big Repticlones were running toward the ship. Beneath their angry frowns, black eyes glittered with hatred. One of them caught my eye and shook a fist at me. I smiled and flipped him off.

The cabin pressure remained the same as the ship went underwater and glided over the river bed. At the point where the Tagus River flowed out into the Atlantic Ocean, the ship picked up speed, zipping over the murky ocean floor. When we were far enough away from the coast, the ship burst out of the water and into the sky at incredible speed. What was truly remarkable was that it simply went straight up, as if we were in a giant, high-speed elevator. My stomach lurched, as if I was on a roller coaster. Other than that, I was fine.

First I saw Portugal's coastline, then the continents of Europe and Africa. I gasped in awe when we broke through the atmosphere. There was no more blue sky! I could see satellites! Tears automatically ran down my face as a deep surge of emotion took hold of me. I was humbled by what my eyes beheld. From my vantage point, Earth was more spectacular than any of the NASA photos I'd seen. I was awestruck by the incomprehensible amount of stars. Each one twinkled like a dazzling miniature sun. I knew that I was a part of this glorious wonder, this biomorphic universe that teemed with precious life. This realization filled me with profound sense of joy and serenity.

The ship gradually changed its course and I spotted the moon. My heart was so full—I was beyond ecstatic. The screen lit up again and Victor's face appeared.

'The white button overhead will make the ship travel at light speed toward home. The cabin pressure will hold, protecting you from within, but what you see with your human eyes may cause motion sickness. There is a silicone bag beneath the seat. Push the button now.'

How practical of Victor to remember my frail, human body. Placing the hi-tech vomit bag on my lap, I took one last look at the amazing scene around me and pressed the light speed button. I was instantly thrown back against my seat with great force. I slowly opened one eye to take a peek. Everything was a blur—like speeding through a lit tunnel. When the expected wave of nausea didn't happen, I opened the other eye.

Victor moaned beside me.

"Victor?" I said, leaning forward in my seat.

He opened his eyes. "Veronica?"

I reached out to hold his hand. "We're in the ship, my love. I'm taking you home."

My words sobered him instantly. His eyes scanned the control panel to check if everything was in order. "You're an amazing woman, did you know that?"

"And you're quite thorough with instructions."

He noticed the wound on my cheek. "Your face…"

"Grazed by a Repticlone bullet. Don't worry, I took anti-venom. You did, too." My eyes welled up. "Oh, Victor…"

His face grew serious. "Tell me what happened."

I told him about the attack on the terrace. I owed Sebastian so much and it pained me that I could never repay him. "Soon after Sebastian saved your life, he was killed trying to protect me."

"Sebastian's sacrifice will never be forgotten, nor will he have died for nothing. The Universal Council will be apprised of the Repticlone rebel groups, and how they have united to support our cause."

"If the truth is revealed to the other Repticlones, won't they join the rebels to fight against the Reptilians?"

"With the Universal Council backing them, I would think so. The Reptilians will have no choice but to transfer to the planet that's been chosen for them."

"And if they refuse?"

Victor frowned. "Force will be used, but only if it's absolutely necessary. I doubt it will come to that."

"And the humans?"

"You've fulfilled the prophecy. Now, it's up to them."

Would the humans take my words and my warnings to heart? Would Earth be saved from ruin? Or would mankind continue toward self-annihilation?

Victor put his hand on my shoulder. "You should get some sleep, you look exhausted."

"I am," I agreed, closing my eyes.

The big black snake slithered through the desert, its shiny surface reflecting outrageous colors. Catching sight of me, it hissed and disappeared into a hole. I searched the vast desert and saw nothing but sand in every direction. I was alone and afraid. The heat of the blistering sun scorched my skin until I fell down face-first. My swollen tongue felt too big for my mouth and my dry lips cracked and bled. The sun's infernal rays were melting my body and boiling my brains. The agony was unbearable. I dissolved into liquid form, then I became vapor, rising into the sky.

I don't know how long I slept, but when I woke up there was nothing but an eerily silent black void around me. I was floating, completely weightless. Where did the ship go? I couldn't see any stars or planets. There was nothing except me and the infinite blackness...

Victor, where are you?

A shrill, piercing sound filled my ears and it wasn't until Victor shook me that I realized the sound had come from my lips. I opened my eyes and we were in the ship, still traveling at light speed through the universe.

"Wake up, Veronica!"

"Oh, Victor," I said tearfully.

"You're okay, little star. It was only a bad dream."

"It's more than that," I countered. "I think I'm losing my mind. I've been dreaming about black snakes…"

"Considering what your mind and body have been through these last few days, it's normal. Your past and present are merging. You'll heal soon, I promise."

"Are we almost there?" I asked, feeling claustrophobic.

"Yes, almost. You've been sleeping for several hours."

Victor clicked off the light speed switch and the ship slowed. He took my right hand and turned it over to expose my wrist, then pointed straight ahead. The swirling constellation of stars and planets in the distance matched the mark on my wrist. The precision of the design was uncanny. Sentimentality crept into his eyes. "Now you understand why your wrist bears Our Mark."

The alluring green planet I had seen in the Lisbon bunker loomed before us. Victor took control of the ship and broke through the atmosphere, which was surprisingly similar to that of Earth except the sky possessed a yellowish hue instead of blue. Hundreds of shades of green loomed below. Trees and plants grew literally everywhere. It wasn't until we were close to landing that I finally picked out several structures. Unlike Earth's cities, these cities blended in with their natural environment. The landing strip was lined with circular lights. I could see other ships coming and going from the area, and assumed this was similar to an earthly airport.

"Welcome to my home—our home," Victor said.

"I want to call your planet by its proper name."

He raised an eyebrow at me. "Your tongue isn't trained to make the sound, remember?"

"Can't you create a human equivalent?"

He thought for a moment and looked amused. "The closest word I can come up with is Eden."

I smirked. "As in the Garden of Eden?"

"Exactly. A lush, green paradise."

Two metallic vehicles hovered toward our ship.

Victor removed his mouthpiece, lifted the helmet from his head, and inhaled a deep breath. I began to follow suit, but he stopped me.

Um, Veronica...the only 'alien' here is you.

Two Watchers in matching black uniforms and helmets with mirrored visors stood outside the door. Judging by their height and broad shoulders, I guessed they were males. Victor opened the door and they bowed to him respectfully before handing him a glass vial. I couldn't understand what they were saying to each other, but when they saw me, they fell down upon one knee.

"What are they doing?" I demanded.

"Greeting the Sacred Oracle."

"I thought I was the Phoenix…"

277

"To us, it's the same thing."

"How do they know it's me, anyway? I mean, I didn't radio in to tell them I was coming."

"The ship is equipped with thermal and retinal scans in order to keep track of its occupants. Everyone has already been notified of your arrival, and there will be a great feast tonight in your honor." He placed the vial in my hand, which contained a silver pill. "You need to swallow this."

"What is it?"

"Our atmosphere is very similar to Earth's with a few minor elemental differences. That pill will enable your lungs to breathe our air without a problem."

I moved my mouthpiece aside to swallow the pill. After about a minute he removed my helmet, thus cutting off my oxygen supply. I took a deep breath of Eden's air and found it to be a bit heavier than that of Earth. Sweeter, too. The density of the atmosphere slowed my heart rate, which made me feel calm.

The Watchers helped me out of the ship, then led us toward one of the hovering vehicles. The ride was incredibly smooth and quiet. Most of the futuristic edifices were constructed of shiny materials that reflected the greenery around them. The curvaceous, biomorphic style of the architecture reminded me of the whimsical village in Vienna designed by Hundertwasser.

"My planet is divided into several regions," Victor explained, cutting into my thoughts. "Each region has a main city where an Elder presides, such as this one. What is your impression so far?"

"I'm amazed," I replied honestly. "You referred to this planet as my home, and promised me an explanation."

His face expressed joy, excitement, anticipation and a bit of concern all wrapped up in one. "I know this is a lot to ask, but can you be patient a bit longer? Everything will soon be revealed to you."

"All in good time?" I teased, quoting him. When he nodded, I added, "What exactly will be revealed?"

"Patience, Veronica. Please, trust me."

I let the matter drop. "Where are they taking us?"

"To the home of one of the Elders."

"Is it far?"

"No, we're almost there. As soon as we arrive you'll be given comfortable quarters where you can bathe and change into fresh clothing."

"Thanks. I didn't exactly have time to pack."

Or say goodbye to anyone...

"Everything you need will be provided."

The immaculately clean streets were smooth and tan in color. Healthy plants grew everywhere. Victor explained that the private gardens on rooftops were for growing food, while the parks below were for everyone's pleasure. These public spaces were adorned with elaborately carved fountains fashioned from materials resembling jade and marble.

The streets were eerily empty. "Where is everyone?"

Victor studied the sky to gauge the time. "The citizens should be arriving at the main arena by now."

Were there sports events on this planet, too? Curious, I asked, "What are they waiting for?"

He chuckled. "You."

"Are you kidding?"

"Not at all."

We pulled up to grand building with green vines adorning the south wall. Unique flowers of every color and shape imaginable filled the wide space between the front door and the pavement. I was struck by the heady scent of their exotic perfume the moment I exited the vehicle.

"This way," Victor said. "Decisions and laws are made here. The Elder resides on the top floor with his consort."

"You mean his wife?"

"Yes."

Big lit circles lined the atrium floor. We stood on one of them and Victor wrapped his arms around me.

"This is our equivalent of an elevator," he explained.

I didn't realize we were floating upward until I looked down and saw my feet dangling. Panic made me cling tightly to

Victor.

"You won't fall, I promise," he assured me. "We've perfected anti-gravity technology a long time ago. The universe's energy is free, clean, and abundant."

We reached the top of the building and alighted directly onto a tiled courtyard boasting a small fountain.

"Our gracious hosts approach," Victor said at the sound of footsteps.

The Elder came out first. His strong features were slightly weathered with age, but his hairless skin was luminous. A set of gold, wizened eyes peered at us from beneath a smooth, prominent brow. His floor-length black tunic was simple in its design, yet tailored perfectly. His eye fell on me briefly before embracing Victor.

The Elder's attractive consort entered the courtyard with quick, light steps. She appeared slightly younger than her husband, her pale skin resembling fine porcelain. She also wore a floor-length black tunic, cut to compliment her slim, curvaceous figure. The only adornment she flaunted was the blue and silver headpiece that covered her bald head. Her eyes held mine for a moment and she gave me a genuine smile before wrapping her arms around Victor.

The mature couple stood side by side, impressing me with their regal demeanor. Victor said something to them, and they each embraced me in turn. My body vibrated with warmth and joy.

"Veronica, I'd like for you to meet my mother and my father," Victor said. "They are so very pleased to see you."

"These are your parents?"

"I wasn't hatched, you know," he joked. "My mother will show you to your room."

The Elder's consort led me inside their home. The interior space was comprised of natural elements like stone, metal, and what appeared to be glass—no synthetic materials. We went through an opening that had no door and I found myself in a room with a spectacular view of the city. My eyes swept over countless rooftop gardens set against a pale yellow sky tinged with the slightest hint of orange. My host nodded and waved her arm, as if requesting my approval. I smiled gratefully and nodded, too. It's amazing how hospitality needed no words.

Before taking her leave, she indicated a silver button inside the room's opening. Curious, I pushed it and a glittering screen appeared, affording me privacy. So, this was their version of a door. The bed, shaped like a big oval, beckoned me. The mattress instantly conformed to my body and adjusted its temperature to make me perfectly comfortable.

Another opening led to what I assumed was a bathroom. I got off the bed and went inside to investigate. A wide glass tube with a drain on the floor served as a shower, and the big polished stone bowl protruding from the wall could only be a sink. The toilet was a bit more complicated, but I managed to figure it out and marveled at their ingenuity.

I stripped out of my clothing and stood inside the smooth glass tube. Within seconds, warm, scented water rained down on me from tiny holes in the stone ceiling; a mini waterfall. I washed my skin and hair, then realized that there were no towels. Since the paperless 'toilet' used water and hot air to wash and dry, I assumed the same technique would be applied to the shower. I was correct.

I stepped out of the shower and noticed a silver panel protruding from the wall. It slid to the side, revealing a pile of neatly folded black tunics. I put one of them on, and returned the bedroom. Victor was seated on the bed waiting for me, also wearing the inevitable black tunic.

"Why is everyone in black?" I asked.

"There are actually two good reasons, and one of them you already know." At my puzzled expression, he explained, "I told you that the days here are short and that we absorb many of our nutrients from the sun through our skin. Black absorbs every frequency of light."

"Oh. What's the second reason?"

"Our planet abundantly produces a plant similar to flax but with black fibers. We use it to make this fabric, which is softer and cooler than linen. We wear colors on special occasions, but most of us wear black on a daily basis out of convenience and comfort."

"The women normally wear headdresses?"

He nodded. "It's like a form of jewelry. Some are made of simple fabric, some are fashioned from flowers, and others are encrusted with jewels, like this one."

He held out a delicate silver crown with shimmering crystals and iridescent beads. Gently, he placed it on my head and turned me toward the ceiling-to-floor mirror in the room. Strands of silver cord strung with crystal beads fell down the sides of my long, dark hair. The crown formed a delicate point in the middle of my forehead from which hung a small tear-shaped crystal reflecting every color of the rainbow.

"Oh, Victor, it's exquisite!"

"I was hoping you'd like it. I've also brought you something to wear for tonight's celebration."

I noticed a white gown on the bed. The garment was long and adorned with countless tiny crystal beads.

I held it against my body and preened. "It's gorgeous, thank you so much."

"Can you manage or shall I have my mother come in to help you?"

"I can manage."

"We'll be waiting for you in the courtyard. Everyone is very anxious to see you again."

Again?

I slipped on my new dress, which gathered at one shoulder and flowed like silk to the floor. A pair of simple silver sandals in exactly my size completed the outfit.

I met Victor in the courtyard. He had changed into a royal blue tunic lined with gold and his father wore one in dark green. His mother wore a long tunic the color of fire with a gold and ruby headdress. Victor's parents each said something in turn to him before beaming at me.

"What did they say?" I asked, accepting Victor's proffered hand.

"They are both overjoyed to see you, and happy that you

arrived safely and in good health. They want to thank you for saving my life, too. My mother has already chastised me for not having stocked Repticlone anti-venom in my Lisbon bunker."

"Your mother is right."

"Do you realize that you look like a queen dressed like that?" he asked, cleverly changing the subject.

"I was thinking more along the lines of Greek goddess."

He laughed. "Come on, Ms. Goddess, it's time to celebrate."

We stepped onto a bright circle of light and took the strange "elevator" down to the atrium. The twilight sky had deepened to a shade of rosy apricot with glowing green streaks blazing across the horizon. Tiny solar lights illuminated our way as we walked toward an enormous arena. The city was silent.

The automatic doors opened upon our arrival. Victor squeezed my hand as he led me down a long corridor. I could see another set of doors with two black uniformed Watchers standing beside them. At the sight of me, both guards fell to their knees like medieval knights. I inclined my head at them, and they stood to open the doors. The moment I stepped into the arena, I froze in shock. It was completely filled with Watchers!

Literally thousands of them stood mingling, the buzz of their excitement rippling through the air. There was a riot of colors as far as my eyes could see; tunics and gowns in every shade imaginable, accompanied by eccentric headdress. When the Watchers in the crowd caught sight of me, they froze, too. Whispers spread as quickly as wildfire until all of them stood facing me in curious silence.

In that moment, I became aware of two things: first, we were on a stage, and, second, I was the only person wearing white. I peeked over my shoulder and realized that we had entered the arena from the back entrance—like rock stars! Victor may be accustomed to this sort of thing as the lead singer of Icon, but I sure as hell wasn't.

I staggered backward only to be caught at the elbow by Victor. His mother came forward to press her cool hands on my arms, caressing them in an attempt to calm me. She whispered unintelligibly, yet soothingly, in my ear. The Elder stepped up to the edge of the stage and addressed the crowd.

"What's he saying?" I asked of Victor.

"He's informed them that we've arrived safely, that you've fulfilled the second prophecy, and that you're finally home."

I frowned in confusion. "I've never been here before."

Victor took hold of my shoulders and kissed my forehead. A cheer went through the crowd and I noticed that everyone looked at me with affection, admiration, and respect. I blushed to the roots of my hair under their scrutiny. What had I done to deserve this honor?

The Elder motioned for me to step forward and stand beside him. Below us, a female Watcher approached the stage, parting through the crowd as if she were Moses dividing the Red Sea. Oddly, she also wore a stunning white gown. Even her headdress was fashioned in silver and crystal, similar to the one Victor had given me. Her eyes locked on mine and she smiled at me in a familiar way, as if she knew me well. I noticed that aside from the lack of hair and golden irises, we bore a strong resemblance to one another.

Now there are two Greek goddesses at this party.

The mysterious female walked onto the stage and gathered me to her chest in a hug usually reserved for the most intimate of family members. She pulled away, her eyes glistening with tears of joy.

What was going on here? I looked to Victor and his parents. The three of them were misty-eyed and emotional, as if they were witnessing a heartwarming reunion. It seemed like everyone on this strange, wondrous planet knew who I was except for me.

A Watcher child with wide, curious eyes came forward and offered me a golden chalice. I glanced nervously at Victor, who nodded encouragingly at me. Bringing the chalice to my nose, I took a sniff. I heard a ripple of laughter from the crowd and peeked at them uneasily. The contents within the chalice resembled water, but it smelled of flowers and tasted sweet. I drank the strange elixir and handed the vessel back to the child with a grateful nod. Everyone seemed to be holding their breath in anticipation as they stared at me.

A stabbing pain shot through my temples and I put my hand to my head.

Oh, no!

Everything around me grew smaller and smaller until there was nothing but a pinpoint of light in the darkness. My knees turned to rubber, and I could no longer feel the floor beneath my feet.

My last memory was of Victor rushing toward me.

CHAPTER 41

Victor's strong arms supported my shoulders as I gradually regained consciousness. Slowly, I opened my eyes. The first thing that came into focus was my beloved's handsome face. My twin sister, the Sacred Oracle, leaned over me, her expression one of concern.

I smiled weakly. "What happened?"

When she replied, she did so in our native tongue. "You fainted, but you're all right now."

Realization hit me and I smiled. "You fed me the Mind Clearing Drug."

My twin grinned and nodded. "I've missed you so much," she declared with great feeling. "I've tracked your every move on Earth from the time you departed until now. I watched your life energy travel through the universe to fulfill the first prophecy, and when you were brutally murdered, I mourned for you—we all did." She made a sweeping gesture toward the immense crowd of onlookers. "We knew your spirit was strong, however, and that your energy would remain near Earth until the time came for you to fulfill the second prophecy."

I sat up with Victor's assistance. "What about the humans?"

"Earth's destiny now lies in their hands," she replied. "We have done our part. Now, we wait."

I wanted nothing more than for humankind to thrive.

She continued, "While you slept, we read your memories. We know about the Repticlones evolving, the rebel soldiers, and the deceitful Reptilian overlords. We also know about the brave Repticlone, Sebastian, and how he saved your life."

"And Victor's, too," I inserted.

"And Victor's, too," she conceded. "The Universal Council has already been alerted by our faithful Elder. Dear sister, your brave sacrifice will go down in history."

I reached out for her hand and squeezed it tightly. We had

many stories to exchange and much to discuss—*all in good time.*

Victor's golden eyes twinkled. "Does everything make sense now?"

I nodded in answer to his question as the memories of my pre-existence flooded me with the force of a tidal wave. My sister and I were twins, both serving the Sacred Oracle for the greater good of our people. The Sacred Oracle referred to the entire body of many individuals, not a single entity. Yet, at the same time, all of us within this special group bore the title of Sacred Oracle. We were one. Each of us had a special gift; some could see the future, others deciphered prophetic dreams, and some—like myself—fostered a deep, intuitive understanding of nature. Together, we assisted the Elders in creating righteous laws that would benefit every living being on our planet.

We knew that Earth was in grave danger after being plunged into The Age of Lost Knowledge. The catastrophe that befell our planet long ago forced our people to return home, thus abandoning mankind. Despite the extenuating circumstance, the Universal Council still forbade direct intervention on our part. The law was clear: each planet had the right to govern itself as they saw fit.

Monitoring the humans and sending envoys to gather information was not enough; it soon became obvious that something more had to be done. The only way the Universal Council would allow us to intervene and prevent disaster was if a volunteer infiltrated the Earth as a human. This legal loophole came with a strict condition: the volunteer's life energy would be wiped clean of any previous memory.

We knew the tremendous risk involved in doing such a thing. Once freed into the universe, the volunteer's life energy may or may not return home. This energy could be tracked and monitored, but it couldn't be controlled or steered into any desired direction. We were also well aware that humans, being a young species and not yet fully evolved, were violent and unpredictable. There was a good chance that the volunteer would be subjected to physical, mental, and emotional pain—

even death.

I knew all of the risks, but none of them mattered when I volunteered for the mission. One life in exchange for many made perfect sense to me, and I was happy to be the sacrificial lamb. The two prophecies regarding my life on Earth came after my energy had been freed, so I knew nothing of them until I became a human.

Several members of the Sacred Oracle had dreamed of me and had seen my future. After the Elders had pleaded to the Universal Council on my behalf, they had agreed to use their power to physically mark me so that a tracker could find me and be sure of my true identity.

I touched Victor's cheek. "You were the tracker assigned to watch over me."

To my surprise, he blushed and remained quiet.

"He wasn't assigned," my sister countered. "He volunteered for the mission. Actually, *begged* would be a more fitting term."

"Is this true?" When Victor nodded, I inquired, "Why? I have no recollection of you whatsoever prior to my existence on Earth."

"I think it's time you told her the truth," my sister prompted.

Victor turned to face me, taking both my hands in his own. "It's true, we've never met here, but I knew who you were. I saw you for the first time in a public garden. You were feeding the tiny creatures by the fountain, and it seemed as if the plants and flowers surrounding you were leaning toward your energy. The way the sunlight kissed your skin took my breath away. You were by far the loveliest vision I'd ever laid eyes on! Back then, I was too shy to approach you, let alone speak with you. It wasn't like you were an ordinary citizen—you were a Sacred Oracle. When I finally found the courage to speak to my father about arranging a formal introduction between us, you had already volunteered your life energy for the Earth mission. I was devastated."

"Oh, Victor," I whispered.

He kissed my fingertips. "Shortly after your life energy was released, the call went out for a volunteer tracker to watch over you and witness the fulfillment of the prophecies. I jumped at the chance and, yes, I begged for the mission. Of course, I wanted to serve my planet, too, but it would be a lie to say my motive was completely selfless. I wanted to meet you, to speak with you, to be near you, and to feel your beautiful energy."

"Thank you," I said to him. "I'm deeply moved by your words. All the puzzle pieces are in place now."

"Our marriage on Earth is not binding here," he reminded me, trying to hide his apprehension. "You're free to serve the Sacred Oracle without any strings attached."

I pondered his words. "I will continue to serve the Sacred Oracle, for it is a privilege, but I will do so while being your official consort."

Crushing me to his chest, he kissed my face. No more words were needed. There came a thunderous approval from the thousands who had witness this exchange. There were no secrets here, nothing to be hidden or ashamed of. Everyone existed as one, with nature, as it should be.

Victor helped me to my feet before I faced the countless pairs of golden eyes. Drunk with joy, I spread my arms wide in a gesture of affection. If I could, I would have embraced every one of them in that moment. A great celebration followed, accompanied by a sumptuous feast. At one point, the voices of my people came together in song to honor me.

This is too much...

Overcome with gratitude, I wiped away a tear. Glancing at Victor and my twin sister, I wondered what the future held in store for us. I would miss Earth, and many of the people I had come to know and care about.

As for Veronica, she would forever be a part of me.

Did you enjoy this novel? The author would appreciate your review on Amazon. Thank you.

Turn the page to read a sample of the eerily suspenseful novel, LILITH: A Tale Set in Old Salem.

LILITH

A Tale Set in Old Salem

C. DE MELO

ISBN-13: 978-0-9997878-5-4
ISBN-10: 0-9997878-5-3

Note from the Author

This is a work of fiction. Some of the dates and people mentioned are accurate, but artistic liberties were taken to create this supernatural historical fantasy. A total of twenty people were convicted of witchcraft and sentenced to death during the witch trials of Salem Village in 1692 (this number does not include those who perished while awaiting trial in jail). Nineteen were sent to the gallows. One was crushed to death. The dates of their executions are listed beside their names.

Bridget Bishop (June 10, 1692)
Rebecca Nurse (July 19, 1692)
Sarah Good (July 19, 1692)
Elizabeth Howe (July 19, 1692)
Susannah Martin (July 19, 1692)
Sarah Wildes (July 19, 1692)
George Burroughs (August 19, 1692)
George Jacobs Sr. (August 19, 1692)
Martha Carrier (August 19, 1692)
John Proctor (August 19, 1692)
John Willard (August 19, 1692)
*Giles Corey (September 19, 1692)
Martha Corey (September 22, 1692)
Mary Eastey (September 22, 1692)
Mary Parker (September 22, 1692)
Alice Parker (September 22, 1692)
Ann Pudeator (September 22, 1692)
Wilmot Redd (September 22, 1692)
Margaret Scott (September 22, 1692)
Samuel Wardwell Sr. (September 22, 1692)

*Killed by *peine forte et dure* method (crushed to death).

"Speak too liberal of the Devil

and his horns will soon appear."

Samuel Taylor Coleridge

PROLOGUE
SAVANNAH, GEORGIA
1750

The packet boat glided down the Savannah River in the golden glow of twilight. Adam Wiseman admired the rosy sky from the vessel's prow as it drifted toward the dock. He had waited years for this day.

"Mr. Wiseman—"

Startled, Adam spun around to face the boat's captain.

"You were in deep thought."

"Yes…"

The burly man cleared his throat while adjusting his cuff. "I normally don't meddle in the affairs of others, much less my passengers, but I sense that your youth and inexperience warrants a bit of cautionary advice. After all, I am old enough to be your father." He paused until Adam nodded for him to proceed. "Whatever your business is in Savannah, stay clear of Dame Lilith. Consider this a friendly warning."

Adam's brow creased. "Sir?"

"My grandfather sailed from England to settle in Salem Village at the onset of 1692…I'm sure you've heard of the witch trials?"

"Yes, of course."

"Twenty people were executed for witchcraft that year. According to my grandfather, it should have been twenty-one." Narrowing his eyes, the captain added, "I'm sure you catch my meaning."

Adam kept his expression neutral. "I appreciate your counsel, sir."

The old man grinned, lighting up his round face. "Farewell and good luck to you."

Adam accepted the captain's proffered hand and shook it.

The captain sauntered off, satisfied with having performed a good deed.

The boat dropped anchor, prompting Adam to gather his things before going ashore. Torches twinkled along the mucky coastline in the gloom of a midsummer evening. A crescent moon, crisp and white, peeked through ashy clouds.

A cluster of curious onlookers eyed him, a few inclining their heads in greeting. Adam touched the rim of his tricorn hat and set off down the main road. He walked with purpose, the way his father had taught him. The orange glow of cooking fires illuminated the interiors of several neat cottages, and the humid air hung heavy with the scent of roasted meat. The mouthwatering aroma caused his stomach to growl.

A boy toting a lantern fell into step with him. "Can I help you, my lord?"

Adam smiled at the lad. "I'm not a lord."

The boy eyed the stranger's finely tailored coat and new leather shoes. "You look like one to me."

Adam extracted a coin from his coat pocket. "Well, I appreciate the compliment. I would be much obliged if you sold me your lantern."

The boy conducted his profitable transaction without hesitation, then ran home. Adam held the lantern aloft and scanned his surroundings. There were no more cottages after a certain point, and the road tapered into a footpath. The feeble moonlight revealed a forest straight ahead of him. Peeking over his shoulder, he noticed human silhouettes standing in open doorways. The villagers didn't move or make a sound, but their collective stares burned into his back, warning him to tread no further.

The tree line of the forest grew in height as the dark shadow of the woods loomed before him. The eyes of owls and marsupials glimmered in the moonlight as he penetrated the rim of trees, but the animals weren't the only beings aware of his presence. Each step attracted more unwanted attention as he cautiously picked his way beneath the thick canopy of branches. Before long, *they* completely surrounded him.

He recalled the first time his father had taken him deep into the forest, far from his mother's prying eyes and ears. Although he couldn't have been older than five, he had never forgotten his father's words: *"Of the many frightening things lurking in the forest, you are the most terrifying of all…"*

The vivid childhood memory melted Adam's fear, endowing him with the needed strength to banish the evil entities. Cicadas, crickets, and toads sang in unison, filling the balmy evening air with night music. Sparks of greenish yellow light flashed in the dark, prompting a nostalgic smile to play upon his lips. He had loved catching fireflies as a boy. One landed on his sleeve and he marveled at the insect's body as it lit up like the sun.

A few golden circles of light emerged from behind the massive trunk of an oak tree. They floated closer to better study him, their tiny faces wary. He acknowledged the fairies with a curt nod, prudently maintaining his distance.

He eventually came to a big circular clearing marked by evenly-placed white stones. Serenity washed over him the moment he crossed the protective barrier. On closer examination, he realized that the white stones formed a giant pentacle. A fine stone cottage stood in its center. Each elongated triangle of the star hosted healthy herbs. Foxglove and hemlock grew along a flagstone path leading to the front entrance.

An attractive dark-haired girl with green eyes opened the door before he had a chance to knock. "Welcome, sir. My mistress is expecting you."

Adam set down his satchel as another pretty girl came forward to take his coat. Bathed in golden candlelight, the home's interior boasted fine furnishings. Bunches of dried lavender, rosemary, and sage hung from the ceiling rafters. Bound with colorful ribbons, they stood out in stark contrast to the blackened wood beams. A sun-bleached ram's skull with curling horns hung above the door, and the table to his left revealed an array of plants, mortars, and pestles.

A third girl turned away from the hearth to set a steaming plate of beef stew on the table. She offered him a dazzling smile while pulling out a chair. He inhaled the mouthwatering aroma with longing.

I wish I had three fine servants, Adam thought.

"I have a total of seven girls."

Adam craned his head toward the authoritative voice. An old woman sat by the hearth arrayed in black silk. Each slender finger of her gnarled hands boasted a large gemstone that sparkled in the firelight. Like the girls, she wore her thick snowy locks loose around her shoulders. Her slightly bent head kept her face in shadow.

"Go on," she prompted. "Take a moment to gather your bearings."

Adam's eyes wandered. An impressive white marble dragon statue dominated the mantel above the hearth. The meticulously rendered scales, claws, and sharp teeth revealed the sculptor's skill. A mighty sword hung above the dragon, its silver hilt embellished with an engraving of a sun and moon. There were animal skulls and horns displayed on walls and many surfaces. Silver candlesticks and copper bowls gleamed in the candlelight, along with oil paintings in magnificent gilded frames, vibrant Oriental rugs, porcelain plates and green glass goblets—treasures befitting a palace, not a cottage in the forest.

"Gifts from admirers expressing their appreciation," the old woman explained, reading his thoughts again.

"Appreciation?"

"For my help, of course."

Where were his manners? "Good evening, ma'am. Please forgive my late arrival. My name is Adam—"

"I know who you are," she snapped. "Come closer. Let me have a proper look at you."

The woman's eyes had been the bane of her seventy-six years, so she deliberately kept her gaze lowered as he knelt before the chair. Pressing her palm against his firm cheek, she allowed a faint smile to touch her wrinkled lips.

Adam looked so much like him…

"I believe my mother wrote to you," he ventured quietly, interrupting her faded memory.

Ignoring his comment, she asked, "She never did get over

your father's death, did she?"

"No, ma'am."

The old woman nodded sadly. "According to your mother's letter, you are a talented writer. Is this true?"

Feeling the heat of his blush, she correctly deduced that he wasn't accustomed to praise.

"I prefer to let others judge my work."

"Humility is an admirable trait, Adam," she said, finally removing her hand from his face. "Your mother also mentioned that you wish to write about the witch trials of Salem Village."

"I'm hoping you will allow me to record your version of what happened in the year 1692."

"That fateful year changed the course of my life…"

A moment of tense silence passed between them.

Adam whispered, "Will you do me the honor of recounting your story?"

Conscious of the impact her eyes would have on him, she slowly met his gaze. He flinched only a little bit, doing his utmost to hide his shock. Having endured such reactions since childhood, she had long grown accustomed to them. Adam's mother had no doubt plied him with admonitions as she wasted away on her deathbed: *don't stare, don't cause offense, don't ask too many questions…*

"Very well."

"Thank you, Grandmother."

"Dame Lilith. Trust me, it's for your own protection."

PART ONE

ALBUS DRACO

"Come not between the dragon and his wrath."

William Shakespeare (King Lear)

Chapter 1
Salem Village, Massachusetts
Spring Equinox 1674

Rachel Healer awoke with the start. Given her excellent reputation, incessant pounding on her door at inconvenient hours had long become a normal occurrence.

"Goody Healer!"

She hastily shrugged into her clothing in the silvery light of the full moon. Two pregnant women in the village were due to give birth at any moment.

Yanking open the door, Rachel frowned. "Lizzy! What are you doing here?"

"My mistress has gone into labor."

"It's too early…"

Grabbing her satchel full of ointments and instruments for aiding women in the dangerous act of childbirth, Rachel fled her cottage with Lizzy in tow.

***

Reverend James Bayley ushered the midwife and his serving girl inside his home twenty minutes later. Barely past the seventh month of a difficult pregnancy, Harriet Bayley writhed in pain upon the bed.

Rachel took hold of the woman's hand. "I'm here to aid you with God's help, Goodwife Bayley. Can you take a deep breath for me?"

Harriet's dark eyes filled with tears as she tried to breathe. "The baby…it's not ready to enter…this world."

The grim-faced reverend hovered over the midwife's shoulder. "Have you ever delivered an infant this early, Goody Healer?"

Rather than respond, Rachel motioned to Lizzy. "Add feverfew and rosemary to the fire."

The girl obeyed and a pungent herbal scent permeated the room. The Bayley children began to cry in unison, so James ordered Lizzy to take them to his aunt's home down the road.

"Stay with them until I come to fetch you," he instructed before Lizzy steered the distraught children outside.

"It's coming, I feel it," Harriet wailed.

Rachel gently prodded the woman's stomach, feeling the baby's position through layers of fat and skin. "Push!"

"Lord, help me!"

"One more time…"

"I can't…I can't!"

James gripped his wife's hand. "Don't give up, Harriet. Think of our little ones. Who will care for them if you die?"

"Pray for me, James!"

James put his hands together and closed his eyes. "Heavenly Father, I beseech thee…"

Rachel positioned her hands between Harriet's meaty thighs while uttering encouraging words. A snowy white head became visible, causing the bewildered midwife to pause in her task. A wave of dizziness overtook her as vivid images of white scales and wicked teeth flashed through her mind. The infant's head emerged, yanking the midwife back to the present. With trembling hands, she aided the tiny soul into the world. She had never delivered such an abnormally pale a baby.

"A healthy girl," Rachel announced in a shaky voice.

James praised God, but the joy on his face was eclipsed by shock when he laid eyes on his daughter.

Seeing her husband's reaction, Harriet panicked. "What's wrong with the baby?"

The reverend's eyes slid toward his wife. "Jezebel!"

"Husband?"

"Who is he?"

Harriet recoiled. *"What?"*

"Calm yourself, Reverend Bayley," Rachel interjected. "I believe your daughter is afflicted with a rare condition that is only superficial in nature."

Somewhat appeased by the midwife's words, James

demanded, "How do you know this?"

"I've heard stories..."

Harriet reached for her husband's hand. "How can you accuse me of such wickedness, James?"

"Forgive me, my love," he offered contritely before bringing her knuckles to his lips. "I lost my head for a moment and spoke without thinking. Blame it on the infant. *Look* at her!"

Rachel placed the baby in her mother's arms.

Tears filled Harriet's eyes. "Lord help us..."

"You have been blessed with a healthy child, Goodwife Bayley. This is an occasion for rejoicing, not weeping," the midwife said, trying to sound convincing despite her apprehension. She knew the strange vision she had experienced a moment ago must somehow be connected to the baby.

Ignoring the midwife's comment, Harriet demanded, "James, what are we going to do?"

The baby began to cry, causing Harriet's nipples to leak milk. Spent from the ordeal of childbirth, she watched the child suckle with an expression of disdain. The moment her daughter opened her eyes, she screeched and plucked the baby from her breast.

"You must feed her, madam," Rachel prompted.

Holding the screeching infant at arm's length, Harriet cried, "James!"

Rachel took the child from her mother. "Hush, little one, don't cry."

James pulled the midwife aside. "I moved my family from Boston to Salem Village two years ago in order to shepherd this flock. My wife's parents are prominent members of Bostonian society and descendants of the English aristocracy. *This* won't do."

His eyes were on the child's downy white hair and she understood his meaning. Every member of the Bayley family flaunted brown eyes and dark brown hair.

"Help us, Goody Healer," James pleaded.

Rachel was taken aback. "Help you? How?"

"I don't know, but the baby cannot remain here."

"You cannot shirk your responsibility as parents. God wouldn't approve—"

The reverend's nostrils flared. "You presume to lecture *me* about God?!"

"No, sir, I only—"

"It is for God's glory and for the spiritual health of His congregation that I must forsake this child. She will only serve as a spiritual stumbling block to others. One look at her, and everyone will assume that I'm either a cuckold or that my family is cursed." Placing his head in his hands, he added, "My in-laws would never approve."

"You could explain—"

"Don't be naïve, Goody Healer! People will believe what they want to believe. My reputation will be tarnished, and my wife will suffer the humiliation of suspicious stares and malicious gossip for the rest of her life."

"What exactly do you intend to do, Reverend Bayley? You can't simply cast the infant out into the street like rubbish."

"I shall tell everyone that Harriet birthed a stillborn."

"Making such a claim is not only dishonest, it would blemish my reputation as a midwife. As a widow with two deceased parents, I'm forced to eke out a living alone."

James nodded thoughtfully to her words. "You are young and strong. You can remarry someday."

"With all due respect, I prefer to be alone."

James cast a glance at his wife, then whispered, "Please, I beg you, go home and take the baby with you. I'll be along shortly to figure something out."

Rachel appealed to Harriet one more time. "Goodwife Bayley, please take your daughter…"

Harriet's lower lip quivered as fresh tears formed in her eyes. "You heard my husband. Get out!"

Rachel bundled the baby in one of Harriet's shawls and stormed out of the cottage. Holding the infant close to her bosom, she marched toward home with angry steps.

What kind of people reject an innocent child?

The Spring Equinox moon hung like a giant pearl in an inky

sky. Rays of moonlight kissed the sea beyond, turning its surface into shards of mirrored glass.

Rachel glanced down to find the baby staring at her. The child's gaze reflected curiosity and intelligence. Two years ago, her abusive husband had slipped off the roof while patching a hole. The fall had proved fatal; a blessing in disguise. Widowed at the age of twenty, she longed for children but refused to risk another violent marriage.

Could this child be a gift from God?

Rachel entered the cottage and set the baby on the table before lighting several candles. She examined the infant, gently prodding the miniature body and checking it for any abnormalities. Everything seemed fine.

She heated up some goat's milk and allowed the warm drops to fall from her fingertip into the baby's mouth.

"There will be two new mothers in the village very soon. Both are goodhearted women who won't mind sharing their milk with you."

The infant smiled, instantly melting Rachel's heart.

James arrived an hour later. Rachel opened the door and regarded him expectantly. "Well?"

He entered the midwife's cottage with a troubled frown. "My wife and I are departing for Boston immediately on the pretense of family illness. Harriet's mother hasn't been doing well lately, so it's a partial truth."

"Goodwife Bayley needs rest. She shouldn't be traveling—especially at night."

"It was *her* idea to leave. We'll tell people that she lost the baby in Boston, so your reputation will remain intact."

"What about Lizzy?"

"She'll be notified that tonight was a false alarm." His gaze shifted to the baby. "Have you examined it?"

The midwife bristled. *It?* "Yes, she is healthy."

"I'm specifically referring to strange markings or moles that are insensitive to touch."

Rachel hid her fury as the reverend unwrapped the infant and lifted her naked little body toward the candlelight. He

303

scrutinized every inch, even the child's most private parts.

"What exactly are you searching for, Reverend Bayley?"

"Devil's marks. Did you know that Satan can suckle vital nourishment from a witch's teat?"

"There is no such wickedness in your daughter," Rachel snapped, retrieving the baby from him. "She is as innocent as a child born blind or deaf."

"I shall concede to your valid point, Goody Healer, for you are knowledgeable in the field of midwifery and healing. I ask that you concede to mine. You must think me a monster for rejecting my own flesh and blood, but this child would only cause problems for me and my household. People would doubt their spiritual leader, perhaps even abandon their faith."

Rachel hated to admit it, but the reverend made a valid point. The child would indeed be seen as illegitimate by the many gossipmongers of Salem Village. Despite this, she said, "You may regret this decision someday, sir."

James sighed. "I know."

After a tense silence, she said, "Very well, the child will remain here with me. I shall raise her as my own."

Relief washed over him. "God be praised. Naturally, I'll assume all expenses. The child won't be a financial burden to you, I promise."

"I need to concoct a believable story before sunrise," Rachel said, pacing the room. "Go home, Reverend Bayley. I need to think."

James opened the door. "God bless you, Rachel," he said before slipping into the night.

CHAPTER 2

The persistent knocking caused Katherine Harwich to curse under her breath. Who would disturb a middle-aged widow at this time of night—or was it already dawn? She squinted at the grayish blue light seeping through the cracks of the window shutters.

Placing the pillow over her head, she cried, "Go away!"

"It's me, Rachel Healer. Open up!"

Katherine sat up in bed. The midwife? *Here?*

Throwing open the door, she demanded, "What's all this fuss about?"

"So sorry to bother you, Katherine, but you're the only person I can trust."

"Couldn't it wait until—*is that a baby in your arms?*"

Rachel nodded. "Before I explain, you must swear not to say a word to anyone. Also, I need your help."

"Yes, now come inside and tell me everything," Katherine urged while leading her unexpected guest to a chair. "I'll stoke the fire and make us some tea."

***

The sun shone brightly in a cloudless sky the next morning, inspiring the good wives of Salem Village to wash their linens. Rachel and Katherine set out amid dancing sheets drying in the sunshine. The younger of the two women toted a basket, which concealed the baby. They waved to the busy villagers as they passed, deliberately informing them of their intention to forage for roots in the forest.

Fearing the child would awaken at any moment and start crying, the women hastened their steps. Discovery would ruin their plan. Twigs snapped underfoot and the tips of branches scratched their shoulders as they followed the footpath past the barrier of trees. Verdant aromas of spring floated on the breeze, and birdsong filled their ears as they entered the green sanctuary.

"Hurry," Rachel prompted.

Katherine lagged behind, her plump cheeks reddening from the exertion.

"Do you hear anything?" Rachel asked when they finally arrived at the clearing.

Huffing and puffing, Katherine cupped her ear. "No."

Rachel set the basket on the plush mossy ground, then sank to her knees and began digging up roots.

The matronly widow leaned against a tree to catch her breath. She smiled at the sleeping infant. "What are we going to call the little one?"

Rachel glanced up from her task. "Lily, like the flower."

"An apt name given her coloring and daintiness."

"Yes," the midwife agreed while shaking the dirt from a root. "Take her, will you? I need to fill this basket."

Katherine carefully lifted the baby from her hiding place and held her close. "Do you think people will believe us?"

"I can't think of a better farce. Can you?"

Katherine shook her head.

Rachel had already named the child *Lilith* in honor of her late grandmother. Lilith had been the matriarch of their family; a strong, capable woman worthy of respect and admiration. She and her husband, Aaron, had converted from Judaism to Christianity in Holland. They had settled in Salem as "Anne" and "Paul," a respectable pair of Protestants.

Katherine said, "Let's do our best to sound convincing, and leave the matter in God's hands."

"Agreed," Rachel said, rising to her feet and dropping the last batch of roots into the basket. "Here, you can carry this and I'll take Lily."

The women exited the forest with the baby in full view. Several curious villagers rushed over to them.

Rachel explained, "We found the infant in the clearing."

Katherine added, "Imagine our surprise!"

The village women studied the strange infant.

"Left by a ruined maid from a nearby village, no doubt."

306

"She's terribly pale. Do you think she's ill?"

"Ugly little thing, isn't she?"

"Lord protect us if she's carrying the plague!"

Rachel endured the unkind speculations with forced neutrality. "I think the reverend should be notified about this at once," she declared in a voice for all to hear.

Predictably, one of the women said, "Goody Healer, haven't you heard? Reverend Bayley and his family left for Boston at dawn."

The midwife instantly matched the voice to the face of Goodwife Tilter, a notorious gossipmonger.

Rachel feigned ignorance. "Did he?"

"Apparently, his mother-in-law is sick." Goodwife Tilter's expression turned sly. "Lizzy mentioned something to my daughter about fetching you last night. Did you tend to the reverend's wife?"

"Ah, yes. *False* labor," Rachel improvised. "The baby isn't due for quite some time, as I'm sure you know."

"It *has* been a difficult pregnancy for poor Goodwife Bayley from what I've heard—and from what the reverend's aunt has told me."

"It has indeed," the midwife confirmed. "I'm sure that all of our prayers are with Goodwife Bayley and her family."

Several women nodded and agreed.

Goodwife Tilter continued, "Well, hopefully, she won't make matters worse during her visit in Boston. Given her delicate condition, it would have been wiser for her to simply stay here and rest, don't you agree?"

"I cannot deny that it would."

The woman's eyes dropped to the baby in Rachel's arms. "You should inform the constable." Narrowing her eyes, she added, "That baby may be a changeling."

A changeling? Rachel hid her anger. "I'm going to the take the child home to examine her first, then I'll tell him."

"That's the sensible thing to do, Goody Healer. In the meantime, why don't I fetch the constable for you?"

"Thank you," Rachel said, breaking away from the group.

Katherine caught up with her friend and rolled her eyes. "I can't believe she called Lily a changeling! Odious woman. Off she goes to spread the news. The entire village will know of Lily's existence before noon."

"I have no doubt of that."

"Goodwife Tilter is a pain in the arse."

"Katherine!"

Rachel glanced around nervously to make sure that no one had heard Katherine's comment. Thankfully, the village women were too busy discussing the abandoned infant. Some of the women followed the midwife to her tiny cottage near the sea.

Rachel made a big production of examining the child for the sake of her audience. Goodwife Tilter eventually appeared in the doorway with the constable. No doubt, he had already heard every possibly version of the story. Rachel ushered him inside and repeated what she had told the villagers earlier, regardless of what Goody Tilter may have told him.

The man listened with a pensive frown while rubbing his chin. Finally, he inquired, "Was she crying when you found her?"

Rachel and Katherine exchanged glances.

"Sleeping," Rachel replied.

"Like an angel," Katherine added.

"Or a changeling," Goodwife Tilter countered, crossing her spindly arms. "One can never be sure nowadays with all the mischief afoot!"

At this, some of the women nodded and whispered. Frightened by Goodwife Tilter's words, they insisted that the constable inspect the child.

Biting back several angry retorts, Rachel held the naked baby up for the constable's inspection. The man brought his face as close to the infant's flawless white skin as possible. A few concerned onlookers entered the cottage without invitation and crowded around the table to gape at Lily's tiny pale form.

The constable eventually backed away with a nod of satisfaction. "No marks."

A collective sigh of relief filled the room as Rachel covered

308

Lily's body with a strip of linen.

He continued, "Goody Healer, will you care for this infant until I can consult with Reverend Bayley on how we should proceed with this matter?"

"Yes," Rachel replied.

***

Reverend James Bayley returned to Salem bearing tragic news: his wife had delivered a stillborn babe while in Boston. People lined up to pay their condolences to the family. Harriet embraced her role as well as any seasoned actor would on stage. She lamented over the loss of her child while shamelessly accepting the comfort of other women.

Meanwhile, Rachel waited patiently for the reverend's expected visit. James eventually arrived at her cottage with an entourage of villagers. Before several witnesses, he declared Lily a "child of God" and blessed the baby.

Goodwife Tilter, who stood at the front of the group, inquired, "Which family will raise this child?"

The crowd began discussing Lily's future, naming one feasible possibility after another.

Rachel cleared her throat. "I will raise her."

Taken aback, Goodwife Tilter exclaimed, "You have no husband!"

The woman's comment sparked an argument.

"Shouldn't the infant be entrusted to a family?"

"Goodwife Johnson has been trying to conceive for years— at least the child will have a father."

Rachel inclined her head in acquiescence to their words, then said, "It's true that I lack a husband, but I've grown fond of the infant. After all, I've been caring for her since the day Goody Harwich and I found her in the forest. As you all know, God saw fit to take my husband before I had the chance of knowing the joy of motherhood…"

The midwife's words softened everyone's hearts.

Rachel continued, "Two women will soon give birth in the village. Surely, they won't mind sharing their milk with Lily."

The reverend's eyebrows shot up in surprise. *"Lily?"*

"Do you approve, Reverend Bayley?"

He nodded, then turned to address the people. "God saw fit for two widows to find this child—not a family or a couple. Who are we to question His wisdom? Goody Harwich has already experienced the joy of motherhood and has a grown son in Virginia. Perhaps this child was sent to comfort Goody Healer. After all, she has always gone out of her way to help those in need, and her conduct is exemplary."

At this, the people nodded in agreement.

Placing a hand on Rachel's shoulder in a fatherly gesture, James added, "You can count on the support and help of this community in the raising of the child."

Satisfied with the outcome of the situation, the people dispersed, leaving Rachel and Lily in peace.

CHAPTER 3

Rachel's cottage was located far from the village square, which made avoiding the Bayley family an easy task. True to his word, the reverend discreetly visited the midwife's cottage once per month. During these nocturnal visits, he would inquire after the child's health, and leave the midwife with a generous sum of money. Harriet, on the other hand, never visited her daughter.

Lily went from a baby who seldom cried to a solemn, contemplative child. Unlike most rambunctious toddlers, she liked to sit and listen to the chirping of birds or the creaking of trees in the wind. With the passing of time, Rachel often found Lily staring at her in a thoughtful manner. The child preferred listening to speaking, and took note of everything.

To Rachel's irritation, a few people still entertained the possibility that Lily was a changeling. Goodwife Tilter often fanned the flames of this fallacy. Brash and callous, she heedlessly voiced her suspicion to anyone who would listen. Malicious adults then instilled this notion into the heads of their sons and daughters. As the years passed, some of these mean-spirited children took perverse pleasure in tormenting Lily after the Sunday service. They teased her for being pale and puny, too.

One day, shortly after her fifth birthday, Lily inquired, "Mama, am I a changeling?"

Rachel frowned in annoyance. "Who called you that?"

Katherine, who happened to be visiting Rachel that day, inquired, "Is Goodwife Tilter up to her tricks again?"

Rachel rolled her eyes and nodded before repeating, "Lily, who called you that?"

"Mary Miller," the child replied.

Katherine waved her hand dismissively. "Pay no mind to that naughty girl, Lily. Even her parents can be insufferable at

311

times."

"Goody Harwich is right," Rachel said. "Ignore Mary."

Lily looked from one woman to the other. "What is a changeling?"

Rachel replied, "It's a fairy child that's been left in place of a human child stolen by fairies."

Lily's smooth brow creased. "What is a fairy?"

Katherine, who grew up in England where such folklore tales were common, replied, "Fairies are spirits of the forest. They usually reveal themselves as small winged creatures. Mischievous little imps, the lot of them!"

Lily's face lit up. "I've seen them!"

Katherine smirked. "Have you, now?"

"Yes. Some glow as brightly as the sun."

"Those are only fireflies, Lily," Rachel countered.

"No, they're not."

"Fairies don't exist," the midwife said, her tone firm.

"But they do, Mama!"

Katherine's eyes crinkled with amusement. "I'm afraid your mother is correct, dear. I've never seen a fairy, nor has anyone else that I know."

"They exist," the child insisted, pouting.

The old widow chuckled. "So, you think you're clever enough to tell the difference between fireflies and fairies, do you?"

Lily nodded, her face serious. "The fireflies never speak to me, that's how I know."

The grin on Katherine's face vanished as her wary eyes slid toward Rachel. "What did you say, child?"

The hair on the back of Rachel's neck stood on end as she took hold of Lily's arm. "Inventing stories is the same as telling lies!"

Lily's eyes glistened. "Mama, I'm not—"

"Silence!" Rachel put her lips to Lily's ear. "Don't say another word."

"But—"

Rachel gave her daughter a pointed look. "Go outside and

play. *Now.*"

Frowning at both women, Lily did as she was told.

"She has such a vivid imagination," Katherine said, her trembling voice betraying her fear as she watched the pale child twirl around beneath the shade of an elm tree.

"Yes, she does," Rachel agreed. "Which is why I ask that you please not repeat what you've heard here today."

***

Rachel was busily washing dishes after supper when someone knocked on the door. Puzzled, she paused in her task. There were no pregnant villagers, so who would be out at such a late hour?

She cautiously opened the door. "Reverend Bayley."

Rachel invited him inside, then closed the door against the cold February wind. She normally asked Lily to wait in the bedroom during the reverend's visits, but he stopped her from doing so this time.

"I'd like to see the child, if you don't mind," he said.

The midwife motioned for Lily to come forward. The little girl studied the man's face.

James knelt before the child and smiled. "Hello, Lily."

Lily hid behind Rachel's skirt and said nothing.

"I didn't expect to see you so soon, sir," Rachel said, for James had already paid her a visit last week.

He stood. "I've come to say goodbye."

"Oh?"

"My family and I are moving to Boston. My father-in-law is ill and needs our help." He placed a large leather pouch on the table and added, "There is enough money there to keep you and Lily comfortable for many years to come. God bless you both."

James took a long look at his daughter, then left the cottage without a backward glance.

Lily tugged on Rachel's skirt. "Who is that man?"

"You know he is the reverend."

"But, who is he *really*?"

Rachel's mind raced with plausible replies as she gently stroked Lily's silken locks. "James Bayley is a man who cares for the well-being of children."

"Is it because I don't have a father?"

"Everyone has a father, Lily."

"Where is mine?"

The midwife busied herself in order to hide her misting eyes from the child. "I don't know, sweetheart. Go on and get ready for bed. It's late."

Rachel eyed Lily thoughtfully. Someday, she would disclose the truth to her daughter. Thankfully, that day was far away.

***

Salem Village, composed mainly of farmers and fields, was located almost seven miles north of Salem Town. James had endowed Rachel with enough funds to purchase a decent home, so she considered moving to the lively port town. Bustling with commerce and transient people, Salem Town would prove an interesting change from dull country life.

In the end, Katherine convinced Rachel to stay put. The practical midwife eventually sold her tiny cottage by the sea and used the money to purchase a bigger home near the forest. The spacious cottage, set farther away from the rest of the homes, ensured privacy. Mature trees lined the far end of the garden, providing plenty of shade for Lily's delicate, sun-sensitive skin.

Living so near the forest enabled the child to forge a special bond with nature. She could easily differentiate poisons from beneficial herbs, and remember the use of each plant. Before long, every sort of creature began showing up on their stoop. Baffled, Rachel watched in awe as Lily whispered softly to the animals while offering aid. She regularly mended the wings of birds and made plasters for injured cats.

"What do you say to the animals, Lily?" Rachel asked one morning as her daughter applied a soothing herbal solution to a dog's mangy coat.

Lily shrugged. "The animals like music, so I sing."

"What do you sing?"

"Hymns from the Sunday service."

Relief washed over Rachel. "Good girl."

People eventually came to accept Rachel's daughter as a

member of the community. Polite and respectful, Lily did her best to remain unobtrusive. Whenever she went out in public, she kept the hood of her cloak low over her strange eyes. In a place like Salem Village, the prudent took great lengths to avoid unwanted attention.

Lily proved surprisingly resilient when plague struck Salem Village in 1680. The malady had already ravaged through Salem Town, leaving almost a dozen people dead in its wake. Several children were bedridden with high fever, yet Lily remained immune. Thanks to Rachel's potent vitality tonics and healing draughts, the lives of many villagers were spared. Of the six people who had succumbed to death, two were children.

Reverend George Burroughs arrived a week after their burials. A gentle man with a kind face, he dedicated his first sermon to those who had lost loved ones. Chapters were read from the comforting biblical book of Psalms, and prayers were offered on behalf of the lost souls.

***

The day before Lily's seventh birthday, Rachel ventured into the woods with her daughter to collect early spring flowers. She set the basket down between them and got to work.

Lily worked alongside her mother, picking dandelions and other plants. Eventually, she got bored and wandered from her mother's side. She loved being in the clearing, for it teemed with life. Frogs, birds, snakes, insects—each one held the power to enchant her.

The child ventured to the pond and leaned over to study her pale reflection. Two long white pigtails dangled over her shoulders. She straightened at the sound of leaves rustling. Turning her head, she saw a pair of brown eyes, sharp teeth, and black fur.

Struck by terror, Lily stared at the bear. Unable to scream or move, she took in the beast's powerful limbs and fearsome claws with awe. The bear looked dangerous, as if it could eat her up in two bites, yet she found it fascinating.

Rachel's scream startled the great black beast, and it retreated into the forest. Lily felt herself being scooped up in

315

her mother's arms.

"Thank God," the midwife whispered, relieved. "Come on, let's go home."

***

Rachel ran through the forest in a panic. The branches of briar shrubs scratched her chest and face as she veered off the footpath into the forest. She finally arrived at the clearing, breathless. Something ran toward her; something big and heavy and dangerous. Hearing snarls and growls, she turned to run but could not.

Run! Run! Run!

Her mind screamed the word over and over, but her legs refused to obey the command. She slowly turned around to face her pursuer. The trees and brush crackled and eventually parted, allowing a magnificent white dragon to emerge. Rays of sunshine burst through the clouds as the beast entered the clearing. Its scales glistened like pearls in brilliant sunshine...

Rachel woke up with a start.

"Albus Draco."

The whisper had involuntarily escaped her lips, but she had no clue what the words meant. Could the nightmare be a result of the shock she had suffered earlier that day in the forest? The memory of the black bear standing so close to her daughter made her shiver.

She checked the bed beside her own and found it empty. "Lily?"

The eerie silence felt wrong. Puzzled, she crept out of bed and went into the main room. The moonlight revealed Lily standing perfectly still by the hearth with her eyes closed.

Without opening her eyes, the child whispered, "Go back to bed, Mama. It's not safe here."

Icy fingers crawled up Rachel's spine. "What are you doing?"

"Protecting you."

"From what?"

When Lily didn't reply, Rachel struck a piece of flint and lit a candle. Sensing an unnatural presence in her home, she shivered. Fierce determination settled across the child's diminutive features as her entire body trembled.

"Lily!"

"Hush, Mama…"

A heavy silence followed.

Finally, Lily said, "Be gone!"

Rachel whimpered in fright at the sound of something swooshing past her.

The child exhaled a long, slow breath and opened her eyes. Looking at the empty space beside her, she whispered, "It's all right now, you're safe. Go in peace."

"Who are you talking to?" Rachel demanded, her voice trembling with fear.

"Zebadiah Wilson."

The five-year-old boy had drowned last year.

Rachel gripped her daughter's shoulders. "Lily Healer, that's not funny."

"No, it's not."

"Explain yourself."

Lily stared at Rachel, debating whether or not to confess the truth. "Someone whispered my name in my ear as I slept. I woke up to find Zebadiah beside me."

"You can *see* Zebadiah?"

"Not anymore. He just left."

Despite her fear, Rachel forced herself to continue the interrogation. "What did he want from you?"

"The monster was tormenting him, so he asked me to make it go away."

"M-m-monster?"

Lily nodded, her face solemn. "Please don't ask me to describe it, Mama, for it will only make you more terrified than you are now."

Rachel stared at the child in horror. "How did you stop the monster?"

"I didn't do it alone, the beast helped me."

A whimper escaped Rachel's lips. "Go to bed and say your prayers."

"Mama—"

"Now."

The midwife swiped her small Bible from the shelf and clutched it to her chest. She went back to bed but sleep eluded her until dawn.

Rachel awoke to the sound of sweeping. Placing a hand on her throbbing temple, she cautiously made her way to the cottage's main room. White sage leaves burned on a copper plate in the center of the table, causing thin wisps of smoke to swirl gracefully in the air.

"Good morning," Lily said with a broom in her hands.

Rachel tore her eyes from the smoke patterns to look at her daughter. "Why are you burning white sage?"

"It has the power to clean the air of bad things."

"Who told you this?"

"No one."

"How do you know it to be true?"

Lily shrugged in response to the question. No one had ever explained the sacred nature of white sage—she simply *knew*. She didn't need anyone to tell her that the act of sweeping drove away evil spirits, or that salt's purifying properties also served as a spiritual protection. She instinctively knew these things to be true, the same way she had known that honey would taste sweet long before it ever came into contact with her tongue.

Rachel's brow creased in thought. "Why do you feel the need to cleanse our home?"

"After last night's—"

Rachel rushed to cover the girl's mouth with her hand. "You are forbidden from speaking about last night to me or anyone else. *Do you understand?* That kind of dangerous talk stirs up trouble. There are whispers of witchcraft in the village, and we need to be careful."

Lily nodded, her eyes wide.

Rachel lowered her hand. "Forgive me, my child. I'm only trying to protect you. Happy seventh birthday, Lily."

***

In 1683 George Burroughs stepped down from his post due

318

to lack of paid wages. Deodat Lawson took Reverend Burrough's place in 1684, and then abandoned the congregation four years later for the same reason.

In time, Salem Village acquired a shameful reputation for not paying their Christian shepherds. Neighboring towns and villages viewed it as a contentious place to live due to its quarrelsome inhabitants. Villagers were required by law to pay taxes in order to support these holy men. Adherence to Puritan practices and precepts were demonstrated by regular church attendance. Without a godly shepherd, these expectations could not be met.

Do you want to keep reading? LILITH: A Tale Set in Old Salem is available on Amazon. Thank you.

Made in the USA
Coppell, TX
08 September 2020

36454343R00185